THE HAND OF SATAN

There was blood dripping down the walls of the living room. Blood—it looked like gallons of it—was smeared on the walls, puddled on the carpet, staining the sofa and the loveseat, dripping off the paintings.

He stepped into the living room, his feet squishing into the soggy, blood-soaked carpet. He smelled an unbearable odor.

Gerry! Where was his boy?

Tony looked around, noticed the crumpled legs sticking out from behind the baby grand. Oh no! Not Gerry! *Oh God!*

Gerry was over behind the piano, as still and silent as his mother had been. There was one gaping hole in his throat, and the whole of his shirt was covered with gore. He held a butcher knife in his hand. The hand, too, was covered with blood. *But why did the hand look so peculiar?*

Also by William Schoell:

SPAWN OF HELL
SHIVERS
LATE AT NIGHT

BRIDES OF SATAN

WILLIAM SCHOELL

LEISURE BOOKS   NEW YORK CITY

A LEISURE BOOK

Published by

Dorchester Publishing Co., Inc.
6 East 39th Street
New York City

Copyright © 1986 by William Schoell

All rights reserved. No part of this book may be reproduced or transmitted in any form or by any electronic or mechanical means, including photocopying, recording or by any information storage and retrieval system, without the written permission of the Publisher, except where permitted by law.

Printed in the United States of America

BRIDES OF SATAN

Prologue

1887
The Nation of Sumara in Asia.

Sister Venicus lifted her head and saw with dismay that her prayers had not been answered. She had not been magically transported to another time, another place, out of this sweltering hothouse they called a train that tore across the isolated terrain like a fire-breathing dragon on metal wheels. She was still inside the railroad car, packed in with those dozens of diseased, ugly people, people with whom she would have to live, and sleep, and break bread, not only here on this train, but in Benpor, their destination. People to whom she would have to minister. She tried to summon compassion for these pathetic wretches, tried to feel something when she saw their hollow faces, withered bodies, the open festering sores, the black, shallow looks of the children. But all Sister Venicus could feel was *disgust*.

Sister Venicus felt so lost. She lifted the withered left arm, the bony, almost useless appendage that had been crushed in a childhood accident—the bones had snapped and her middle finger had been severed when a wagon overturned on her—and realized with some irony that in spite of her affliction she was perhaps the healthiest person on board the train. It was bad enough for the other passengers, who were garbed only in sheets and sandals, but Sister Venicus was stifling under the heavy robes she had to wear at all times. Her hand reached beneath the enveloping wimple on her head and wiped away dripping streaks of dirt and sweat.

For a moment Sister Venicus smiled. So many people mistook her for a Catholic nun. The sisters of the Holy Messianic Church—some of them, at least—were nothing like the nuns of the Roman Catholic Church. They only had to *pretend* to be. Sister Venicus again felt a flash of bitterness, and yes, hatred, as she recalled the last conversation she'd had with the Mother Superior in England before embarking on this terrible journey to nowhere.

They were in Sister Angelica's chambers, a dark octagonal room with a multitude of clocks and tables full of papers. Arch-shaped globs of light came in through the windows, dissecting the chamber into several sections, and criss-cross shadows littered the floor. "I'm afraid, Sister Venicus," the Mother Superior said, "your request for a transfer has been denied." She held up a finger, her warning that the sister was not to speak until permitted. "I know how much you've been wanting to join the Order of the Mourning Sisters. And I know why you wish to join them. But I'm afraid we have decided you do not have enough spiritual balance to be of use to the sisters of that order. The Mourning Sisters have a very special place in our church. They are sacred and revered, and knowledge has been imparted to them that none of the rest of us can share. In short, Sister Venicus, we find you unworthy. I am sorry."

Sister Venicus bristled. She knew what the real reason was. She had been too critical of the Mother Superior, she had dared to speak out when she saw how badly the woman ran things, the mistakes she made in matters of faith and discipline. Unworthy? The very idea! She knew that she was, in fact, one of the worthiest, far more so than the Mother Superior. She was being punished, that was all, being punished for daring to have her say.

"We have decided that you should be assigned to mission work in Sumara," the Mother Superior continued. "There is an epidemic there; many people need assistance. You are to be sent

to an outpost, a hospital they have opened for the victims in the town of Benpor." She smiled. *"It will be good for you, Sister Venicus. It will keep your mind off things. It will draw you out of yourself and strengthen your religious principles. All of us sisters need at times to go out into the field and share our love of God, show our love to the sick and needy."*

Sister Venicus had barely heard of the small Asian nation of Sumara, and certainly had no desire to go to such a useless, filthy country, especially one where the dying outnumbered the living. But there was nothing she could do. Sister Angelica's words were final.

The memory faded as Sister Venicus stared out the window and watched the bleak monotonous scenery passing by. Acres of unending desert relieved only by occasional patches of brush and cactus. Those vast, forlorn mountains in the distance. How she hated this country! The journey so far had been unbearable. The miles of travel through countless foreign nations. Then waiting with the throngs of the sick in Asapon, Sumara's capital city, for the final stretch to the hospital outpost in Benpor. The train was overcrowded. Everywhere you looked there were people, scores of them, filling up the rows of uncomfortable wooden seats, the narrow slice of aisle, hanging out the windows for room or just a tiny smidgen of air.

Sister Venicus had to share her seat with four others; two skinny boys with ribs showing through their flesh, a weary, heart-heavy mother, and a small female child—a baby, really—who kept flopping over onto Sister Venicus' lap. Sister Venicus looked at the little girl, so frail and weak from hunger she was barely alive, and tried to feel pity for her. She thought of trying to comfort the mother, to do what she had been sent here to do. Yet she felt nothing for the savages of this tiny underprivileged nation but a kind of pity and revulsion that forced her to think of them as things instead of humans. Most of them were practically dead anyway.

She didn't want to be here. She was not supposed to be here. She stared out the window and tried to keep from crying. How could she help these creatures when she could barely help herself? How could she give them love or guidance, when she felt only hatred and resentment? She was only twenty-two, God help her, so young and frightened, a child herself. She should not have been sitting here sweltering in this oppressive passenger car, stifled by the heat, terrified lest some germ or infection enter her body and kill her. She had no idea what to do or say to these people. She wanted nothing to do with them. She didn't care if they lived or died; she just wanted them to leave her alone.

Sister Venicus, a small, light-complexioned woman, was not unattractive—the small, close features of her face formed a pretty and delicate composition—but the look of hate and horror upon it made the nun seem almost demonic. Her pale blue eyes bulged from their sockets; her thin white lips were pressed together from tension, her nostrils were wide and flaring. If only her God would send her some comfort, tell her what to do. She felt so insignificant and helpless, completely unable to fulfill the task she had been sent here to do. She closed her eyes as tears ran down her cheeks, and let the wrenching despair enter her heart and mind and soul.

In the small town where she came from, the Convent of the Penitential Sisters was not only the largest structure, but the one which had the most influence over the people. The Holy Messianic Church was not nearly as powerful as once it had been, its membership steadily dwindling, but in Brosolov, Romania, it was the religion and the law. To become a sister of the Church was the highest honor. Sister Venicus' parents had died of disease; her widowed aunt had tried to raise her but was ill herself and poverty-stricken. It was a blessing the day the young woman who was to be called Sister Venicus decided to enter the convent, to take her holy vows and become God's bride. Truth to tell, Sister Venicus had done it primarily because she knew the sisters' gardens. Their rich stock of cows and chickens would keep her well-fed; it was preferable to surviving on a bowl or two a day of hot gruel with her dying Aunt Beatrice.

After a few months, the ambitious Sister Venicus was transferred to a larger order in the English countryside. One day, through another older sister who had become fond and protective of her, Sister Venicus discovered that there was another church, an inner circle, hidden deep inside the outer one. Rumor had it that most of the members of this inner circle had gone to America, and now belonged to the mysterious, isolated Order of the *Mourning* Sisters. Sister Venicus believed that *theirs* was the true faith, and wanted desperately to go to America to join them. Instead, she had been punished, sent to this godforsaken outpost to preach a gospel she no longer believed in, to bring Christianity to heathens, to force them to accept something which in her heart she could no longer accept herself.

It wasn't fair.

And worst of all was the loneliness. She was twenty-two, but she felt ninety and was convinced she looked forty-five. The dark rings under her eyes, the puffy flesh on her cheeks. She knew vanity was a sin, in their church if not hers, but she didn't care. She didn't even have the other sisters for company any more. She could not make friends with the diseased rabble all around her, no matter how hard she tried, and whatever missionaries or Catholic nuns she met in Benpor would undoubtedly bore her. Their religion was not hers. Besides, Catholic sisters were quite suspicious of the sisters of the Holy Messianic Church. Everyone knew how intolerant the Catholics could be of those outside their faith. They would not welcome her with open arms, of that she was sure.

While the train continued on its journey—*clickety clack clickety clack*—pulling her inexorably to a fate that was unkind and unjust, it was quickly growing dark outside. Sister Venicus had visions of herself climbing through the window, flinging herself out into the desert where she would die and her corpse feed the vultures that were constantly circling overhead. Wouldn't death be preferable to this? Wouldn't it be faster than succumbing to a sickness and wasting away like these pathetic animals?

I'm only twenty-two, she thought. *Only twenty-two.*

Suddenly a great wailing rent the air. The middle-aged woman next to her was sobbing, shaking her child, crying out to her God for mercy. Sister Venicus saw what had happened—the baby girl had died in her sleep. The nun's eyes met the tormented eyes of the grieving mother. The mother saw the sister's tears and thought they were tears of sympathy and compassion for her and her dead child. Sister Venicus was touched for an instant by shame, sharp and biting and terrible. The mother reached out her arms, holding the child up to Sister Venicus. She wanted her to take the child, to breathe life into it, to help her as only one of God's brides could. Sister Venicus blanched. No, no, she couldn't. She *couldn't*! She was sorry for the child and mother but she simply coudln't touch it. Take it away! *Take it away*, she said, there was nothing she could do. She thrust out her hands in revulsion. As the mother shrieked in horror, the baby girl tumbled out of the woman's arms and fell onto the floor of the train.

In abject mortification, Sister Venicus jumped to her feet, almost stepping on the child as the mother wailed in misery and reached down to retrieve her bloodied daughter. The baby had fallen out of its coverings and lay in the filth on the floor, its glistening scars and running sores revealed in all their ugliness. Sister Venicus had to get off this train! She could not stand another moment!

In a panic, she brushed roughly past the sleeping, lying, leaning hordes of the sick, sweating, odorous passengers, and tried to push her way to the front of the car. A wave of nausea hit her; tears streamed down her face: tears of misery, tears of hatred for herself and these people, tears for the child and its mother and the whole rotten world they were dying in.

She had only traversed halfway along an aisle littered with passengers, when the train was suddenly rocked on its tracks and a fearsome rumble filled the air.

The train was beginning to slow down. The passengers, many of them awakened by the noise, began to murmur and chatter amongst themselves. What was happening? Sister Venicus felt an unreasoning fear, a desire to cling to life even when it was at its most worthless. She only knew that she *did not want to die.*

A hot, foul blast of air suddenly swept in through the windows, momentarily raising the temperature to such a degree that some of the passengers actually fainted. The train continued at its slower, jerking pace, steadying itself. Suddenly there was no more rocking or rumbling and the passengers began to settle.

Then without warning there came a burst of blinding white light that lit up the train and the outside area until it totally enveloped the countryside—an unearthly glare that vividly illuminated every bush, every furrow, every fissure in the soil.

What was that? The passengers were muttering and crying, but Sister Venicus could barely understand their language. Why did Sister Angelica have to send her here, damn her!

Pushing aside the passengers in her path who were too weak to resist, Sister Venicus made her way to a window and nervously peered outside. The chattering of the passengers was increasing in intensity. They were scared, apprehensive, as terrified as she was. Where was the light coming from? Even as she tried to protect her eyes from the glare, the light was getting warmer and more brilliant, steaming the air and bathing each of them in a glow that washed out all individual details and features.

The passengers began to shout and whimper.

Sister Venicus prayed.

The train suddenly came to a complete stop.

And as Sister Venicus stood there and wept for her short, unhappy existence, the light got hotter and brighter.

Until it completly engulfed the train and everyone on it.

The following morning:

The tall brown man called to his fellows and told them to hurry. They had found the train. There it was, sitting quietly on the tracks, about halfway between Benpor and Asapon. "We've found it," he said. "Come, let's see if they need assistance."

The tall man and his companions chattered amongst themselves as they approached the engine. There must have been a breakdown of some kind. The cars themselves looked untouched and undisturbed on the tracks, so there could not have been an accident, derailment or fire. Funny, where were the passengers? You'd think they would have wanted to get out of the sweltering confines of the railroad cars, if only for a moment. Then again, in this heat, perhaps staying indoors out of the sun was a better idea.

The tall man climbed up into the locomotive, a black obelisk with a huge funnel in the front, and entered the forward compartment. After a second he looked back at the furnace. Odd. There was no one about.

He called to his companions. "No one's here. Let's check the other cars."

The first car they entered was empty. So was the second. As they made their way through the two remaining passenger cars and into the caboose at the end, their amazement and confusion began to mount. *Each* car was empty of passengers. The possessions were there, flasks and bottles and bags, and even—and this was the strangest part—people's clothing laying about in disarray, but there was not a *single soul* on board in any of the railroad cars.

Where could several hundred people have disappeared to?

"Must have gone back the other way on foot," one of the men suggested.

The tall man shook his head. "In this heat? After so short a time?"

"Well, then, where are they? People don't just up and vanish."

The tall man sighed and wiped his forehead. He didn't know what to say.

"They'll turn up," another man assured the others. "Have to. They might have gone off into the mountains."

"And leave behind the food and medical supplies on the train? What for? They'd only die quicker up there."

The man didn't answer.

There was no answer.

None of the train's passengers were ever seen again.

Part One: *Désirée*

1

1940.
Greenwich Village, New York.

Désirée Fontana walked across Bleeker Street in such a state of depression that she didn't see the blue car bearing down on her until it was almost too late.

"Hey, lady! Watch where you're going!" As the blue roadster sped past only an inch or so away from her body, a greasy-haired kid in the driver's seat hollered obscenities at the top of his lungs.

Désirée composed herself and continued walking.

It was not as if it mattered, after all. It might have been a blessing had the automobile run over her. Anything to terminate this endless sense of futility and hopelessness. She was hungry. And weary. And there were times when she felt so alone.

She knew she was wrong to feel that way. After all, her roommates, her friends, Janice and Paul, felt the same way she did. They, too, were aspiring artists. They, too, went to endless rounds of auditions and struggled to make ends meet. Why, if the three of them didn't share an apartment she didn't know how they'd ever manage.

She climbed up the steps of the brownstone where they lived. Once, many years ago, it had been a private home. The building was at least seventy years old and looked it. It had been divided into twelve units, and turned into a boardinghouse where you paid rent by the week. It might not have been glamorous, but it was cheap.

She climbed the stairs to the second floor as quickly as she could, hoping to enter her apartment without being seen by the landlady. Bad enough they were behind in the rent. But since Paul had moved in—a man, a *black* man besides—Mrs. Prout, the landlady, was watching them like a hawk. The suspicion was finally entering her mind that Paul was not just a friend of theirs who visited frequently but a bona fide occupant of the building. Two women sharing a studio were one thing—but with a man? A *negro*! That simply would not do!

Désirée made it inside the door without mishap. She took off her hat and coat, shivered a little, and went over to the kitchen area to put some water on the burner. A nice hot cup of tea would do her just fine. While she waited for the water to boil, she collapsed into the nearest chair, shoved off her shoes with first one foot then the other, and ordered herself not to cry.

This was not the way it was supposed to have been. Not the way at all.

She looked at the top of the kitchen table as a cockroach skittered across it and disappeared into an open bag of cookies. When would that slob Janice learn that everything had to be wrapped up tight? Well, Désirée hadn't the energy to shoo the bug out of the bag. Let Janice find it and have a screaming fit later. Désirée was just too tired.

The water boiled. She got out a bag and cup and prepared the tea, wondering if Janice or Paul had had better luck than she did. That audition director had paraded the girls about while making whispered comments that carried up to the stage, reasons why this one or that one wouldn't do—too fat, too tall, too ugly. Thank God she hadn't heard whatever he might have said about her. All that abuse—and just for a job as a lousy extra in a crummy off-Broadway play.

She had wanted that part so badly she would have killed for it.

As she sipped the tea her eyes looked around the depressing apartment, and her mood, if possible, worsened. Désirée didn't think she could even remember what it was like to be working steadily. This was not the way things were supposed to have turned out for Denise Steinbeck of Valley Stream, Long Island. By now—twenty-five years of age and getting older—she was supposed to have been successful, with a glamorous career like Katherine Cornell or Helen Hayes, and a wonderful husband to share it with. She'd have a wealthy, interesting circle of friends, and plenty of money. She'd eat at the plushest restaurants and hang out at the most elegant bars, become a real somebody in theatrical circles. Her apartment would be a penthouse or duplex—perhaps she and her husband would even own a townhouse. People would know her and love her. They'd see her and say, "Do you remember that dumpy Denise we went to school with? Well, just look at her now."

Yes, just look at her now. The one source of comfort she had was that she was *not* dumpy little Denise any more. Now she was tall, attractive, willowy *Desiree.* The name Désirée was more chic than Denise. The Fontana she'd derived from Lynn Fontaine, though people told her she more resembled Joan Fontaine. The duckling had spread its wings and become a swan. She was pretty, maybe even beautiful, and men seemed to find her attractive. Unfortunately, the men she encountered in her dizzy rush to stardom were either sleazy hustlers, bogus producers, or nice young boys whose feelings for her would never go beyond brotherly affection.

Désirée had a good figure and long, shapely legs. Her features were small and delicate, but sensual. She wore her hair down to her shoulders, a style which was not quite as becoming as she might have thought. Her makeup was a bit overdone, but she felt it made her lips seem fuller and it did highlight her tiny blue eyes.

No, a "lovely little princess" like her—her mother's words —did not belong in a dump like this. The apartment consisted of one fairly large main room, with a narrow, cramped bathroom to the side, and a large walk-in closet beside the doorway from the hall. There were two beds, cots really, one against each of the longer side walls, with a coffee table and two old easy chairs between them. The space on top of, around, and between the beds was filled with a messy flood of discarded garments and theatrical scripts—mostly Janice's. Désirée's orderly nature was repulsed by her roommates's slovenliness, but she had long since given up on trying to clean up after her. Who could deal with the chaos?

The "kitchen area"—a tiny nook in one corner of the apartment—consisted of a stove, sink and small refrigerator. There were also a kitchen table and four matching chairs. There were three windows, one in the bathroom, one to the side of the kitchen sink and one at the opposite wall between the two beds. Although the white walls had been freshly painted only a year or so before, they looked terribly streaked and dingy. Every day for the past few weeks Désirée had been spotting more and more bugs. She was sure that Janice's failure to wash dishes and take out the garbage would only help hasten their inevitable advance.

Their friend, Paul Wilson, slept on a rug and pillow placed between the two beds. Every night when he went to sleep he would simply fling all of Janice's scattered possessions aside to make room for his body. The girls had let him move in with them out of friendship and necessity. He'd been thrown out of his apartment for nonpayment of rent and had no place to go except park benches or the hideous men's shelter. His family had no room for him. However, due to the odd jobs Paul got from time to time, he might be able to manage to pay at least a third of their rent. Janice and Désirée, eternally broke and always underfed, were fond of Paul and desired his company, so they offered him a place to stay and wouldn't take no for an answer.

But if Mrs. Prout discovered him, they'd all be out on the street, she just knew it. At the very least the old woman would raise their rent, and they could barely manage it now. Too many weeks went by when their income was virtually zero. Janice could have gotten more money from her family out in Iowa, but she didn't want them to know how poorly she was doing. Paul's family had no money to give him. And the former Denise Steinbeck had been told by her parents that if she ever found it necessary to ask for money, the only way they'd give it to her would be if she packed her bags, left "that awful place" and moved back home where she belonged.

Twenty-five. Living with her parents. No, there was no way she would ever admit defeat, settle down for a life of boredom and complacency, watch her folks getting older and listen to them tell her how she should forget the foolishness and get a job in the local dress shop as a clerk. "Wait for some nice boy to come along and marry you," they'd tell her. Some nice dull boy with a nice dull job and nice dull, nobody friends. She didn't know what scared her more. The very thought of such a boring life, or the comfort it sometimes gave her when she thought she could always fall back on it if worse came to worst. She shuddered. It would be so easy, so easy to fall into the trap and settle for the path of least resistance.

The tears were beginning to drop out of the corners of her eyes when a knock on the door made her stop sniffling and collect herself. Who could that be? She wiped her eyes, got out of the chair, and went to answer the door.

It was Mrs. Prout.

There was no keeping the woman out when she wanted to get in. She forced her massive bulk inside the door before Désirée even had a chance to fully open it. "Somebody's finally home in this place," the old woman said. "Took a look in here this morning and just about couldn't believe my eyes."

Désirée hated the idea of the woman being in their apartment, sniffing around, prying when no one was at home. She said nothing, waiting for the woman to get to the point.

Mrs. Prout was of indeterminate age, but had to be at least over sixty. She was grossly fat, the folds of flesh on her face obliterating whatever traces of prettiness may have existed in her past. The sweaty little ringlets of her sparse black hair seemed, to Désirée, like loathsome little worms that were burrowing into the old woman's scalp. Her lips were thick and blubbery, and she had an enormous brown beauty spot on the left side of her mouth. On the few occasions when the woman had the audacity to wear makeup she resembled nothing so much as a preambulating bulldog in drag. Her arms and legs were puffed up sausages of liver spots and greasy, hanging flesh. Her massive breasts hung down obscenely beneath the stained folds of her housedress, within whose confines she seemed to spend every waking hour. She had been a widow for the last ten years and was likely to remain so.

"Disgusting!" Mrs. Prout said, surveying the room with her arms folded together in front of her chest. "Look at this place. Just disgusting."

Désirée mentally cursed her roommate. "We all had early auditions and interviews this morning, Mrs. Prout," she explained. "You know how it is. Both of us were late." She bit her lip and hoped that the old woman wouldn't wonder why she'd first said "all" instead of "both." "Neither of us had time to clean up and I just got home myself."

Mrs. Prout let out a snort of disapproval. To think that Désirée had at first found the old woman motherly. Well, motherliness could turn to savagery when you were a few weeks behind in your rent.

"Don't give me any of that," Mrs. Prout argued. "This place is a pigsty. A pigsty, I tell you. This mess wasn't made in a single morning. Whatcha think, I'm stupid? You think I'm stupid, girl? Is this the way your mother raised ya?"

The old cow was chewing gum so fiercely that some of her words were unintelligible. "Now you clean this place up or else. I want this place to look decent. This is the kind of mess I'd expect a man to make, not two little girls like you and your friend." She paused. The edges of her mouth turned up a little, the closest her sour face would ever get to a smile. "Little girls shouldn't make messes like this."

At times Mrs. Prout's scolding could almost become affectionate, without warning, and Désirée always did her best to capitalize on it. *Play up to her, engage her sympathy, get her off balance. Keep her from asking about the rent.*

"Well," Désirée said, "you know how young ladies are. Especially we girls in 'the theater.' Always rushing off to some place or other. We're sorry, Mrs. Prout. I'll start cleaning up immediately." She looked around the room and giggled. "Why, it really *is* a mess, isn't it?"

"More like a man's mess than a girl's."

Oops. She was back on that again. And then Désirée was

sure she knew why Mrs. Prout had been up in their apartment that morning. She'd been looking for signs of another roommate, a *male* roommate, looking for masculine objects, clues, anything to use as an excuse to throw them out into the street. "Lots of people need these apartments," Mrs. Prout was fond of saying. "I could rent this one just like that." And then her fingers would snap like the crack of doom.

Désirée bent down to pick a blouse up off the floor, bracing herself for the prying questions that were sure to follow. But Mrs. Prout had gone from one of her scolding motherly moods to one of introspection. She was talking about her late husband again.

"That man. That Mr. P., I tell you. Now *there* was a slob. He made messes like this. Never put the cap on the toothpaste. Had to holler at him to get him to comb his hair."

While the old lady droned her way down memory lane, Désirée made the appropriate appreciative noises; how she *enjoyed* Mrs. Prout's stories! After awhile she simply tuned out and started cleaning the apartment in earnest. She would have to convince Janice to be more careful. Look what trouble they were in already! While she put the place in comparative order, she looked to make sure that there *weren't* any obvious traces of Paul's presence. She didn't think so. What few clothes he had were safely hidden away in a suitcase under one of the cots. The peach fuzz on Paul's twenty-two-year-old face was so insubstantial that he only had to shave infrequently, and when he did, used soap lather instead of expensive shaving cream. A man's toothbrush didn't look any different from a lady's, except perhaps for the color, and Paul was using one of Janice's spare pink ones. Paul was not a remarkably masculine man; he blended in with the feminine scheme of the girls' apartment without making a noticeable ripple. Even Mrs. Prout's "masculine clutter" had actually been created by Janice.

Désirée had almost forgotten about it all when the old lady suddenly stopped droning and abruptly said, "Where's that black boy who's been hanging out around here?"

"Oh, him. He's just a friend of ours. I met him in acting class last year. A nice fellow, Mrs. Prout."

"And where does he live?"

Désirée feigned disinterest. "Up with his family in Harlem, I guess."

Mrs. Prout was never one to drop an unpleasant subject. "Well, he's around here an awful lot. Yesterday I saw him on the outside steps about to come into the building. He shot off down the street the minute he caught sight of me. What's he so afraid of?"

"He probably just forgot something. He's always doing that. We practice together, do parts for our acting classes."

"Well, he seems harmless enough, not like some of them, but if you let him hang around here too much, people will talk, and that's something we can all do without, understand?"

"I guess so, Mrs. Prout." She was tired of the old woman, tired of the cross-examination. "Paul won't be any problem, believe me. He's a very nice guy."

Mrs. Prout unfolded her arms and put her hands on her hips. She twisted her mouth into a vulgar sneer and said, "Well, he doesn't look the type to knock a girl up, but you can never be too careful."

Désirée stopped working and stood there facing the woman, a pair of stockings dangling from her hand. She hoped the expression she wore was as disgusted and weary as the old woman's was. For a period of about ten seconds or longer they simply stared at one another, the unspoken implications of the woman's remark hanging there in the air like an ugly, translucent phantom.

Then Mrs. Prout snorted, shrugged her shoulders, and said, "Well, you just see this place is cleaned up, and keep it that way." She started for the door, then turned around. "And don't think I've forgotten about that rent you owe me. I'll give you five more days to cough it up, or it's—" She drew a line across her throat and gurgled dramatically.

"Yes, Mrs. Prout. Thank you for giving us the extra time."

The woman left and closed the door behind her. Désirée could hear her huffing and puffing her way down the stairs and couldn't help but hope that she might have a heart attack and wheeze her last breath right then and there as Désirée gleefully listened.

Désirée was surprised. The apartment was already looking

better. If only she knew exactly where Paul was now. She could call him and tell him to stay out late, to come home after nine o'clock when the fat old lady was asleep.

So far a catastrophe had been averted.

But for how long could you cheat fate, she wondered.

Paul Wilson sat in the subway car and tried desperately to keep from crying. What would the people on the train think if they saw him like that? That middle-aged white couple who sat across from him, looking past him and around him as if he didn't exist; the gaggle of young black kids at the far end of the car, trading jokes and insults, staring at a pretty black lady who could hear their obscenities but pretended they didn't faze or offend her; the heavyset man with the Irish mug and the red blotchy face who breathed heavily, coughed up phlegm and stared down from his perch of insignificance with stony, counterfeit indifference. They would have no sympathy if they saw him crying. They would see the weakness there, the fatigue and pain and hunger, and they would hate him even more than they already did.

It wasn't easy being a *nigger* who had the audacity to want to be an actor.

Or a dancer or a singer or just a simple entertainer. Paul would have painted his face, put on a silly hat, made like Stepin Fetchit; he would have done an imitation of "Rochester," screamed like a fool at men in white sheets and acted like an old negro jackass if he thought it would get him a job. This was no time for pride. There he was: broke, humiliated, so desperate and hungry he'd been forced to move in with two white girls just to survive. This was no time to be offended by the simpering roles he was offered—*might* be offered; right now no one was offering anything—the roles that made blacks look like fools and ninnies and idiots, the roles that the black actors in Hollywood had eagerly accepted just to keep themselves and their families fed. Now he understood why you had to take anything they gave you, why you had to be a clown, a fool, an asshole. Kiss the white man's behind. Anything to keep from starving, anything to keep the roof above your head.

But today had been the final straw, the ultimate humiliation. They had needed a black actor for a tiny bit in an off-off-Broadway drama, just a teeny-tiny role with a couple of lines. God knows the call for black actors came so infrequently that every negro in the city with the slightest thespian leanings had showed up for the audition. Most of them supported themselves with other, more sensible jobs. Even the white actors were mostly waiters and bellboys.

But not Paul, no sir. Paul couldn't handle those kinds of jobs, at least not on a regular basis. Paul was too proud—as his mother and his uncle always told him—too proud to shine shoes or sell papers or do jobs that most negroes were only to happy to do. Paul fancied himself the new Bill Robinson; hell, the new Paul Robeson. Why be humble? He had read about Hattie McDaniel winning her Oscar for *Gone With the Wind* and gotten some idea that the negro's day had finally come. His uncle had viciously reminded him that Hattie had only played a mammy, after all, and surely Paul couldn't do that? Or could he? And then Uncle Moe had guffawed and slapped his knee, laughing at Paul until he caught his sister's half-scathing, half-pleading looks and stopped.

It would have been bad enough if Paul had wanted to be a jazz musician, play in a band in some of the Harlem nightspots—even that would have been tough enough to break into. But he wanted to act, to emote, to *be somebody*. How dare he have such nerve! Why wasn't he content to accept his lot with the rest of the "little people?"

He'd almost gotten that part today, that's what hurt the most. His reading had been good, damn good. He'd ignored the faint snickers he'd heard from some of the others auditioning. The stage manager, Tod Bolton, an acquaintance of Paul's, was an intense white boy who always seemed to expect more of Paul than Paul wanted to give. Tod had overheard the director and playwright talking about Paul after the audition. Later, over a cup of coffee in Horn and Hardart, Tod told Paul that they'd crossed his name off the list of "suitables."

Although he had couched it in compassionate terms, Paul sensed that Tod had enjoyed giving Paul the bad news. "They felt you weren't quite right," Tod explained. "They wanted someone a little . . . tougher, dumber. You're too smart, everyone can see that. And also . . . well, maybe I shouldn't say this . . . but they thought you were a little, y'know, girlish. Y'know. You're slender, kind of willowy. You know. Not enough meat on your bones."

Maybe I shouldn't say this. Why did people always say that first when they knew they were going to hurt you? Why did they say anything?

Not enough meat on his bones, was that it? Paul knew what they had really meant, and had probably said. The stage manager, a beefy, muscular type and ex-sailor, could "pass." Paul could not. He had ignored the sexual insinuations—unsure himself if they were true or not, and not even sure if he cared—and said, "There'd be more meat on my bones if I got enough to eat."

The futility of his life hit him as the train wound its way down toward Greenwich Village. What had made him think he could possibly make a living as an actor? He had *at least* three strikes against him. He was a negro. He was "girlish" and intellectual when they wanted someone manly and stupid. And, perhaps the worst of all, he was a secret epileptic.

He told no one about his illness. Absolutely no one, even though it was not a big problem for him. His attacks had always been of the milder type, *Petit Mal* at worst, and even poor people were given a drug called dilantin to keep their condition under control. But often he was haunted by the thought that he'd finally get his break and that opening night on the stage he'd have a fit—*Grand Mal*, the most serious—and he'd snarl and foam at the mouth and contort his body like a maddened, howling dog, maybe even lose consciousness. It would be the performance of his life, all right, his final one. Boy, would the audience get their money's worth! Watch the freak make the ultimate fool of himself in front of several hundred people.

Oh Lord. He put his head in his hands and tried, tried, to keep the sobs in. What made him think he had any kind of chance? The haunting specter of the shoeshine stand—the one his uncle had worked at for forty years—kept getting closer and brighter and more vividly frightening in its emptiness and defeat than it had ever been before.

New York was really lovely in the winter. So lovely. Sure, it was cold, but what did that matter? There was something about Manhattan when a chill was in the air. . . .

Janice Evans walked gaily down the street and pretended that her heart wasn't broken. *That's life, Janice,* she thought. *You win some, you lose some. There's no use crying over it now.*

That handsome guy she'd met at the club last Friday had promised to meet her for a drink that afternoon at three. She'd rushed from her acting class to make it on time, almost breaking her neck as she galloped down those rickety stairs, racing to catch a crosstown bus she'd seen pulling up to the corner from the window of the studio. She'd arrived with moments to spare, ordered a drink at the bar, and sat there for over an hour waiting for the man to appear. Finally she got up the nerve to dial the number he'd given her after their memorable night of passion.

It was the number of the Federal Savings Bank.

No, they had no employee named Peter Sortsky. *But she bet they had a depositor by that name, a real creep who gave out the number of his bank to anxious broads he didn't want to see any more.*

Serves you right, she told herself, for thinking that this one was any different. He'd been so handsome, with his straight nose, perfect teeth, and glossy black hair. And a real humdinger in the bedroom. A great lover, sure, but a miserable human being. Did he *have* to make that date with her? Surely he'd known at the time that he had no intention of keeping it. If he had, he would have given her his real home number. Was it some sort of cruel rite of passage he had to go through, something he had to inflict on his pick-ups, the women he slept with, before he could feel completely like a man?

She began to swing her arms back and forth as she walked, hoping the extra bounce in her step would give her a lift that she really didn't feel. Anyone seeing her would think she was the happiest girl in the world. Look at me! Pretty. Successful. Popular. Aren't I the envy of all the world? Who wouldn't want to be in my shoes?

Said shoes were getting holes in the soles. And her clothes were last year's models. And wasn't she getting too old for this game?

The folks back home in Iowa thought she was doing real well. Goodness knows, she certainly didn't tell them the truth. Mommy and Daddy thought that their little girl was the most wonderful, the most beautiful and chastest young lady in the whole wide world. Apparently they didn't notice the slightly crooked teeth, the too-large nose and too-thin lips, when they looked at her face. They didn't know about all the men she'd slept with.

Taken individually, Janice's features weren't really that awful, but collectively the effect was less than stimulating. Désirée was the one with the looks, the one who could keep a man interested even if she dared to say "no." Janice knew she wasn't really ugly—a lot of men had told her just the opposite—but she lacked that certain "something" that a woman needed if she were to get ahead in show biz. Not that looks were everything. After all, pretty Désirée wasn't doing any better than Janice was.

Though she had hardly any money, Janice stopped to splurge on a small box of cookies at the corner market. They would make her feel better. Paul and Désirée liked them, too, so she wouldn't eat all of them herself and get fat. That was one thing she was grateful for—a slender figure and good boobs. She sometimes thought men weren't interested in her, only in her boobs. Men like Peter What's-his-name.

Taking a cookie out of the box and munching on it—she remembered to keep the smile on her face, that dizzy look of fun and gaiety that would fool all of the passers-by—she turned the corner onto Bleeker Street and walked up West Fourth to the brownstone where she resided.

She had a history of picking the wrong men, like they were magnets and she a mere metal female who clung irresistibly to their surface. First there was Sam Mason, her hometown sweetheart, who turned her off for good because he only had "one thing" on his mind. (Boy, if he could only see her now.) How she had adored that boy. And how close she'd come to "giving in." If she *had*, she might have become *Mrs.* Sam Mason—and been married to a man who was serving several years in the penitentiary for armed robbery.

Then there was Joe Forrester, the stagehand who had a

beautiful voice, sensuous eyes, lots of money and charm to spare—and a wife and three kids back in Scarsdale. He had nearly driven her to a nervous breakdown, that one. She swore after that: No More Married Men!

Lastly there was John Rutherford, the director of the one and only play she'd ever appeared in. Not truly handsome, but manly and attractive, with a big chest and arms to match and a swagger that had her swooning at the very thought of making love to him. Finally, when her agony had become obvious to the entire company, a kind and more sophisticated soul than the little hayseed from Iowa took her aside and explained that the nice athletic fellow who did the stunts in the second set and was John's roommate, was *more* than just John's roommate.

Janice had been stunned; she'd only heard rumors about such things. She'd thought only men who were kind of feminine like, well, Paul, could possibly be "that way." And she shouldn't really think that way about Paul because he had never said anything about it one way or the other, and anyhow it was really not her business. It was all beyond her, she was afraid. But it *was* 1940 and she supposed a thespian in New York City should be tolerant of such behavior.

She reached the brownstone and climbed to the second story, trying to put on a fresh, sunny face before she opened the door and greeted her friends. She was sure they, too, would have bad news, and she hadn't yet decided whether she would share hers with them or not. Things were dismal enough as it was without them having their rock, their own little comedienne, Janice, fall apart on them.

She hadn't realized how late it was. Paul and Désirée had already finished supper. What little there was of it.

"Hi! I've brought dessert."

Paul rushed over and kissed her. "Sit down," he said. "We're going to do something wonderful tonight."

What was going on? Nobody looked upset and Paul was all excited. For a moment Janice's gloom dissipated.

"We're going to have a *seance!*" Désirée said, jumping up from her chair and hopping around like a rabbity two-year-old.

And just for a second—it was intangible, really—Janice's

wall of optimism opened just a crack and looked out upon a big, black pit of fear and apprehension. *Something awful's going to happen.*

Then it was gone.

"Really!" she said, taking off her coat and laughing. "Why, that sounds like a lot of fun!"

2

"Whatever gave you two the idea to have a seance?"

Seances. Those strange sessions where people sat around and held hands and the lights went out and suddenly these spooky voices—voices of the people's dead relatives—started talking out of nowhere. The mere thought of it gave Janice goosebumps. All she knew about seances was what she had seen in creepy old movies.

Désirée, ever the practical one, was the first to answer. "It doesn't cost anything," she said.

"My Aunt Bessie used to hold seances for people before she died," Paul explained. "I was just a boy then, but I remember how she did it. I think she somehow faked it all. But sometimes . . . sometimes you just couldn't be sure."

"Did she make a living that way?"

"Sure," Paul said. "Enough to keep Uncle George in whiskey, at least. She once confessed to me—I was about seven at the time—that *most* of what she did was trickery; she only gave the customers what they wanted. But sometimes, for friends and relatives, she did try to call up real spirits. She believed that once or twice she had actually made contact." He hunched over, widened his eyes comically, and spoke in a stumbling dialect that was as far away as possible from his own superb elocution.

31

" 'Son, things have happened that even I, even your own Aunt Bessie can't 'splain. Things no one can 'splain. And dat's the truth.' "

Janice, intrigued, sat down on her cot and said, "Like what things?"

"She said she heard voices. They all heard voices, things she swore she wasn't responsible for." He widened his eyes again. " 'Some people got the power. Some's got a little and some's got a lot. I only got a little, but mebbe, boy, mebbe you got a *lot*.' "

Désirée's eyes twinkled. "Paul might be on the verge of a whole new career."

"Hell, it couldn't be any worse than my acting career."

"Now, now. We're not going to talk about any of that. Tonight we're just going to forget. Forget everything." Désirée turned to Janice. "We left some supper on the stove for you. Not much, I'm afraid. But we'll let you have most of the cookies. And there's some of that wine left over in the refrigerator. We can finish that, too. Folks, we're going to have a regular little party."

Although she knew what they were trying to do, Janice's curiosity got the better of her. "Listen, didn't *any* of you guys get good news today? Even an inkling?"

Paul came to a standstill. Désirée rubbed the back of her neck and stood with her head crooked to one side. "*No*, Janice. It was a really crummy day."

"Same here," Paul admitted. "No luck." He shrugged and added, "Not yet, at least."

Désirée told Janice about Mrs. Prout's untimely visit. Then she blinked her eyes and perked up a bit. "Never mind our troubles. Tell us about the date you had with that good-looking guy. How did it go?"

Janice shrugged, trying to hide the hurt. Finally she just blurted it out. "He stood me up."

"Oh, Janice, we're sorry." Paul came over and reached his hand gently toward her, as if he were hoping to siphon off the pain and disappointment.

"Relax, guys. It's okay. No harm done. He was a creep anyway. Halfway there I almost turned around and went home. Seriously, he didn't interest me all that much. I just didn't want to hurt his feeling by not showing up." She rolled her eyes. "I might have known."

Désirée came over and hugged her, patted her back. "He's not good enough for you. He probably knew you didn't like him that much and figured you wouldn't come." A little white lie, they both realized, but a nice one.

Paul smiled. "Tonight we'll call down the spirits on him, okay, girls?"

They laughed. "Are you sure we have enough people for a seance? Don't you need at least seven?" asked Janice.

"No, you're thinking of a coven. My aunt would sometimes have only three people, sometimes five or more. Doesn't make much difference. In fact, if there's too many people the spirits might get confused."

Janice didn't know if he were kidding or not, but she was certain he knew more about the subject than she did. Although she was willing to try anything to take her mind off her troubles, she still wasn't sure about this. "Do either of you actually believe in the spirit world?"

Paul and Désirée glanced at each other for a second, then looked at Janice. "Let's just say," Paul replied, "that I believe in the *possibility* of the spirit world."

"There are more things in heaven and earth, Horatio, than you dream up in your philosophy," Désirée giggled, "or something like that."

"Stop butchering Shakespeare," Janice said, "and tell me how a seance is going to pay our rent, get us jobs, and keep dear Mrs. Prout off our backs."

"Now, Janice," Désirée scolded, "Enough of the doom and gloom. We said we weren't going to think of any of that tonight. Tomorrow morning our troubles will still be here and we can face them then. We'll put our heads together and think of something. But there's nothing we can do about it tonight, so why can't we have fun?" A desperation had crept into her voice that surprised even her. "Look," she said, "usually we just sit around reading books or studying lines, wrapped up in ourselves, staring into space in our separate little corners, feeling awful and not knowing what to do about it. Paul and I talked about it over supper, Janice. We *need* to try something different. Just for tonight. Going out is too depressing because we haven't any money for a restaurant or a movie, and besides it's too cold.

So let's forget our misery and give this seance a try."

Janice had to admit that she couldn't argue with Désirée's logic. "Okay. I'm game. What do we do first?"

"It doesn't have to be just the three of us," Paul said. "We could call up some friends and have them come over."

Janice liked the idea, but Désirée vetoed it. "No. Most of our friends are just as broke and depressing as we are. You know what will happen. We'll start to talk about the theater and trade notes on our horrible experiences, and before you know it the whole purpose of the evening will be forgotten. We don't *want* to talk shop and get depressed tonight. They'll be asking us how we're doing, and maybe one or two of them will even have gotten a job . . . which will depress us even more. *No*.

"Besides," she said, "What other friends—real friends—do the three of us have? Besides each other?"

There was a moment of silence that was as comforting as it was awkward, a realization that Désirée's words were pathetically correct, but that in spite of that they could truly depend on one another.

"Okay, let's start," Paul said, rubbing his hands together. His fingers were long and slender like a pianist's, the palms unblemished and pale. "We can use the kitchen table. Let's get out a couple of candles and turn off the lights.

"Wait a minute," Janice said. "Isn't it a little early for this? Aren't seances supposed to start around midnight? And I haven't had dinner yet."

"We can have a seance any time. Doesn't even have to be at night. Isn't that right, Paul?" Désirée said. "But we *should* let you have dinner first. It is awfully early."

Paul agreed. "Okay. Désirée, why don't you finish the rest of the wine while Janice has her supper?"

Désirée went to the refrigerator and took out a gallon bottle of cheap chablis. It had been left over from a party they'd had several weeks earlier, though no one could recall who had brought it. Janice spooned herself some franks and beans while Désirée got out wine glasses and poured them each a splash of the chablis. It wouldn't take much of the stuff to get them high, as neither of the girls could be called heavy drinkers. Paul never touched liquor.

Almost two hours later the wine was almost gone and all of

them were feeling quite good. They had come dangerously close to starting the forbidden "shop talk"—comparing notes on auditions and the like—when Paul reminded them of what they had promised to do earlier. Janice brushed her teeth—she was compulsive about that if nothing else—while Paul and Désirée prepared for the seance.

Janice wondered why she couldn't shake the bad feelings she had about it. Just a few minutes ago, as they'd finished up the wine, she thought they'd forgotten all about it and been relieved.

She dried her mouth on a towel and thought that underneath her cheery demeanor she had to be the most melancholy person in the world.

By the time Janice got out of the bathroom the apartment was dark except for two lit candles that had been placed on either side of the kitchen table. Désirée had even gone so far as to place a red linen tablecloth—"looks so mysterious and demonic, doesn't it?"—on the top of the battered table top. janice sat down near one candle while Désirée sat across from her near the other. Paul, the medium, sat between them in the middle.

Désirée picked her pocketbook up off the floor and started rummaging through its contents. "Turn the lights back on," she said. "I have to fix my face."

Janice laughed. "What do you have to do that for, silly? Who do you want to look good for, the ghosts?"

Désirée realized Janice was right. Why keep them all waiting when they were anxious to start? She just hoped this would work. She hoped it would keep them from enduring their nightly ritual of collective self-pity. The misery in this house was so rich and thick there were times she swore that she could smell it. A putrid stench of fear and panic.

Désirée watched Paul's face as they grasped hands across the table and held onto each other tightly. He was a good-looking man, his color a deep, rich brown and his eyes deep-set and pensive. His cheekbones were almost too high, giving him a pretty look, but his full lips and strong chin were perfect. Sometimes Désirée felt a strong, confusing attraction for him, a desire to caress his face, to *touch* his prettiness, and she was glad it was unlikely he'd respond to her if ever she did. It would cause complications, and her life had enough troubles as it was. She wondered if Paul realized how much strength there was under his delicacy, how much pride and persistence and steeliness came through beneath his fluttery outward manner.

She looked at Janice. Her friend was the same age as she, though she looked a little younger. Janice's face was given color and character by the candlelight. Désirée knew she herself looked awful in candlelight; it only highlighted her very worst features. She hoped her makeup would compensate. Yet if she couldn't show her worst face to her very best friends, then who could she show it to? Janice, on the other hand, was made prettier by the fire glow; the darkness covered her blotchy cheeks and forehead, and she almost looked exotic.

Paul had begun his chanting. The girls couldn't help giggling and neither could he.

"Stop it," he mock-scolded. "The spirits will never hear me if we don't take this seriously."

Désirée burped, eliciting a few chorus of howls.

"Do you think the spirits were responsible for that?"

"Not the kind of spirits we're trying to raise," Janice replied.

They settled down again and promised one another to behave. Paul closed his eyes, gripped their hands with renewed determination, and lifted his head toward the ceiling.

"Spirits of the darkness, do you hear me? We are open to you, we are calling you. Will you give us a sign that you are listening?"

The girls' giggling was abruptly silenced by the sound of something shattering in the bathroom.

Janice screeched and Paul let their hands drop. "What the hell was that?"

Désirée got up and investigated, not even willing to entertain the notion that something supernatural might have been responsible. She called from the bathroom. "Janice, you left your perfume bottle too close to the edge of the sink." It had slowly slid across the sheath of water on the porcelain.

"Oh no," she groaned. "That stuff cost me a bundle."

"Clean it up later," Paul said. "I know it sounds crazy, but I feel like I'm really on to something. That if we concentrate we can really make contact."

Désirée turned out the bathroom light and came back into the room. "Have you considered what might happen if we actually *do*? Make contact, that is. Aside from running out of the room?"

"Spirits won't hurt you," he said. "I saw some spooky things when I was a kid at my aunt's seances—half the time I never knew if they were real or not—but though I sometimes got really scared I never felt I was in danger."

"What exactly is supposed to happen?" Janice asked. "How will the spirits appear? How will they get in touch with us? I mean aside from knocking over perfume bottles?"

"Well, they might appear as a vague figure made of white light hovering in the air above the table. Or ectoplasm may form; we might actually see somebody or something standing nearby or at the other end of the room. Ectoplasmic forms normally keep their distance from humans."

Janice laughed. "Thank goodness for that."

"Or they might communicate with us by taking over my body. I'll go into a trance all of a sudden, and the spirit will talk to you, answer your questions, through me. My voice will sound funny, a combination of the spirit's voice and my own. I may even speak in a different language. But whatever you do, don't try to snap me out of the trance. And don't be frightened. It will be a wonderful opportunity. Just ask me whatever questions come to mind."

Désirée thought it sounded as if Paul might be setting them up for something. Well, who cared? This was fun.

"But *what* spirits will take you over?" Janice asked. "Whose spirit?"

Paul shook his head. "It could be the spirit of someone who once lived in this room. Died here, that is. Or the spirit of a loved one, one of our own relatives who passed on. It won't be anyone who means us harm, believe me."

Désirée shivered. "I hope you're right."

"Say, couldn't we accidentally conjure up a demon or the devil?"

"*Janice!*"

Paul waved away the suggestion. "Don't be silly, girl. We probably won't get anything. It would take a medium a lot more powerful than I am to do something that bad."

Désirée got a glimpse of something emanating from Paul just then, something in the eyes or around the shoulders, something in his very core that made her wonder. Sure, this was a game, an amusement, for him just as it was for them, but part of him was taking it quite seriously. She could understand. The poor fellow had so much defeat in his life it was no wonder he welcomed the opportunity to be something special, to be able to do something no other person—or at least very few people—could do. But calling up the spirits? She wondered if this was the expression of some long-repressed voodoo heritage or something like it, then chided herself for being so silly.

They clasped hands again. From that moment on Désirée really hoped it would work, that they'd call up someone and get a glimpse of life beyond. It would be nice to know there really was something after death, the possibility for some happiness and peace after a lifetime of disappointment and struggle.

She knew all three of them had entertained thoughts of suicide, had thought of taking that way out of their dreary, nowhere lives. None of them had ever come right out and said it. But did they have to? It would be nice to know, if they ever *did* give in to the ultimate act of self-destruction, that there might be something waiting for them on the other side. Perhaps it was just the wine, the alcohol warmly circulating through her system, but she hoped that Paul was successful. Like him, she closed her eyes. Perhaps, if she really concentrated, it would help.

He was chanting again, different words from before, and Désirée knew it was more than a performance. He was trying to make contact, real contact, with the spirit world. She opened her eyes a slit and saw that Janice had closed her eyes, too. That was it. They would carefully focus their energy and freely give Paul their assistance.

The low chanting and clenching of hands seemed to go on forever. Désirée couldn't get over how seriously they were all taking this. Not one of them giggled or broke the chain. Not one of them said, "Look guys, isn't this enough?"

And then from somewhere near the floor came a low steady rumbling.

It's just the subway, Désirée thought. The IRT may have been a block away but the vibrations traveled all the way up the street. Up to the second story, though? Maybe Mrs. Prout was having company, or had the TV up too high. *It had to be the subway.*

Janice was murmuring something as the tension from her grip

increased. *"Janice, you're hurting me,"* Désirée said. When there was no reply and no diminishing of the tension, Désirée realized with a start that she'd only said the words in her mind.

The rumbling of the floor was getting louder and she swore she could feel a chill in the air. Was the table moving—or was it just her foolish imagination?

She was about to tell Janice to let go of her hand, out loud this time, when Paul's chanting began rising in pitch. His grip, too, was tightening. Désirée thought that perhaps it was time to put a stop to this silliness, but she was transfixed by Paul's performance. Janice was whimpering again; she was really scared and Paul was doing it to her.

Désirée found her voice. "Paul," she said. "*Paul!*"

Paul didn't answer. From far down in his throat came a deep vibratory grumbling. It should have been impossible for Paul to make a sound like that. Could it be happening, really happening? Had Paul's mind been taken over?"

"Paul. *Paul.*" She was about to say, "You're frightening us," but she'd be damned if she'd let him know that he was fooling them. *Actor's pride*, she thought—even now there was a tinge of envy of each other's ability.

But somehow, somewhere deep inside her, she knew that Paul was not giving a performance, and that whatever was going to happen had already gone too far to be stopped. This time she swore the table *was* shaking. Was Paul doing it with his knees? The rumbling had temporarily receded, but the air was still chilly. Had Janice opened the bathroom window? Désirée hadn't noticed when she'd been in there before.

The growling noises issuing from Paul's mouth were slowly turning into vowels and consonants, a crazy, unintelligible language made up of impossible phrases. Désirée couldn't understand a word.

"Désirée?" Janice said, her eyes wide and pleading. "Is Paul joking or what?"

Désirée ignored her. "Paul? Paul! What's happening to you? Is this for real? 'Cause if it isn't you're really scaring us and we wish you would stop."

The strange words, the weird language, kept gushing from his mouth in spite of the fact that his lips weren't really moving. Désirée could tell even in the candlelight that now his teeth were actually clenched together. How *could* he be making those noises? Could he really be in a trance?

Sitting there in that dark apartment on West Fourth Street, stuck between those four barren walls, Desiree had a sudden sense of The Universe. All the dark things that walked behind the walls, hid in all the cramped, hollow spaces were suddenly visible. She had a sense of the enormity of experience, could see the hidden corners that were normally closed off from human mentality. Beyond the paltry glare of the candlelight it seemed as if the apartment had been swallowed up: the beds were gone, and so were the chairs and the rug and all their belongings and the world outside that they represented. It was a strange new dimension, one of enormous size and shape, as well as one with an entirely different set of physical laws and sciences.

Désirée fought to hold on to reality, to convince herself that what she seemed to perceive was truly just an illusion, that in the darkness beyond the table everything was as it always had been. But with Paul sitting there with his head back and the horrible noises coming from his throat, and with Janice wide-eyed and trembling in her chair, with the chill in the air and the rumbling below their feet, it was hard not to admit even a little bit that there was more to the World Beyond than she might ever have imagined.

Janice had let go of both Désirée's and Paul's hands, and Désirée finally followed suit. That did nothing to make Paul stop. If anything his yowling had gotten worse. He was like a growling animal struggling to make speech but lacking the basic ability to do so. Luckily he was keeping his volume down. If he got too loud it would wake up Mrs. Prout downstairs and they'd really be in a fix. Where would they put Paul if she came prying —in the bathtub?

Paul. Stop it now. This has gone far enough.

But then Désirée realized that his actions so far had only been a mere prelude to the performance that was to follow.

It had to be the candlelight, Désirée told herself. It had to be a trick of the light, a distortion caused by the flickering flame. Paul's face couldn't really have changed that way. That look in his eyes. That ghastly paleness. Had he somehow managed to hide a makeup kit under the table, made up his face to look like Dracula while she and Janice had their eyes closed?

Janice had seen it, too, and she was quivering in terror. "Désirée," she said. "What's happened to him, Désirée? What's going on?"

"I don't know, Janice. Do you?" Was this a trick they were both playing on her? Désirée swore she'd kill them both if it turned out Janice had a hand in it, too.

"No. And I'm scared. Paul, stop it!" Janice screamed. "You're scaring us!"

No it wasn't a trick. Paul had wonderful diction and breath control, but he couldn't lower his voice to such a deep, inhuman register, no one could. There hadn't been time for him to apply white makeup to his face. And the eyes—God, the eyes. All Désirée could see were the whites. And there was foam pouring out of his mouth, thick and yellowish, like no saliva she had ever seen before.

Désirée screamed and shot out of her chair. She raced over to the sink, splashed some cold water on her face and turned on the light above the kitchen table. Maybe with the light on it wouldn't be so scary.

She was wrong.

It was worse.

Paul's whole body was quivering. His cheeks were swollen and that pus-like stuff continued pouring out of his mouth, more it seemed than he could have held comfortably within his jaw. The pus dribbled down his chin and plopped onto the table. His eyes were two white sunken spots surrounded by pale brown flesh. The flesh was mottled with what looked like stains or sores. On his forehead ridges had appeared, rippling ridges that made it seem as if something were moving beneath the skin, or as if his brains were expanding and about to burst right out of his head. His head was visibly growing larger, too, his mouth opening, unleashing more and more fluid, and his jaw widening to an impossible width to accommodate the flood. Then the outpour stopped and his full brown lips came together again. He stood up with that horrible look on his face and turned to confront the two women who were standing in horror-struck silence by the door. *This was no act. It was real.*

"Oh my God, Désirée!" Janice screamed. "Something's happened to him. My God—something's happened to Paul! And look at his hand. What's happened to his hand?"

Désirée reached out an arm, but stood her distance. "Paul. Paul, tell us what's wrong." She noticed the hand then, Paul's left hand, which he had raised in the air and thrust out toward the women like a menacing scimitar. The fingernails were long and sharp, the flesh bumpy and mottled. *It looked like a claw.* And there was something else. . . .

Désirée knew that Paul had to be seriously ill, but she was too terrified by his appearance and his actions to go over to him and administer aid. If this was a trick, then Paul had to be the greatest stage magician in the world, and she knew that was not the case. Was he having some kind of fit? One night when he'd been groggy and semicoherent, hadn't he mentioned something about childhood epilepsy? He'd never elaborated on it and she'd had enough tact not to press him. Maybe he needed a doctor, and the two of them were standing there hollering like a couple of raving idiots.

"Paul?" Gingerly she approached the table. "Paul, is there something we can do, some way we can help you?"

Janice wrenched open the door to the hall and said through her tears, "I'm going to get a doctor." There was a phone on the floor near one of the beds, but she was clearly too scared of Paul to go past him to use it. It was understandable—he looked as if he wanted to kill them. Désirée told Janice to run downstairs and use the pay phone in the hallway.

A moment later Janice was gone and Désirée was alone in the room with Paul. Though there was no more foam on his lips, his growling had intensified. Some kind of sixth sense warned Désirée that she dared not approach him. She backed away from Paul even as he started moving in her direction. Before she knew what hit her he had lunged and grabbed her by the arm.

"Paul, stop it!" Désirée wriggled out of his grip and headed for the doorway. There was no medical condition she could think of, epilepsy or anything else, that could make a man start behaving in this manner. Had Paul gone "mental?" Was it rabies?

Or was he really possessed by a demon?

Paul was now hollering at the top of his lungs, screeching how he had to kill her or be damned, describing with hideous intensity the horrible things he'd do to her if he caught her. The demon had finally found its voice—for it could not be Paul's voice that was saying such things and in such bestial tongues. As Désirée darted into the hall, the thing using Paul's body ran after her with a cackle.

She stumbled on the top step of the staircase, and felt a moist, heavy hand grabbing her by her hair. "Help! Help me!" She could hear the voices of Janice and Mrs. Prout downstairs, her roommate explaining the incredible situation to the landlady. She could hear other people in the building stirring, too, even though it was one a.m., could hear voices and doors beginning to open. "Help me!" *Oh, Paul, why are you doing this? Don't you know what they'll think? Colored boy attacks two white women in their apartment. Don't you know what they'll do to you? Don't you realize what they'll say about Janice and me? We only tried to be your friends—*

But she was only trying to keep from accepting the obvious. That it was not Paul Wilson who was dragging her along the corridor with one hand and beating her on the head and face with the other. That it was not Paul Wilson who was muttering curses and breathing hoarsely and heavily like a malevolent dragon. That it was not Paul Wilson who was doing this to her.

When he tried to pull her back into the apartment, he had to turn, and his attention was momentarily diverted. Désirée managed to get to her feet as his grip on her hair briefly loosened. Before he could grab her again she was halfway down the hall, looking for something to defend herself with. Her face was bruised and battered, and blood was running from her nostrils. *You bastard!—Paul or whoever you are—damn you for doing this to me!*

She saw the fire axe in its holder on the wall.

Even as she lifted it up and off of the hooks that held it in a horizontal position, she wondered if she could ever use it on her dear friend Paul. No, not Paul. Not kind, gentle Paul. How could he have become this monstrous engine of destruction? Wouldn't someone come and save her, save *him* from her attempts to protect herself?

She raised the axe, preparing to swing it into his arm or shoulder, just enough to stop him without causing grievous injury. In the end, though, she couldn't bring herself to do it. She lowered the axe as he advanced on her and resorted to pleading and crying. That was her undoing.

The heavy axe dropped out of her hands as Paul lunged at her again. His fists kept opening and closing, as if the demon's mind in his body weren't sure if he wanted his man-slave to strangle the victim or beat her to death. At times the expression on Paul's face indicated that the man was struggling to fight off the influence of the alien consciousness, but it was a battle he didn't seem to be winning.

Désirée ran into the apartment and closed the door behind her. She remembered catching a glimpse of Mrs. Prout and Janice at the bottom of the stairs. They wanted to come to her aid but were too afraid to come closer and put themselves within the raging man-demon's reach. Désirée couldn't blame them, but she wished somebody would come to her rescue.

She should have known that even a locked door would do no good against this kind of opponent. There was a terrible, startling SLAM, followed by a chopping, rending noise. Paul had taken the fire axe she'd dropped and was using it to batter through the wood. Splinters flew into the room and into her face as one stroke after another began to tear the door asunder. Finally a hand reached through the jagged hole in the wood and got a grip on the doorknob. Désirée turned around in a panic and ran toward the window between the beds. Somehow she had to get out!

Paul got to her before she could climb out and drop into the alley behind the building. She was so close, so very close to safety. Her last thoughts were of her parents, the grief this would cause them, the pain. As the axe came down again and again, she felt the warmth of the spattering blood and could not believe that so much of it had once been circling around inside her. In some dim, distant corner beneath the waves of wrenching agony, she knew that this was not the kind of ending that she deserved. Surely she had not been as evil as all that?

What sort of lurid headlines would they write about her? Would they revel in her anguish and her blood? Would people riding the subway on their way to work read about her? Would they shudder and shake their heads and ask themselves what she had done to invite such a grisly demise? Would they think that she must have asked for it? Would they ever concede that she might have been someone as nice as their wife or their daughter, someone who hadn't deserved to have this happen?

The last sound she heard besides the relentless chopping of the axe was Janice screaming and screaming. . . .

. . . screaming and screaming. Janice was looking at him and screaming her head off. What was wrong with the girl? She wasn't acting normal at all. And God, her carrying on had woken up the fat old landlady. Now they would catch it! Now they would all be sleeping on the sidewalk. *Janice, would you please stop screaming!*

Mrs. Prout was hollering at him and pointing in his direction. She called him terrible names, "nigger" and "jigaboo" among them. Two cops were walking into the room, guns out, looking at him as if he were a bull and they matadors. The cops hated colored boys. What had he done to bring this on? They had only been sitting at the table having a quiet seance. Where was Désirée? She was always calm and rational; surely Désirée could make things right.

Then he looked at his feet and *saw* Désirée.

She was all slashed up. Her face was covered with blood and bruises. One arm seemed nearly severed. Her clothes were torn and soaked with gore. There were raw, gaping wounds in her body. . . .

Désirée!

Paul Wilson started to gag. *My God, who did this? That can't be—*

The cops were pulling him away, cuffing him, hitting him on the side of the head and grimacing hatefully. Someone was shouting, "Murderer, MURDERER"—but he wasn't sure if it was Janice (*not Janice, no, not you*) or fat Mrs. Prout. It could have been any one of the throng of spectators standing outside in the hall: the building's other residents as well as neighborhood ghouls who'd been attracted by the police cars in the street.

"What happened?" he asked, tears for Désirée streaming down his face. "What did I do? Where did I get that axe? It was only a game. Sweet Jesus, it was only a game. I did nothing, I tell you. I don't remember anything. Not a thing!

"It wasn't me," he pleaded, as they led him down the hall. "You must believe me—I would never have hurt Désirée. . . ."

He would stick to that story until the day two-thousand volts of electricity were shot through him and his crazy tale of demons

45

and devils would die with him.

Paul Wilson would die for a crime he had never committed.

He would die without knowing what had really killed Désirée Fontana.

Part Two: *Vicious*

3

1963.
New York City.

Anthony Winteroth sat up in bed and studied the woman who was dressing by the mirror. This was one he wouldn't have minded seeing more than once. Part of this was her fault, he thought, the brazen little thing. During the interview she had been constantly flirting with him, touching him in little suggestive ways and telling him he was handsome enough to star in one of his own movies. If she hadn't been so blatant in her attention to him he wouldn't be in this hotel room with her now, while his wife and son were waiting patiently for him back at their townhouse.

Anthony Winteroth was a good-looking man of forty-seven who kept his figure slim and had the kind of scholarly bearded face that some women found irresistibly virile. But the main secret to his charm was the enormous power he wielded, at least in Hollywood circles. He didn't bother telling his bed partners that the old adage—"only as good as your last picture"—applied as much to him as it did to everyone else.

Winteroth always preferred his lovers to leave before he did. It was never good to rush out of these things. He had to have time to prepare a good cover story, appraise himself for any incriminating evidence, particularly anything—such as scratches on his back—that couldn't be wiped away with a kleenex.

The reporter finished applying a fresh coat of lipstick and came over to the bed. She pursed her bright red lips and said, "It's been fun, Tony. Thanks for a good interview." She winked. "And for everything else."

Winteroth kept this suite at the Clinton year round for a variety of reasons. He preferred entertaining business associates at the hotel. It was hard to get rid of long-winded fat cats and studio heads if they decided to overstay their welcome at his townhouse—he couldn't just throw them out of his home. But if meetings went on for too long at the hotel, he could make up some story about another meeting, or family business, and duck out while the others finished their drinks and cigars and let the maid clean and lock up behind them. The suite served dual roles as his business office and trysting place. It came equipped with a private bath and bedroom, the latter of which had its own toilet as well as a separate entrance. Winteroth found the place useful for engaging in adulterous relations. It was very unlikely that his wife, Suzette, would ever come to the office suite, and in any case, she had no key to either door that led into the bedroom. And the heavy walls at the Clinton were practically soundproof.

The reporter handed him a slip of paper with her phone number on it. He smiled, blew her a kiss, and watched her as she let herself out.

Winteroth stretched and let out a mighty yawn. Throwing off the covers, he hoisted his trim, naked body out of the bed. He strode into the bathroom and relieved himself, then studied himself approvingly in the mirror. Forty-seven and still no gray. His black hair was as thick and smooth as it had been in his twenties. He brushed a hand through his wavy locks and went out into the bedroom to get dressed.

It really had been a fortunate moment when Don Ramis, a screenwriter with whom he had worked on several pictures that Winteroth had both produced and directed, came up with the idea of dramatizing the famous Désirée Fontana murder case. The storyline had everything. Beautiful, racy women. A dark, psychotic villain. A hint of mystery—that young man had insisted on his innocence to the very end. Things that were still unexplained and unresolved. Hints of occultism and demonism, devil-worship, even. Who could resist a package like that?

This was the picture that he really needed. His last one, *The Lady Strikes Back*, had been an ill-conceived attempt at comedy, a first—and last—for the normally somber Winteroth. And it was a fairly well-kept secret that *Outcry*, the one before that, hadn't even made back its costs. That was the last expensive war film he'd do that had its emphasis on philosophical talk instead of action. The people wanted blood and bombs, not sentiment. They didn't want to think, they wanted lots of color and movement. Well, *this* picture was going to give them all that and more. This one would get him out of his slump, if anything would. And he was prepared for, even *welcomed*, the inevitable "antiviolence" backlash it would engender.

He was startled out of his reverie by the sound of the phone ringing. He picked it up on the fourth ring, and said, "Anthony Winteroth speaking."

He heard a man's deep, gravelly voice say, "Mr. Winteroth, this is Barry Phillips. Perhaps you remember—we met at Estelle Hardy's party in Los Angeles last week."

Estelle Hardy was one of the most successful agents in Hollywood, and her expensive parties were legendary in the business. "Oh yes, Mr. Phillips. It was a pleasure. Tell me, what can I do for you?"

"Well, frankly, you mentioned something about an interview. Said I should look you up here in New York before the premiere. Unfortunately, I was delayed out in L.A. until this morning. I know it's awfully short notice, what with the premiere in just a few hours, but if you had the time I sure would like getting—"

Winteroth didn't even let him finish. "Of course, of course, Mr. Phillips. No problem. If you want an interview, I can give you one this afternoon. Where are you calling from?"

"Uh, the lobby, as a matter of fact."

"Good. Why don't you come up right now? Just give me a second to alert the desk."

"Thank you, Mr. Winteroth. I really appreciate it."

"What do you drink? I'll order us something in the meantime."

"Scotch and soda," Phillips replied.

"Scotch and soda it is. See you soon."

Winteroth hung up and rubbed his palms together. He called the desk and told them it was okay to let Phillips come up to his suite. They had on occasion had trouble with hopeful young starlets and anxious screenwriters who tried to wangle their way up without an invite. Then Winteroth rang room service. The liquor supplies in the suite were running low.

As he finished dressing he thought what a stroke of luck it was that Phillips had arrived when he did. For one thing, Winteroth wanted as much publicity about his new picture as possible. For another, this sudden, unexpected interview would be just the thing he needed to cover up his encounter with that pretty reporter. He would explain his lateness due to Phillips' unexpected appearance. He would not have time to shower, but hopefully the lingering traces of the lady's heavy, overspiced perfume would have faded away by the time he got home.

A few minutes later he was ensconced in the suite's living room, handing Barry Phillips his Scotch and soda. Phillips was a slim, bespectacled man with a narrow face, deep-set eyes, and a swarthy complexion. While the two of them made genial small talk, he took pad and paper out of his suit coat pocket and got ready to ask the first question. Finally Phillips leaned back into the couch and said, "I—and a lot of other people—are curious about the title, Tony. Why did you decide to call the picture *Vicious*?"

"That was actually Don's—Don Ramis, my screenwriter's —idea. *Vicious* seems to get right to the point, I think. It's a vicious crime that's committed—the axe murder of the young girl. Society has a vicious response to such an antisocial crime. This current of viciousness runs right along the whole storyline, right up until they pull the switch and send the juice through the murderer's body, frying him on the spot." That didn't actually happen in his movie, but he thought it essential to mislead people at this point.

Before Phillips could ask the question that was already forming on his lips, Winteroth continued. "With *Vicious* I'm trying to make a statement about the eroticism, the *voluptuousness* almost, of violence, the link between our sexual natures and the expression of savagery in society. I think this will be my most controversial film ever." He had said much of the above in slightly altered form for the dozens of reporters he'd been interviewed by during the past few weeks, but a quotable comment was well worth repeating.

"Would you say that *Vicious* is a plea against capital punishment?"

"No, no, not at all. The man commits a fiendish murder—society has no other way in which to register its disgust and disapproval. No, I have no problem with the capital punishment aspect. His death is comparatively humane compared to what he does to the girl." *Wonderful.* In every interview he took the writer in the wrong direction, knowing that when their publication's readers finally saw the film, the surprise at the end would be that much more effective.

"Then you're not one of those people who feel that Paul Wilson, the actual black man who committed the murder in real life, may have been framed or railroaded, that at worst he needed psychiatric help but not a death sentence, that—"

Winteroth cut him off. This line of questioning always made him uncomfortable. He was not really interested in Paul Wilson or any of the true facts or theories of the case. He had never bothered to read any of the articles or the two nonfiction books that had been written on the subject, relying instead on popular myth and Ramis' secondhand input. "You must understand, Barry. This picture is fiction, pure fiction. True, it was *inspired* by an actual murder case, but it is not a documentary or even a reenactment, as such. We took great liberties with the storyline. Our characters only loosely resemble the actual parties involved. We've changed their names, their descriptions, their relationships to one another. The actual Désirée Fontana case was even steamier and more horrible than we've presented it. I found we had to tone things down. Our primary aim—my primary aim—is not to comment or proselytize, but simply to scare the pants off the audience."

"Then *Vicious* is a horror film?"

"I would not call it so, no. A psychological thriller would be the best way to describe it, I suppose. We want to scare people, yes, but also give them something a little classier and more thought-providing than the usual vampire film or monster movie.

Phillips smiled. "Anthony Winteroth does not make 'horror films,' in other words."

"Let's just say that this will be An Anthony Winteroth Film, both produced and directed by yours truly, and the audience knows what to expect."

"Is it true that the budget for *Vicious* was much smaller than what you're accustomed to?"

Winteroth hedged. "Uh, no, not really. It wasn't a tremendously big budget, as there are no major stars in the film. I wanted a fresh approach to the acting style, no household names that come with preconceived audience expectations. We had few sets and did some location shooting in Greenwich Village. Costs were kept down simply because this was not a tremendously expensive picture by its very nature, not because I was on a restricted budget per se. I could have spent much more. There was simply no need to."

"You say this is a fictionalization, only 'inspired' by the infamous Fontana case, but what attracted you to that story in the first place?"

"Don Ramis had read a piece about it in a crime magazine and thought the story had all the elements of a good cinematic thriller. He approached me with the idea. Neither of us was interested in doing a straight, fact-based treatment. I like linear stories with clear beginnings, middles and endings. I didn't want to go into the politics of it. We changed the Paul Wilson character into a white man for one thing, removed a lot of the sex element. Hollywood wouldn't touch a lot of what went on there, so what was the point in doing a true story if we had to fictionalize or obfuscate in the first place? So instead I asked Don to take the basic elements of the story but write an original screenplay around it: his own characters, his own situations. People will be able to recognize the murder, sure. They'll know what it's based on even if they didn't know it before they entered the theater. But *Vicious* is basically fiction and nothing more. We even updated it to the 1960s."

"What about the actual murder scene? There are rumors going around that you've presented it quite graphically."

"Yes. Yes, it's quite graphic. I saw no other way to do it. It's so graphic I almost thought of filming it—at least that sequence, the murder sequence—in black and white. But audiences expect color these days. It's very bloody." He never failed to mention this during interviews, knowing that it would practically guarantee hordes of morbidly curious customers.

"Is that why you've allowed no press previews of the film? Afraid bad word of mouth about the murder will turn off prospective viewers?"

"Not at all. This picture is an *event*, that's all. I wanted everyone to see it for the first time together. Let the critics come see it with everyone else. That will give them a better chance to gauge the audience's reaction, and, as you know, the audience's reaction is nine-tenths of it. These critics who isolate themselves in screening rooms have no true way to judge what kind of an effect a film has on the average member of the audience."

"Then this is a real 'audience participation' picture?"

"That's not a bad way to describe it, yes."

"If you had to sum up your feelings about the finished film, what would you say about it?"

"*Vicious* is nothing that's been done before. It's going to shock a lot of people. The bedroom murder, the axing of the girl. We don't spare the audience. They've come to see a girl be murdered and they will see a girl be murdered. They must be prepared for that. *Vicious* is going to infuriate a lot of people." His eyes twinkled as he smiled. "And delight a lot of them, too."

Phillips caught him by surprise with his next question. "You need a hit very badly at this point, don't you, Tony?"

"Well, Barry, uh—" Winteroth tugged self-consciously at his tie. "Everyone wants their pictures to be hits. I'm no different from anyone in that respect."

53

"But your last picture was a flop. And *Outcry* was so expensive that in spite of pretty good business the studio didn't make a dime on it. In fact, they lost money. And the three films before that—while all admired by the critics—were not the kind of commercial successes you might have hoped for. How does Anthony Winteroth feel as he approaches fifty with such an uneven track record? How important is *Vicious*' success to you? Isn't it true that you're deliberately pandering to the audience's lowest tastes in the hopes of making a profit?"

Winteroth was stunned. Phillips' manner had been so low-key throughout the interview that he was completely unprepared for the abrupt change in the columnist's manner. What made it worse was that Phillips had not really raised his voice or narrowed his eyes, or adopted any kind of hostile or defensive attitude, but rather sat there as calmly as before, asking these tough questions in soft, well-modulated tones like a wolf in sheep's clothing. The bastard!

Winteroth, however, was not so unflappable. "I think that's a little unfair, Phillips," he said grouchily. "Thrillers are perfectly acceptable, even respectable, films to make. They're a real challenge for a director, too. *Vicious* may be controversial. But I consider it one of the best pictures I ever made, and I will certainly not make apologies for it." He got to his feet. "And as for my career as I—how did you put it?—approach fifty, I'm in the enviable position of being able to choose my own projects and work with some of the best talents Hollywood and overseas have to offer. I have long since stopped worrying about box office and critical opinions." He rubbed his chin and coughed. "Now I'm sorry I have to cut this short, but it is getting late and I'd like to have a leisurely supper with my family before the premiere."

Phillips also got to his feet, but as he shoved the note and pad back into his coat pocket he couldn't resist a final sally. "But do you really think that showing a woman being chopped to pieces is entertainment, Tony?"

Winteroth ignored him. "See the picture, Phillips. Judge for yourself."

Phillips held out his hand and Winteroth took it reluctantly. "Thanks for the interview," he said. "And on such short notice. I appreciate it."

"My pleasure," Winteroth replied. But his eyes said something different.

After Phillips exited, Winteroth picked up the bottle of Scotch and poured himself a double.

Damn columnists. Why couldn't they just ask their dumb questions and do their jobs and act like the publicity cream puffs everyone knew that they actually were? He hated it when they dared to make value judgments. The Scotch was smooth, almost sweet, and went down quickly to fill the cold spot in his stomach.

"Damn columnists," he said.

Suzette Winteroth sat in front of the vanity and tried to turn herself into a raving beauty. Having a husband in the movie business did nothing for a woman's ego; there were days when she was confronted with an unending parade of the world's most beautiful women. When Mrs. Winteroth had simply been Suzette Chambers, only daughter of the Boston banking Chambers, she had never felt any insecurity whatsoever about her looks. She'd always thought of herself as being extremely attractive. But whereas once her long, thin face had seemed fashionably slender, even elegant, at forty-two it seemed merely gaunt and bony. Her nose was much too long, her cheekbones too high, her chin and eyes too large. She threw the eyeliner down on the table and let out a sigh of exasperation.

Nothing she did to her face seemed right this afternoon. And it was so important that she look good tonight, that she be standing by Anthony's side, a living refutation to those horrible rumors about his unfaithfulness. How did such things get started? That awful woman at Estelle Hardy's party last week, so drunk and vulgar in the ladies room, telling Suzette that she'd "better keep an eye on her husband," that he was "getting it everywhere but home." And those veiled references in the gossip columns—"Winteroth seen dining with starlet."—"Is so-and-so's husband getting jealous of a certain bearded director?"—how could people be so vile? Just last week one writer had dared to imply that the Winteroths' marriage was "in trouble."

She couldn't understand why everyone was out to get them. "It's just jealousy," Tony kept telling her. "Jealous people who hate the thought of what we have. A good marriage, a fine son. They hate my success, and they hate your attractiveness. That's just the way people are."

Suzette understood that Tony was a busy man. People had no idea how much wheeling and dealing was involved in the movie industry, all the people he had to see, all the actors whose work he had to witness. Story conferences and script revisions and time spent soothing the hurt feelings of actors and writers. She understood why Tony had so many meetings and was so often out of town. They flew back and forth across the country every other month it seemed, occupying their townhouse in New York or their mansion in Beverly Hills for weeks at a time until Tony's work forced them to pack up their bags and travel somewhere else again.

On either coastline, Suzette spent too much of her time alone. If it wasn't for their son, Gerald, she thought, she'd probably have gone out of her mind. Gerald was seventeen—as attractive as his father was, although he looked more like his mother—and had his mind on cars and girls and the usual teenage obsessions. But he was always there when his mother needed him, and she appreciated that more than he'd ever realize. She'd once been close to her brother, Stephen, but his work always kept him so busy.

Suzette was not yet satisfied with her appearance; she wasn't even sure if she'd wear this dress—an unassuming but quietly tasteful strapless white gown—or change into something more striking. But she was not in a mood to fuss any more. She got up and left the bedroom, hoping that Tony would get home soon so they could have a quiet supper together—just the three of them—before leaving for the premiere. There would be time enough later for them to surround themselves with hundreds of adoring film fans, to be hurled into the midst of a great throng of Tony's admirers at the party at Loudon's cafe. Always Tony's admirers. Now she just wanted to relax and enjoy the quiet.

As she walked into the living room the front door opened and Gerald walked in, his dark hair and dark pensive eyes in vivid contrast to the paleness of his skin. He had been given a variety of odd jobs to do on the set of *Vicious*—how she hated that name—and both parents assumed that any day now he'd express his own desire to act or direct. So far his interest had been surprisingly perfunctory; hanging out on the set with his famous father was just something to do. In a year or so, she expected, that would change.

"Hi, Mom," he said. Though he went to school in L.A. and had to stay there most of the year regardless of where his parents were, they had let him come to New York this trip as a reward for his academic diligence. Luckily he was not the type to take advantage of his freedom. He threw his jacket on the couch where the maid would find it and said, "Is Dad home yet?"

"No. I expect the interviews took longer than he thought they would."

"Oh." For some reason he averted his eyes from hers. He went over to the mirror in the hallway, whipped out a comb, and fussed with the slicked-back hair that she thought he wore too long. He looked like a juvenile delinquent, a baby-faced Elvis Presley. Suzette supposed all teenagers had to go through their little phases. Just because *she* had been a Goody Two Shoes. . . .

"Are you excited about tonight?" she asked, sitting down on the piano bench and flipping absently through the sheet music.

"I don't know. It's not as if this is Dad's first picture or anything like that."

"But he's never had a big 'star-studded premiere' like this before." Suzette cocked her head in that cute little way of hers that said she wasn't being entirely serious.

Gerry smiled. "*Ashes in the Wind* had a 'gala premiere' in Hollywood, remember?"

"Yes, but you were only five years old then. We had to leave you with the babysitter. Anyway, I'm glad he's premiering the film in New York. There's something *about* this city. . . ."

"What?"

"Oh, it's got . . . class. Whereas Hollywood is so—" She shrugged.

"Gee, Ma, you're really articulate these days, you know."

57

"Don't be fresh," she said, smiling.

He put his comb away and studied himself in the mirror for a second. Such a cocky boy. He rubbed his chin and frowned. "Are you looking forward to tonight, Ma?"

"I suppose so. But like I told your father, I can think of other pictures of his that *should* have had this kind of treatment, pictures of his that are better than this . . . *Vicious*."

"You haven't seen it yet."

"It chills my blood just to think about it." She shivered for dramatic emphasis. "Bodies. Murders. *Ugh*."

"I think it's neat. Dad has made an honest-to-goodness horror film."

"Don't let your father hear you say that, Gerald."

Her son laughed and headed toward the kitchen. "When are we eating?"

"Betty has everything ready and we'll eat as soon as your father gets home. Don't go ruining your appetite now."

She watched him as he moved down the hall. God, how was it possible that she could have a son so big? She was too young to have a full-grown boy, wasn't she? Where on earth had the time gone? She got up from the piano bench and went over to the couch.

She had just made up her mind to stop flipping through *Vogue*—so depressing—and go back and finish with her makeup so that she'd only require a touch-up after dinner, when the door opened and her husband walked in.

"Hi, hon," he said. He gave her his warmest smile. Coming over to her side, he bent down and kissed her cheek. His lips were cold from the frigid February air. "Are you all ready for tonight?"

"Just about. Do you like this dress?" His approval had always been important to her.

He gave it a cursory glance. "Sure, looks fine." He looked around the room. "Where's Gerry?"

"Hanging around the kitchen probably. Tony, we're all starving. What kept you?"

"Barry Phillips. Skinny guy we met at Estelle Hardy's party last week, remember? He wanted to do a last-minute interview."

"Oh yes. The columnist with the glasses. I thought it was

something like that." She didn't want to think about Estelle Hardy's party.

"Say, are you sure you don't want to eat out tonight? It *is* a special occasion."

"Tony! Betty's prepared a wonderful meal for us. Besides, it'll take too long to fuss around at a restaurant, you said so yourself last night."

"Yeah, yeah, you're right. Just thought you might like it. Well, let me go get washed up and I'll join you in the dining room in a few minutes."

Gerry was coming up the hall from the kitchen just as Tony started moving down from the living room toward the stairs at the corridor's midway point. "Hi, son," Tony said.

"Oh, hi Dad," Gerry replied, moving past him without saying anything else, without the usual hug or friendly jab that they always used to exchange.

Was it just that Gerry had grown too old for such stuff? Or was there a noticeable cooling in his attitude toward his beloved "Daddy." And if so, why? He'd told his mother he thought *Vicious* was "neat." Why wouldn't he tell his *father*? Well, Suzette would have to worry about all that tomorrow when things were a little less hectic.

She leaned back and studied the room for the fiftieth time since they'd arrived in New York. Creamy white walls, gold carpeting, antiques in every corner. She really *should* think about redecorating, though. They had completely redone the house in California. She felt certain that a change every few years was good for one's soul and well-being.

She went and told Betty that the whole family was finally together and that she could start serving the warmed-up dishes in just a few minutes. She told Gerry to wash up, sat down at her place at the table to the right of her husband, as always the dutiful wife, and waited for the others to arrive. The smell of the soup from the kitchen was delicious.

She sat there and waited and wondered why she felt as if her life were falling apart.

How strange.

4

The Tivoli moviehouse on West 46th Street had been chosen for the premiere because of its theater district location and its cavernous dimensions. While not as large as Radio City, it was far vaster and more decorative than the majority of movie theaters in Manhattan. Many years before, it had been home to revues and Follies, leggy dancing girls and baggy pants comedians. Today, unruly crowds of teenagers threw popcorn at the screen and traded drugs in the men's room. The high vaulted ceilings, sweeping red curtains, loges, balconies and abandoned private booths at the sides of the theater were wasted on the unappreciative.

Winteroth had left all the logistics of the premiere to the proper parties. Aside from checking to make sure that the correct print had arrived from Los Angeles, that everything was in tip top shape in the projection booth, and that plans for the banquet at Loudon's afterwards had been finalized, he did nothing but sit back in his orchestra seat in the theater and wait with several hundred other people for the world premiere of his latest motion picture.

He had to admit, even if only to himself, that he was more nervous about this than he let on. *Vicious* was a real departure, even for a director with so eclectic a style. He thought he had a good picture, one that would really shake up the audience, but he wasn't *certain* how everyone might react. Would they understand why his boldness had been so necessary, why he had to do things the way he had done them? Oh, he expected a certain amount of outrage—there was no getting around that—but would the more sophisticated members of the audience tolerate his visual audacity, or would they merely label him a ghoul and storm out of the theater in protest?

He reminded himself that this was not exactly an ordinary crowd. Many of these people were invited members of the press, fellow members of the motion picture industry, people who would at least sit still to the end out of common courtesy and respect for an artist no matter what they might personally think of the picture itself. He wouldn't have to worry about them. *Well*, he told himself, *you wanted a film that people would love or hate, and that's what you've gotten. As long as no one is bored. . . .*

Suzette sat on his right and Gerry on his left. His wife was as loving and supportive as ever, although he sensed she wasn't crazy about this latest project and had no idea how she'd react to the picture itself. Even though he had employed Gerry part-time on the set and spent as many hours—or as few, he thought guiltily—with him as ever, he sensed that he and his son were drifting apart. No, that wasn't it. Gerry was *pulling away* from him. And Tony wasn't sure why.

He knew that rumors of his many extramarital indulgences must have gotten around town, but was sure that Suzette was too trusting to suspect him. Could he help it if he had extremely strong sex drives? He was constantly thrown together with some of the world's most beautiful actresses, forced into intimacy with them like Svengali with a string of Trilbys. Those little flings had nothing to do with his life with Suzette; he was still sincerely and deeply in love with her. But he knew it was something she would never understand.

He wondered if his son had heard stories about him. The kids at Beverly Hills High were sophisticated and most of them knew who was fucking whom. Was that what this was all about, the cause of Gerry's silence and sulkiness whenever Tony was around? He'd have to have a talk with the boy to reassure him. *He'd have to lie to his son.*

Suzette was pulling on his arm. "Tony, honest. That woman in the outer aisle in the green dress. Is that Veronica Hamilton?"

He put his distance glasses on, which he hated to wear in public but would need just to see his movie clearly, and looked where his wife was pointing. "Yes, that's her." Veronica was a bosomy starlet he had worked—and slept with—once.

"She's gotten fat."

"Now, now," Tony said. "Don't be catty. Only a pound or two, I'm sure."

So far the evening had gone well. Although there were no superstars in *Vicious*, enough of them were in attendance in the audience tonight to ensure that plenty of their screaming fans lined the sidewalk outside. Tony had managed to get past the news reporters waiting with the starstruck rabble without stumbling on his words, losing his temper—as he had nearly done with Barry Phillips—or getting too defensive about his movie.

And now the lights were dimming and they were off.

Crossing his fingers, Winteroth thought, *if it does turn out to be a bomb, I can always blame it on Ramis' screenplay.*

What the audience saw for the next hour and forty-five minutes was a dark psychological suspense story that was totally gripping from the first frame to the last. One could tell from the very first scene that Winteroth had lost none of his power to hold an audience's attention; he was as sure of his technique as ever. *Vicious* began as the story of a young woman —an aspiring actress—who works at a sleazy downtown stripshow and has trouble fending off the advances of men as well as making ends meet. When she gets fired from the job for refusing to sleep with the manager, she is unable to pay her rent and must advertise for a roommate.

The early scenes detailing the young woman, Clara's, life were sharp and gritty, done in a naturalistic style that captured the girl's desperation and hope and contrasted it vividly with her depressing lifestyle and surroundings. Winteroth looked around and studied the audience. There was absolutely no talking, and very little rustling or coughing. He had them in the palm of his hand. They were spellbound, anxiously waiting to see what would happen next.

About a third of the way through the film, another major character was introduced. Yvette Cummings, a bouncy, promiscuous brunette who moves in with Clara and introduces the more conservative girl to a variety of men and occupations. Right away Hal Mellison's rich and melancholy musical score made it clear that Yvette is going to lead Clara down the path of destruction. The film, if anything, became richer and more sinister. The audience knew what was coming—they all knew about *Vicious*' connection to the Désirée Fontana affair—but none of them would be quite prepared for what Winteroth had in store for them.

A little over halfway through the film the next major character was introduced: Ed Halsey, a sexy, athletic young punk with slicked-back hair, intense dark eyes, and a magnetic personality. He is picked up in a bar by Yvette, but it is clear from the first that he and Clara are the ones who are setting off sparks. Winteroth had to smile at the thought of all the twists and turns and sinister implications Don Ramis had put into his screenplay. He had taken the Fontana case and exploited it for all it was worth, developing every possibility with the sure hand of a master. Better yet, since everyone assumed that Winteroth had complete control over, and a hand in writing the screenplays for his pictures—not always true—he knew that he would get the credit for most of Ramis' innovations.

As the film proceeded through the second half, the audience watched as Halsey slowly moves into and takes over the girls' lives, manipulating them through his sexual hold on them. Tension begins to develop in the relationship between the two roommates; it is implied that Halsey is sleeping with both of the girls, Winteroth driving the point home as well as possible without outraging either audience or censors. He could feel the current running through the Tivoli: what was going to happen next?

At this point the film introduced its pseudo-demonic aspects. The Halsey-Wilson character believes in the occult: the ouija board, tarot cards, astrology. He is convinced that he has a demon in his brain that is trying to take over his mind and which he has to constantly keep under control. That was one aspect of Ramis' script that Winteroth had had to tone down. Ramis meant to suggest in a subtle way that perhaps Halsey-Wilson had really been under the influence of demonic possession. Winteroth preferred to let the audience reach their own conclusions. Besides, considering the ending they had cooked up, it was all a red herring anyway.

Winteroth tensed. Now came the time for the *piece de resistance*, the thing that would keep the audiences coming in droves. The dreaded bedroom murder. If this worked, if it had the effect he intended, the picture was guaranteed to be a success no matter what everyone thought of the rest of it.

Clara is alone in the apartment. She's just come out of the shower. She steps into the bedroom, wrapped only in a towel that reveals all the sinuous curves of the actress' magnificent body. She is about to remove the towel and start dressing, when a shadow fills the entrance to the room. She turns, screams. Close up of her mouth. A dark figure advances into the room, clutching an axe. Close up of the axe.

This next shot Winteroth loved. It was filmed from above, showing the figure slowly approaching Clara, waving the axe high in the air above its head.

The next few shots showed the assailant making repeated swings at the girl with the axe. She keeps dodging. The axe hits the bedboard, cuts into the mattress, chops violently into the wall. *The girl's screams. The assailant's guttural breathing.* Mellison's provocative music swelled to fill the theater, expertly matched to every spine-tingling frame.

And now the actual murder began. This time the axe hit the girl's body. What followed was a brilliantly and breathlessly edited series of shots, an assault on the audience's senses, as they watched what appeared to be a young woman being slaughtered in front of their eyes. Winteroth knew they would all think (those who kept their eyes open, that is) that they were seeing every detail of the murder with charnel-house accuracy.

Actually he had inserted only one shot of an axe striking, penetrating, human flesh, one that lasted only a fraction of a second and was almost subliminal. Through clever editing and pacing he made it seem as if every blow to the girl's body was recorded, when in reality all the audience saw was reaction shots of the girl screaming, quick flashes of the axe rising and falling in the air, and droplets of blood—much less than there would have been in real life—splashing across the walls of the bedroom, on the mattress, and across a pink pillow. The ultimate effect, he had to admit, was extremely gruesome. He had gone further in the depiction of murder than any other director in the history of the cinema.

He shivered involuntarily. He had really done it. The sequence was superb. No one who had ever seen *Vicious* would ever get undressed in their bedroom again without getting a chill of remembrance.

He looked around the theater quickly. His wife sat deep in her chair with her hand across her mouth. A hasty glance up and down the row confirmed that many of the women in the audience had adopted a similar position, and a few of the men as well. Some members of the audience looked pale, disgusted, even faint. Others were unabashedly admiring the audacity and technical virtuosity of the sequence. Good. No one was walking out, although he did hear a few disturbed mutterings from the balcony.

The tone in the theater had undergone a peculiar metamorphosis. Some of the audience's tension had been released; the infamous murder scene they'd heard rumors about was over and they could relax. But others were more nervous than before, as if they were wondering what new horrors might await them.

The film moved very quickly from the bedroom murder to the finale. The main character was dead so the picture intercut between Halsey and Yvette, who was apparently not aware that her roommate had been murdered. She and Halsey were going to leave town together. The audience cried out in silent sympathy for the poor dumb brunette. Sure, she may have been a tramp but she didn't deserve to get axed by that slimebucket Halsey.

And then the penultimate scene: Yvette and Halsey in the motel. The audience bit its collective fingers, waiting for Halsey to do the chop-chop routine on Yvette. Yvette gets Halsey to confess that it was Clara he really loved, but that he had to get away from her when he realized her feelings for him didn't go beyond lust. Yvette is enraged.

"I thought for sure when she was dead you'd belong to me!" Yvette screams, taking the bloody axe out of her luggage. *Surprise!* She's about to hack up Halsey—as she had Clara—when the door opens and the manager, alarmed by the crying and screaming, comes in with a cop who subdues the woman and takes her away to the nuthouse.

The final shot is a close-up of Yvette staring into the audience. She has assumed her dead roommate and murder victim's personality. "I love you, Halsey, I love you, Halsey," she says in Clara's voice. Her face turns ugly and brutal—*"I love you I love you I love you"*—until it becomes a raging, hate-filled growl on the soundtrack. There comes the faint, chilling sound of an axe *chop–chopping* in the background.

THE END

For nearly five full minutes the audience applauded ferociously.

Winteroth sat there with his wife and son—both of whom were completely silent—and let the congratulators swarm over him as the rest of the audience moved delightedly out of the theater. Whatever they thought of *Vicious*, no one was quiet about it. They'd had the reaction he'd been hoping for. And everyone had been taken completely by surprise by the twist at the end.

"So Yvette was the killer!" a producer said, clapping Winteroth on the back. The old fellow had turned down three opportunities to work with Tony during the early years, but now he was certainly humble. "A masterstroke. A masterstroke!" Winteroth did not remind the man that the idea for the twist had come from the screenwriter.

He shook a few more hands and accepted the compliments like a prince receiving the members of his court. He looked around for Ramis, the lead actors, and others associated with *Vicious*, but they were scattered all over the theater. Well, he'd catch up with them at Loudon's. He put on his coat and said to his wife, "Let's see if we can get out by the side door. Or else we'll be here all night." There was still a mob in the aisles and in the back of the theater overflowing into the lobby.

He knew better than to ask Suzette what she thought of the picture. If she liked it, she'd tell him so later. If not, she'd never say a word, ever the picture of politeness. He did wish that Don hadn't decided to name the murderess Yvette. It had finally hit him that it was much too similar to Suzette, and his wife was already paranoid enough as it was.

Winteroth looked over at his son, who was busy fussing with

the buttons of his coat, more fussing than was necessary. Once upon a time, Gerry had been his father's greatest supporter. How Tony wished his boy would look up at him and say, "Gee, dad, that was really *neat*." Tony realized with a bit of a shock that he might have been subconsciously driven to do a—dare he say it?—horror film in the hopes that it would make his son feel close to him again.

But as he looked around the room trying to spot a few of his favorite starlets, Gerry said nothing. He didn't even acknowledge his father's presence. Well, Winteroth rationalized, Gerry had been on the set of *Vicious*, a few of the scenes anyway. He had pretty much known what was going to happen. But that didn't make Tony feel any better.

As they made their way to a side exit, Winteroth shook a few more hands and accepted the compliments with a casual humility, but the disapproval of his wife and son made it all seem like so much dross.

For a moment *Vicious* did not exist for him.

Just as the actual participants in the Fontana murder case—Désirée, Paul Wilson, Janice Evans—had never existed for him.

5

Winteroth was in his element.

The big banquet room on the second floor of Loudon's was filled with dozens of people, all of whom were paying homage to the director of the year. "You'll get an Academy Award nomination for this one," a studio head whispered in his ear.

"Let's just hope I win one for a change," Tony replied.

The long tables on either side of the room were heaped with delicious hors d'oeuvres and hot dishes. There were salads and barbecued chicken pieces and chunky pigs-in-blankets. At the end of the room there was a bar with two handsome aspiring actors pouring every conceivable kind of liquor into large ice-filled goblets. Behind the long food-filled tables there were several round ones where the less hardy could sit for a spell.

"I wouldn't worry about the reviews," Chuck Addis, a booker for a national theater chain said as he introduced Winteroth to his extremely sexy wife. "*Vicious* is going to do socko business no matter what."

Winteroth winced somewhat when he overheard someone in the crowd say, "The critics always hate horror films but the public goes for them anyway."

Where, *where*, were the interviewers? He wanted to make it perfectly clear that *Vicious* was not a mere horror film. What did they think he was, some hack like William Castle or Roger Corman?

He had had two whiskey sours and was feeling good about himself again, about his life and his picture and his career. So what if Suzette and Gerry didn't like the movie? He thought it was one of the best, and certainly one of the most newsworthy things he'd ever done. What any true artist needed most was the recognition of his talents. Anything else was unimportant.

Joan Luanna, the associate producer, came to Tony's side and told him that a photographer from *Life* wanted to get a group shot of all behind-the-scenes talent in the corner. The starring actors were being interviewed over at the bar by reporters from the tabloids and local news programs. Winteroth hoped the three of them appreciated the fact that *Vicious* would turn them all into overnight celebrities, stars even, if they played their cards right.

Tony looked around for Suzette and Gerry but they were lost in the sea of flotsam surrounding the banquet tables. He let Joan, a chubby, fortyish spinster with thick round glasses and a pleasing personality, escort him across the room to where the others were congregated.

There was handshaking, congratulations all around. Don Ramis looked spiffy in a sleek dinner jacket and a bold green tie. He was a short man with a curly receding hairline, glasses, and a small head that was broad in back and became increasingly narrow as it tapered forward to the point of his chin. His dull wife hung at his side, a pale, sweet blonde in a light green dress and too much makeup. Hal Mellison, the film's composer, was holding on to his cocktail as if it were his security blanket. Though one of the finest composers of symphonic musical scores in Hollywood, and a frequent collaborator of Tony's, Hal was extremely shy and almost always quiet. He was very tall and slender, with a sagging, bloated face that hung down from age and alcohol, and a very bulbous nose that seemed like the Creator's comic afterthought. He wore a crimson bow tie against a starched white shirt that smelled vaguely of Clorox.

Teddy Anderson, the cinematographer, was blowing his nose noisily and looking bored. He was the least "Hollywood" in the bunch, a dour, sour-faced professional who knew his job and did it and didn't understand why there was always so much fuss made over things. He was of medium height, totally bald, and at least sixty-five, though his browned, athletic body belied his maturity. He looked like everyone's idea of a broken down boxer, a stereotype sent by Central Casting. Laurence Edwards, the dapper, gentlemanly film editor—and the man who was most responsible for the effectiveness of the bedroom murder whether he knew it or not—sipped his Scotch slowly and wore a beneficient smile as he watched Tony and the others preen and posture for the cameras.

Once the photographers were through, the men all shook hands again, congratulating each other on a job well done, patting each other warmly on the back. Off the set none of them were friends with one another, but they did have respect for each other's professionalism and vision. Tony suspected that each of them thought *Vicious* would be the biggest film they'd ever worked on. But then he'd been wrong before.

He finally spotted Suzette. She was coming towards him, balancing two plates in her hand, while Gerry followed behind her holding his own plate and a drink. Tony swore under his breath. If only he could read those two—did they like the picture or not? What would they say if an interviewer asked for their opinion? He told himself again that their opinions didn't matter, but it nagged at him just the same.

"I brought you some food, dear," Suzette said. "Try the Swedish meatballs. They're really good."

"We had a big dinner," Tony reminded her. "I'm not the least bit hungry."

"I thought so, too, but it has been hours since we've eaten. Just have a bite for a snack. You know you'll be hungry later."

He waved the plate away and she put it down on a nearby table. Gerry stood there munching some celery, avoiding his father's gaze. Suzette returned and said to her son, "Isn't this exciting, Gerry?" She was smiling, but her eyes were dead. She didn't find it exciting at all.

"Yeah, it's nice." He was as sullen and distant as ever. What was eating the boy?

Suzette and Gerry continued eating in silence, while Tony looked around for someplace to which he could escape. His family was being a drag, and this was one night he didn't want to feel down. Ahhh, Betsy Van Sloan, the Hollywood columnist, was heading in their direction, pencil waving in the air to attract his attention. Tony took a few steps away from Suzette and Gerry, catching Betsy at a midway point. He didn't want the woman asking his wife or son any questions.

"Tony, *Tony!*" Betsy said, pushing out her pinched little face topped by a bee's nest of unruly brown hair and kissing the air beside his cheek. "Fabulous film. *Fabulous.* And so gruesome. Goodness, I would have lost my lunch if I hadn't closed my eyes."

Tony said nothing. They'd spent a whole week filming that sequence, two weeks in the editing room painstakingly putting it together, and this bitch closes her eyes! He just smiled and waited for her questions. "Have time for a mini-interview?" she asked coquettishly. It was absurd behavior coming from someone who, like most people on the fringes of the business, was so dumpy and unappealing.

"Always time for you, Bette," Tony said. He knew she loved to be called Bette. It made her feel like her idol and favorite film star Bette Davis, who had recently made a big comeback with Joan Crawford in a horror film directed by the elephantine Robert Aldrich. Tony had it on good authority that La Davis thought Betsy was a cunt.

A moment later Tony had forgotten all about his insubordinate wife and son and was saying: "With *Vicious* I'm trying to make a statement about the eroticism, the *voluptuousness* almost, of violence, the link between our sexual natures and the expression of savagery in society . . ."

Out of the corner of his eye Tony saw Suzette sneak away to the bathroom.

She almost didn't make it in time. Something on that buffet table had given her the runners. Suzette collapsed onto the toilet seat and gratefully relieved herself, dismayed at how loud it sounded, and hoped the small ladies room would stay empty until she was through.

The worst of it was over when the bathroom door opened and someone entered. Two someones. Suzette watched them through the crack in the door. She couldn't see their faces, but they were slender, youthful (judging from their voices), and dressed in attractive but inexpensive clothing. They began fixing their faces at the mirror. *All this fussing in mirrors*, Suzette wondered, *does it ever end for us women?* She herself had not changed a thing about her face after dinner, fed up with her futile attempts to look lovelier and ten years younger. Why should she care? She was not the celebrity, after all, Tony was. She wasn't a movie star. In fact, she wasn't anybody. Just a wealthy housewife, really. And though she knew she ought to be supremely grateful just for that, she often felt like a worthless supernumerary.

What was that? Had the women said something about Tony? Well, why shouldn't they? The party *was* in his honor. Never mind everyone else who had worked on the picture, everyone else who'd helped Tony look good, *he* was the man of the hour. Even she knew enough about the film business to know that movies were team projects, no greater than the sum of their parts. She knew Tony was a great director—she'd seen enough bad pictures made by other men to know the difference—but she also knew he always had help.

She hoped he didn't come right out and ask her what she thought of *Vicious*. She had really hated it. His worst film ever. Movies were so unromantic these days. All that violence and bloodshed. That horrible murder. Tony had left nothing to the imagination. It was beneath contempt, she thought, and in the worst possible taste. All her life she'd hoped never to see anything like that, nothing gruesome or terrible like she read about in the papers, and now her husband was filming it in living color and showing it on movie screens a hundred times larger than life. A girl practically being dismembered. Disgusting.

What had happened to the nice pictures they used to make? Ginger Rogers and Fred Astaire. Claudette Colbert and Clark Gable. All that love and romance. Suzette liked pictures to be about the sunny side of life; she liked movies that made the bleak world seem happier and brighter.

Tony had never been one for pictures like that, too obsessed with rape and torment and seething courtroom drama. Too obsessed with *significance!* Well, the only thing different about *Vicious* was that it was the clear sign of a man who was desperate for attention. Still, she supposed she'd have to defend it if any of the reporters asked her what she'd thought. After all, he was her husband. She wasn't supposed to criticize his work.

She'd just say something about artistic integrity, make some statement about "voluptuous violence"—wasn't that how he always put it?—and let it go at that. She didn't have to make sense, she just had to seem supportive. Hadn't her mother always said that?

Tired of thinking about *Vicious*, she involuntarily let the words of the two women outside the stall sink into her consciousness. Were they still discussing Tony?

"And was he *good*, Sondra?"

"The best."

No, they couldn't be. It had to be someone else.

The first girl let out with a vocal leer. *Disgusting*. Girls these days were such—

"So Tony Winteroth is a great lay, huh?"

"He's got a big penis, too."

"More than a mouthful, huh?"

Suzette felt her world collapsing. She was sitting in a toilet with diarrhea dripping from her ass and two sluttish women that she didn't even know were carelessly ripping her life into tatters. She would have laughed had she not been so filled with despair.

The second woman cackled like a hyena and said, "All during the interview he could hardly keep his hands off me. You know, he has a *bedroom* right next to that office of his!"

Tears falling out of her eyes, Suzette put her face closer to the crack in the door and tried to make out their faces. The second woman was patting her hair. "I *know*," she was saying.

"You *know* about the bedroom?"

"Also about his big dick."

"Lucy, how—?"

"You think you're the only woman who's been to bed with Tony Winteroth? Join the club, honey. That man has made it with more chicks than Presley and Beatty put together."

No, no! These were just two tramps. They knew nothing, had seen nothing. They must have noticed Suzette walk into the bathroom and had, in their jealous, vindictive way, decided to make her life miserable. How she hated them! She had a good mind to walk out of the stall and surprise them, tell them that their nasty plan hadn't worked.

"I don't believe you, Lucy. You've never been to bed with

Tony Winteroth."

"Wanna bet? You know what I really loved about him. That cute little scar he's got right beside his belly button."

Sondra gasped.

So did Suzette.

"Not to mention the mole he's got next to his balls."

Suzette clapped a hand across her mouth. *They musn't hear her.*

"Lucy, you bitch. You *have* made it with him!"

As the two women fell into each other's arms and howled like wanton banshees, Suzette Winteroth put her head in her hands and prayed that they wouldn't hear her sobbing.

Tony Winteroth had followed his son around until he'd cornered him at the end of one of the banquet tables. Two more drinks made Tony feel a lot braver, in the mood for confrontation. Damn it—*Vicious* was just the kind of picture his boy should have liked. Wasn't he always raving about *Macabre* and *Homicidal* or some low-budget shit like that? Wasn't this the kid who still had models of Godzilla and the Wolfman and the Phantom of the Opera in his bedroom? Hadn't he been noticing bosomy blonde ladies in the past couple of years, indulging in adolescent fantasies and sneaking in friends' copies of *Playboy*? Didn't he have two volumes on Jack the Ripper and *Great Crimes of the Past* on his bookshelf, not to mention a book on the world's most infamous psychopaths? *Vicious* should have been right up his alley. Murders, maniacs, and beautiful women. What was wrong with the kid? *Vicious* was a hundred times better than *I was a Teenage Werewolf*, for Pete's sake. Wasn't it?

Tony went up to him and boldly said, "What did you think of *Vicious*?"

"Uh, Dad—"

Gerry didn't get a chance to go any further. Suddenly the full, sensual face and figure of Veronica Hamilton was looming over them, her powdered cheeks and pursed red lips hanging in the air between them like a hot and heavenly vision. She had one hand on Tony's shoulder and the other on Gerry's and her tremulous breasts were bobbing like massive melons.

"Hi, Tony. Loved your movie. And who's this fellow, huh?"

"Veronica, this is my son, Ger—"

"Your son! Oh, he's adorable." She leaned over and gave Gerald a hard, noisy kiss, leaving a round red smear on the side of his face. She probably would have rustled his hair had it not been so plastered down with tonic. Gerry's eyes kept wandering up and down from Veronica's mouth to her breasts. She didn't look as good under this light as she did in her pictures, but she was still one of Hollywood's major beauties.

"Gerry," Tony said, "I'm sure you recognize Veronica Hamilton."

"Yeah, *sure*." The boy was more alert than he'd been in weeks.

"Keep me in mind if you do a sequel, Tony," she squealed. "You could chop me up with an axe anytime." She winked, squealed again, and tottered off to bother someone else.

"Well, as you were saying, Gerry—wait a minute." Smiling broadly, he pulled out his handkerchief and wiped Gerry's cheek. "Can't have you walking around like that, can we?"

Gerry's face reddened. "It's okay, it's okay." He grabbed the handkerchief out of his father's hand and finished the job himself.

"I'm still waiting to hear what you think about *Vicious*."

Gerry shrugged. "I don't know. It was okay, I guess. All of your movies are okay. What do you want me to say?" He handed the handkerchief back to his father. "All right," he said grudgingly. "I liked it."

Tony smiled. "Wait, you didn't get it all off. Stop groaning. There, now you're all right." Tony shoved the handkerchief back into his pocket. He winked. "Veronica's quite a woman, isn't she?"

"Well, if anybody would know, you would," Gerry said.

"What is that supposed to mean?"

"You know."

"Gerry, how much punch have you been drinking tonight? You're not making any sense. Look, you've been moping around like a spoiled brat for months now. I want to know what it is that's bugging you and I want to know now."

Gerry turned away, grimacing, as if he wanted to spit it out but had to hold back. The guests all around them were loud and raucous, dancing to piped-in music, consuming great quantities of food and liquor, and no one was paying any attention to the little family drama in the corner. "The guys on the set, they talk a lot, you know. Sometimes in front of me. They didn't know who I was . . . or didn't realize I was there." He looked straight in his father's eyes and said, "You've been sleeping with every woman you could get your hands on. You've been treating Mom like—" In one instant he rebelled against his disciplined upbringing and all his mother's training and burst out *"shit!"*

Tony had to control himself to keep from slapping the boy's face. So, that was what this was all about. Damn it—if only the boy were older. He was probably still a virgin. He didn't understand, couldn't understand, the compulsions, the natural urges of married men, the innocent little indulgences that had nothing, everything, to do with married life. None of those women meant anything to Tony—but here Gerry was doing a scene straight out of *Death of a Salesman*, acting like his father was the only one in the world who had ever slept with someone other than his wife.

"Son, you don't understand. It has nothing to do—"

Neither of them knew where she had come from, but suddenly Gerry's mother was there, looking pale and red and weary as if she had just been having a good, long cry. Had Gerry been talking to his mother? Tony would kill him!

"Suzette, is something—"

"I don't feel well," she said, but her words were directed at Gerry. "If you're having a good time you can stay here with your father, but I'm taking a taxi home now."

She was studiously ignoring her husband. "Suzette?"

Gerry looked at his father with some guilt, but he seemed as surprised and disturbed at his mother's condition as Tony was. "No, it's okay. I'm getting tired. Do you mind, Dad?"

"No, by all means see your mother home. This is only your father's big night. Why should he want to have his family spoil —I mean, share—it with him?" Then an expression of grudging concern crossed his face. She was his wife, after all, and he loved her. "Suzy, are you really not feeling well?"

"You were right," she said, addressing Tony but not looking at him. "I ate too much, too soon. There's something wrong with the potato salad. I just want to go home. I really don't feel well."

There *was* something wrong. The few times that Suzette had gotten sick at parties she had been all apologetic, wanting to stay and stick it out regardless, not wanting to spoil her husband's

77

good time or embarrass him in front of his associates. But tonight, she clearly wanted only one thing—to get out of there and away from her husband as soon as possible. Damn it. Gerry *must* have gone to his mother with his suspicions.

Tony didn't need the two of them here moping and sobbing and ruining his reputation, causing a scene in front of everyone. He kept his voice down, stayed calm, turned to make sure no one was listening. "Gerry. Take your mother home."

As he watched them make their way to the staircase leading downstairs to the exit, he had no way of knowing that that was the last conversation he would ever have with either of them.

6

In New York it was only the theatrical producers who sat up all night waiting for the reviews to come out, but Joan Luanna had decided that she and her associates from Hollywood would steal a cue from Broadway. The party at Loudon's would go on at least until the early morning editions of the local papers went on sale.

At midnight Joan came up the stairs to the banquet room with fresh-off-the-press copies of the *Post*, *News*, *Times*, and others. The expression on her face revealed nothing. Many of the guests had already left the eatery—not wanting to hear bad news perhaps—and the festivities had quieted, but there was still a party-like atmosphere in the restaurant. Joan came right over to the table where Tony and Don and the others were sitting, anxiously waiting, and said, "Haven't read them yet." She handed the papers to Tony. "Well, producer-director. You want to do the honors?"

Tony had made his family's excuses an hour ago—a headache for Suzette, and Gerry had school to attend; both obvious lies. "I think we should forget the reviews," he said. "It's not as if *Vicious* is a Broadway play, dependent on the whims of the critics."

"I know," Don explained, "but we're all still curious anyway.

Right, fellows?"

Tony shrugged. "Okay. Here we go." He opened the *Times* and turned to the review section. NEW WINTEROTH SHOCKER OPENS read the headline. He scanned the five or six paragraphs that made up the review. "Crowther didn't like it. Oh, he liked some of it, liked your music, Hal. But that's about it. Old fart. He's had it in for me for years."

The *Post*'s Archer Winston was a little kinder. "Strictly a slice-'em-up melodrama for the more lurid tastes of the audience, but told with sophistication and Winteroth's usual flair for the (melo)dramatic."

The *Mirror* and the *News* grudgingly respected the artistic values of the film, but hated the storyline. "Psychologically dubious, with a twist ending that stretches belief and numbs the senses," read one write-up.

None of the critics liked the bedroom murder. "The most disgusting, horrendous, and repulsive murder scene ever recorded on camera. Winteroth wallows in every death gasp of the beautiful blonde victim, and shows us every chop of the hatchet, every drop of the splattering blood. Yes, the axe comes down and we see it slashing and hacking as newcomer Melanie Fortune screams her head off. Screaming for a better agent, perhaps?"

All that work, all that effort, Tony thought, and those damn fools couldn't even see the hand in front of their faces. They acted as if *Vicious* were just another trashy horror film. They had made up their minds as to what they would say before they had even entered the theater.

"Don't worry," Joan said, putting down the *Mirror* and picking up her drink. She patted Tony's hand. "*Vicious* is critic-proof. It's a masterpiece," she assured him. "The public will see that. The critics for the periodicals and film magazines, the weekly papers, will see that. The critics hated the subject matter, not the movie. You're going to be redeemed. Just wait and see."

Yes, he thought, she was right. Of course she was right. The critics for the daily papers were notoriously bourgeois, lacking true knowledge and appreciation of film as an art form. He had nothing to worry about. *Vicious* was going to put him on top again. He was too shrewd to make another bomb. The public would eat it up.

In bad taste . . . repulsive . . . disgusting . . . outrageous . . . toilet-probing . . . the words of the critics came back to haunt him. But like a shining beacon through the fog of whiskey sours pickling his brain, one savage opinion seemed to matter more than any other.

You've been treating Mom like shit.

He lurched to his feet, grabbed his suit coat off the chair where he had hung it, and said, "Sorry, folks. Keep partying. But I'm afraid I've got to get home."

The other people at the table could only stare at each other in puzzlement.

"What got into him?" Ramis asked.

Joan smirked. A touch of frustration and bitterness played across her lips. "The question is," she said, "who will *he* be getting into?"

It was raining outside and the window of the cab was spotted with dripping streams of grayish water, liquid smog falling from the sky. Tony sat back in his seat and tried to formulate a plan, caught between going home and having it out with his wife and son, and telling the cabbie to turn around and take him to the nearest bar and grill. What had possessed him, rushing out of Loudon's like that? What was he going to say when he got home? What could he say? He almost told the driver right then and there to stop at the Killarney Castle at the end of the street. He could just drink himself into oblivion and face all of this in the morning.

But part of him was eager to repair the rips in the fabric of his life before they got to be too wide. He couldn't let the negative feelings of his wife and son fester until the morning. He had to assure his wife that he was still a loving husband, had to convince her and Gerry alike that the talk they had heard was just talk. There was no question but that he would have to lie. There would be no saving his marriage, no regaining his boy's love and respect, if he should admit his infidelities. The only place wives forgave their philandering husbands was in torrid Swedish films with English subtitles.

The taxi turned onto a street in the East Sixties and headed crosstown toward Fifth Avenue. In only a few minutes Tony would be home, and he'd better have something to say. It was too much to hope for that they'd both be asleep. Gerry had been staying up late watching movies while they'd been in New York, not having to worry about going to school in the morning. And Suzette could never get to sleep when she was upset. Of course, they'd both been drinking tonight, and the alcohol might have made them drowsy.

No, he hoped they weren't asleep. He wanted this business settled tonight. Betty, their traveling maid and cook, had family in Queens, and had had the rest of the evening off to visit them. She wouldn't be in the way.

The taxi turned onto Fifth Avenue and, sooner than Tony expected, the townhouse was looming in front of him. It was an old, distinguished edifice on the corner of the block, three stories high, square and firm, with a brick front with stone facing, and a spiked fence running around it. There were several broad stone steps leading up to the front doorway. Tony told the driver to stop at the corner, pulled out a five dollar bill, and flipped it over the front seat toward the cabbie's outstretched fingers. "Keep the change," he said. He opened the back door and disembarked.

He stood there watching the cab drive away as he got himself together and steeled himself for the ordeal that was to follow. He would have to give an Academy Award performance. A little voice inside him said, "You've never won an Oscar for direction, what makes you think you can win one for your acting?"

He put his key in the front door and turned the lock. As he swung the door open carefully he was struck by the silence. Did that mean they were asleep? He walked into the foyer and removed his jacket, hanging it up in the closet. He took off his suit coat and stripped off his tie. Now with his sleeves rolled up and his mind still buoyed by the lingering effects of the alcohol, he felt sure that he could face anything. He was positive all he had to do was retread the same old line, the old formula with a clever new twist, and Suzette and Gerry would believe him. "Everyone knows *Vicious* is going to be a hit. You know what a cutthroat business it is. Now that I'm back on top the bastards have to get out and sharpen their knives. If they can't attack a man's career, they attack his family. . . ."

There was blood dripping from the walls of the living room.

Was this some kind of joke? He moved in cautiously for a closer look.

Blood—it looked like gallons of it—was smeared on the walls, puddled on the carpet, staining the sofa and the loveseat, dripping off the paintings Suzette had chosen with such care.

He knew there was bound to be a backlash against *Vicious*, but would his opponents have gone as far as this? To break into, to invade his house, to *desecrate* . . .? Or had Suzette and Gerry gone crazy, been so maddened by his infidelities that they resorted to. . . . No. It couldn't be them.

He stepped into the living room, his feet squishing into the soggy, blood-soaked carpet. He smelled an unbearable odor.

He knew what fake blood looked like, smelled like. He had used plenty of it in *Vicious*.

This was not fake blood.

And then he saw the body.

Oh my God! He rushed over to Suzette, her motionless form crumpled brokenly behind the sofa. She was lying on her side. *Oh please be faking. Let this be a horrendous joke. You'll get up and laugh and I'll scream and scold you, but in the end I'll take you in my arms and say I forgive you.*

He knelt beside the body. No—it looked bad, it looked real, the wounds looked real. It was one thing to imagine this sort of thing, to imply it happening with the tricks of his camera and all the tools of the cutting room. It was another to actually see it, to see someone you loved lying there dead and so horribly torn and twisted. God help him. Was this some kind of *punishment*? Had he gone too far?

"Suzette?" He shook her by the shoulder, then stopped.

The head was leaning at an impossible angle. Tony saw that it had nearly been severed. There was no way this could have been faked. He had abruptly stopped shaking her body in fear that her head would entirely separate from the neck and roll away across the floor like an anthropomorphic marble. There were jagged cuts in her clothes revealing raw, ragged slashes in her flesh. No blood came from the wounds.

She was dead.

He screamed. *"Suzette!"*

Phone, have to get to the phone, call the police, ambulance. Maybe it isn't too late. He knew he wasn't thinking rationally, but how else could a husband act? Must have been a burglar, a stinking, lousy burglar, surprised them when they walked in the door. Don't care what he stole, I only want my wife back. Suzette! He hoped the police would catch the guy and kill him.

He was about to lift the receiver off the hook when he remembered his son.

Gerry! Where was his boy?

Tony looked around, noticed the crumpled legs sticking out from behind the baby grand. Oh no! Gerry, too! *God, no!*

Gerry was over behind the piano, as still and silent as his mother had been. There was one gaping hole in his throat, and the whole of his shirt was covered with gore. He held a butcher knife in his hand. The hand, too, was covered with blood. *But why did the hand look so peculiar?*

Sobbing with despair, Winteroth collapsed at his boy's side and held him in his arms, not caring about the blood or the anger or anything but how much he had loved him.

Fifteen minutes later he called the police.

Lt. Detective Joseph Anderson had braced himself for the worst as he always did when he was called out to a homicide. Once he'd worked in the city's poorer sections, and though he'd seen a constant flow of death and murder and misery, at least the slayings in that part of town had been simple and direct. It was always for money or love, always one or the other. Someone mugged, stabbed, for a few dollars change. Or a jealous husband slamming a wife on the head with an iron and hitting the woman too hard.

But death in the land of the Rich and the Famous always had an extra nasty edge to it. Aside from cases when burglars—most of whom only wanted to get in, grab what they could, and get out as fast as possible—had to shoot the occupant of the home they were robbing to avoid capture, murders among the Upper Classes had some pretty devious and sinister complications. And they were often especially vicious. It was as if the wealthy had the time and the imagination to go about murder with a peculiarly savage flourish.

Well, he'd seen worse. He wasn't a big movie nut, but he'd read in the papers about *Vicious* and he had to admit that this was the most chilling piece of irony he'd come across in a long time. Anthony Winteroth, looking like a receptacle for all the shit and torment in the world, had sat in the kitchen numbly answering questions. The bodies themselves remained dead and stationary in the living room while the squad of experts dusted for fingerprints, took pictures and made measurements, all in the hopes of catching the maniac who did it.

But it looked cut and dried to Anderson. Only in detective novels did bizarre facts and strange twists come out with the evidence. Usually, things were exactly as they seemed to be. And his trained eye couldn't help but notice that Mrs. Winteroth's wounds appeared to have been made by a butcher knife, the same kind of butcher knife that Gerald Winteroth was holding in his hand, the same kind of butcher knife that had sliced into the young man's neck. It looked like a self-inflicted wound. Yep, when the evidence was in he was pretty sure he knew what it would say: Gerald Winteroth had gone on a rampage; excited into a frenzy by his father's nasty movie, he had slashed up his mother with a large kitchen knife. Then, horrified by what he'd done, he'd stabbed himself in the throat and died gurgling in his fluids. Murder. Suicide. Common in upper-class households. Anderson knew that money was no cure for psychosis; often it only aggravated it.

But Anderson also knew that there was one thing the medical examiner wouldn't be able to explain.

He called his partner, Murphy, over to his side and asked, "Did Winteroth's son have any physical disabilities?"

Murphy knew what the other man meant. "We've all been wondering about that arm, Joe. Winteroth says he can't explain it, his son's arm was always perfectly normal."

But it wasn't normal now. The hand that had held the knife, Gerry's left hand, was shriveled and bony and gray like that of an elderly woman. A skinny wrist, in vivid contrast to Gerry's healthy right one, stuck out of the boy's blood-soaked sleeve, attached to a hand that was bony but strong. A hand that was missing the middle finger.

A hand that looked more like a *claw*.

Part Three: "Vicious Two"

7

Early summer 1987.
New York City.

Dorothy Hunter wished for the second time in an hour that she had had the good sense to take a taxi. Taxis were an extravagance, she knew—much of her not insubstantial income had to go to paying her share of the rent alone—but they were certainly a convenience when time was short and she wasn't in the mood for being trampled on and pressed against hordes of New York City's huddled masses.

The man sitting next to her on the bus was so overweight that he could have easily taken up two seats and have enough left over for half of a third. In direct violation of the transit rules, he was smoking on a smelly cigar, and his body odor was not to be believed. It was the b.o. that kept her from insisting that he put out the cigar. The smoke covered up the man's personal odor and was infinitely more agreeable.

The bus moved over to the curb to make another stop, and more people began piling aboard. Every seat was taken and the aisle was so full of passengers that Dorothy couldn't see out of the opposite windows. Where were they now? She wondered. If she had missed 51st Street she'd really be angry. She took a quick look at her watch. She was already late for her appointment. The bus was not air-conditioned and she felt woefully overdressed in her becoming brown suit. She knew it made her seem businesslike, formal and efficient—cute, even—but it was not the kind of outfit made for eighty degree weather. She mentally kicked herself for not having the foresight to wear something frillier and cooler.

Dorothy was an attractive woman in her early thirties. Her wavy brown hair was medium length, and she had large brown eyes and high cheekbones. There was much of her mother's Irish perkiness in her face: the thin, wide lips, the too-broad chin, the short, narrow nose, the determined look she wore without half trying to. It had always caused her some consternation that she had her father's stocky build—albeit a feminine variation of it—instead of her mother's tall, slender sensuality. She was not crazy about being five-foot-four, but as her lover always reminded her, she was really not short for her sex, and she did have a very good figure. Dorothy kept her weight down and had a nice, full bosom. Perhaps she was more handsome than beautiful—damn this suit—but in the right clothes and makeup she could look as dainty and feminine and pretty as any other woman.

Well, she thought, she may not have been a raving beauty, but she'd gotten almost everything she'd ever wanted out of life in spite of it. True, she was not a Pulitzer Prize winner yet, but she made a good living as a professional writer and had a steady income; no mean feat for a free lancer. True, she was not married and had no children—time would soon run out for that—but she did have a good relationship with a live-in boyfriend who was attractive, kind, and, in his own way, sensitive. She really hadn't anything to complain about.

Now if only she could permanently banish the melancholia, the crushing darkness that crept into her thoughts at odd times of the day and night and stole away her joy and her complacency. If only she could keep away the screaming and the blood. . . .

She tried to peer in through the space between the two women standing in front of her, and thought she saw the big black building at 1515 Broadway through the window. Just in time. She reached up, pressed the buzzer, then rose to her feet with an aggressive, unabashed thrust. "Excuse me. Please, excuse me. Getting off. Excuse me." She squeezed her way through the obstructing bodies and inched down towards the front of the bus. She arrived just as it came to a halt at the corner with a pneumatic wheeze. She stepped down out of the bus and exhaled with gratitude. Freedom, at last!

As she headed into the large lobby of the building and up the escalator to the elevators on the second level, she thought again about how lucky she was to have this enviable position with *Woman Now* magazine. Although she had been offered a staff position several months ago—after turning in four topnotch assignments—she preferred the freedom she had by simply being one of the publication's top free lance writers. She had the time and wherewithal to work on other projects, could take off whenever she wanted to, didn't have to adhere to office hours. Once every few weeks, however, she had to go into their editorial offices to talk over new projects and decide with the editor which ones she'd be most suitable for. It had gotten to the point where the editor, Joyce Ramsey, was giving her ideas, instead of the other way around. They liked her work that much.

She stepped off the elevator on the seventeenth floor and walked along the vivid green carpeting until she reached the suite at the end of the hall. She opened one of the double wooden doors and stepped into the reception area. The woman behind the desk recognized her immediately. "Hi, Dorothy. Go right in," she smiled. "Joyce is waiting for you."

She walked down a narrow corridor, turned to the right, and stepped into a spacious office with light blue wallpaper and attractive brown furnishings. As usual, Joyce stood up and shook her hand.

"I'm sorry I'm late," she told the editor, sitting down on the chair beside the desk and opening her briefcase. "Made the mistake of taking the bus."

Joyce laughed. "Never take the bus when you're in a hurry. Anyway, it's only five after three. You're a lot more punctual than some of my writers."

Joyce Ramsey was an attractive fortyish woman with a square face and a short, nicely-styled haircut. She had a little stub of a nose and tight lips that, when they were stretched in an infrequent smile, made her face seem warm and sparkling. Her big green eyes, always full of an inquisitive twinkle, seemed to penetrate even when merely glancing. Joyce, too, was wearing a dark suit today, though she normally wore jeans and sweaters; nothing was very flattering to her rather chunky figure. She was likeable, but kept her distance. Though she and Dorothy had worked on many stories for the magazine together, there was no way you could have called them friends.

Dorothy had her pen and paper out and was waiting for Joyce to start. The older woman always took a while to get her thoughts together. She was running a finger over the blotter on top of her desk, carefully thinking over what she would say.

She had just opened her mouth to speak when Gladys Edwards poked her head in the door. Dorothy always thought that Joyce's secretary looked like an owl. She was a tiny, big-bosomed woman of thirty-five with curly black hair and an enormous pair of glasses that made her eyes seem twice the size of most people's. Perky without being especially pleasant, she gave an impression of incompetency but was really quite efficient. "Would either of you like coffee?" she asked.

Joyce rolled her eyes and shook her head in self-rebuke. "Oh, of course! Forgive me, Dorothy. You want coffee, don't you? Yes, Gladys, thank you. There's no hurry."

The secretary darted away from the doorway and disappeared.

Joyce was never one to beat around the bush or make needless small talk. She collected her thoughts for a moment or two, then said, "I like that idea we talked about on the phone. About the movies. The—what do you call them?—*splatter* films?"

"Yes. Splatter films, horror films," Dorothy said. "The increasing misogyny in films of terror, I think I called it."

Joyce's pencil *tap-tapped* on the blotter. "Not a bad idea," she said. "I remember at the time that I was afraid it might be a little dated. There's been a lot of talk on the issue, an awful lot written about it."

Dorothy had a new slant on the piece and she was anxious to talk about it. *To get it over with*, was more like it. "Yes, I know," she said, but—"

Joyce interrupted. "I've changed my mind." She leaned back in her chair and looked straight in Dorothy's eyes. "Tell me, have you ever seen the movie *Vicious*?"

"Winteroth's *Vicious*? I've heard of it, of course. It's a very famous picture. But I've never seen it, no."

"Well, you were probably just a child when it came out. I saw it on a date when I was in high school."

Dorothy frowned. "That's the one with the famous 'bedroom murder,' isn't it?"

"That's the one. And, of course, Winteroth's own wife and son were killed on the night of the premiere. Supposedly his son murdered his mother and then committed suicide. Though there have been other theories. And the movie itself was based on another famous murder case. The Désirée Fontana murder of the forties. Anyway, a lot of people think that Winteroth's film ushered in a new age of . . . 'cinematic violence,' made gore and graphic murder respectable. That it started the whole trend of women as victims in thrillers. Exaggeration, perhaps."

"I hadn't thought of that," Dorothy admitted. "I was just going to go into the modern day stalk-and-slash pictures like *Body Count at Buzzard's Bay* and"—she snapped her fingers in an effort to recall some others—"and *Maniacal*? There's just so many." She rushed ahead with what she wanted to say before Joyce could interrupt her again. "Joyce, I wasn't really going to do a piece on *movies* as such. It was going to be something much more personal. Something that would explore my feelings toward these pictures, the trend in violent entertainment, as well as my feelings about something that happened to me personally."

Joyce raised her eyebrows.

"I don't talk about this very often." She paused, looked down at her lap. "I was raped once." She looked up again. "Violently raped. I still have nightmares—"

"Here we are," Gladys said, walking in with a tray filled with steaming coffee, cups, sugar, and a tiny pitcher of cream. Leave it to her to pick the worst possible moment.

The expression of interest and concern remained on Joyce's face while she gave Gladys a perfunctory thank you. She spent a few moments fixing her coffee while Dorothy did the same, then sat back and waited until Dorothy was able to continue. "I know I'm not unique. Unfortunately," Dorothy said. "Lots of women have been raped. But," she gave a brief, humorless smile, "not all of them have had their parents murdered by psychopaths."

"Dorothy! Is this true?"

"Yes. It happened when I was in junior high. Do you—do you remember the 'Slicer?' "

"Yes. The guy who went berserk on streets and subway trains with a meat cleaver."

Dorothy nodded. She had told herself she wouldn't cry, but already tears were forming in the corners of her eyes. "Well, two of his victims were my parents."

"Dorothy. I'm so sorry."

Dorothy wiped her eyes and continued. "It's been years, and though you tell yourself you've gotten over it I suppose you never do."

Joyce nodded. "Of course."

"Anyway. All of a sudden I see these movies—at least I see the ads for them and read the reviews of them—that present people being slaughtered, hacked up, dismembered. As *entertainment*. I think about my parents, about the reality of it," she struggled to find the words, "and I just find it so hard to accept." She wiped her eyes with a handkerchief and continued. "My boyfriend loves these things, these 'splatter' pictures, goes to see them all. By himself, I don't have to add." Joyce smiled. Dorothy cocked her head and asked, "Am I making any sense?"

Joyce folded her arms. "You want to write the article about these movies from a personal point of view, describing how these pictures appear to someone who has actually experienced—at least in an indirect manner—the kind of horror that these movies present as entertainment."

"Yes, *yes*, that's it! I know that my perspective isn't entirely a normal one—I mean, not that many people have loved ones who've run up against monsters like the Slicer—but I think it's . . . valid. I think maybe I can explain what's wrong with these movies—"

Joyce unwrapped her arms and lifted her hands in the air. "Dorothy, it's a wonderful idea, like all of your ideas, but there's one thing that concerns me." She shifted in her chair and sat up straighter. "I have no doubt it will be a wow of a piece, and one that will be important and make a lot of people think—but do *you* think you can handle it?" She added softly: "Do you think you can handle the pain it might cause?"

Dorothy sipped her coffee and put down the cup. "I don't know. But I have to try. Look, if you think it's a bad idea, that it'll get messy and self-defensive and hysterical or maudlin, just say so and I'll understand. I know there are a lot of good ideas generated in this office, and I'd probably enjoy doing any one of them. But this is a piece that I really want to, have to, write. How I feel about this issue is stuck in my craw and it has to get out sometime."

"Dorothy, you've sold me on the basic idea, but . . ." She put down her coffee cup and looked Dorothy straight in the eye with that unnerving, penetrating glare of hers. "The piece will only be an anecdote—a very moving and very tragic anecdote, but an anecdote, nonetheless—if you don't look at your subject from both sides of the issue. Now this is going to sound inhuman and terribly cruel, Dorothy, but if you want to discuss the pain of your parents' deaths in the context of today's horror movies, you're going to have to—you're going to have to sit through some of those movies. I'm a hard, tough, mean-minded editor, but you know I like balance in my pieces. That's what keeps *Woman Now* from being a carbon copy of *Ms.* You're going to have to *sell* me on the idea that these films are immoral and sexist.

"Now, now, that doesn't mean that I don't already agree with you. But you know a lot of feminists disagree with the stance of the antiporn and antisplatter-movie contingents of the movement. I want you to know exactly what you're talking about. I'm not trying to make this harder for you—I just want a better, more accurate and stronger piece of work from you. Get out there and talk to the people that make these movies. Tell them about your parents; in this instance your subjective viewpoint is invaluable, which is why I wouldn't assign someone more objective to this piece. Ask them how they justify doing what they do, chopping actors up on camera with such grisly realism, making murder seem like fun. That's the only way I can see this from becoming just another, albeit more personal, crime story from the victim's point of view. I want something that *hasn't* been done before."

Dorothy had trouble sorting out her feelings. Part of her understood and agreed with Joyce. Another part of her was appalled. Was she being unfair to Joyce? Was Dorothy bothered by the editor's suggestions, or merely annoyed at the thought of the extra work it might entail, the time it would consume, the pain that Joyce admitted she'd have to go through? Well, the pain would be there in any case, no matter how she approached the article, whether or not she even wrote it. She was not crazy about the idea of sitting through those awful movies, however, especially with the cretins who normally went to see them. Her idea had been so simple: a woman who lost her parents to a "mad slasher" gives her opinion of mad slasher films and the effect that their very existence has had on her morale. Joyce had made it much more complicated and she wasn't sure she should thank her for that.

"I can see you're not entirely thrilled with my suggestions," Joyce said, smiling. "Well, let's bat it around. I can be wrong."

"It's not that. You know what kind of piece you think would work best for the magazine, that's why you're the editor. It's just that I was wondering . . . you've given me a lot to think about. I have to give it time, get it into focus. And, as you said, there's the pain. . . ."

"Well, there's no hurry. Think about it for a couple of days and get back to me." She waved her hand over a pile of papers on her desk. "There's plenty of other pieces you can do, believe me. A lot of issues that need exploring. If you don't want to do the piece as I've suggested, or can't come up with an alternative we can agree upon, we'll just move on to something else. However, before we drop this, there's another element I haven't mentioned yet."

"What's that?"

Joyce dug through the debris on her desk and pulled out a folded newspaper clipping. "This was in one of the columns." She handed it to Dorothy.

Dorothy reached out and took the paper. It was an item about a new movie. Something called *Vicious Two*.

"They're making a sequel to *Vicious*," Joyce said. "As you say, there has been a trend of late, an increase in films that present violent crimes against women. The original *Vicious* did. Is the sequel going to continue the trend, intensify it, or is it something entirely different? How would you like to cover the making of the film, from a feminist's point of view? Get in there and ask the tough questions. Relate it to your feelings about your parents' deaths. The original *Vicious* was about an almost mythical murder case. Your parents were . . . murdered . . . by an equally mythical monster." She paused. "Am I being too morbid, too insensitive?"

"No. It's just that you keep bringing up *Vicious*."

"That's only because that movie was one of the biggest things to come out of Hollywood and it started the whole trend that we've been talking about. Like I say—and I say this with concern and affection, Dorothy—this subject may not be the one for you. It may be more than you can handle. You'll have to see *Vicious*, you'll have to find out about *Vicious Two*. Has the trend come full circle? Call me exploitative and sensationalistic, but that movie has always gotten some pretty heavy reactions from people, particularly from women, our readers. I want to do a story on it. Either you or someone else. But it would be the perfect context within which you could write the kind of personal but well-rounded, well-researched piece you've been suggesting. How about it? If you need some time to think about it, be my guest.

"Look at it this way. Without in any way diminishing your parents' deaths or the tragedy you endured, this will give you an opportunity to enlarge the scope of your original idea, to really do a job on the whole subject, an in-depth look like nothing that's been done before. Take 10 . . . hell, 20,000 words. We could make it a series. There's no end to the possibilities. I think it sounds exciting."

Yes, Joyce, you're being insensitive. I don't find any of this "exciting."

"You know *Woman Now* hasn't got the kind of budget that would pay for a trip to L.A. where they'll be filming, I'm afraid. Phone calls we can pay for, but not planes or hotels. Yet sometimes on a really strong cover article that we think will generate a lot of controversy and sales, we do pick up a percentage—a small percentage—of the bills. You'll get paid above our usual editorial rates, too. Of course, there's no real need to leave New York. Phone interviews and letter responses can be substantially rewarding. A talk with the producers and director—they're all named in that clipping I gave you—good quotes from the writer and actors, particularly the female actors, would give us the balance we need." She swiveled in her chair and started to get up, her signal that the meeting was over. "Think about it. Let me know by the end of the week."

But Dorothy already felt defeated. What a comedown. From writing an article about her beloved parents to doing a write-up on something as obscene and idiotic as *Vicious Two*.

She put up a brave front when she left Joyce's office, but her mood could not have been bleaker.

James Radley's favorite part of the week was the editorial meetings.

He sat on the left side of the table, tucked in between Gloria Hernandez, an editorial assistant, and Robert Harrington, the Senior Editor. There were eight of them in all, ranging from Executive Editor Bart Hamilton, down to Leslie Rhodes, the newest Assistant Editor. James felt good today, confident, then he happened to look down at his shirt and realized with dismay that sometime during the morning, he'd spilled coffee all over himself. Damn! He hated when that happened. What a slob!

James Radley had been a contributing editor of *Frames and Directions* for six years before being given a full time staff job and the title of Associate Editor. Not only did this give him input into what went into the magazine, its editorial slant, but it gave him first choice at the most interesting assignments. Of course he was still basically just a writer; aside from feature stories every couple of months, depending on how much time and effort an individual piece might require, he also contributed reviews of current films and books, and put together brief write-ups for other sections of the magazine. *Frames and Directions* was one of the glossiest and most prestigious film publications in the nation, if not the world.

Ever since he'd been a little boy, James had loved all kinds of movies, but particularly terror films. Because of this there was a lot of good-natured kidding in the editorial office; every time some gory low-budget thriller came out someone would always say, "Did you see that one yet, James?" Occasionally the question would be voiced in a condescending manner—the staff of *Frames and Directions* did not take horror films very seriously—but James' good writing, the in-depth critiques of everything from serious dramas to profound foreign-language films that he was always submitting, soon made it clear to the offender that he was a film reviewer and historian to be reckoned with. The idea for a new feature that he planned to bring up at today's meeting was right up his alley. Yet, he still thought it would surprise and intrigue everyone present.

Bart Hamilton, a balding fifty-five-year-old man with thick brown glasses and a taut, wrinkled face, brought the meeting to order. For the first half hour they talked about how work was progressing on various stories, whether the stills they'd ordered for a certain feature had been dug up, bought, or copied from the Museum of Modern Art's extensive collection, how plans for the layout and illustrations were coming along. While each person on the team had their own particular duties to complete, Bart liked to have a lot of input from all his staff on virtually every aspect of the magazine's production.

Debbie Schuster, Articles Editor, shook her head and said, "I think we're going to have to postpone the profile of Clarissa Harvard. I think Kerrigan's having trouble with it. He keeps promising it for the fifth, but he's missed deadlines before."

"Any suggestions on what to replace it with?"

She bit her lip, thought a while. "The Welles piece, I suppose. James, do you have a backlog?"

James put down his coffee cup and licked his lips. "I might have something. The analysis of *Lord of Light* is in rough form. I suppose I could polish it up in time for the deadline. And my piece on *Now Voyager* still hasn't been used."

"That's an inventory piece," Bart said. "For when we really come up short. Unless you want us to run it immediately as a courtesy, Jim. Otherwise, really, it's not the kind of material that's likely to date."

"No, there's no hurry on it."

Debbie bit the end of her pencil. "What are we going to have from you for next year's special spring issue, Jim?"

"That's what I wanted to talk about today. I wanted to do something on—get ready, gang—the 25th Anniversary of *Vicious*."

The group's reactions came fast and furious:

"Has it been that long already?"

"God, that picture gave me nightmares. That bit in the bedroom. . . ."

"*Vicious*' anniversary? Say, that's not a bad idea."

"Yes, but is it really that important a film?"

"It's considered a masterpiece," Jim countered when the room had quieted down. "Not only of its genre, but as an example of pure cinema. Well, I don't need to defend the film. You've all seen it, you know how famous, how good, it is. Most of you, at any rate. We all know how much influence it had on pictures that came afterwards. Whatever you may think of the movie I think it would be remiss of us to let twenty-five years go by without having made some mention."

"What exactly would you go into?" someone asked.

"The critical reactions at the time, how they've reversed over the decades. The public outrage—and why the film was a box-office smash in spite of it. The precedents it shattered. Its influence over the years. The bizarre real-life twists: Winteroth's son murdering his mother and killing himself the night of the premiere. It was a murder as shocking and bizarre as the original case that inspired *Vicious*."

"The film opened in February 1963, right?" Bart asked. The Executive Editor had a funny smile on his face and James couldn't figure out why. Perhaps because this really was such a typical suggestion of his after all.

"Yes. So this would be perfect for the Spring issue."

Leslie Rhodes repeated her cute habit of raising her hand before she spoke as if she were still in high school. "Did Winteroth make any films after *Vicious*, Jimmy?" she asked.

"Yes, two or three, I believe. But he never recaptured what made him great. The death of his wife and son just about did him in, as you can imagine. And then he died in 1970 of liver trouble."

Sensitive Leslie looked as if someone had just told her that her dog had been shot. "Poor guy."

Bart looked around the table. "What do the rest of you think about this?"

No one had any strenuous objections. In fact, to James' surprise, most felt it was a natural. He had forgotten that even non-horror fans greatly admired Winteroth's bloody achievement.

Of course, the final arbiter was Bart himself. He looked over at James and said, "I like the idea, Jim." That funny smile was back on his face again. "But I'd like to expand upon it."

"Expand upon it?"

"Yes. I want you to write about the original *Vicious* in relation to the making of its sequel."

"Its *sequel*?"

"Yes," Bart was grinning broadly now. "I just got confirmation this morning that Avalon Studios is going ahead with *Vicious Two*."

"*Vicious Two*? I thought that was just a rumor."

"Not any more. Livingstone Stoner is directing. And filming begins in a few weeks."

"Are you sure is isn't a *remake*?" asked Debbie Schuster.

"A sequel!" Bart said emphatically. "*Vicious Two*." He turned back to James and said, "Jimmy, my boy, you planned to go to L.A. on your vacation, right? Why not drop in on the set of *Vicious Two* and write us up a firsthand report? We're going to have full coverage of *Vicious Two*, complete with color photos, in the Spring issue."

Though he couldn't have said just why, James Radley was more excited than he'd been in years.

8

The shadow-man was climbing all over her, his breath foul and moist, his hands hot and sweaty. She kept hoping he would get it over with, just get it over fast so she could get up and get on with her life. She prayed that he'd be satisfied with this humiliation, that he wouldn't feel the need to kill her. It was so dark, how would she ever recognize him? But maybe he didn't care; maybe he was one of those sick, perverted creatures who wasn't satisfied with merely abusing a woman, maybe he wanted to torture and mutilate her, too. . . .

Dorothy woke up, drenched in sweat, shivering. No, it was all right. She was in her bedroom. Even in shadow she could recognize the bureau against the wall, the rocking chair by the window. She was safe. *Safe.* The dream. That damn dream. The one wherein she relieved that awful ordeal, where she felt that scumbag's greasy hands all over her and. . . .

She was alone in the bed. Where was Jimmy? She looked at the luminescent dial of the clock on the nighttable. 4:15. Much too early for him to be up. He was either in the bathroom or getting a snack. She sat up in bed and rubbed her eyes, waiting for the memory of the nightmare to recede.

"What's the matter, honey?"

James Radley walked into the room, naked except for his

cotton briefs, holding a half-empty glass of orange juice in his hand. "I thought I heard you cry out."

"Nightmare," Dorothy said. "It's over. What are you doing up at this hour?"

He shrugged. "Something woke me up and I couldn't get back to sleep. Thought I'd have something to drink. Can I get you anything?"

"No thanks."

James sat down on the bed beside her and continued sipping his orange juice. With his free hand he rubbed the back of her neck. Dorothy was always reminded in little ways of his quiet affection for her, something perhaps deeper and more enduring than passion.

She was glad James was her lover. They had been introduced to one another five years ago at a party and started dating almost immediately. Their relationship became an intimate one right from the start. Within a year they had both stopped seeing other people, and a few months later they each left their own studios and moved into a more spacious apartment on the Upper West Side together. For almost four years they had lived together—happy, comfortable, caring. The thought of marriage came up now and then but things were so terrific the way they were there was some resistance from both sides to changing things. Still, marriage was something that no longer filled Dorothy, at least, with panic. Maybe someday. . . .

James' stroking intensified; he had magic fingers, she always told him. He bent down and kissed her lightly on the lips. In the darkness the planes and angles of his face were deepened, softened; he seemed even handsomer than he was. Although he always protested that he was nice-looking but not a "hunk," as far as Dorothy was concerned he was the best-looking man in the universe. He was not terribly tall, but tall enough for Dorothy to look up to. His hair was short and wavy, his face long and narrow. He had a long, straight nose, high cheekbones, a set of even white teeth, even a dimple in his chin. As he slowly approached forty, the boyish impishness of his face was being superceded by an attractive maturity. He had one of those faces that got better with age, something Dorothy often noted with a certain quiet envy.

"Think you can get back to sleep now?" James asked in a

husky whisper that she always found sexy.

"I don't know. But I'll try." She leaned back, nuzzling the pillow. "Ummmm. Yes, I think I can go to sleep now."

James finished his orange juice in one gulp and put the glass down on the nighttable. Dorothy didn't want to scold but she was afraid the unwashed glass would attract roaches. As James got up to go rinse out his mouth, she told him, "Don't forget the glass."

He slapped her stomach playfully and did as he was told. "Yes, master."

Dorothy was asleep again almost before she knew it. *Jimmy had come back to the room carrying another glass of orange juice, only the glass was full of blood. He had a sneer on his lips, and his hands were the hands of her rapist. Suddenly the bed split in two and Dorothy was plunged into a pit in the floor. Plump pink hands rose out of the fissure to grab her, and she felt something gnawing on her leg. Please don't kill me, she screamed, do what you have to, you bastard, but don't kill me, please. And the wall above her head turned into a face, and the face said, "It's just a sequel, my dear. We're making a sequel to your nightmare. This is a remake of your rape. And when we're done with you, we're going to kill your parents again. This is just a movie, my dear."*

Dorothy woke up feeling so ill she was afraid she might throw up all over the bed. James was still sleeping, deeply, and the sound of his breathing reassured her. She touched his back, touched her face, tried to control her quivering and gasping. It was getting worse. The dreams were getting worse.

And she thought she knew why.

"I'm not so sure I can take that trip to Hollywood," she said calmly at the breakfast table a few hours later. She looked awful. She had slept only fitfully since awakening from her last vivid nightmare. "I'm not sure I can do it."

James, who looked as fresh as a daisy in his clean white shirt and nicely pressed trousers, closed the refrigerator door and came over to the table where she was slumping over her cereal. "Dorothy, I thought we had gone all over this."

Yes, they had gone all over it. She had come home last week after her meeting with Joyce and told him about *Vicious Two* while preparing dinner. James had seemed inordinately interested, then had surprised her with the news that he was also going to cover the film for *Frames and Directions*. It seemed like suck a happy coincidence. Since he would have to go visit the set in Hollywood, she might just as well go with him, though she had not been too crazy originally with the idea of their vacationing together in grubby Los Angeles. But they could travel together, stay together, be together the whole time. Although they'd be covering the story from different angles, the advantage to that was that they could supply each other with fresh and opposing viewpoints, provide a challenge that would deepen their perspective and be reflected in their articles.

Like *Woman Now*, *Frames and Directions* did not have a tremendous budget, but could supply a larger percentage of the traveling fees. Jimmy's vacation was coming up in a few weeks —near the end of *Vicious Two*'s three-month filming—and he had always wanted to show L.A. to Dorothy. As a free lancer Dorothy could take off whenever she pleased. It would be a combined pleasure and business trip. Everything had seemed so perfect.

But that was before Dorothy's nightmares had started intensifying.

James sat down at the table across from her and sipped a cup of coffee. "Well, tell me what's wrong? What's happened?"

"Nightmares," she said.

"You've always had nightmares."

"Yes, but not like these. Oh, Jimmy, it's not the nightmares I'm worried about—I can handle them, I suppose. It's what they're telling me about my mental state. I feel like I'm getting some kind of warning. The nightmares have gotten worse ever since I accepted this assignment—"

"We've talked about this," Jim said. "You're letting it get the better of you. Treat this assignment like you would any other. Handle it like the professional you are. If you don't, you'll be emotionally stunted by what happened to you and your parents for the rest of your life."

Dorothy had heard this before, and she knew he was right. But at the same time, it hadn't happened to him. He could never really understand how she felt.

"I've had enough violence in my life," she said. "I don't need to go out to Hollywood to wallow in it."

"You won't be 'wallowing' in violence, Dorothy. How often do I have to make that point? You'll be wallowing in moviemaking, in fantasy, in *feminism*, for God's sake—your favorite subject. Look at this subject in the same intelligent way that you look at every other subject. Exorcise the demons, Dorothy. Don't let them take control of your life."

He put down his coffee cup and leaned over the table toward her, touching her hands and staring deep into her eyes. "Come on, Dorothy. Everything's been arranged. We're going to have a lot of fun. During a week or two out in Los Angeles we'll have plenty of time to go out, eat at nice restaurants," he grinned, "see the stars. Wouldn't you like that? All we have to do is interview the people working on the film, write about *Vicious Two* from our own special viewpoints—hell, it's not as if you're going to have to sit through the movie. At the most all you have to do is watch them shoot a few scenes. Nonviolent scenes, if you prefer. Come on, honey. What do you say?" He pinched her cheek playfully. "We'll have a great time, I swear. And you've still got a few weeks to prepare yourself for 'the ordeal.' "

"I . . . don't know."

"I'm not unsympathetic to what happened to you," he told her. "I really do understand. Or at least I do as far as it's possible for someone else *to* understand. Think of this job as therapy, a chance to come to terms with your fears, to banish your nightmares forever."

"Nothing is ever that simple. Besides, it's not just a question of going to the set and talking to people. That I could handle. But if I'm to do an in-depth treatment on this subject I have to do my homework. That means sitting through *Vicious* and at least a dozen other films just like it. How can I criticize horror movies if I don't know what I'm talking about?"

"You've watched enough of them with me on TV to have developed all this outrage—how many more do you have to sit through?"

"Enough to have a good, solid grasp of the field. I can't condemn an entire genre just because of a couple of movies. I know that I've read enough reviews and commentaries to know what's going on in stuff like *The Woodshed Murders* and *The Dead Diabolical*—"

105

"*The Diabolical Dead*," he corrected.

"Whatever. But until I've seen these movies for myself I can't really write about it."

She pulled her spoon out of her soggy cereal and slapped it down on the kitchen table. "And I don't *want* to see that stuff. I don't want to see people being killed, dismembered. I should just call Joyce and tell her that I reject the whole assignment."

Jimmy sighed with infinite patience and wiped his upper lip with his finger. "Honey, if I've said it once I've said it a thousand times. You're not seeing real people being murdered. It's all make believe. Once you understand how the special effects are accomplished, it loses all sense of reality."

"I know, I *know.* But it still sounds disgusting."

"Look, we'll rent a few videotapes. Sit as far away from the TV set as you can, distance yourself from it. I'll sit with you every minute and hold your hand. When it gets to be too much, you can close your eyes. And I'll give you an accurate, blow by blow description of what you've missed so you'll know what you're talking about if anyone asks."

"Yuchhh."

"Well, it's better than not knowing what you're arguing against, isn't it? Look, I don't even agree with you about these movies, but I'm willing to help. Once you actually sit through some of these pictures, see how silly and phony they are, they'll stop having a hold over you. You won't be frightened any more."

"Phony? You keep telling me that the effects are so realistic you can hardly tell them from the real thing."

"Yes, in some cases. But they're exaggerated, comic-bookish. You can't take it seriously."

"I *hate* violence, can't you understand that? I read the papers and I get sick to my stomach. I hate the thought of people being murdered! And not just because of what happened to my parents. I would like to think that I would have enough decency and compassion—"

"Compassion has nothing to do with it. We're not talking about real people, about items in the *Daily News*. That stuff— real life, real people, real murders—upsets me, too. But movies and fiction do not."

"Don't those movies make sick people want to go out and

imitate the things they see?"

"*Sick* people, yes! But sick people can get excited into acts of violence by *anything*. Hell, they could see something on the evening news that'll set them off." Before she could reply, he threw up his hands and exclaimed: "I've got to get to work. I can't hang around here all day. I don't have time for this argument." He stopped in his tracks and pointed his finger at Dorothy. "Y'know, Dottie, you have this habit of letting the tragedies of your life give you an insurmountable advantage in every damn argument. No one's opinion can *possibly* be as important as yours."

"That's not true! That's an awful thing to say!"

"It is true. I have to handle you with kid gloves all the time. Dorothy, what happened to your parents was horrible, monstrous. And if I ever caught that guy who raped you I'd kill him with my bare hands. But I do not now and will never agree with you—and your whacko friends—on this issue, this bug in your bonnet about horror films and porno mags and their treatment of women. I really hate censorship, Dorothy. I think because of your multiple tragedies—which you never let anyone forget, by the way—you have lopsided views on the issue. Enjoying a horror picture doesn't make a man a psycho. Enjoying a skin mag—and yes, Dorothy, I admit I like to look at *Playboy* centerfolds now and then—doesn't make a man an 'M.C.P.' I like women, I like to *look* at women, particularly women who have been well paid—"

"You're dragging in another issue entirely—"

"—and who have *willingly* consented to pose in the buff. I will not be branded a 'sicko' by a bunch of neurotic, loveless—"

"Not a sicko, a *ghoul*," Dorothy shouted. "You're a *ghoul*! You don't like women, you like to see women being chopped up and shot at and tortured. Some of the things that go on in those movies—"

"Which you haven't even seen!"

"Which I've read about, heard about, been told about, seen pictures from . . ."

"They're entertainment. Horrible things happen to people, men as well as women, in horror films because they *are* horror films, not Doris Day movies. Will you get that through your thick skull? You have been brainwashed by all those crazy, man-hating—"

"Oh, don't be stupid, James. That's the sort of remark some narrow-minded meathead would make, not a man who likes to think of himself as being open-minded—"

"Open-minded, yes. Can *you* say the same thing? Sit through some of those movies, Dorothy. See for yourself. Don't let the staff of *Woman Now* or anyone else make up your mind for you. Do you have the guts, Dottie?" He stepped closer to the table, still wagging his finger. "And there *is* a link in some women's minds between skin mags and horror films, whether you like it or not. Aren't they calling some horror movies the 'new pornography?' Now, *you* wanted to tackle this issue. You brought it up to *them*, that's what you said. Well now have the guts to go through with it. Because you're right—you can't go out to L.A. and do a job on *Vicious Two* just because you don't like horror films, just because you can't and won't look at them objectively. You have to keep things in perspective or you'll just be writing 5000 words of crap propaganda for a lot of know-nothings to cluck about."

Before Dorothy could respond to his irate remarks, he added, "Oh, the whacko radical feminists will eat it up, all right. You'll be their heroine, they'll carry you around on their shoulders. But all the time you'll know the truth. That what could have been a piece of fine, objective journalism, was instead turned into a piece of subjective drivel. Which will it be, Dorothy? Fine, objective journalism—or the easy way out?"

He swiveled on his heels and headed out of the kitchen. "Now I've got to get to work. I can't just sit around here all day the way you do."

Dorothy shot up out of her chair, so angry she could have throttled him. "That's a low blow, Jimmy, and you know it! I work, too, even if I do it at home instead of in an office. You're not paying my bills, Jimmy, and I always pay my share of the rent and everything else. How *dare* you imply that my free lancing is less important—"

He tried to placate her. "I'm sorry, I'm *sorry*. You're being too sensitive—"

"I'm not your wife. And I wouldn't expect you to support me even if I were. Go to work, Jimmy. I'm sure they can't do without the most important man in the office."

For a few beats, he just looked at her. Then he abruptly turned his back. "Ah, the hell with it."

When he was gone she wiped her eyes and swore she wouldn't cry. But though she begged herself not to let it happen, the memories came flooding back, the memories and the sense of loss and the painful, wrenching wave of emotion. And with them, all the tears, so many tears. . . .

The Slicer, as the newspapers referred to him, was a pitiful, deranged Irish-American, born Lawrence O'Connell. He was an unemployed alcoholic who had been living on welfare in an SRO hotel in downtown Manhattan. Many years before his ultimate comedown, he had been married, with two children, a girl and a boy, and had been gainfully employed in a factory on Long Island. It was the drinking, the lack of satisfaction—both sexual, emotional, and financial—in his life, that drove him to ruin, that started eating away at the fabric of his mind and slowly turned him crazy.

His drinking bouts led to wife beating and child abuse. When he drunkenly tried to molest his own daughter—thinking she was an old girlfriend, or so he said—his wife clobbered him with her boy's baseball bat and called the police. The next day she had him thrown out of the house and filed for divorce. By this time, most of his friends and his own dear children had completely turned against him.

Lawrence got bald, Lawrence got fat, Lawrence's booze-ravaged face with its jowls and rotted teeth looked like a suppurating blister. The tipsy colleens in the neighborhood taverns no longer had any use for him, and a few bouts with crabs and the clap had turned him off prostitutes. Besides, the whores had gotten big for their britches and raised their prices, and he found he could no longer afford them.

He got thrown out of one rooming house and residential hotel after another, for bad behavior, spent a few nights in jail for petty offenses, and got his share of summonses for urinating on the sidewalk and the like. Now and then he made threatening calls to his wife and children, until they got an unlisted number and finally moved to Boston out of reach. Lawrence's mind and body continued to deteriorate.

The final stroke: he lost his job. The management, as well as his co-workers, had had enough of his antics. And often he would not show up for days at a time. Enough was enough. He stayed sober enough to apply for unemployment. A drinking companion steered him to a cheap semi-welfare hotel in Manhattan, which was appropriate, as when his unemployment ran out he had to go on welfare anyway.

It was hard to say what finally set him off. He spent most of his time either drunk or asleep or enmeshed in lurid fantasies. His sexual appetites increased, but prostate troubles made it painful for him to ejaculate. Driven mad by sexual tension and the utter defeat of his life, he decided to murder anyone who got in his way, anyone who seemed happy and satisfied while he was so miserable. Somehow he got his hands on a meat cleaver from the diner where he had what few meals he consumed, and set out to take his revenge against society.

Half of his assaults and killings were on the city streets and the other half in the vast subway system of New York. He would get on a train at one stop, pull the cleaver out of his coat and chop at whatever unsuspecting party was closest, then dash off the train as soon as it pulled into the following station. He did this at least three times before a fairly accurate description of him could be circulated.

Out of seventeen initial victims, most received only superficial wounds before O'Connell ran off for one reason or another. However, five were seriously injured, and three were killed, two of those succumbing to shock and blood loss, and the other committing suicide after losing a limb. It was O'Connell's last nighttime foray into the subway that was the most sensational, when he cornered a middle-aged married couple on the IRT and savagely mutilated them in front of several horror-struck witnesses. He was so engrossed in his chopping and smashing that he failed to get off the train once it had pulled into the platform, which gave passengers—some of whom were still to this day unhinged by the experience—time to run for assistance. The train was delayed until officers could come and subdue the now-enervated maniac. His clothes, the subway car, were totally drenched with blood. Pieces of his victims were scattered everywhere.

The couple, who had simply gone out for an infrequent night at the theater, were Myra and Joseph Hunter of Glendale, Long

Island. Apparently they had been calmly sitting in a corner when the Slicer got on. Without warning, he pulled out his cleaver and chopped straight down in Myra's head, killing her instantly. Joseph tried to defend himself but was unable to stop the savage strokes that tore into his body one after the other. Even after the Hunters were dead, O'Connell continued his butchery. The jaded police had never seen anything like it.

Fifteen years old at the time, Dorothy had been watching the Late Show with her Aunt Maggie when the police drove up outside. She stayed in the living room while her aunt spoke to the police in the foyer. Dorothy heard a terrible wailing erupt from the hall. She knew instantly what must have happened—an accident of some kind. She assumed her parents were injured, but wasn't ready to hear that they were dead. She was never told exactly what had happened—the true, repulsive *ferocity* of the assault—only that they, against all odds, had become the latest and last victims of the now-identified Lawrence O'Connell. She and her aunt had held each other for the longest time. The TV had kept on blaring, but the sound and the movie and the commercials had receded into a twilight world of sanity and normalcy that could no longer exist for the two shattered women. Uncle Bert got home from his poker game and turned white with horror upon receiving the news. Things like that just didn't happen to people you knew, he said, to people you loved. They just didn't happen.

Dorothy had been telling herself that for almost twenty years now. And what had happened to her parents still didn't make any sense.

Lawrence O'Connell had had nothing personal against her parents. They had just been in the wrong place at the wrong time.

Back in those days, 1966, there was less tolerance for insanity pleas and plea bargaining and all the tricks and shenanigans of the legal profession. People still cared about victims. Lawrence O'Connell was put away for life and died in prison. The irony was that, unlike so many contemporary criminals who beat the system, O'Connell was genuinely crazy. Dorothy was taken in by her loving aunt and uncle. And the grief didn't truly hit her until she was nearly sixteen.

Even now, a grown woman, Dorothy could still not believe it

had happened. She thought about James with some bitterness. Perhaps if it had happened to him, he'd understand.

She got up from the kitchen table, feeling numb, convinced she should simply call Joyce and tell her that the story was off. She could get someone else to do it. Someone who hadn't suffered as she had and could look at stuff like *Vicious Two* as a good time instead of the sickness she was convinced it really was. Her hand was almost on the receiver when she froze.

Is is really your parents that are bothering you? Or is it what happened to you a few years later? Coming home from the store to your first apartment. Sensing the stranger stepping out of the shadows along the pathway. Feeling his hands around your throat, covering your mouth, pulling you back into the bushes. The knife blade at your jugular. The hot breath in your ear. His words of vulgar endearment. Wondering how many pieces he'd leave you in when he was through, if he'd be satisfied with just raping you or if he'd have to watch your death throes to come to climax.

How could people, as many actually did, think rape could be enjoyable? Didn't they realize that it was hard to "enjoy" anything when a knife was at your throat, when fists were battering your face and body, when you were jabbed insanely with all the love and affection of a jackhammer? Enjoyment? They were crazy! How could you enjoy what was essentially an act of violence; how could you enjoy it when all the time you were praying that the violence would end when the rape did and that you wouldn't wind up a collection of body parts scattered in garbage cans across the city.

The hardest part for Dorothy to deal with was that they never caught the guy. All her humiliation, all her outrage, and they never even found out who he was.

James didn't understand. *She* had been a victim of misogynous violence, had felt the hands and breath of the rapist, had felt his *hatred*, his anti-female vileness filling her to the core.

Damn Jimmy. She had thought her lover had been different, one of the few men she could make love to, give herself completely to just as he gave himself completely to her—without trembling in memory of that loathsome experience. But he was still a man, like all the rest, and couldn't, wouldn't, understand.

Still, she had known Jimmy for five years. She knew that he

was *not* like other men, that he was more sensitive and less "macho," without being prim or prissy. She had to remember that both of them said things in anger that they didn't really mean. . . .

Or was she just making excuses for him? The confusion was bringing on a headache.

Oh, Jimmy. Jimmy. Why can't all these things be less complicated?

Him and those damn movies.

She went back to the kitchen table and sat down. The cereal looked most unappetizing but she'd try to finish it anyway. She had to smile in spite of herself. Jimmy's tastes were so charmingly . . . unrefined. His reading tastes leaned toward horror and suspense, while she found nothing more satisfactory than cuddling up with the latest historical novel or biography. Jimmy watched *Star Trek* reruns while she relished *Masterpiece Theatre*. Jimmy loved all those gruesome horror pictures that he had to go see by himself. When those films were by chance on cable —on regular television with all the gory parts cut out she could stand them—she'd retreat to the bedroom and put on her headphones while Mahler or Beethoven issued from the stereo. Jimmy, Jimmy, Jimmy. Just like a kid. He especially loved to watch monster movies. Those she could tolerate—except even they were too disgusting these days. Made her sick to her stomach.

Yet, Jimmy was clearly not an idiot. He was well-educated, literate, knowledgeable in many fields, could appreciate fine music and theater. Perhaps it was that a part of him had never grown up. Perhaps there was a dark side of him that needed violence and bloodshed. Well, Dorothy had had enough of it in her lifetime, the *real* thing. If Jimmy had had her experiences, he might not find such amusement in matters of a morbid nature. There was more than enough violence in the real world to suit her.

She was feeling calmer now. The argument had diminished in importance, become just another one of their frequent, silly set-tos. It didn't mean anything, really. Jimmy was so protective of his interests. She would dare to speak out against the things he loved—like horror movies—and he would take it as a personal attack.

Well, she had to admit she was the same. Often she knew his remarks about *some* of her feminist friends and their ideas were right on target, but damn if she'd agree with him. She was no traitor to "the cause." If she conceded on just one item, he'd never let her forget it. Still, he had always seemed reasonable when it came to women's issues, more understanding, certainly, than the average man. And she was sure he understood how she felt about horror films. Why couldn't the two of them just *admit* it to each other, *give* a little, meet the other halfway?

Maybe she *was* wrong to turn her hatred of horror into a big feminist issue. Maybe she should just look at it personally without involving other women. Hadn't that been her original idea? *Curse you, Joyce Ramsey*. Should she refuse the assignment and do another version of it for a different publication?

No, she had made up her mind. She owed it to herself, to Jimmy, to their relationship, to women, to murder victims and their families, to *everyone*, to investigate this subject and do a complete and thorough job on it. No, there was no turning back.

After all, she figured, once you've lived through the horror yourself, how bad can a movie be?

9

Late Summer, 1987.
Los Angeles and environs.

Vivienne Cherneau woke up and wished she were dead.

Some foolish tenacity in her system kept the "old battleaxe," as she privately referred to herself, going on long past the point where life had any purpose. There was nothing on this earth more ridiculous than a glamour queen who'd outlived her usefulness, of that she was convinced.

She rolled over in her pale pink bed in her pale pink bedroom and studied the soft lavender light coming in through the dainty crimson curtains. Her agent and friend, Harry Fagan, kept telling Vivienne—born Vivian Hope Maxwell in Pittsburgh, Pennsylvania—that she was on the verge of a sensational comeback, that appearing in *Vicious Two* was a golden opportunity. But she'd long since had her fill of gruesome two-bit horror films, and even though *Vicious Two* promised to be a little more expensive and a little bit classier than the usual, she was not much looking forward to the experience.

Sound investments had kept her from going the way of some of her peers, broke, desperate, alcoholic hasbeens who lived in crumbling hotels and spent their last days lost in the oblivion of booze and fading memories. Some of them—God! She couldn't understand what kept them going. She had to admit she was a lot luckier than most. She no longer had the Beverly Hills palace she'd lived in during her heyday, but she did have a nice little condo in Los Angeles, a live-in maid and companion who was a godsend and could even speak English, some money in the bank —more than enough—and she even managed to keep getting jobs in the movies. Jobs? What a joke that was.

She had to face it. Not much mattered any more since Charlie, her devoted husband, passed away. There was no one to share or remember things with. No special person to take care of her or to care about. Nothing much to live for, really. By now the loneliness had settled in her bones.

Hester, a skinny, teenaged maid with cute bangs and crooked teeth—the only hired help that Vivienne could afford—came in with a tray and a nice, warm smile. Such a treasure, even if she insisted on continuously mispronouncing her employer's last name. "Good morning, Miss *Chernowww*. I have something nice for you this morning."

No, no, it's Cher-know, you idiot! "Goodie. What is it, dear?"

"Eggs Benedict. Just the way you like them."

"Wonderful, Hester. That's just what I was in the mood for." Well, if you had to wake up wishing you were dead, at least life could offer a few compensations. Yes, she was luckier than most.

The maid also produced a package. "This came by messenger for you."

The script. About time. They began shooting in a couple of weeks and she'd yet to receive the finished revised version of the screenplay. (Though there had been times Viv hadn't seen a finished shooting script until two days after shooting began!) Long red fingernails tore open the manila envelope. *Vicious Two* by Douglas Longbank *and* Livingstone Stoner. Apparently director Stoner had felt Longbank's version needed a few rewrites. She'd had a splitting headache when she'd read the original screenplay and barely remembered it so there was no way Vivienne could judge if this one were generally better or worse. Only one thing mattered: was her part bigger or smaller?

She flipped through the script while nibbling on her eggs and fried potatoes. Hester's coffee was always good and hot. She wished she could say the same for the screenplay.

It looked as though Vivienne wouldn't have much to do now until the final quarter of the movie! She was playing the character of Yvette, the murderess in the original film—God, how Winteroth's picture had scared her back in '63—who is now twenty-five years older and has managed to escape from the asylum. The actress who'd originally played the part had died in an automobile crash in 1967, and none of the other two principals had been available or interested in reprising their roles (in the man's case) or playing another character (in the woman's.)

Instead of the one gruesome killing that the first film had offered, *Vicious Two* had no less than seven grisly murders. She forgot about her eggs and rushed through to the ending. She was hoping that at the very least Yvette had been made the killer this time. Or was it still someone else as in Longbank's original story?

Before she could find out, the phone rang. *Damn*. She picked up on the second ring. She didn't like Hester answering the phone; she was terrible at getting messages straight. "Yes?"

"Vivienne. It's Harry. Did you get the script yet?"

"Yes. I'm reading it now."

"Now look, Viv. It's still a good juicy part."

"Yeah, with about half the lines I had before. I take it you got your copy this morning, too."

"Yes. Came by messenger thirty minutes ago. Nice of them to finally get around to it."

"Well, since you interrupted me, perhaps you can tell me if Yvette did it or not."

"Did what?"

"The murders, Harry. The Murders! Did I do them or *not*?"

"Well, my copy of the screenplay is missing the final few pages, so I really couldn't tell you. They have a tight lid on security, I guess. What about yours?"

"Wait a sec." She put down the phone and flipped to the end of *Vicious Two*. Missing! She didn't know who the killer was, damn it!

"Mine's missing, too. I'm so tired of this crap. Are they really afraid I'm going to leak the ending to every reporter I run into?"

Harry sighed. "You know how they are. Besides, what difference does it make? It's a good credit in a first-class production."

"Well, I don't know about *that*."

"Look what a big horror hit did for the careers of Bette Davis and Joan Crawford back in the sixties?"

And a lot of other desperate old broads, Vivienne thought bitterly. But she wasn't and never had been Davis or Crawford. She'd starred in more than her share of pictures—mostly "B"s—but she'd never achieved the kind of superstardom that Davis and Crawford had, not even in the forties or fifties when she'd been more beautiful than both of those women put together.

"I'm tired of horror films, Harry. I want to do something different. Right now Shelley Winters and I are running neck and neck for the title of actress who's appeared in the most rotten movies. Harry, you gotta get me out of this rut."

"Vivienne, I try, I try. But you know how it is. Darling, I try my best."

Yes, she knew "how it was," she thought, looking down at the eggs benedict congealing on the pretty china plate. She had let herself get too old and too fat. Face lifts could hide wrinkles, but they could only do so much for double chins. Her closet was filled with a colorful collection of ever-enlarging muumuus, clothes tailored to hide her enormous weight gain. Jane Greer and Ann Blythe, actresses who had never been as popular as she had been, could get supporting parts on nighttime soaps and daytime "continuing dramas" because they were still presentable. People looked at them and said, "See how good she looks," or "doesn't she look marvelous for her age!" They looked at Vivienne and thought: "Goodness—what a *mess*!"

Vivienne's round pretty face, with its enormous yellow eyes and bright auburn hair, was bloated and wrinkled and blotchy beneath her makeup. She usually wore a succession of old-fashioned wigs, but her own hair, worn medium length, swept outwards at the sides in dingy little curls. Her nose was a rounded stub and her chin and cheekbones three large, prominent protuberances under a ton of rouge and face powder. You could never have convinced her that she looked better without the cosmetics.

She mentally calculated the probable calories in eggs benedict and reminded herself to give Hester a scolding. Dumb broad—Vivienne kept saying she wanted *diet* food, palatable, tasty, diet food. Was that so difficult for the idiot child to manage?

Harry had thought of something positive to say after the awkward pause. "I think there may be a part for you on *Miami Vice*. A good showcase, Viv."

Vivienne frowned. *As what, a blimp?*

"And you're welcome back on the *$99,000 Answer* any time you're willing. There's even the possibility of a guest shot on Carson."

"Really?" Just as long as Rivers wasn't guest host. Vivienne knew the brassy comedienne wouldn't resist taking pot shots at the size of her body.

"And there's always the *Joe Franklin Show* the next time you're in New York."

Vivienne sipped some more of her coffee and swallowed so hard Harry heard it over the telephone. When was he going to get her a guest shot on *Dynasty* or *Dallas*? Sure, she was fat and she knew it. But wouldn't her fans—and she did hear from hundreds of them all the time—just love to see her on some popular prime time program? Was she doomed to be cast in penny dreadfuls and creature features for the rest of her existence? *Charlie, where are you? I need you, Charlie.*

"Will you be all right, Vivienne? Shooting starts in a couple of weeks. Are you keeping yourself in shape for *Vicious Two*?"

She decided that the cold sticky eggs looked palatable again, and started spooning them, along with the sauce and the bread, into her mouth. "Mmmmmm," she mumbled through her lips, finally swallowing the masticated morsels. "I'm getting a new hairdo, new clothes—"

"Don't go overboard. In the film you'll mostly be wearing a mental hospital uniform and an inexpensive wig."

Shit! They'd never give her a chance to show off whatever of the old glamour remained, would they? Talk about Vicious! One of these days she'd be the most vicious bitch in Hollywood, and *then* would she say a thing or two about the way the old producers' nephews were running the show.

"Harry," she said. "Will you please find out if I'm the killer or not? Now, goodbye!" She hung up the phone.

The mood she was in, she hoped for once that she *was* the maniac. Kill everyone, that's what she'd like to do. And she'd love every minute of it.

It was another sunny morning in the suburb of Sherman Oaks, California. Inside a split-level ranch house with a large front lawn and a pool in the back, Douglas Longbank sat up in bed, ran his hands over his balding pate, and groaned.

Virtually every time he woke up he thought of what had been done to his screenplay and felt sick to his stomach again. Damn that Livingstone Stoner! He was only a hack director who got lucky and now fancied himself another Anthony Winteroth, a Kubrick, a Hitchcock. The fool! What was worse, the final straw was Stoner's insistence on rewriting large sections of Longbank's *Vicious Two* screenplay. His work was decidedly not an improvement.

Longbank's wife, Edna, poked out from under her pillow and smiled. "Is it morning yet, darling?" She was a pretty, perky redhead with chipmunk cheeks and large front teeth that somehow worked in her favor instead of against it. Longbank stroked her belly affectionately and said, "Yes, it's morning." He smiled. "Go and make my breakfast."

Laughing, Edna said, "Go and make it yourself. And I wouldn't mind pancakes, either."

He flipped himself out of bed and stuck his feet into his slippers. "Whatever you say, my darling." He stood up and patted his own naked belly this time. Forty-four—and in pretty good shape. He looked a damn sight better than that jackass Livingstone Stoner—what a silly name!—and Stoner was almost ten years younger. Why was it always the children who called the shots in Hollywood? He even bet that messy mop of curly hair that Stoner had on his head was a wig, for Christ's sake. He snorted out loud and headed toward the kitchen.

Longbank was a nice-looking man with bright blue eyes and clean-cut features. He had already sold several screenplays, watched five of them be made into movies, and seen three of them actually released to other than home video. Most of his films had been family dramas and comedies, but it was his work on a thriller titled *Jigsaw* that had won him the *Vicious Two* assignment. He had started out as a short story writer, inspired by the likes of H.P. Lovecraft, Fredric Brown, and Robert Bloch, then had sold three novels. It wasn't long before he realized that the real money was out in Hollywood. He'd only intended to make enough to support his literary endeavors, to keep the wolves away from his door, but he'd been out here for eleven years now, found a wife, had a daughter—who was now out visiting Doug's sister in Long Beach—and realized he liked his life just the way it was.

Vicious Two—in crass, commercial terms—was to have been a major breakthrough for him. He had approached the material the same way the late Anthony Winteroth, and Winteroth's screenwriter, the retired Don Ramis, had approached it. Strong characterizations, a hint of mystery and the occult, a serious study of the effects of sexuality and environment on violence. The main character in his screenplay had been the murderess, Yvette. The movie had really been about her, her attempts to fit back into society, to start a new life for herself, without succumbing to the madness of the past.

Yvette was not a heroine in the classic sense, but she was a fascinating character nonetheless, a haunted, tormented individual who finds reminders of her horrible—now regretted—actions everywhere she goes: movies, books, plays, topical jokes and parodies—everything reminds her of the night she killed her roommate. The script suggested that she might be cracking up all over again, due to a new set of pressures.

There were two on-screen murders in Longbank's screenplay, another off-screen, but the emphasis in them had been on surprise and suspense, not in gruesome carnage. The killer at the end had turned out to be a friend of Yvette's, a nurse she had known at the institution who had been driven mad by her years of dealing with stress and insanity, and had been striking out at those she perceived as a threat to Yvette's security.

But Livingstone Stoner had decided the screenplay needed to be "punched up" a bit. He added many more murders, each of them more hideous than the one before, clearly under the influence of the success of the "stalk-and-slash" summer camp movies like *Body Count at Buzzard Bay* and all of its sequels and imitations. Much of the psychological subtlety was completely jettisoned when Stoner rewrote fifty percent of the dialogue, making character motivations too obvious, too hackneyed, and at other times, totally inexplicable. New, pointless characters were introduced, only to be beheaded or run over a few pages later. Clearly Stoner was not interested in a classy suspense picture like *Vicious Two*'s predecessor. He wanted to make a plain and simple splatter film. Longbank was convinced that Anthony Winteroth would turn over in his grave if he knew what that one "bedroom murder" of his had wrought.

Incredibly, Longbank didn't know who Stoner had decided—arbitrarily, he was sure, without thought of logic or clarity—to make the murderer this time. The character of Yvette's nurse friend had been reduced to a scene or two, so all the comments Longbank had been making about exposure to insanity begetting insanity were completely lost, along with the whole point of making her the killer. Only Stoner himself knew who the maniac was going to be now—assuming he had even decided at this point. Not a single released copy of the finished screenplay included an ending. Maybe Stoner was even stupid enough to film the movie *without* a denouement, probably thinking this novel approach would be akin to some sort of contemporary genius. What a fool!

Edna came into the kitchen while Douglas poured batter into the frying pan. "Is that your stomach grumbling or your mouth?" she asked, kissing him lightly on the cheek.

He put sliced pieces of apple into the pancakes and turned up the heat. "All this business with *Vicious Two* has given me an ulcer. I should have never have demanded to see a copy of the revised script."

She kissed him again. "I know, I know. I've already given you my advice, Dougie."

"I know," he sighed, holding his spatula and watching the pancake batter start to bubble. "Take the money and run."

Jocasta Sullivan waited dejectedly in the trendy restaurant on Montrose Avenue and wondered what she had done to be placed in such an awkward position. She didn't want to come off like a jealous shrew, certainly not to her own daughter, but she thought she certainly had a bona fide grievance. Stay calm, she told herself, and handle it like you would any other problem.

She sat back in her seat, biting her fingernails, and pointedly studied her surroundings. No sense getting herself into a state before her daughter even arrived. The restaurant, called Somethin' Else, had only just opened recently, but was already a Los

Angeles success story. Jocasta had had no trouble gaining admittance, even without a reservation. She basically liked the place's ambiance, although she personally found the abundance of mirrors, plants and plastic coverings a bit too artificial.

"More coffee, Ma'am," the waitress said, a skinny red-headed lady who seemed all bones and bangs.

Jocasta declined. She'd had three cups already. Damn that daughter of hers; why wasn't she ever on time? She tapped the square, glass table top with her spoon.

Jocasta was a pretty, middle-aged woman of forty-seven with short brown curls across her forehead and neatly-styled hair that curved inward at her chin line. Her bright, perfectly made up eyes were blue with flecks of green. She wore an attractive white dress, simple, and a pretty pearl necklace, fake.

It really was a cosmic joke, she thought. Something that could only happen to her. She had struggled along as a bit player during her younger years, then had finally become a reasonably well-known character actress at forty. Two years after that she lucked into winning the lead in the film version of the bestseller *Starburst*, playing a faded actress addicted to drugs and the wrong men. After winning an Oscar for "Best Actress" that year, Jocasta had been sure that her luck was finally changing. Five years after that and the flurry of attention she'd enjoyed after *Starburst* was all but over. There were few parts for serious older actresses, and her pride wouldn't let her take bit parts or supporting roles even if she'd been offered them.

But the widow of a poor provider would eventually have to swallow her pride, and that's what she had finally done, telling her agent to consider any offer, as long as it was fairly respectable. *Vicious Two* was heaven-sent. Of course it was trashy— but she was shrewd enough to know that this project was definitely the one to get her back in the public eye. And the role of Sarah, the nurse, was a juicy one. Or at least it had been.

When she'd received Stoner's new version of the screenplay this morning she'd nearly developed catalepsy. What had he done to her part? It had originally been a good solid supporting role; now she had only a walk-on or two, maybe one good scene and that was it. And without those all-important final pages she didn't even know if she was still to be unmasked as the homicidal maniac, thereby ensuring at least a few good final moments.

What made it all the worse was her daughter's part in it. She hated being the kind of mother who had such negative thoughts about her own flesh and blood, but her sneaking suspicions would not go away. Jocasta had gotten the role because of her friendship with *Vicious Two*'s Executive Producer, Harold Watson. Watson had been out of favor with the studios for the longest time—right when Jocasta could have used him—but, as with everyone else, sooner or later his fortunes had changed, and Jocasta had been willingly dragged along on his coattail. Livingstone Stoner had been suitably awed—to a diminished degree, admittedly—by having an Oscar-winning actress of such talent and stature interested in appearing in his picture and immediately gave her the role.

Then there was talk about finding a suitable young actress to play Pamela, the beautiful young woman who becomes the maniac's first victim in what was to have been a kind of latter day "reprise" of the classic bedroom murder (which had wisely been excised from Stoner's revised screenplay.) "Why not Ellen? Ellen, my daughter?" Jocasta had suggested. Ellen, the bright, sexy, twenty-three-year-old who had kept her late father's name and called herself Ellen Rue. Wouldn't Ellen be perfect? Jocasta said to Harold.

Too perfect. When Ellen met Livingstone it was instantaneous lust. She got the part. She also won his heart. Before long they were inseparable, the darlings of the columnists. So much the better, thought Jocasta. I've done my bit to help my dear aspiring—not terribly talented—daughter. The rest is up to her. Oh, how Jocasta had suffered through all those summer stock shows and supper clubs and dreadful Grade Z revues in which Ellen had appeared. Ellen had the tits and ass—she was far more attractive than her mother had been at her age—but as an actress she was just about zero. Plenty of presence, but not a dollop of skill. But who needed skill when you looked like that?

Ellen, wearing a tight pair of designer jeans and a light blue blouse, walked bouncily into the restaurant, holding her black patent leather purse in her hand. Oh, she looked like such a wiseass. One good part and she thought she was Madonna. How Jocasta would have liked to wipe that smug, conceited look off her face. Ellen spent all her nights getting fucked by Livingstone Stoner. Jocasta would have had to have been blind not to notice that in Stoner's new script Ellen now had a much bigger part, as well as more lines, than her mother.

The tension at the table as Ellen sat down was so thick you could hardly have cut it with a chainsaw.

"How are you, mother? I'm sorry I'm late."

Jocasta pulled it out of her handbag. "Have you seen it? This? Your boyfriend's new screenplay?"

Ellen was hesitant. "Uh, yes. What about it?"

Jocasta was so mad she could hardly talk. *Look at her sitting there on her tush like a total innocent. What has she done to deserve such a break? I was the one who studied for years, who worked hard, who starved and who waited on tables while waiting for a chance, any chance. I'm the one who's paid my dues. And now—with my help—she just waltzes into a major movie role and takes over, using her influence with the director to reduce her mother—her own mother's part—to nothing. To think I carried her, bore her, nursed the brat, and frankly I would rather have been out making rounds.*

Jocasta stood up abruptly and shoved the script back into her bag. Forgetting her own advice, she succumbed to temptation and emotion and sneered into her daughter's face. "Ellen, you may be my daughter. But I happen to think you're a Grade A, number one *bitch*."

And with that she stormed out of the restaurant.

Eddie Petrano, a short, slender, dark-haired man of thirty-eight, heard his mother coming into the living room and quickly closed the book he was leafing through. He slipped it into his briefcase—but not before the old lady had seen what he was doing.

"What's *that*?" she asked in her gravelly, accusatory tone. "Something you don't want me to see?"

The old lady stumbled across the living room in her walker, her head shaking and her lips working even when she was silent (which wasn't very often.) As she walked she looked about the room—green, weatherbeaten rug, battered brown sofa, yellow wallpaper, shelves full of china and pictures—as if making certain that nothing had been stolen during the night. Her hair was a mass of scraggly white lint, and her face a pale, mottled blotch of wrinkles and liver spots. "Something dirty, is it, Eddie?

Something about naked women? I told you, I won't have that trash in my house."

Eddie opened his mouth to reply, then thought better of it. What was the use of saying anything? The old lady hadn't her marbles any more so it was like arguing with a wall. She had always been close-minded and stubborn—dumb, too—even when she had been younger. What was the point of saying anything?

"Filthy magazines. You can read them all you want when you're at some tramp's house, but I won't have them in my house."

Yeah, well, who do you think pays the rent on your "home," you crazy old bitch. It sure as hell doesn't come from your pitiful income.

He braced himself. Any second now she'd start in on her second favorite topic. "Of course, what can I expect from someone who works on the kind of movies you do. You were always a strange child, Eddie, always a strange little boy. You and your monsters and your. . . ."

As usual he found the best thing to do was tune her out. That was the only way he would hold on to his *own* sanity.

Guilt made him live with his mother. Guilt made him pay the rent and let her keep what little she had of her own. Guilt kept him from putting her in a home—which would have eaten away all their savings in any case. And guilt made him spend time with her when he would rather have had her rattle on to a paid companion or nurse. He'd tried hiring two of those in the past few months, but neither had worked out. One had even quit in objection to the "goodies" she saw tacked up on his bulletin board when she blundered uninvited into his workshop.

You see, Eddie had killed his father. Eddie had made his mom a widow. Eddie had taken her precious husband, Joe, and her son, Wilfred—the one she'd always loved the best—away from her, leaving her alone and miserable. Wasn't it his duty to stay with her, to watch out for her and see that she was happy? Hadn't his brother and pa told him not to drink so much on that fishing trip, knowing he was the only one who could drive them home? Young Willy didn't have a driver's license yet, and their father's leg was so stiff there was no way he could have sat behind the wheel.

And wasn't Eddie drunk when they started back home on the highway, when they ran off the road into those trees? And wasn't Eddie alive—God surely did look after drunks and fools—while Willy and Pa had been instantly obliterated in the crash? *Obliterated.* Parts of them had been seemingly strewn everywhere, but mostly it was just blood. So much of it. Eddie still drank at times because of what he'd seen. It was their side of the car that hit the tree.

So he took care of his mother out of guilt. Even so, there were limits.

"I can put up with the monsters, the sick stuff you got in your workshop, but I will not put up with smut," the old lady was droning. "Will not have smut in my house. I see you reading those books and magazines whenever you get the chance, hiding them when you think I'm not looking. Well, one of these days I'm gonna find that trash, and I'm gonna throw it right out of this house."

"Ma. Stay out of my workroom!"

"Don't care about your workshop. I never go in there. That's your space, your private space, and a boy's got to have a little space of his own, just like your father did. But that doesn't mean I gotta put up with smut in the rest of the house."

"It isn't smut—oh, what's the use? Ma, do you want a snack? I'm going into the kitchen."

She had finally made her way to the easy chair she liked and was slowly sitting down in it like a Queen Mary coming into dock. In a moment she'd remember that she had forgotten to turn on the TV set first and Eddie would have to do it for her. Anticipating her request, he turned on a game show on channel seven.

"Nah. I'm not hungry now. When is Mrs. Blim coming?"

Mrs. Blim was a middle-aged next door neighbor he paid to babysit Ma when he was out. Ma thought Mrs. Blim was a good friend, a true blue friend and the only one she had, but the truth was Mrs. Blim just needed the money. "Mrs. Blim will be over later this afternoon to fix your supper. You're going to be seeing a lot of her, Ma, once I start my new picture. I'll have to spend a lot of time at the studio."

Mrs. Petrano grunted. "What kind of picture"—she pronounced it "pitcher"—"is this, as if I need to ask. Another one of those trashy things that everyone gets murdered in every other minute? I wish you'd make a picture I could tell my friends about, a picture with Miss Lillian Gish or Jean Arthur. They knew how to make pictures when I was a girl. Maybe something with Irene Dunne."

Eddie went into the kitchen to make himself soup and a sandwich. The old woman never let up on the kind of work he did, not since she'd bought a video cassette of *Body Count at Buzzard Bay Part Two* behind his back a couple of years ago—when she was still fairly mobile and more lucid than she was currently—and sat through the film with increasing agitation. "Where's the plot? Where's the characters? Where's the sense to it?" she'd asked afterwards. "Disgusting! Had to close my eyes through half of it."

What got Eddie's goat was that *Body Count* did have a plot, albeit a slim one, of a maniac hacking up campers—not to mention a twist ending. It was not as if it was just one murder after another without any connecting storyline. Was it any different from all those murder mysteries she watched on television? They were always the same: some creepy guy gets killed and an old woman has to figure out which of the greedy relatives did it. Was *that* supposed to be a plot? Even worse, his mother had absolutely no appreciation for what even the pic's severest critics had called his "clever" and "brilliant" makeup effects. When a director wanted realistic-looking wounds and monsters, the man to call was Eddie Petrano. He was the very best at what he did and he knew it. He made damn good money, too. But would Ma ever give him any credit? Never.

He worked hard to imbue his effects with realism, even going to the point of studying anatomy books, textbooks on pathology, noted works by famous medical examiners. A friend of his had even got him some pictures of accident, gunshot and mutilation murder victims from special police files. He had a nifty collection of actual shots of hacked up corpses, including the infamous subway car shot detailing the havoc that the old New York Slicer had inflicted on his final two victims. He nearly lost his lunch on that one. The only way he could handle looking at the things was by forgetting that they were pictures of actual people, by reminding himself that he needed them for research and accuracy. Mom thought he had a collection of pornography

—"naked women." Well, yeah, some of the victims were nude, all right, but they were not exactly looking their best. . . .

And of course he also had his memory to rely upon, his memory of Dad and Willy and the blood all over the tree and the battered Chrysler. . . .

He heard a clicking noise coming from the other room, so loud and distinct he could tell what it was over the voices on the TV set. It was the sound his briefcase made when it was opened.

Damn that old woman. Always going into his things. He should have known better than to leave the case in the living room. If she fiddled around in there she'd undoubtedly find the book, the one with shots of bullet-riddled corpses, actual autopsies in bright living color. He smiled. No doubt his mother would prefer they were shots of naked women.

There was a scream, a cry of "Oh, my God. Horrible. Horrible!"

Eddie laughed.

His mother had opened the book.

10

Fall 1987.
Los Angeles and environs.

For the fifth time since they left New York, Dorothy leaned back in her seat and wondered why she was flying to Hollywood. She looked out the window, saw only black clouds, and hoped it wasn't an omen. The airline food was not sitting well in her stomach, and James was busy reading, even though he knew she wanted to talk. Talk was the only thing that would keep her mind off the ground far below, off of all the many terrible things that could happen to people who were miles in the air where only birds and asteroids belonged.

"Jimmy?" she whispered. "Do you have any of that gum left?"

He was really into his book. "Uh hmmm," he muttered, not looking up. His eyes stayed on the printed page the whole time as he dug into his pocket and lifted out some Juicy Fruit. "Thanks," she said, pulling off the silver wrapper and stuffing the gum in her mouth. "It's such a pleasure to have a conversation with you."

"Uh hmmmm."

She decided there was no point in bothering him. Reading

was his way of forgetting he was in the air, and she should be glad that he, at least, had found some comfort. Both of them hated to fly, as Dorothy was sure any normal person would. But as she looked around the cabin she realized that few of their companions could have been normal. They all seemed so matter-of-fact and accepting of it all, as if they did this every day. Well, maybe they did. "Excuse me," she said to Jimmy, getting up and squeezing past him. "I have to go to the toilet."

In the tiny ladies' room she looked in the mirror and tried to pretend that she was already at the hotel in downtown L.A. It didn't work. She splashed water on her face and wished she could spend the rest of the trip on the toilet. There was always something comforting about bathrooms, as if engaging in such a private, indelicate function isolated and protected you from the world.

Well, no harm in sitting down for a minute or two. At least it was a change from the nonchalant passengers and overly grinning stewardesses.

She was really trying, she had to give herself that. She was determined to see her way through this assignment for *Woman Now* even if it killed her. She had let Jimmy go out the week before and rent a few videotapes from a place around the corner. He'd come back with an even half-dozen, *Vicious* and *The Woodshed Murders* and *Body Count at Buzzard Bay*, not to mention *Bloody Day of the Diabolical Dead*. What a treat! "We'll just look at parts of these tonight," he said, "so you can get a feel for these things."

First they looked at *Vicious*. That had been the litmus test. She left her eyes open during the bedroom murder and was surprised at how tame it seemed—by today's standards, at least. Still, it bothered her a lot. Shots of the swinging axe, the screams of the woman in the movie, kept mingling in her consciousness with visions of her parents. She almost got up and left the room. Instead she forced herself to cling to Jimmy and sat there with tears streaming down her face for the rest of the picture.

She had cared about that character, that struggling young actress. She wondered about the real person, that Désirée Fontana, and thought she knew how Fontana's parents must have felt at the time of her death, the grief and shock and outrage—finally the deadening acceptance, the numbness—that always came in the wake of tragedy.

When *Vicious* was over she dried her eyes and Jimmy turned on the light. "I thought you should see all of *Vicious*," he told her, "seeing as how you'll be writing about the sequel. What did you think of it?"

"Well, it was obviously done by a talented filmmaker. It was more sensitive and poignant than I expected. I *felt* for all the characters. They seemed so pathetic. The horror, the murder, almost seemed gratuitous. Not in the cinematic sense, as you would put it; this *is* supposed to be a thriller. But they had a good story there, even without the murder; good, interesting things going on."

"Go on."

"But the murder, the psychological motive behind it—the twist ending with Yvette being the killer—that all seemed a bit dubious, silly, invalid even. All that stuff diminished the film's impact—for me. Made it seem like a pulp thriller instead of a work of art."

"Well," Jimmy said. "*Vicious* is essentially an entertainment, escapism, not something deep or profound. Oh, Winteroth had his pretensions, in countless interviews he tried to make the film sound more 'socially acceptable' than it was, but it was basically meant to be a very slick, very cinematic horror pic. On that level he succeeded, don't you think?"

She nodded. "Yes. It really wasn't bad. But still, I saw undertones, misogynous undertones." Had Jimmy rolled his eyes? Or had she imagined it? "The sleeparound girl gets wasted. She was promiscuous, had premarital sex. Bingo—she deserves to die."

"Ah, I think you're reading more into it than there is, really. You're looking at it and assigning all the contemporary jargon—"

"Maybe. Maybe you're right. I'm not saying that was Winteroth's intention. I'm just saying, there's a tacit disapproval, morality, in there, that I found disturbing. But no, basically I liked the picture well enough. I just wouldn't want to sit through it again."

He showed her parts of two other Sixties horror films, both of which were steals from *Vicious*. It was the late Seventies and early Eighties that interested them most, reportedly the dawning of the stalk-and-slash and splatter movies that were incredibly explicit in their depiction of violence against women.

Surprisingly, *Body Count* was not one of those movies. It *was* very gory, with extremely realistic depictions of violence during which Dorothy had to close her eyes (no matter how much she promised Jimmy she wouldn't). They had practically raised the re-creation of death to an art form. But *Body Count*'s victims were both male and female; the killer was not a misogynous sleazeball getting back at "bitches," but a widowed school teacher who felt her teenaged victims had been responsible for killing her son in a drunk driving accident. Feminists were always decrying *Body Count*, using it as an example of sexist horror-porn, but that was simply not the case. Jimmy was right about one thing. *She* would have to know what she was talking about if her piece were to have any impact.

"Now this one," Jimmy said, as he inserted a new cassette, "is definitely a sexist horror pic. It's not one I like but I think you should see it. This is the sort of stuff that gives Gloria Steinem the shivers."

It was called *The Woodshed Murders* and was about a scuzzy middle-aged janitor who snatches nubile young ladies from the streets, rapes them, tortures them, then uses various implements in the shed to murder them with. The film was total sleaze from start to finish, radiating a contempt and hatred for women that was alarming, to say the least. "You paid good money to see that in a theater?" she asked Jimmy.

"Yes. There's another one similar to this—*Co-Ed Death Drop* —that I thought was pretty sick, too, but I enjoyed it in spite of that. It was skillfully made, had a lot of atmosphere. *Woodshed* is just thrown together by a bunch of nerds out to make money."

"Let me get this straight. You enjoyed *Co-Ed Death Drop*?"

"Honey. You know I don't hate women. I just have a love of . . . the macabre. Not real death. I would never get into snuff films or war footage or autopsy movies like some people do. It's the effects I admire. *Death Drop* was a real kick in the pants. I would have preferred it had some of the victims been men, had the attitude toward women not been so nasty . . . I never said it had socially redeeming value." He must have been afraid they'd argue, because he let the matter drop right there.

Dorothy had seen enough bloodshed for one night. She turned the lights back on and stretched, vaguely disgusted with

Jimmy, wondering why she wasn't as angry with him as she should be. Perhaps because she knew he was being honest when he said that he didn't hate women, unless those feelings were so ingrained or repressed or deep-rooted that he didn't even know he had them. "We've sat through nearly five hours of movies," she said. "That's enough for tonight. I'm not sure I want—or need—to see any more of them."

"Are you convinced that not all contemporary horror films are sexist?"

"Yes. Yes, I am. There *is* a difference. But don't you think, Jimmy, that stuff like *Woodshed* and *Co-Ed Death Drop* only serves to bring about or even increase the frequency of violent attacks against women? Don't you think there's a corollary?"

He rubbed his palms together. "Look at it this way, Dorothy. Women have been the victims of violent assaults since the dark ages and before. Were horror films responsible for it then? Désirée Fontana, the real victim of *Vicious*, was actually murdered in 1940—twenty-three years before the film that's generally looked upon as the one that started the gory, exploitative trend in horror films was even made. Was it a horror film that brought about her death? When we blame horror films for violence in the streets, aren't we looking for an easy solution to a complex problem?"

Now who was using "contemporary jargon," she wanted to say, then realized she couldn't argue with his point. But as she got ready for bed, she thought that she'd really have breathed a lot easier if she lived in a world where there was no *Woodshed Murders*, nobody who had the urge to make, appear in, or witness a picture like it or the atrocities it depicted.

A red light went on in the airplane lavatory, shattering her reverie. Seatbelt time.

She got up, opened the door, and went quickly down the aisle to her seat. A heavyset woman had been waiting outside to use the toilet for who knows how long, and now had to trudge gloomily back to her spot. Dorothy hoped the poor thing's need hadn't been too urgent.

"Where have you been?" Jimmy asked. "I was worried about you."

"Worried about me! The way you've been engrossed in that novel I'm surprised you even knew I was gone."

"It's not a novel," he said, handing it to her so she could see the front cover.

She read the title: *Don't Go in the Bedroom: A Study of Horror Films Since "Vicious."*

"You oughta read it," Jimmy said. "It'll give you some perspective."

"I will read it. If you're ever through with it."

He leaned over and kissed her. "Just think, Dottie. We're in Hollywood."

"Los Angeles. Hollywood is only a district."

"You're so disillusioning. Anyway—just think of the nice dinner we'll be having in an hour or two."

"Dinner? How can you think of dinner after eating that airplane food?"

"Come on. It wasn't that bad."

She smiled. Five years together—and already they sounded like an old married couple.

Several hours later Dorothy and Jimmy were ensconced in the Hotel Bellmore on Yucca Boulevard, a small, but fairly respectable hostelry with a long gray lobby and a weary old desk clerk. The neighborhood was rather sleazy, but no worse than the lesser areas of midtown Manhattan. As long as you watched your wallet, held on tight to your purse, and avoided the seedier characters in the street, you'd be okay. The hotel room itself was small but comfortable, American standard, with a large bed, a long mirror, and other old but functional furnishings.

Dorothy had decided that the easiest way to approach the film people was to say that the making of *Vicious Two* had reviewed an interest in the Désirée Fontana murder case and that she was writing about it for *Woman Now*. That seemed to her to be the only way to get around the fact that she was working for a feminist publication, and to reassure them that she wasn't there—as far as they were concerned—to do a hatchet job on the picture or horror films in general. She was sure they must have known about the campaign to eradicate gory movies that many feminists were supporting. Jimmy had been talking about how he would handle all the arrangements ever since they'd gotten off the plane—he'd been in L.A. before, after all—but she was determined to show him how self-reliant and resourceful she could be, even when she was out of her element. She waited until he went into the bathroom, then reached for the phone. Would he be surprised!

It was a bad idea. The publicity head for Avalon Studios said to her over the phone: "*Vicious Two* has nothing to do with Désirée Fontana. Even less than the original *Vicious* did. It's a completely new storyline, in fact. Don't see how we can be of help."

Dorothy knew that she had to change tactics. "Our readers will still be interested in the movie, I'm sure," she said quickly. "I'm sure there are female characters in *Vicious Two*, maybe even a female murderer? The magazine I write for uses a lot of general interest pieces. I'd really appreciate it if I could interview some of the people connected with the movie, some of the actresses, perhaps? For a bit of background, local color. It will make my piece so much more interesting and contemporary."

The man reluctantly agreed to see what he could do and get back to her. *Woman Now* was not as well-known or prestigious as *Ms*, after all.

Coming out of the bathroom, Jimmy saw her putting down the phone and asked her what was wrong. When she told him, he chided her for impatiently jumping the gun. "I told you I'd handle it. You've never dealt with the studios before."

"Yes," she admitted. "But I'm not exactly an amateur." The phone conversation, those hours on the plane and in traffic from the airport, had not put her in the best of moods. She didn't even want to be in Los Angeles. What she'd seen in L.A. so far had been dirty and vulgar and spaced so far apart that it seemed more like one giant collection of suburbs than a city.

"I never *said* you were an amateur," Jimmy protested. "For crying out loud, will you give me a chance to *finish*?"

Exhaling her tension, Dorothy sat down on the bed and was quiet. She had to stop snapping at Jimmy. "I'm sorry. Go ahead."

"All right. It's like this. You're a top pro and we both know it. You've interviewed everyone from housewives and feminists to heads of corporations and heads of state. But when it comes to film writing, writing about movies, dealing with studios and the like, you're a babe in the woods. That's my specialty, will you grant me that? Forget about publicity heads. Forget about *Woman Now*. Will you let me get in touch with the people that we both need to see? Okay?"

She now saw no harm in letting him handle all the details, but asked, "How do you propose to do that?"

He took out a little black book.

"Say, I've seen that around," Dorothy said. "I thought it was full of your former girlfriends' addresses, but I valued your privacy and never once took a peek."

"That's nice of you. But you would have been disappointed. Or relieved. There's nothing in here but contacts I use for *Frames and Directions*. Names such as Livingstone Stoner, actress Jocasta Sullivan—and their numbers—Harold Watson's office number *and* home phone. Ellen Rue's manicurist—"

"Ellen Rue's manicur—Come on!"

"Just joking. Rue is Jocasta Sullivan's daughter, by the way."

"Figures. The only actors who seem to get anywhere these days are related to somebody." Though she had yet to appear in a major role in a picture—*Vicious Two* was her first big assignment—Rue was already a celebrity due to her relationship with Livingstone Stoner and all the assorted items about the couple that had been planted in the press.

Jimmy went to the phone. "I'm going to give Harold Watson a call. It just so happens that I've interviewed him before. He even wrote to tell me what a nice job I had done."

"You interviewed him for *Frames and Directions*? Wow. He's one of the biggies, isn't he? He's head of the whole shebang!"

Jimmy smiled. Dorothy knew he was probably thinking that what she didn't know about movies could fill the Paladium. She had to confess she paid as much serious attention to *Frames and Directions* as he did to *Woman Now*. Well, they said that often the best relationships were based on people who had nothing in common. Although, to be fair, she and Jimmy did share a lot of different interests.

"Yes," Jimmy said. "Watson is the Executive Producer of *Vicious Two* and just the man we want to talk to. Harold is finally pulling himself back up again after falling on hard times. Now that he's a big shot he may not even deign to speak to us."

"You really think he won't?"

"Actually, I'd be surprised if he didn't; he's a nice fellow. But you never know in this town. Now that they're so close to finishing the picture, things may be very hectic out here."

Dorothy knew that Jimmy had worried about showing up in L.A. so late in the filming, giving other mags a chance to scoop *Frames and Directions* and interview the principals before he did, although *F and D*'s coverage was usually so special and extensive it didn't matter what other mags printed. Also from past experience he'd learned that the last couple of weeks on a set were often more relaxed for certain of the cast and crew—they were bored, anxious to get it over with and go on to something else. They had had a chance to form strong impressions of their colleagues, and were not as skittish about speaking their minds. Besides, other projects at *F and D* had necessitated that he delay his trip to L.A. until now.

There was no problem with Harold Watson. The Executive Producer consented to meet with them the following afternoon at the studio, and promised that he would try to assemble some of his associates on the film. Jimmy told him that Dorothy was a free lancer who wanted to ask him some questions from the "woman's perspective."

"Corny, but he bought it. And please, go easy on him, Dottie. At least, at first. He's a really good contact for me and I don't want to offend him."

"I'm not a rank amateur," Dorothy repeated. "I know how to talk to people, even hostile ones."

"I know that. But you do ask awfully hard questions. Sneak up on them tomorrow. Catch them unaware. But keep the smile on your face all the time. Remember, you get more with honey than with—"

"Vinegar," Dorothy said. She nodded deliberately in a little girl fashion. "Yes, daddy. I would *never* have thought of that myself. Not after only *ten* years of interviewing—"

"Okay, okay." Jimmy smirked. "Don't take offense at everything I say."

Dorothy went over to the desk and pulled a pen and paper out of her bag. She started jotting notes feverishly, trying to remember all the questions she'd thought of on the plane and the exact way that she had phrased them.

Jimmy raised an eyebrow.

"You know how we amateurs like to be prepared," she explained.

The executive dining room at Avalon Studios was everything Dorothy had expected it to be. Plush, exciting, crowded yet quiet, full of mostly nobodies with a smattering of movie stars. The walls were painted a warm shade of beige and the tables were covered with brilliant white tableclothes. There were several booths along the side walls and pictures of movie stars and producers hung above them.

A maitre d' led them over to Harold Watson's table, a booth in the corner with places for at least eight people. Watson stood up and greeted Jimmy warmly, then took Dorothy's hand and kissed it.

"This fellow," he told her, "this fellow is an angel. He did the most wonderful interview with me a few years ago. Just wonderful." He scrunched up his wrinkled face with sincerity. "And not bitchy or gossipy or mean-spirited. Honest, with integrity, that's what it was. And believe me, my career was not at its highpoint then; it was nice of Jimmy to do the article on me and remind people of my winning streaks instead of my failures."

For many years Watson had been co-owner of Watson-Berghorf Associates, and along with his partner, Manny Berghorf, had turned out dozens of vivid, low-budget, independent exploitation features that cost hardly anything and brought in tremendous profits. But then came the split between Harold and Manny, the accusations, recriminations, with the result that Harold was eventually forced out and had to struggle his way back up to a position of preeminence. He had just formed a tenuous association with Avalon when Jimmy had done his interview with him. Now, years later, that association had blossomed into a full-fledged love affair. Watson had had a winning streak, one hot picture—with large budgets yet—after another.

Watson was a tall slender man in his late fifties. He had an elongated face with rubbery cheeks and a full lower lip, and carried himself with an exaggerated but amiable cockiness. His green eyes were tired and bloodshot, showing the effects of defeat and struggle even as his smile tried so hard to deny them. He introduced the man and woman sitting to his right, neither of whom had risen as Dorothy and Jimmy approached, and who did not do so now.

"This is my Associate Producer, Bethany Carraval. Bethany

is a godsend. Let me tell you, this lady knows her business."

The "godsend" was an attractive—very attractive—redhead with long wavy tresses down to her shoulders and a rather haughty impatience about the eyes. She smiled curtly and nodded like a princess at the newcomers as both of them briefly shook her hand.

The third person was the director, Livingstone Stoner, a not unattractive fellow with a bushy mustache and curly black hair that did nothing to hide the essential babyishness of his bland, well-modulated features. He looked much younger than his thirty-six years, and projected a kind of pliable insolence that seemed partly defensive and partly theatrical. He wore a casual blue denim suit with a white shirt and a slim beaded tie. He accepted Jimmy's and Dorothy's hellos with gracious indulgence.

Watson ordered drinks for both his guests, and another round for his associates, who had apparently arrived about half an hour earlier to talk shop. Watson was skillful at making people feel at ease, blending disparate personalities together so that an awkward social occasion could become an affair to remember. He had also learned the hard way how to handle the press.

"Harold, I really appreciate this," Jimmy said. He looked around the table. "And I want to thank the two of you for coming."

Stoner grinned. "We're ahead of schedule. At least for today. So I've got time. Besides I've always wanted to be interviewed by *Frames and Directions*. I feel like I've finally made it."

Bethany turned to Harold. "These people do realize that we're not going to reveal too much about the plot of *Vicious Two*."

Watson smiled tightly. "Of course, Beth, of course. Jimmy knows there are certain things we can't discuss. But he's promised us that *Frames and Directions* is going to give *Vicious Two* quite a play-up in an upcoming issue, so let's try to be as cooperative as we can."

Dorothy didn't know much about Bethany Carraval, only that she had worked with Watson on a couple of previous films as a production assistant or whatnot. In fact, Dorothy wasn't too sure exactly what it was a producer did, even though last night Jimmy had mentioned something about how they were in charge of virtually every aspect of the filmmaking process. As for the difference between "executive producer," "producer," "associate producer," and so on, Dorothy could only assume it had something to do with the delegation of duties.

She had read a copy of Stoner's filmography that Jimmy had brought home with him from the office. Stoner had made a couple of low-budget films that received little attention from either critics or public, and would likely have continued on that disappointing course had he not decided to film a friend's screenplay entitled *Thanksgiving*. Deceptively titled, *Thanksgiving* was about a masked maniac attacking small town residents with a hatchet, giving them the treatment normally reserved for holiday turkeys. *Thanksgiving*, the movie, however, was no turkey. Made for less than $800,000 it became a surprise hit through word of mouth and eventually made a profit of several million. Stoner then found himself being plied with offers to direct a variety of thrillers, much more in demand than he'd ever anticipated.

Jimmy had told Dorothy that *Thanksgiving* was not a terribly good picture, and that it was the money men—not the creative artists in Hollywood—who decided that Stoner was the one to direct the sequel to *Vicious*. In between *Thanksgiving* and *Vicious Two*, Stoner had made no less than eight imperfect horror films, each grislier than the one before. His three films about killer zombies stalking the living—the *Diabolical Dead* series—had not broken box office records as *Thanksgiving* had, but quickly became modestly profitable cult items nevertheless.

Jimmy started the ball rolling by asking the usual questions about budget, shooting problems, how the cast members were chosen, and how Stoner was approaching the material. Stoner, of course, did most of the talking, though Watson and Carraval jumped in from time to time.

During a minor lull in the conversation, Bethany looked straight at Dorothy and said, "Are you here as an *observer*? Or what?"

"No, I'm, uh, here to do a free lance piece on *Vicious Two*. In fact, if you want to relax for a minute Jimmy, Mr. Stoner, *I* have some questions for Ms. Carraval."

After glaring at her for a second, Jimmy acquiesced with a taut, frozen smile. Stoner looked bored. Watson's face was as polite and inscrutable as ever.

woman, or because of twisted sexual motives. There are no rapes. None of my films have ever been misogynous. Not one. My *Diabolical Dead* movies are considered classics of the genre. They're held up as examples of the finest, most artistic achievements in macabre cinema," he boasted, "but both the zombies and their victims come from both sexes. In my films," he said, completely shutting out any input from Bethany or Watson, "I explore the fabric of reality that separates the real world from our nightmares. I examine the thin line between the sane and the insane, how close we all—that is, each of us, the average person—come to committing acts of violence for the most trivial of reasons. . . ."

Dorothy couldn't believe this pretentious babble. Did the man think he was directing Shakespeare? And Jimmy was scribbling down every word. She certainly wouldn't bother.

"In *Vicious Two*, which I've completely rewritten, I've fashioned an exercise in morbid curiosity, one that implicates the audience as well as the characters." He scrunched up his face in almost comical puzzlement. "Which of us is ever truly innocent? I present characters at odds with their environment, almost *driven* to violence by the circumstances of their lives. It will be a tough, penetrating film, one that asks questions about the world we live in, and perhaps, will give us answers that we may not be prepared to live *with*. Are all of us not murderers?"

Watson broke the sudden silence. "*I'm* not a murderer," he said. Dorothy could tell the man was as confused by Stoner's rhetoric as she was. Was Jimmy really taken in by all this drivel?

Then Bethany started up. "In *Bloody Day of the Diabolical Dead* Livingstone examined the needs and hypocrisies of the consumer society. In *Vicious Two* you might say we'll be looking at that same society's emotional hang-ups."

"Yes, yes," Stoner said hurriedly, apparently not disagreeing with her but distressed that she hadn't phrased it better (or better yet, let him say it.) "Emotional hang-ups, and the emptiness of human existence."

"Are you trying to say," Dorothy asked, her lips stretched out in a tight semi-smile, "that *Vicious Two* will be along the lines of Dickens or Williams or Steinbeck?" She pressed on. "Eugene O'Neill, perhaps?"

Stoner looked at her with complete seriousness and said,

"Go ahead," Bethany said, giving an edge to the simple words that made them seem like a challenge.

"Ms. Carraval," Dorothy said. "And Mr. Stoner—perhaps you'll have an opinion on this, too. You've probably heard some of the uproar some people have made over contemporary horror films and their continual use of women as victims. *Vicious* featured a scene wherein a woman is chopped to pieces with a fireaxe—"

"More was implied than shown," Stoner said, as if showing them he'd done his homework.

"Yes, but that isn't so true today. Nothing's implicit any more, but explicit." She tried to keep the edge out of her own voice. "Tell me, Ms. Carraval, Mr. Stoner—will *Vicious Two* feature assaults against helpless females, and how do you, Ms. Carraval, as a woman, feel about working on a film that might contain such material?"

Ms. Carraval stubbed out her cigarette and rolled her eyes. "Oh, *please*, not that again. I am so sick of that shit!"

Jimmy jumped in before another word could be said. "Dottie's only playing devil's advocate, Ms. Carraval. She's just telling you what *other* people are saying. Isn't that right, Dottie?"

For a moment Dorothy was stunned by his interruption, more so than by what Ms. Carraval had said. How dare Jimmy butt in like that! She had let him hog the show for over half an hour and now he presumed to speak for her! She bit her tongue and hoped that Bethany would continue without prompting. Dorothy didn't trust herself to speak just yet.

"Yes, well," Bethany said, "I've worked on a number of horror films, some of which were written and directed by women. Always these crazy ladies from NOW or some nutty coalition try to say we're demeaning women, encouraging crimes against women. That's crazy. We're making movies, not shaping real life. We're not responsible for the crazy things these nut cases get into their heads. Somebody gets carved up by a maniac—who's responsible? A movie—or the maniac?" She snorted with disgust. "It's just not worth discussing, frankly."

Stoner blew out a puff of smoke and said, "Actually, the murders in *Vicious Two* are pretty much divided between men and women. Not a single woman is killed simply *because* she is a

"*Vicious Two* will be my *Mourning Becomes Electra*."

Dorothy tried to keep from laughing as she finished her drink and announced her intention to visit the ladies' room. She couldn't believe she was sitting here, seriously discussing this nonsense with presumably educated people. It was as if clowns had taken over the movie industry and the only thing they could churn out was cartoons.

Cartoons about people being chopped into hamburger, she thought ruefully. Images of her mother and father skirted across the edges of her mind as she ran to the bathroom where she could then decide whether to laugh or cry.

11

James got out of the taxi and started up the concrete steps to the apartment house where Eddie Petrano lived with his mother. He was really looking forward to meeting Hollywood's premiere makeup man. And he didn't mean Max Factor.

True to his word, Harold Watson had done his utmost to make things move as smoothly and as quickly as possible. Right after they'd finished the interview at the studio, Harold had taken Dorothy and Jimmy on a tour of the soundstage, but it had not been a very good day to be there. As Stoner had said, they were ahead of schedule; an unsatisfactory set was being refurbished and most of the cast and crew, excluding carpenters and the like, had already been dismissed for the day. Harold suggested that it would be an excellent opportunity for Jimmy to interview makeup artist Eddie Petrano at his apartment. "If you try to talk to him when he's on the set, it will be impossible. The man lets nothing interfere with his concentration."

Petrano was not needed at the studio that day and, as usual, spent the time off tinkering on his designs in the workshop at his apartment. There was a workshop set up at the studio, of course, but Petrano often preferred working at home in order to jealously guard his secrets and experiment with new, improved methods of, say, taking someone's head off. He told Watson he'd be happy to talk to Jimmy.

Now if only I could smooth things over with Dorothy, Jimmy thought, walking down a clean white corridor and studying the numbers on the doors that he passed. Boy, had she been angry with him. He could still hear her yelling as they left the studio and waited outside the gate for a taxi. "You hogged that interview, barely let me get a word in edgewise. Such a patronizing manner you had, they all had. That awful woman. That ridiculous director. The only one I had any use for was Mr. Watson." He tried to calm her down but he knew there was no dealing with Dorothy when she got into one of her moods. Normally he would match her histrionics volume for volume, but he was finding her frequent outbursts increasingly tedious.

Of course he had realized that Livingstone Stoner was only giving them a heap of bullshit. "The thin line between sanity and insanity," "the violence in us all"—nothing but a lot of hoary cliches. And that bit about *Mourning Becomes Electra*! He'd been tempted to say to him: "Cut the crap, Stoner. Why don't you just admit you're making another honest-to-goodness horror pic just for the fun of it. And the money." It was Anthony Winteroth all over again, except that Winteroth had been genuinely talented and had imbued his picture with more atmosphere and characterization than was found in the usual chiller. But what had Dorothy expected him to do? Ignore what the director was saying? He had to have quotes for his article, didn't he? And if Stoner came off looking like an asshole, why should Jimmy care?

He wondered if goading Dottie into taking the assignment had been the right thing to do. He remembered when he'd first found out about what happened to her parents—while they were first dating. She'd resisted his attempts to take her to horror films and he'd assumed it was simple squeamishness on her part. When he'd learned the real reason he'd been shocked and frightened for her. He dropped the subject of horror films altogether, kicking himself for his earlier, inadvertent insensitivity.

But as the years went by he'd come to the conclusion that it wouldn't be healthy for either of them if he continued to treat her like an invalid. She had spells of deep melancholia and during one of them finally blurted out the story of how she'd been raped. No one as lovely and delicate as Dottie deserved to have had such tragedy in her life. But somehow she had to get over it, confront her fears, or there'd be no end to her internal misery.

Formerly he had treated her as if she were made of eggshell, wincing if he should accidentally mention rape or violence, as if he'd told a blind man there was a movie he should *see*. He realized lately that that was the wrong approach; it was only making things worse. He decided no longer to shield Dorothy from unpleasantness, from reminders of her past. That was the only way she'd come to grips with her problems. But had he gone too far in the other extreme?

He was haunted by what Dottie had once said to him during a "spell." She looked up at him, tear-stained, trembling, and said, "It never goes away, Jimmy. *It never goes away*." Even professional help didn't seem to do her any good.

Jimmy found Apartment "F" and rang the bell. The door, which had a number of dents in it, was painted a creamy beige color and was apparently made of metal. Judging from the number of locks, Eddie Petrano's home was a miniature fortress. Well, he did a lot of experimentation in his private workshop, and undoubtedly his rivals would have given their right arm—perhaps *literally!*—to get a look at some of his material.

As he waited for someone to answer, Jimmy wondered what Dorothy was up to now. After she'd returned from the bathroom at the studio, she'd tried several times to steer the conversation back to her particular métier, but was unsuccessful. Jimmy had done his best to help her, trying to keep from angering Stoner and the others, thereby saving the interview for both of them, while also trying to provide a neat segue via for Dorothy. Perhaps he *had* been a little too abrupt in the first place. Well, he wasn't perfect.

God knows he wasn't unsympathetic to her viewpoint, to all the pain and suffering she'd had to endure. And admittedly, even he found some of the movies they made today rather unsettling. In fact, there was an area in the back of his brain that often wondered just why he enjoyed them as much as he did. Yet he also knew that Dorothy was approaching the whole issue from a highly emotional and subjective plateau, that because of it she had a tendency to be overly and constantly simplistic. But try and tell *her* that.

She'd gone off in a taxi by herself, muttering something about sticking to her own methods and getting things done her own way. Well, he hoped she was successful. He did not expect her to come around to his way of seeing things, just to look at both sides of the issue clearly and objectively and write about it as honestly as she possibly could. No matter how much she might have believed otherwise, he would never derive satisfaction from her failures.

The door opened and there stood an impish Eddie Petrano. His black hair was thick and wavy, and he had a thin, lean face with hawk like features. He had the oddest little grin on his lips.

And he was holding a severed arm in his hand.

"And this is a little creature that I made for *Nightmare Agony*," Eddie told his visitor. He frowned. "But they cut it out of the final version." It resembled a man-bat with a glandular problem: a bigger-than-usual mouth, large feet like an eagle's, antennae that poked out above the nose and gave it an almost comical appearance. "They thought it was too silly. I guess they were right, huh?"

Jimmy smiled. "I think it's kinda cute myself."

Eddie liked his visitor. The writer was a nice guy, really enthusiastic and appreciative, without any of the condescension that a lot of other people exhibited when they visited this workshop. He'd had a good-natured reaction to the joke Eddie had pulled at the door, too. Seeing him holding that bloody sawed-off replica of an arm, Jimmy had looked at Eddie and said, "So you thought I'd need a hand, did you?"

Yes, Eddie liked this fellow. He could always tell when people were sincerely interested in his work and when they were just humoring him.

Jimmy patted the homunculus on the head and asked his next question. "There's been some flak about the inevitable overlapping of makeup effects and special effects, hasn't there? I mean, in the old days there were makeup men who made the starlets look pretty, and makeup men who made people look shot up or stabbed or just plain dead, and then guys like Jack Pierce who created the looks of the monsters like Frankenstein and The Wolfman. Now makeup has been extended to the creation of nonhumanoid creatures, too. You guys don't just create the wounds and the hacked off limbs and the disembowelments, you also build the monsters that *make* those injuries."

"Yes, there's more and more of that," Eddie agreed, "and it's caused some resentment, union problems and the like. I suppose models like these aren't in the strictest sense what you'd call a makeup problem, but," he reached behind a box on his work table and pulled out a very realistic-looking severed human head, "it's not such a big step from this,"—he indicated the head —"to this." He pointed to some of the monster masks and tiny figures cluttering the rectangular room he'd converted into a workshop.

The den was medium-sized, with a long wooden table that bisected the room, and several smaller wooden tables and benches surrounding it. A variety of grotesque masks hung down from every inch of the four walls, and one of the corner tables was littered with an alarming selection of assorted body parts. Up against the wall there was a bulletin board upon which was tacked grisly photographs of what appeared to be murder victims, though if they were genuine or not, Jimmy couldn't tell and didn't particularly want to know.

"Look," Eddie said, "I've gouged out people's eyes, cut off people's heads, disemboweled and gutted people, aged them from twenty-five to a hundred in the space of ten second's screen time. I constantly need new challenges. My monsters aren't elaborate mechanical contraptions or three dimensional hominids that they animate with stop motion photography—that kind of stuff *would* fall under special effects. But," he gestured to the monster material on one of the cluttered benches, "what *I* do is make models of casts, I make puppets made of rubber or plaster of Paris. We use these bladder contraptions to make the things move instead of expensive animation effects. It's a form of makeup, though a lot more complicated than before. There's no limit to what we can do if we set our minds to it." His eyes were alive and fiery, reflecting the passion he felt for his vocation.

Jimmy looked around the workshop appreciatively, trying not to linger on the table of human limbs or other less savory exhibits. "This stuff is just amazing, Mr. Petrano, Can you describe for me some of the effects you'll be working on for *Vicious Two*?"

Eddie had been told by Stoner to keep his mouth shut. But there was no harm in giving out a little sneak preview as long as it didn't give away any of the surprises, was there? Besides, even Eddie didn't know who the killer was going to be. Only a few days of shooting left and Stoner still hadn't revealed that information, melodramatically leaving the disclosure for the final day when the climactic scene would be shot. "Well, I can't tell you too much, Mr. Radley, but somebody's going to get run over and I have to build a head that will—kind of explode—on impact. It'll really be effective. There'll be a number of stab wounds, a slit throat, the usual stuff." He held up the head again. "And I'm sure we'll find a use for this, or something very much like it. Pretty convincing, huh?"

"It's, uh, terrific, Mr. Petrano."

"Call me, Eddie, please."

"Okay. Eddie, I have something that's—well, it's a little difficult to ask you. Looking around his workshop, having seen many of the films you've worked on, I know that you're a fine craftsman, in fact your effects are often the best thing in the picture."

"Yeah. I've been told that. Thanks."

"But . . . does it ever bother you? All this . . . gore and graphic violence. You said a minute ago you have to build a head that'll get squashed on camera. I mean, does it ever get to you, make you wonder where the motion picture industry is heading . . . ?"

Eddie felt conflicting emotions. He hated being asked this because there was really no way to answer it, but he liked Mr. Radley and wanted to tell him how he really felt. "Yeah. Yeah, sometimes it bothers me. That's why I do the monsters. All this hacking up bodies, this stalk-and-slash stuff, is gonna get tiresome after a while. Look, I'm not saying I mind it. I'm not saying it's immoral or anything like that. I mean, it's all so exaggerated, so—I don't know—you can't take it seriously. It's almost morbid humor, I suppose."

Still holding the head with his free hand, he walked over to a bench and lovingly stroked what appeared to be a chubby human hand in need of re-skinning. "It doesn't really bother me —I mean, the bloodshed, that is; I can stomach that. I have to study pictures of corpses to get the right effect in my films, and once you've seen what real people can do to one another, there isn't nuthin' in the movies that can disgust you. But yeah, sometimes it bothers me. But it's a living. And I'm good at my job. I enjoy it."

Jimmy thanked him and shook his hand. "Thanks for the interview, Eddie. I really appreciate it. And thanks for the look at your chamber of horrors, too." Eddie laughed.

The makeup man led Jimmy to the door, shook his hand once again, and said goodbye.

That guy had been respectful, Eddie thought. He hadn't looked at him as if he were a groundslug or earthworm, the way his mother sometimes did. That impressed him a lot.

Ma had been cool to him for weeks now, ever since she opened that book in his briefcase. That had been funny. He'd realized then how little power she really held over him, how little her threats and protestations amounted to. What could she possibly do to him anyway?

In a moment she'd be calling for her supper. Mrs. Blim couldn't come in today on account of a "backache," though Eddie was sure the bitch had boozed too much the night before and had a hangover. Some nursemaid she was.

He looked at the head he still held in his hand. It was so lightweight he'd carried it all the way from the workshop to the foyer when he'd shown Mr. Radley to the door without even realizing it.

Eddie got an idea.

Mr. Radley may have only been being polite. There was one sure way to see how convincing the severed head was.

Chuckling wickedly, he dropped the head onto Ma's easy chair, and put the little colored throw pillow on top of it. *Just wait*, he thought, *just wait*.

His mother was still taking her daily nap. He went into the kitchen and fixed himself a snack. After a while he could hear her thumping her way from the bedroom into the living room with her walker, sighing and wheezing and groaning with each step.

Now! he thought. She was just about to sit down in the chair, about to move the pillow to make room for her body.

"Ahhhhhhhhh!"

This time her scream was even better than the last one.

You naughty boy, he thought guiltily.

But he simply couldn't stop smiling.

Vivienne Cherneau sat on her balcony overlooking the boulevard and tried to convince herself that there was really no reason for her to throw herself off. But one look at the jetsam and flotsam, the bums, punk rockers and sleazeballs walking up and down the street below was enough to keep her from jumping. Who would want to land among *them*?

It was simply the most awful thing. Her problems with *Vicious Two* were as nothing compared to this. Here it was, a day off when she could relax at home, paint her toenails, sit about all afternoon eating chocolates and not have to spend a single minute thinking about that awful picture she should have been starring in. And look what happens! She could still hardly believe it.

The awful day had begun when Hester walked into her bedroom at eleven a.m. with another scrumptious breakfast tray and a copy of the *Hollywood Reporter*. The maid heard an ungodly shriek come from the bedroom a few minutes later, and probably thought that her employer was either having a heart attack or had discovered a cockroach in her coffee.

"Mrs. Cherneau! What is it? What's wrong? Do you need a doctor?"

"A lawyer is what I need!" Vivienne held up her folded, disheveled copy of the *Hollywood Reporter*. "This—this is mortifying. The most outrageous—"

Without thinking, Hester grabbed the paper out of Viv's hand. She noticed her mistress' name in prominent black lettering on the lower half of the page.

"They've taken out a half-page ad," Vivienne said, clutching her bosom and crying. "An *ad*, they've taken out!"

"Mrs. Cherneau! How wonderful!" Hester said. "It says here you're going to win an Oscar!"

"No. No, you idiot!" Vivienne grabbed back the periodical and tried to swat Hester with it. The girl went rushing out of the room—she knew better than to be around when her employer was on the rampage—as Vivienne grabbed up the phone and dialed her agent's number.

But Harry had been out of the office at twelve, at one, at two, three and four—or so that skinny bitch with the eyebrows and all the hair who worked as his assistant kept telling her. Finally, at four-thirty her phone rang and an apologetic Harry was on the line.

"Viv, I'm sorry. I had to spend all day in conference with Troy Paddon." But he knew what she wanted to talk about, allright.

"Harry, Harry! You simply must do something. You must sue them, I tell you. Sue them!"

"Sue them? Vivienne, honey, come on. It's only a publicity gimmick. By tomorrow the whole thing will be forgotten. Who knows? You may even *get* a nomination for it."

"Don't make jokes," Vivienne hollered. "I don't want to hear jokes. Not now, Harry. This is the most humiliating, disgraceful thing I have ever—oh, I can't even talk about it."

Several months ago Vivienne had made a cheap little gore item named *Sweet Psychotic*, in which she portrayed the maniac's bloated, half-crazy old mother. She had only two scenes, and from what she saw of the rushes, neither presented her in the light she would have wanted to have been remembered by. She had this tendency—particularly in these dreadful horror films that she only did for the money—to overact worse than Bette Davis and Anne Baxter put together. And her figure! She no longer resembled Shelley Winters in *The Poseidon Adventure*. She now resembled the *boat*!

She had gone on a diet—lost twenty pounds, still weighed about forty too many—and vowed never to play another psycho or psycho's mother until the bill collectors were literally nipping at her heels. That was until the "prestigious" *Vicious Two* had come along and her agent assured her that the part was pretty juicy. She had forgotten all about *Sweet Psychotic*, ignoring the ads in the daily papers when it finally was released a week or so ago, until she read the ad in today's *Reporter*. The producer of *Sweet Psychotic*, a child of twenty-three who fancied himself the new Steven Spielberg, had apparently had enough money left over in his trust fund to place this idiotic half-page ad in the paper:

WE PREDICT:
VIVIENNE CHERNEAU WILL WIN AN ACADEMY
AWARD NOMINATION FOR HER WORK IN—

"SWEET PSYCHOTIC"
Ranson-Morrell Associates

If was so horribly embarrassing. People would be *laughing* at her from one end of this town to the other. Was she to be stripped of every last ounce of dignity? People would go to see *Sweet Psychotic* out of curiosity, expecting to see Vivienne giving a performance along the lines of her nun in *The Story of Sister Maria* or the deaf-mute in *Joey and Sarah* or the tormented nymphomaniac in *Lest Love Be Forgotten*, the few "A" films she'd made before being consigned to Hollywood's "Poverty Row."

Instead they'd see this aging harridan, this elephantine wreck of a woman, giving her worst performance in the worst movie she'd ever made. *Sweet Psychotic*. Ugh. Her big scene had been when she had to do in her own insane son by taking a hatchet and slicing off the top—only the top, *yuchhh*—of his head. They'd stuffed sausages or animal offal into a dummy head and had her whack off the top of it and the stuff had gooshed out all over her, bits of bogus brains and bona fide innards, and she'd had to run from the set to throw up before anyone could see her.

"Harry," she whined into the phone. "I don't want to be laughed at. Is that so much to ask? I can put up with having to take the *dregs* to keep my career alive, I can put up with the loneliness. I can put up with the nights when I toss and turn and live over old regrets and wish I could go to sleep and never wake up again. I can even put up with being without Charlie. But I don't want to be laughed at. Is that so hard to understand?

"My last day on the set of . . . *Sweet Psychotic*"—she pronounced the words as if they referred to fecal matter—"I told those fools, those children, I worked with, what real acting, what real movies, were about. And they laughed at me. They made snide remarks. Said I wouldn't talk about 'real acting' if I'd bothered to look at *all* the rushes. They were right. I was terrible. Harry, I was hoping only the usual loonies would go to see this picture, that it would disappear from theaters after an *hour* or two, that no one of any consequence would even *hear* of it—"

"Vivienne, you've already made a dozen of these things. . . ."

"But none quite so bad, Harry. None in which *I* was quite so bad. I had reached the end of my rope, you see. I just wanted to do my scenes, in a hurry, no retakes, and *get out*. It was amateur hour, Harry. Even me. Yes, even me. They even shot it in sixteen millimeter, don't you remember? Had to blow it up for theatrical release. Such lousy sound quality. And I was bad, so bad. A rotten actress in a rotten movie."

"You are not a rotten actress!"

"I have to go now, Harry," she said, hysterical, distraught. "I'm going to cry." She felt damned and demeaned and on the verge of being demented.

She hung up and sobbed into her pillow. *Oh, Charlie, Charlie!*

What would you think if you could see me now?
What would you think if you could see what's become of me?

Doug Longbank sat watching television in the bedroom. Edna, his wife, was making sandwiches in the kitchen. The night was remarkably hot, even for California, and they even had the air conditioners on. *They didn't hear the tinkling of the glass as the window on the backdoor of the utility room smashed inward with one blow.*

Edna Longbank whistled a commercial jingle while she spread liverwurst over the low-cal whole wheat toast. She wrapped the wurst up again, put it in a baggie, and deposited it back on the shelf in the refrigerator.

Edna sensed that someone was standing in the doorway to the kitchen, blocking her exit to the hall. She turned and confronted the intruder.

"Dougie, where on earth did you get that crazy outfit?" He had put a sheet over his head and looked like a specter of death. That *was* her husband, wasn't it? *Silly, who else could it be?*

Dougie was holding something in his hand. Something curved. The flourescent lights in the kitchen ceiling glinted off of it. Metal?

"Dougie? What are you—?"

"Dougie" had raised his arm.

The thing in Dougie's hand slashed down and *whacked* into Edna's body.

Edna stood there and watched in disbelief as something flew *off of her* and into the air, coming to rest on top of the range where it sizzled. She'd just taken the teapot off the burner.

The thing on the stove was Edna's right arm.

The plate of sandwiches in Edna's left hand clattered onto the linoleum floor.

Edna Longbank felt incredible pain. She screamed. She still couldn't believe what had happened. It was as if she were viewing it from miles away, watching it happen to somebody else via closed circuit television. It had been so sudden, so terribly swift and easy, the way her arm just *parted* from her body and flew across the room in a blood splattering arc like a gruesomely dripping boomerang.

Edna's tears rolled down her face as fast as the blood gushed from the stump of her arm. Why would Doug have done such a thing? She expected him to throw off the sheet, if that's what he was wearing, and yell: *"Oh my God, Edna! It was a joke! What have I done? Oh, God, what have I done?!"*

But he didn't. And for the first time since her assailant's appearance Edna considered that the person in the sheet might not be her husband.

"Dougie?" she asked.

Edna was feeling faint, getting dizzy, starting to tumble to the ground from shock and bloodloss. Everything that had happened so far had happened in the space of an instant. In the next instant she thought about Kerry, their daughter, realized that she would never live to see her daughter grow up, go to college, get married, never see if she would ever become famous. All her hopes and plans were dematerializing as her lifeblood poured across the floor in what seemed like raging torrents.

The intruder raised the weapon for another savage stroke. Just before Edna blacked out, she wondered—*what's happened to his hand? What's happened to Dougie's hand?*

Down the hall Douglas got off the bed and switched from the *Tonight* show to a rerun of *Space '99*. His stomach was really bothering him. He had wanted to gobble a few rolls of antacid, but Edna had insisted that a sandwich alone would help settle his stomach. Some ulcers, she'd insisted, were like that.

He heard a noise coming from out in the hall. At last! Edna had sure taken her time with those sandwiches. He hoped she'd brought him some soda or a beer to go with it.

He turned and looked over at the doorway, wondering what could be making that peculiar rustling noise.

The figure in the doorway looked familiar.

Who was it? *What* was it?

It was the grim reaper, that's who it was. It was dressed in a sheet, or costume of some kind, and the sheet was stained with a dripping wet liquid. It had eyeholes to see out of, and came equipped with a small metal scythe. Cute. The grim reaper, yes. Wasn't something like that in Stoner's revised script for *Vicious Two*? The maniac dressed up in an outfit just like that and murdered a couple of people. Yes, that was it. He laughed.

"Edna, come on." She knew how the whole *Vicious Two* thing had been driving him crazy. She'd hoped to make him laugh at it all by making fun of the movie. Good for her. Maybe it was just what he needed.

Only Edna wasn't built like the figure beneath the costume. In fact, he couldn't even tell if it were a man or a woman under that bulky outfit.

"Edna? Is that you?"

As the intruder advanced into the room, Douglas tried to find some kind of weapon, just in case. Just in case it was not one of Edna's friends under the sheet, some relative or neighbor she'd put up to it. *And where did they ever get that fake hand, the one that looked like some kind of monstrous claw?*

While his back was turned the scythe sliced down into the side of his leg, narrowly missing his testicles.

"*Aghhhhh!*" He turned back, lifted his arms to defend himself.

The scythe swiveled and suddenly dug upwards, ripping into Doug's abdomen. Tearing and slicing, it unleashed a flood of steaming, odorous offal.

"*Oh My God!*"

Doug went into shock as the contents of his belly slid through his fingers and fell onto the floor.

And the scythe went up and down and up and down, cutting and tearing, rending Douglas Longbank limb from limb.

12

"Yes, yes. A horrible tragedy. Yes, I can understand. Just terrible. Shocking."

Dorothy woke up to hear Jimmy mumbling into the phone; he was trying not to wake her. She was about to ask him what was wrong when she wondered: *Am I speaking to him or not?*

She'd been furious with him at the interview at Avalon Studios the day before. While he interviewed Eddie Petrano she'd done a little sightseeing on her own and come back to the hotel room very late. He was not in the best mood, either, so they'd said very little to one another, knowing one wrong word would start a fullscale argument that would wake the neighboring guests. A lot of Dorothy's anger had been directed at herself. She'd been so intimidated during the interview, listening to the others talking about the moviemaking process in technical terms that she didn't understand. She'd learned her lesson. From now on she'd only interview people *by herself*.

Yesterday, Saturday, he'd gone off to the studio early while she slept late. She finally got around to some productive activity in the early evening. This time Jimmy came back to the hotel at an ungodly hour after a full day and night of interviewing and kibitzing. They'd barely said three words to each other the whole time. Well, she supposed it was okay to end this silly silent treatment if he would, too.

When Jimmy finally noticed that she was awake, he raised his eyebrows significantly and gave her an unreadable look.

Something was wrong. Words like *horrible* and *tragedy* came back to her and she thought to herself, *No, it can't be happening again.*

Finally Jimmy was off the phone.

"What is it? What's wrong? Tell me."

"Brace yourself."

Please don't let it be anyone I know, not one of my friends or Aunt Maggie.

"Doug Longbank."

Dorothy sighed with relief and felt guilty for doing so.

"The guy we were going to see this afternoon out at his house? The screenwriter for *Vicious Two*?"

"Yes?" *An accident, a suicide, a mugging?*

He was holding back, Dorothy could tell; he was wondering how much she could take, how much detail she could handle. "He and his wife were slaughtered in their home last night by an intruder."

"Oh my God."

"That was Harold Watson on the phone. He found out about it last night."

"Who was it, Jimmy? Who would do such a thing?" *The Slicer?*

"They don't know. No one knows. It's a pretty freaky coincidence, I tell you. It's too early for the police to have come up with anything, I'm sure."

"Poor man. And his wife, too. Did they have any children?"

"A young daughter. She'd been spending the weekend with her aunt. A next-door neighbor found the bodies. Anyway, the girl is only seven or eight. Her aunt drove in from Long Beach to look after her and make arrangements. Terrible business. At least the girl wasn't in the house when it happened, thank God."

Yes, thank God. Now all she had to do was live with the agony of losing her folks and growing up without them. *Terrible business. Such a tragedy*—all of the words you were supposed to, could only, say at a time like this seemed so completely inadequate.

And then the tears came. Dorothy thought of another little

girl who had been safe at home with her aunt, another little girl who had lost her parents in one hideous evening. "The poor child. God help her."

Jimmy came over and held Dorothy, tried to comfort her as best he could. She tried to push him away.

"No," she said. "Don't hold me. I don't deserve it. I'm crying for myself, not for that child. For *myself*. It's just that she reminded me. . . ."

"Honey, I've lived with you for years, and part of you may well be crying for yourself—that's only natural—but you're crying for that kid, too. Hell, I feel like doing it myself."

"There must have been a reason for it. What exactly happened?"

"Are you sure you want to know?"

She shook her head. "No. No, don't tell me. Just hold me." She clung to him for a moment, crying, then after a few more minutes started pulling herself together.

"Enough. I'm all right now. I swear. I'll be okay. I didn't even know the Longbanks. Still, it's awful. That poor girl. I know just how she must be feeling." She wiped her eyes and nose with a tissue and said, "What else did Mr. Watson have to say?"

"He was pretty upset. Said he'd be in touch tomorrow with more details. It was thoughtful of him. Would have understood if he'd forgotten all about us. He was afraid we might not see it in the paper. Didn't want us rushing out to their house and—y'know . . ."

Somebody had to say it. "I guess this means the end of *Vicious Two*." But from the look on Jimmy's face Dorothy could tell he thought otherwise.

"I don't mean to sound callous, but why?"

Dorothy threw up her hands. "Jimmy, a man and his wife have been butchered, a man who *wrote* this movie. It's in the worst possible taste to continue—"

"Honey! It was a coincidence, nothing more. It's a terrible tragedy, but frankly, Doug Longbank's work on *Vicious Two* has long since been over. His death won't stop the movie. Why, the filming is almost over. Why shouldn't they finish?"

"But surely—out of respect for the man—they'll at least postpone for a while. A week or so? At least?"

"Harold Watson explained it to me. They're on a schedule,

163

they have a tight budget. They have to finish on time. They'd have to pay the entire cast and crew for all the days off. Honey, what happened to Doug and his wife is a horrible thing, but moviemaking is a business like any other. Things have got to continue."

" 'Life goes on,' I know."

"Watson did say that the production will shut down on the day of the funeral. For a few hours at any rate."

"That's the least they could do. I still think—"

"Some maniac killed Longbank. It has nothing to do with the movie."

"Which is *about* a maniac killing people!"

"Like a thousand other books and movies, Dottie. Maniacs are a part of life, as ridiculous as that may sound and as awful as it may be." He stopped short, probably wondering how much he could say without bringing on the usual tears or hysterics from Dorothy. *For a brief instant Dorothy realized how much of a strain her problems and attitudes had to be for him.* Then the moment passed and she was back safe and sound in her teary self-absorption.

"I know all about maniacs," she said softly. "One of them took my parents away from me. And now this—this poor child's parents. Making movies about them is—"

"Sick and tasteless, I know. But Longbank and his wife might have been killed even if he had never written this screenplay, even if there had never been a *Vicious Two*. Honey, lousy things happen to people. It's crummy and it stinks but there's nothing you can do about it. And you sure as hell can't blame it all on sleazy movies." He looked at her for a second, exhausted, then went back over to her side.

He took her in his arms and kissed her on the eye, the nose, sweetly, tenderly. Dorothy felt herself responding. They hadn't made love since they'd been in California. The funny thing was that that was not what Jimmy had had in mind when he'd embraced her, she was sure of it. She was the one who was altering his message.

"I know what you're going through," Jimmy whispered, touching her hair with his fingers. "You, my dear, have the misfortune of being one of these kind, sensitive souls who wishes she could just snap her fingers and make all the pain go away. All the pain in the world. Sometimes I think you have this crazy idea that if you could only isolate the cause of the world's misery, you could eradicate it and make the world a better place. It'd be nice if it were that simple."

"I know it's not that simple," she said, writhing out of his arms. He had killed the moment, treating her like some idealistic infant again, like a baby he had to diaper with words instead of linens.

"Now what's wrong?"

"Nothing. Next you'll be giving me your 'life isn't fair' speech."

"Maybe, but it's the best I can come up with right now." He bent his head down to look directly into her eyes and poked her playfully under the chin. "How about it? Do you feel better now?"

"I don't know. What I want to know is, what do we do now? Write about Doug Longbank and his wife as if they're some kind of afterthought, a bit of background for an article on some horror film?" She adopted the pose of a typically addlepated television entertainment reporter, and said, "Oh by the way, during the filming of this major motion picture, two human beings just happened to get killed. But I bet you folks would rather hear about the movie.' " She resumed her own identity and asked, "Are our values so backwards these days?"

Jimmy shook his head sadly and said nothing.

"I'm hungry. Let's get dressed and go down to breakfast." She still felt rotten. Depressed and nauseous. Violence, senseless violence, how awful it was. Maybe a good hot meal would help cheer her up.

Jimmy rubbed his tummy. "Yeah. That sounds good. Say, I meant to ask you, what were you up to yesterday?"

As usual they made up after arguments by pretending they'd never happened. "I got out my own little black book and made a few phone calls," she replied, grabbing up the clothes she could find and looking for the rest. "I went to a meeting of a local woman's group that's been trying to secure a copy of *Vicious Two*'s screenplay. It was invigorating, Jimmy. I kept in mind a lot of the things you said, and I've learned to recognize the intelligent, concerned, open-minded women from the whackos who only believe what they want to believe. A few of the women there were horror movie fans themselves and only wanted to determine if *Vicious Two* was sexist or merely gruesome."

"I guess we're rubbing off on each other. When I interviewed Eddie Petrano I thought of you and asked him how he felt making movies about people being murdered. He admitted he had mixed emotions."

Dorothy was pleased. "After the meeting I spoke to a few of the group's organizers. That took up about an hour. Then I realized I hadn't had dinner. I called the hotel but you weren't here. I went to a place near where the meeting was held and tried to get my thoughts together. Jimmy, I think I'm getting a handle on this assignment; it's all coming together for me. And it will encompass everyone's viewpoint."

She sat down on the bed. "At least I'd *thought* I'd made some sense of it all—until *this*, that man and his wife being murdered. It's so strange. It's like there's a jinx on *Vicious*. First Winteroth's family, now Douglas Longbank and his wife. Jimmy," she said with determination. "I want to go to their funeral."

"I've no objection," he replied. "But you didn't even know those people."

"But I feel a bond with them." She looked down at her hands. "And you know why."

He embraced her again, squeezing her with affection.

"Jimmy. When I got back to the hotel you still weren't there, so I started reading." She went over to the night table on her side of the double bed and got a book from the shelf underneath. It was one of the nonfiction studies of the Désirée Fontana murder case.

"When did you get that?" Jimmy asked her. "I didn't know you were that interested in the Désirée Fontana murder."

She smiled. "Why says I don't do thorough research? I got it out of the library before we left, didn't I tell you? I figured everything begins with this murder: the first movie. This movie."

"The murders of Doug Longbank and his wife, too?" The look on his face indicated that if she thought that she had to be stretching it.

"I don't know if there's any connection to that. But the original case is so fascinating. And horrible. Reading this after seeing *Vicious* is a revelation. That movie portrayed those two women as a couple of sluts, sharing the same stud; they seemed to do nothing in the second half but think about sex. They were quite different from that in reality. Désirée Fontana was nothing like her fictional counterpart."

"*Vicious* wasn't supposed to be a documentary."

"I know. But still, it was inspired by an actual event. *Vicious* went so far as to imply that Janice Evans might have murdered her roommate. Not Paul Wilson, who was black, by the way. A black homosexual, a talented, sensitive actor according to this account, not a sleazy white ladies' man with the I.Q. of a chipmunk." A dreamy look came over her face. "Janice Evans is the only one of them who's still alive, assuming she hasn't died since this was written. I wonder what she must think about all this?"

Jimmy's stomach was growling. "C'mon, let's get something to eat before I starve to death."

Dorothy put the book back down on the table. But her mind was working, working.

As they waited for the elevator, Jimmy told her some of his impressions of Eddie Petrano. "He reminded me a lot of myself in some ways. But he especially reminded me of Lonnie Mason."

"Who?"

"Lonnie Mason was a kid I knew when I was in grade school. The two of us sort of became friends because we had a common bond. A troubled homelife. My parents were divorcing, and his father was dying. His mother drank too much because of it. And we both loved comic books and horror movies. One day he let me see his prized possession—this cute pet hamster he had. When he looked at it I saw all this intense love and affection in his eyes. We used to play with that hamster for hours.

"Then one day he was all depressed and teary in school, and I thought his father might have died. But it was his hamster. I went home first to change my clothes, then went to his house afterwards. He was fussing with something in the workshed. I thought he was burying his hamster, but instead he was *dissecting* it. I was totally grossed out. I ran out of there and never went back again."

The elevator came. They got on and Jimmy continued. "I think by dissecting that animal Lonnie was rejecting his pain, avoiding it, pretending the hamster didn't matter and its death didn't bother him. It was his sad, lousy childhood that made him morbid and introspective.

"Do you think that's why you came to like horror?" Dorothy asked. "Because of your parents' divorce?" He had told her all about the messy, screaming, *jangling* breakup his parents had gone through when he was eleven.

"I don't know. That's probably too simplistic. I had the basic interest even before then. Lots of well-adjusted, nonneurotic people are horror fans. It isn't necessarily unhealthy."

They got out of the elevator and walked into the lobby.

"Lonnie Mason," Jimmy said. "I wonder whatever became of him?"

"He's probably a mortician," Dorothy said. She winked at Jimmy and he broke into a smile.

She had to surprise him now and then, Dorothy thought. Kept him on his toes.

In her sprawling home in Beverly Hills, Jocasta Sullivan relaxed in her living room and tried to concentrate on the novel she was reading. She sat on a long white couch beside a short glass table with a shaggy white rug underneath it. The rest of the floor was polished black tile. The walls were painted white and gold and adorned with a number of paintings. There were frilly curtains, billowing from the slight breeze, over the windows. This was the house that her wise investments following her *Starburst* triumph had bought. It was for this house that she would have to keep appearing in stuff like *Vicious Two* if she wanted to keep it.

Jocasta heard a sound. Someone putting a key in the front door, opening the door, and entering the hallway. *Shit!* She should have taken the key from the brat years ago when she'd moved into her own apartment.

Jocasta looked up from her paperback and saw her daughter coming into the living room.

"Where were you last night, mother?" Ellen said. "I called you and called you and there wasn't any answer."

"What difference does it make where I was?" her mother snapped. "I don't have to account to you for my time."

Ellen sat down on a chair across from the couch Jocasta was sitting on and said, "Mother, we have got to talk this out. I'm tired of your avoiding me. You haven't spoken to me for weeks. You never return my phone calls. And you leave your dressing room at the studio the moment I come in to say hello."

Jocasta said nothing. She sat rigidly in her chair—as always, watching her posture—and pretended to read page 83 of the novel as her daughter continued.

"Mother, what do I have to do to prove to you that changing the script was not my idea. I would think you'd be happy for me, for my getting such a great part. I'm sorry that they cut so many of your scenes. I didn't want to get somewhere at your expense. Mother—are you listening to me?"

Jocasta finally put the book down and said, "Yes, I'm listening to you and now you're going to listen to me. You only got that job in *Vicious Two* because I brought your name up to Harold Watson. Livingstone Stoner wouldn't have known you were alive if Watson hadn't introduced you. And you used your influence—and your body, no doubt—to get him to rewrite the script. Your part was enlarged and mine practically reduced to nothing."

Jocasta reached out for her pack of cigarettes. "So don't tell me that you're 'Little Miss Innocent.' Even if you didn't have a hand in it you've never insisted that Stoner go back to the original script, have you? You've never threatened to leave his bedside until my part was fully restored. I'm sorry, Ellen, but I've been fucked over all my life by dumb, pretty little starlets. They got the parts I wanted because of their chest size. Your father fooled around with half a dozen of them while he was living. I'm not about to sit still when my own daughter does it to me."

She lit the cigarette, puffed at it furiously. "By the way, why aren't you by your lover boy's side now? I thought with your new role you'd have to be on the set every minute. I, on the other hand, suddenly find myself with *hours* of free time."

"Mother, I—"

"Oh, I know you may not have *intended* for this to happen, but it did. And all because of your meddling—"

"Mother, you've been drinking again." She caught sight of the bottle on the lower shelf of the glass coffee table. "With your high blood pressure! You know what the doctor said."

"If I have high blood pressure, it's because of ungrateful children—"

A flash of anger and enlightment crossed Ellen's genuinely concerned face. A flash of exasperation and petulance. "Mother, you're jealous! You're jealous of me, I finally see that. But that's so silly. You're the famous actress, not me. You're the Oscar winner, not me. Are you so envious of me because of one tiny little break?"

Jocasta slammed her fist down on top of the table. "I had to work damn hard to get 'one little break,' and you should be damn glad I've done my part for you—unlike some other movie star parents I could name." She reached down under the table and started pouring herself another drink. "But I see how you're going to do it, you little tramp. You're probably going to marry the guy, that Livingstone Stoner—*if* that's his real name—and get yourself juicy parts in all of his lousy movies. Then when you've made a big enough name for yourself, you'll divorce him and shack up with someone else who can do for you. I know how it works in this business. Everyone else does it, so why not you?"

Ellen's lower lip trembled. She held back tears of frustration and resentment and said, "Is that what's troubling you, Mother? That at nearly fifty years of age you've finally realized that if *you* had played it that way you might now be a major movie star with lots of lovers and money instead of a lonely old has-been with a worthless gold statue on her mantel?"

Jocasta got up and slapped Ellen in the face so fast that the younger woman didn't even realize what had happened until the dregs of her mother's drink were splashing across her cheek.

"You bitch!" Jocasta screamed. "Get out of here! Go back to your apartment! Go back to your lover and leave me alone!"

Ellen picked up a cocktail napkin and wiped her face. Her voice was surprisingly calm as she said, "You're crazy, Mother, you know that? And you've had too much to drink."

"Not *enough*!" She looked her daughter smack in the eye and gave her a wicked, boozy grin. "You know, somebody chopped up *Vicious Two*'s original screenwriter. And his wife, too. Left them in a dozen pieces. Maybe somebody has a grudge against this movie."

Ellen's eyes widened in horror. "Mother! Is that true? Stop raving! I haven't heard a thing about it."

"Oh, I'm sure Livingstone will tell you when you see him.

Harold Watson called me this morning and by now it's probably hit the papers."

Ellen looked a bit ashamed as she asked, "They're not canceling the movie, are they? Not when they're so close to finishing?"

Jocasta gave her daughter an evil smile. "No, my precious, they're not canceling the movie. But before you walk out of here *too* happy let me remind you that whoever killed the Longbanks may not be satisfied with just two victims. He might want to get the director as well as the writer. So if I were you I wouldn't spend too many of my evenings with Livingstone Stoner. 'Cause he may be next on the list."

"Oh Mother! You're horrible!"

Jocasta watched her daughter run out of the room, wondering why she didn't feel nearly as triumphant as she ought to.

Harold Watson tried to join his wife for lunch as infrequently as possible, but sometimes there was no getting out of it. He always tried to wait until she was through, by pretending to be caught up in some paperwork or talking on the phone, but sometimes his stomach would grumble and his hunger would get the better of him. If he waited too long to eat he'd always get terrible gas pains. Now and then he'd try to grab a bite before Mrs. Watson ate, whenever she was out shopping or preoccupied elsewhere in the mansion, but then she'd give him hell for not waiting. It seemed he spent much of his time trying to avoid the woman.

He groaned inwardly as she entered the dining area and saw that today he had not delayed long enough. Lauren had barely touched her sandwich. Their maid, Bobbie, a perky middle-aged blonde with a heavy backside and an enormous bosom, bounced out of the kitchen and asked Watson what he wanted. "Tuna, like Mrs. Watson?" she asked. "Or perhaps some salad?"

"Just a nice salad will do," he told the woman, sitting down across from his wife and smiling. "How are you feeling, dear?"

"Glad you could join me, Harold," she said. "I'm better today. Much better. I think those pills Dr. Foster gave me are doing the trick."

Harold had quite forgotten what it was that had been ailing his wife now. It scarcely made a difference. He would simply get the usual bill each month that Foster sent for dispensing his placebos. What a ninny the woman was, what with all her assorted complaints and illnesses.

Lauren held up the daily paper. She was a pretty, slender woman with short gray hair and a long narrow face. "It's in this edition," she said. "They hardly spared a detail. Awful, just awful. And such a young couple. What kind of people are there in this world, to do such a thing?"

Harold had told Lauren about the murders. The police had called him late last night. They were questioning neighbors, relatives, and associates of the Longbanks. Douglas' sister, Elizabeth, had apparently known for whom her brother had toiled on his last complete screenplay.

"No, I have no idea who would have wanted to kill him or his wife," he told the police. "Certainly no one connected to *Vicious Two*." *It only was the other way around*, he said to himself. After what Livingstone had done to Longbank's screenplay, it was a wonder Douglas hadn't wanted to kill Stoner, as well as Bethany and Watson himself for their complicity.

Lauren was saying something. The only way he could deal with her incessant chattering was to ignore her, but sometimes she simply wouldn't be shut out. "Do you think the murders have anything to do with the movie, Harold?" She was all wide-eyed and breathless.

"No, no, no, a thousand times, no! The damn reporters will have a field day with this—"

"But the way they were butchered!" She went right on chewing on her tuna fish as if they were talking about car wax or linoleum.

"Lots of people get butchered in this city. The Longbanks must have surprised a burglar, that's all. I feel dreadful about the whole thing, but I simply will not give into hysteria and assume this has anything to do with the movie." His blood pressure was rising, he was sure of it, and he was beginning to feel warmer. "They just chose a bad time to get murdered, that's all."

God, he couldn't believe he had just said that, but his dear wife hadn't even heard him. Everything he said to her went in one ear and out the other.

"I still think it's terrible," she muttered, having the last word as usual.

Bobbie brought him his salad and he attacked it hungrily.

172

There, now he felt better. All this talk of murders and mayhem. He hadn't known Doug very well personally, but still the whole thing had hit Harold terribly hard. He didn't like bad things happening to people, tragedies enveloping his associates. A strange business, this. But he was convinced it really had nothing to do with *Vicious Two*. A movie was a movie. Real life was real life.

Lauren was droning on about something else again. He wondered for the fiftieth time just when it was that he had suddenly found her so tedious. She had never been a great brain, true, had never had a sparkling wit or an ability to do anything other than make the most vapid of small talk. But she'd been so pretty when he'd married her, bright and alive, the perfect thing to accompany him to parties and the theater.

Lauren was a dutiful little wife, too, although as the years rolled by she had assigned more and more of her duties to the servants. It wasn't her fault if she couldn't have children. Watson had never particularly wanted them anyway. She had given a quite respectable showing of herself in the bedroom, though they had by now reached a point where sex with each other was the *last* thing they desired.

Watson realized that what he really wanted now was to be a bachelor. To have his own space, his own home, his own life, no responsibilities, no one to phone home to, worry about, or explain himself to. Now if only Lauren had felt the same way. Surely she no longer felt any great love or passion for him, not after all of these boring years? Why was she so insistent that they play at being a happily married couple? Why did he have to eat with her and listen to her and pretend that he was concerned, as she was, with the drapes and the carpet and furnishings? Why did he have to account for his comings and goings? *That's* what he hated the most. He was having no affairs, but Lauren always thought he was. He couldn't understand why the silly woman *cared* one way or the other.

"You were out late Friday night, Harold," she said, wiping her thin, dainty lips with a napkin. "Did you go anywhere special?"

He almost said, "Yes. I was fucking Bethany Carraval," though it would have been a lie. He wouldn't have minded fucking Bethany Carraval, but he doubted if she were interested, and he had no intention of chasing her around like some silly, oversexed schoolboy. "Nowhere special," was all he said.

"Oh." The expression on Lauren's face made it clear that she did not consider that a satisfactory answer. Once she had accused him of going to "whore bars." Now she simply damned him with her silence.

Harold asked for the paper and read the stories about the murders. For a brief moment he felt sorry for the Longbank's little daughter. Then he concentrated on finishing his salad.

"Where am I? Will someone please tell me where I am?"

George Piedmont opened his eyes, looked around, and realized he was talking to no one. The room was completely empty. He'd lived in this same cheap studio for forty years now, and always woke up in it no matter where he'd been the night before. Yet every morning when he lifted his groggy head for the first few seconds he had no idea where he was.

"Boy, that was a scorcher."

George got out of bed and looked for his clothing. He was a short man in his seventies with large round eyes, thin lips on a wide mouth, and almost no chin whatsoever. His hairline was receding, but the dark hair in back and on the sides was thick and wavy.

George used the term "scorcher" not to refer to hot days, but rather to the severity of his drinking bouts. The drunker he got, the "hotter" they were. He had really tied one on last night, mostly because he knew he'd have to control the drinking once he was on the set. He didn't have much to do in *Vicious Two*, but his scenes were all being shot during the next couple of days. He was going to be a murder victim, that's all. Someone was going to bash in his face with a hammer. The thought of sitting in that chair for hours while these people made wounds in his face and poured on sticky fake blood was enough to make him head back for the nearest bar. He'd been "killed" before, and it was always such a messy, boring procedure.

He found his clothes scattered about the room, and started dressing. A nice hot brunch at the diner down the street was just what he needed. He didn't live in one of L.A.'s better neighborhoods, but he was used to the place, had pretty decent neighbors, and a rent he could manage even during those frequent periods when he wasn't working.

He was lucky—word had not yet gotten around about George Piedmont's drinking. There were few enough parts for a seventy-two-year-old washed-up character actor as it was. But at least he stayed off the hooch—within reason, that is—while he was working, and he always got praise for his performances. He'd had a tiny part in the original *Vicious*, as a patron in a sleazy bar. It was for reasons of nostalgia that they'd wanted him to do a small bit in this one. Funny, in the sequel his part would actually be bigger than it was in the original. Funny how life worked.

He locked up his apartment and started down the rickety staircase. He remembered to check his wallet for his money, and realized that he'd gone through nearly forty dollars the night before. When and how had he spent that much? It was getting scary, the way he couldn't remember what he did. It was happening more and more often, too. Blackouts. A blank space in his memory that offered up none of its secrets. Aside from the drinking, he had no idea what he might have done, who he might have seen, where he could have gone to spend so much moola. Normally he dropped about ten to twenty dollars on cheap beer, more than enough to have him, with his low tolerance, staggering out of the barroom. Oh well, it *had* been a scorcher. He was lucky he had lived to tell of it.

Before he entered the diner, he bought a paper from the newsstand at the corner. "Hello, Jackie," he said to the little guy selling papers. Once, many years ago, the midget had been an actor just as George was. As little boys they'd worked in silent films together.

"How goes it, George?" the little guy said. His smile seemed a little tight, guilty, as if he had something on his mind. Something he was hiding from George.

It was after George had ordered his usual eggs and coffee and opened the paper that he realized what it was that Jackie had been tense about. Doug Longbank. His wife, Edna. The terrible irony of their murders. There wasn't much solid information, but what little they had the paper played up. 'VICIOUS' TRAGEDY STRIKES AGAIN read the headline. Jackie knew that George had a part in *Vicious Two*.

George asked for God's forgiveness: but he couldn't help but wonder how this would affect the picture and his part in it. He would have to give his agent a call. The man might have tried to reach him this morning, but when George was sleeping off a drunk he was dead to the world.

Dead to the world, ha. He shuddered. He had to be crazy, he thought, wandering around this city in the middle of the night stoned out of his mind. Awful things happened to people in this city at night.

He looked at the paper again.

He didn't need any more proof than that.

13

The words of the minister were as ineffectual as ever. What could anyone say that the two closed coffins covered with flowers at the front of the church did not? Dorothy was glad she had come nonetheless. She would have felt remiss otherwise. She had never met the Longbanks, but she felt she owed them something.

She tried to focus on what the minister was saying, but instead it all came back to her: the day of her parents' funeral. *The two coffins up front contained not the Longbanks, but the Hunters; the pale, little girl in the second row with freckles and pigtails was not seven-year-old Kerry, but fifteen-year-old Dottie. The woman sitting by her side, sobbing, holding the little girl's hand, was not Elizabeth Longbank, but Aunt Margaret.* All the pain came rushing back, and Dorothy's tears for Kerry mingled with tears for herself. Her parents were dying all over again.

And Dorothy knew it was worse for Kerry Longbank. Dorothy had been fifteen when her parents died. Young enough to be devastated, but still old enough, a young lady really, to adjust to being without them. But Kerry was just a child. How could she even *understand* this?

Jimmy noticed her tears. He squeezed her hand, expressing

silent concern and support. Right at that moment she loved him more than ever. He was not, could not be, the ghoul which she had accused him of being. He was human, loving and kind. She had to hold on to that. It was so nice of him to accompany her today to the funeral of two people he had never even met.

The funeral was beginning to be too much for her, but she knew it would be rude and unseemly for her to walk out at this point. She was hardly a grieving relative whose behavior might be excused. Instead she tried to tune out the funeral by focusing on the events of the past two days. The minister, the music, the slight sobbing from the pews began to recede, and memories, recent memories, started to take over.

Things had been hectic since Sunday. She and Jimmy had continued the rounds of interviews, disheartened to see that the deaths of the Longbanks had barely made a ripple. Few people in the cast or crew of *Vicious Two* had known Douglas Longbank well; many had never even met him. No one had wanted to talk about the murders, but they were spooked, she could tell. A few mentioned that they thought the killings were a bad omen, but left it at that.

Livingstone Stoner seemed frailer and more weary than he had during the interview on Friday, but his frazzled condition might have been due to production problems, a tight schedule, or even drug addiction—and not a superstitious nature. He allowed them onto the set again to watch some filming. Dorothy found it surprisingly dull and routine, even disappointing—so many delays and retakes and pauses. At least the scenes they'd witnessed had not been bloody. Livingstone seemed to like Jimmy, though he was wary of Dorothy. Harold Watson and Bethany Carraval fluttered in from time to time looking officious.

Jimmy asked everyone a lot of questions about the technical side of things, while Dorothy concentrated on talking to the women on the set. Among the crew they were few and far between. Out of the cast members, there were several to choose from. She tried to talk to Ellen Rue, but whenever the young lady wasn't working she was literally hanging onto Livingstone Stoner. After her experience in the Executive Dining Room, Dorothy was determined to talk to the ladies when the men weren't around.

Ellen's mother, Jocasta Sullivan—she'd always been one of Dorothy's favorites—was not wonderfully cooperative. She answered a few questions before saying she had a headache. Vivienne Cherneau, on the other hand, also seemed preoccupied but gave a good interview nevertheless. She deplored current horror fare but was forced to appear in it in order to make a living "But this is not a sexist film," she pronounced in stentorian tones. "I personally have been liberated for decades." Dorothy heard a lot of people joking about some Academy Award nomination Cherneau had received or something along those lines, but she never did find out what it was about.

Dorothy gave Joyce Ramsey, her editor back in New York a call. She told her about recent developments, assured her that the article was coming along nicely, that she'd have a lot of good material to submit. Joyce congratulated her on her progress.

Dorothy also attended the meetings of a few more local women's groups, including *Women Against Violence in the Cinema*. Unfortunately, she found them a little creepy, a literal materialization of Jimmy's worst fears, a bunch of smug, sour housewives who really objected to too much sex and immorality. However, she went back to the first group she'd investigated and made a few friends. It was called *L.A. Women Together*, and consisted of a group of feminists devoted to various causes. They were particularly interested in providing support for women in all kinds of trouble: battered wives, rape victims, women who needed a sister's help in getting their lives in order.

She'd really called Joyce Ramsey to assure her that slowly the article was beginning to come into focus; simply by merging the three main themes—women, violence, cinema—Dorothy would eventually find her angle. All she had to do was talk to people, men and women, who had intelligent thoughts on one or more of those subjects, preferably all three. She saw it this way: first she'd write about violence against women in general. Then how it was caused by, or reflected in—she still hadn't decided—contemporary "horror porn." Then she'd go into how, even when horror films weren't sexist, they were still basically insensitive—and she hesitated to use the word, it had so many bad connotations—immoral. That was where her parents' deaths would come in.

It sounded good. Even though her conviction in regard to the "evil" of horror films was beginning to weaken. Due to Jimmy's friendly—and not so friendly—battering, she supposed. Still, she wasn't convinced all *that* easily.

The only sour note in all this was the reason why she was in this church. What had happened to the Longbanks was so ghastly and unbelievable. She hadn't expected the funeral to happen this soon, assuming the police would need days to comb the bodies for clues. But once the autopsies had been completed, the findings jotted down and officially recorded, there was no reason not to release the Longbanks for burial.

Finally the service was over and people began filing out. She saw Watson, Bethany, Livingstone Stoner, a few other familiar faces among the crowd. Well, why not? she thought cynically. They all had the afternoon off, didn't they?

"Are we going to the cemetary?" Jimmy whispered.

"No. That should only be for close friends and relatives."

He seemed relieved.

They were almost out of the nave and entering the foyer, when they heard a commotion near the doorway. Livingstone Stoner seemed to be in the middle of an altercation. Holding onto Ellen as if she had sprung out of his rib one morning and was now a permanent part of his body, he was nodding angrily at two figures who were standing in his way.

"That's Liz Longbank, Douglas' sister," Dorothy whispered. "I saw her picture in the paper."

As they got closer they could hear what the argument entailed. Elizabeth was hysterical, sobbing, hugging the Longbanks' daughter to her side in a bizarre parody of the embrace in which Stoner held Ellen. The little girl, dressed in a fine white dress and polished black shoes, looked partly confused but mostly deadened. Her eyes were red from crying, and it was apparent that her aunt's outburst was only upsetting her further.

"Why didn't you leave it alone?" the woman was saying. "My brother worked so hard on that script. Why did you have to ruin it? His last days were hell because of you! He couldn't sleep nights because of you!"

God, the *script*? Was *that* what she was yelling about? The man was dead and about to be buried, and all she could think of was the script for *Vicious Two*? "I can't believe this," Dorothy muttered.

There was no way out of the building. Livingston and Elizabeth were blocking the exit as they quarreled, preventing the few who remained inside from leaving.

As Douglas' sister poured out her invective, it became clear to Dorothy that it wasn't the script for *Vicious Two* that the woman really cared about. It had been days since the murder and still the police had no leads. This shattered woman had lost her brother; she needed someone to blame, somebody to hate. Livingstone Stoner had become her scapegoat. Her brother had hated Livingston and what the director had done to his work. It was clear that Elizabeth had loved her brother and supported him in all that he did. It was as if she were striking out against his enemies because he himself could no longer do so.

Livingstone Stoner broke through her steady barrage of cursing and hollering and shouted back at her: "Your brother's script was no damn good, lady!"

A collective gasp came from those trapped inside the church, the unwilling witnesses to this messy tableau. How could he say such a thing? At the man's funeral, no less.

"It stunk, lady. His script was pretentious and boring. The jerk writes a script for a splatter pic and puts in speeches that make fun of horror films. How could I use that, you tell me. It was a stupid screenplay. A pile of horseshit."

Elizabeth let go of the girl and beat Stoner on the chest with her fists. He backed away, trying to swing Ellen into the path of the battering hands. Dorothy felt someone brush past her and rush over toward the melee. It was Jocasta Sullivan. Dorothy hadn't realized that the actress had been behind her.

At first, Dorothy thought that Jocasta had come to protect her daughter from the violent actions of the bereaved, but it was soon made apparent whose side she was on. Stoner had backed away, pulling Ellen with him, either to get her out of harm's way or to use her for a shield again, should Elizabeth continue her assault. Jocasta stepped between the combatants and turned to Stoner and her daughter. She was as high as a kite, tottering on her heels. Her blazing eyes were red and boozy.

"She's right! She's right!" she shouted at Stoner. "Your script sucks. It *sucks*!" She turned to her daughter and sneered at her. "All because this tramp wanted a bigger part, that's why." She looked over her shoulder at Elizabeth. "Your brother had more talent in his little finger than this *jackass* has in his whole body!"

Elizabeth, a short, dumpy woman with beady hate-filled eyes, thin lips straining with fury, must have seen her own behavior mirrored in Jocasta's—and it filled her with mortification. Reddening, humiliated, she grabbed the child by the arm and hurried out of the church.

The minister came rushing up the aisle from the chancel. "Please! Please! What is going on here. Remember you're in a church!"

Jocasta stopped screaming at Stoner and Ellen and turned in the minister's direction. He strode up to her and exclaimed: "This is a funeral. What kind of animals *are* you people?"

"*Wounded* ones," announced Jocasta.

From the *National Inquisitor:*

HAS THE *VICIOUS* CURSE STRUCK AGAIN?

Over forty years ago a young woman was brutally murdered with an axe, and the true story became the basis for the sensational horror pic, *Vicious*.

When *Vicious* was made 23 years later, the director —Anthony Winteroth—came home from the premiere to find that his son had butchered his mother, Winteroth's wife, and then committed suicide.

Now the gory legacy of *Vicious* continues as police investigate the grisly murders of Douglas Longbank, and his wife Edna, who were slaughtered by an intruder at their home in Sherman Oaks Friday evening.

Longbanks is the screenwriter of *Vicious Two*, the long-awaited sequel to *Vicious* that is currently being filmed at Avalon Studios.

Is there a curse on *Vicious Two*?

"The murders have nothing to do with the movie," says Harold Watson, *V2*'s Executive Producer, but others aren't so sure. Speaking from her home in Los Angeles, Vivienne Cherneau, one of the actors in *V2* and a star of the current thriller *Sweet Psychotic*, was concerned.

"Yes, these murders have disturbed me. I'm afraid to go out at night. I thought they might shut down the picture, but they haven't. I think *Vicious Two* was jinxed right from the start."

Yet Watson insists that this is a lot of nonsense. "What happened to the Longbanks is a terrible tragedy, but we do live in a violent age. There are cast and crew members who will be out of work early if we cancel this movie.

"We shall continue making the picture—with grief and regret in our hearts over the terrible tragedy that has befallen the Longbanks."

Reports indicate that Longbank's work on the film had been over before his death, and that his script was considerably rewritten by the movie's director, Livingstone Stoner.

Stoner has been around town in the company of luscious starlet, Ellen Rue, who has a pivotal role in V2 along with her mother, actress and Academy Award winner Jocasta Sullivan.

Lieutenant Detective Jerry Chalmers of the L.A.P.D. says there are no leads in the murders of the Longbanks, who are survived by a seven-year-old daughter and Longbank's unmarried sister, Elizabeth, who is currently caring for the child.

"We expect it was a particularly savage intruder that the Longbanks stumbled upon. We're investigating several possibilities," says Chalmers.

Through a source close to the investigation, The *Inquisitor* has learned that the police do have a few clues, however.

The killer entered the house by breaking the window of the back door. A sheet with eyeholes cut out of it, drenched with blood, was found in the Longbanks' bedroom, where Doug Longbank's body was also discovered.

The intruder left no fingerprints. Security patrols reported that no suspicious persons were seen in the area at the general time of the murders.

The murder weapon is presumed to have been a common scythe used for cutting weeds that the killer may have removed from the Longbanks' garage. It was left behind with the sheet, which may or may not have come from inside the Longbanks' home.

The police say they are looking for "a man or woman who is powerfully built, probably athletic, and remarkably strong."

There have been reports that some of the blows delivered to the Longbanks were so powerful that the scythe sliced through bone and flesh and partially dismembered the bodies.

Jimmy got back to the hotel room to find that it was empty again.

Darn it. Where was that woman? Night after night she'd disappear somewhere even though they'd made plans to go out and sample L.A.'s nightlife together. He knew he was always late getting back from his appointments, but he couldn't help being fascinated by what was happening on the set. She could have waited for him; hadn't he gone to that funeral with her yesterday? She knew he loved moviemaking. Additionally, he was doubling as photographer and it took time to set up the best shots.

Of course, today, when they'd filmed one of the murder scenes, he'd felt a little queasy. Hacked up bodies and squirting blood did little for the appetite as it was, but coming so soon after the Longbanks' murders. . . . Well, he was understanding how Dottie felt about things more and more each day. He wished the police would catch the creeps who did it. Having people like that on the loose wasn't helping anyone sleep better.

Dorothy had left a message that she had waited for him as long as possible, then decided to go out. Who knew where she could be? Even back in New York she liked to go off by herself a lot, go someplace where she could be alone with her thoughts. He wasn't necessarily sure that was healthy, not for a person with a background like Dorothy's. But he could hardly chain her to a chair in their apartment.

When she still wasn't back after supper he decided to go out and have some fun. Normally he either went to see a film or had a drink or two at a cocktail lounge. Tonight, he would investigate L.A.'s crazy club scene whether Dottie was with him or not. On his previous trips he'd only driven past Hollywood Boulevard, the famous Sunset Strip and its sidestreets. Tonight he wanted to *walk* it. He knew it was sleazy, but it couldn't be worse than Times Square. He'd hit every dive on the strip, get plastered for a change. Normally he imbibed very little—alcohol was not one of his vices—but every now and then he had a need to go off on a toot.

Hollywood Boulevard was every bit as garish, loud, seamy

and vulgar as he'd hoped. Painted hookers and flamboyant transvestites made kissing sounds as he went by, motioning with their fingers as if to say, "Have some fun for some moola." Though he had no moral objections to their profession or activities, he had no interest in risking VD from an encounter with either a male or female prostitute.

There were people on the street that he didn't want to look at, let alone brush up against. Seedy-looking characters, dirty winos, slithering pickpockets. Kids with leering, nasty faces. Hard women in black leather jackets who clung to the sides of men with greasy hair and whiskers. There was a multiplicity of languages: English, Spanish, street talk, jive talk; black, brown, red, white and yellow faces mixed together. Hot dog stands and pizza parlors issued a variety of spicy smells, some fragrant, some repulsive. Eyes were always looking out of alleyways.

He was hoping to find some wild clubs or discos, though Dorothy would undoubtedly have said he was a little too old for that scene. He doubted if any of the clubs on the strip were that exclusive, the "in" places, but on the other hand, that meant they wouldn't be too expensive. He tried several as he progressed down the boulevard. A hooker's den. A gay place. A joint full of smoking teenagers.

Finally he found a place that seemed halfway decent. The ages were mixed, and the crowd seemed a bit more respectable, better dressed than the others. There were a lot of sexy-looking women wandering around. For a moment he thought the place might offer a different kind of danger and almost backed away. But he had no intention of waiting around in his hotel room.

He went up to the art deco bar, ordered a gin and tonic, and leaned back to watch the dancers undulating beneath the flashing multicolored lights of the dance floor. The disco beat was intense and pounding. The ultraviolet "black" lights above the bar made white shirts and teeth shine like they were radioactive.

He ordered two more drinks in quick succession—they were weak and jammed with too much ice—and looked at the gorgeous, flashy females that moved through the crowd, danced, and stood in corners with their boyfriends.

He and Dorothy hadn't had sex the whole time they were out here, and he had to admit he was horny. He hadn't any urge to cheat on Dorothy—not out of guilt, but out of the knowledge that few women could mesh with him in bed as well as Dottie could—but he certainly didn't mind looking. The girls today were all tight jeans and lip gloss, shapely asses and pretty pink mouths. *He wanted to rub his fingers all over them and kiss them hard on the lips.*

One of the girls detached herself from the many-headed monster that was the crowd on the dance floor and walked in his direction. She was leading someone else by the hand. Just as Jimmy was wondering why the girl looked so familiar, he recognized her companion as Livingstone Stoner. And wasn't that lady Ellen Rue? *Slumming*, Jimmy assumed. Livingstone saw Jimmy, waved, and came over to the bar to say hello.

"Where's your ladyfriend tonight?" asked the director, giving Ellen a squeeze. Apparently Ellen felt no anger over his fight with her mother or at the way Livingstone had practically thrown her at Doug Longbank's sister to ward off the angry woman's blow. Of course, Ellen would still have to make nice-nice with her boss if she wanted continued help with her career.

"Dorothy's out pursuing her story, I guess," Jimmy said. He smiled at Ellen. "You two look as if you're having a good time."

Ellen was well on the way to being drunk. She wiggled her body provocatively and spoke deliberately like a Valley girl. "The most." She nuzzled the director's neck and giggled. Her mouth was a round, wet pink circle the color of bubblegum. *Delicious.*

They made giddy small talk for a while until Livingstone went off to relieve himself. Ellen looked Jimmy up and down playfully, licked her pink lips, and said, "Wanna dance, handsome?"

He wasn't crazy about disco dancing, but he didn't want to offend her. "Okay," he said. "Let's go."

Out on the dance floor he felt rather silly. He was not adept at doing this contemporary "boogie." The beat was irresistible, though, hard and pounding, laden with a driving sensuality. There also seemed to be a *violence* to it, a hypnotic ferocity that underlined the erotic explicitness of the lyrics with a promise of unending torture. Of course, much of the menace that rock music radiated was purely hallucinatory in nature, perhaps ingrained in his consciousness, the result of society's insistence on equating eroticism with evil. Yet, some of the songs he'd heard, disregarding their lyrics, had under-tones and vibrations that seemed sinister and unhealthy, in contrast to the music's message of lust without guilt. Still, he had to admit he dug it.

Jimmy chided himself. *I'm beginning to think the way Dorothy does.* Finding evil in the most innocuous places, interpreting every song and movie as a message of misanthropic hatred, a conspiracy against humankind in general and women in particular. How horrible to be so constantly defensive, so utterly incapable of experiencing joy in anything. A sharp pang of resentment at Dorothy's anhedonia ran through him for a second.

After all these years he'd finally realized that Dottie was not the freeswinging, spirited liberal he'd always taken her for, but a conservative family-type Puritan masquerading as a "modern woman." She tried to be unconventional, but it just wasn't in her. He once thought that her parents' deaths, her being raped, might have turned her that way, but now he wondered if she only used that as an excuse. Could she really be as stuffy and unbending as she seemed?

The funny thing was, he agreed with ninety percent of her attitudes on feminism. Some women *did* have a raw deal, who could argue with that? But Dottie and others like her refused to concede that it was frustrating for many fellows, such as himself, that everything today was centered on "women's role" and "women's problems" as if men, too, weren't often locked unfairly and unwillingly into utterly abhorent roles. Everything was black-and-white, simplistic and simple-minded. The whole brouhaha over porn, and now these movies. Attacking what was at best a reflection of sexism in society but not a cause of it. Dot and her companions carried a flag of feminism, but what they were really after was censorship together with some stilted definition of morality.

But in spite of it all, he loved her. Yet . . . ?

It also bothered him that Dottie never seemed to see beyond her own pain. Oh, she could cry for Kerry Longbank—who couldn't?—but she'd never concede that *he* might suffer from time to time. No, he had not lost his parents to a maniac. Neither had he ever been raped. But he had been subjected to a horribly disorienting custody battle during what they quaintly called his "formative years," had been shunted back and forth from a drunken father to a borderline schizophrenic mother, neither of whom really wanted him. He was just the prize in their frantic, pointless struggle.

Even so, when Dad drove his car into a concrete highway buttress, and Mom had to spend more time in institutions than out of them, it was awfully hard to cope. He'd learned to be self-sufficient at an early age, an age of constant loneliness and insecurity, an age where building plastic models of cars and monsters was his frequent occupation, an age when either his drunken father or raging mother would destroy all his toys for no reason that he ever understood. Now Dad was dead and Mom shared an apartment in the Bronx with her sister. She was a stranger.

Relaxing, letting it all wash out of him, he moved in time to the beat, wallowing in the frank sexuality and earthiness of the music. It didn't matter that his dancing was no good. He was content to surround himself with these beautiful, sinuous people and watch the sultry Ellen twist and turn to the rhythm like a voluptuous Circe singing to the sailors. God, how he wished he could have held her while they danced, felt her chest against his, her arms around him, *her bubblegum lips pressing down on his own.*

The music was getting him hot. The music made him feel alive. There was an energy and a joy to it, a luxuriant message of enjoying one's body and the moves it could make on both the dance floor and in the bedroom. It was mindless, yet primal. Primitive, yet derived from the highest technology. Exciting and carnal and emotional—and yet cerebral in the sense that one's thoughts and sensations were given over totally to unabashed orgiastic pleasure. The bodies of the dancers were reflected in the mirrors along the walls, as garish, glaring lighting effects flashed and dazzled across and over them; it was a dizzying orgy of limbs and beat and color.

As the song ended, Ellen saw Livingstone wading his way through the crowd from the men's room to the bar. She laughed and gave Jimmy a hard, wet kiss on the side of his mouth. He licked sweet bubblegum off his lips. He was about to follow her off the dance floor, when a lovely oriental girl with flowing black hair cornered him and pushed him back into the writhing throng.

Jimmy again felt that vivid flood of resentment toward

Dorothy. She and all the others like her. Stunted people who spread a message of shame: shame about your bodies, shame in your thoughts, shame and prudery and censorship. Shame in enjoying the things you enjoyed. He supposed those friends of hers at that women's group where she'd spent practically every night would think his present behavior a scandal, that he was a chauvinist and a pervert for admiring the sensuous pull of the music and the beauty of the women all around him without apology. But the oriental girl had just given his ass a squeeze, and her obvious attraction to him was hardly any different from what he felt for her.

He made up his mind to stay until closing time, oppression be damned.

He had to be free from—*of*—Dorothy and her gloom and accusations and negativity sometime in his life.

Bethany Carraval was just about to take a hot bath when the doorbell rang.

She made sure her robe was fastened securely, then went down the pretty pink hall through the attractively furnished living room and over to the door where she looked through the peephole. She was surprised to see who her visitor was. Such lousy timing, too. She didn't really want anyone bothering her tonight.

She opened the door, putting on what she hoped was a cool, even discourteous, expression. Maybe the visitor would take the hint and go away. "Yes, what can I do for you?"

Her visitor asked to come in. Her visitor was carrying a shopping bag and seemed to have some kind of problem. She couldn't very well turn away someone who needed help, could she? She led the visitor into the living room and the two of them sat down on the couch. "Are you all right?" Bethany asked. "You really don't look very good."

Bethany had decorated her little home with dozens of plants: they hung from the walls and the ceiling. They cluttered the glass table in front of the sofa. They seemed to occupy every bit of space, as if the woman was hoping a sea of greenery would give some substance to her life, something for her to care for. The messy divorce she'd suffered through was no secret to anyone; she'd even lost the children. Cocaine, that's what had done it.

Thank God that part of her life was over.

"Perhaps some water will do the trick," she said to her guest. "Or maybe a drink. What do you take?"

The visitor was giving her the creeps. As she made the drink that had been requested, Bethany wondered when her guest would get around to telling her what the problem was. She really dind't like to deal with people, whether she knew them well or not, when she was at home. That's what she had an office for. Her apartment was her haven. Bethany's guest was not saying anything, breathing harshly as if on the verge of a stroke and it was really freaking her out. "Say, do you think you need a doctor?"

When Bethany turned back with the drink in her hand, expecting a reply, she saw that the visitor had removed something from the bulky shopping bag.

It was a small electric power drill. The kind for outdoor use that ran on rechargeable batteries.

The visitor flicked the switch into the "on" position.

Bethany's heart jumped. "What on earth are you doing with that?" She couldn't take her eyes off that revolving drill bit.

The visitor got up, moving slowly toward Bethany. The drill bit *whirred* and *whirred* in its chuck. Bethany backed up and tugged at the lapel of her robe.

"Stay back, you! This isn't funny!" She held out her hands and ordered her guest to retreat. "What do you think you're doing with that thing! What have I ever done to you, for Pete's sake? If this is a joke, you crazy fool, I'm warning you I don't like it!"

At first she didn't make any serious connection of this bizarre incident to the deaths of the Longbanks. Someone had broken into their house, an intruder, while this was someone Bethany knew and had willingly admitted. *Could her visitor be the one who murdered the Longbanks?* But if so, *why*?

She backed away from the visitor who was steadily advancing, holding the drill out in front and leering with menace. Bethany almost laughed—how could she take this spectacle seriously? "Stop it! Stop it this minute. I don't think you're funny. Put that thing away and get out of my apartment!"

Growling, the visitor suddenly lunged at Bethany with the drill. Bethany cried out in terror and tried to get out of the way.

Something was blocking her path—the wooden table near the hallway. The drink she'd made for the visitor tumbled to the floor, along with two or three large potted plants. Her bare feet stepped into moist dirt, crushing the plants, as a shard from a pot dug into her heel and drew blood.

Bethany screamed as the four-inch drill bit entered her body at a point directly above her left shoulder. It cut through the flimsy material of her robe and punctured her skin; a gushing red spot of warm flesh and blood spurted out.

Oh my God. It was happening. It was actually happening.

The visitor pulled out the drill bit almost at the same time that Bethany reacted to the pain. It had only gone in about an eighth of an inch, but that was more than enough. She screamed and clapped her hand over the wound.

"Stay away from me! Please, *please* leave me alone!"

There was blood coming out of the hole and she was getting dizzy. But she knew if she fainted she'd die. She'd be totally at her assailant's mercy. *Why was this happening to her?* She tried to run past the maniac and get to her phone. The maniac grabbed her robe and pulled her back, sending her tumbling over and onto the sofa. *The visitor's strength was incredible.*

"Please *please!*" But there was no reasoning with her pursuer. Bethany would have to put up a damn good fight. She grabbed as many plants as she could get her hands on from the table and threw them at the maniac. Some of the plants smashed against the maniac's body, others fell short and scattered across the rug. She had to stop this lunatic, had to save herself somehow.

Before she could get away from the couch, the maniac had reached her side and was pummeling her with a fist. Bethany looked up and pleaded with her killer, tried to reach some core of common decency. *This just didn't make any sense!* The hand that held the drill was very close to her. She saw that something was funny about the hand. She hadn't noticed before, but something was *wrong* with it. It was missing the middle finger, *and it was all gnarled and shriveled like a claw.*

Bethany was so startled by what she saw that she almost missed an opportunity to escape. The visitor had stopped punching for a second in order to turn the drill on again. Bethany wriggled away from her assailant and darted toward the hallway. *She had to get to the bathroom and lock herself in!*

Her feet crunched over the shards of the pots lying in her path and she almost skidded on her own blood as she slid hastily down the corridor. Just as she was almost at the bathroom door, she lost her balance, bounced against the wall, and slipped helplessly down to the floor. Wracked with pain and terror, unable to get a full breath, she began to *crawl* to the bathroom, inch after agonizing inch, desperately hoping she could get inside and slam the door shut before her assailant arrived to stop her.

Too late! She could feel the visitor kneeling at her side as she continued to drag herself forward. *Owwww!* The drill! The assailant was teasing her, tormenting her, pricking and puncturing the delicate skin of her legs—her thigh, her ankle, her calf—with the spinning drill bit as she tried to get away. She realized there also was pressure on her legs; her assailant was kneeling, squatting on top of her, preventing her from moving.

The killer began to climb up and over her, the drill bit whirring in macabre counterpoint to its wielder's chilling *giggling*. Bethany reached up behind her and scratched and clawed, tried everything to stop, to *hurt*, her attacker.

And then the drill bit was thrust deep into her shoulder, all four inches going straight through flesh and bone, deeper and deeper into her writhing, hysterical figure. An enormous spurt of blood gushed out as the visitor removed the drill bit.

Bethany fainted.

Nonchalantly, unhurriedly, the visitor used the drill again and again, boring deep, bleeding holes into Bethany Carraval's unresisting body. After awhile the blood stopped pumping, stopped *jumping* out of her skin like miniature geysers. The legs stopped kicking in involuntary spasms.

The visitor put down the drill and dragged Bethany into the living room. Rummaged in the shopping bag. Came up with a foot-long hacksaw.

The visitor went over to the body and started to hack and cut, hack and cut, giving a good *wrench* now and then until something pulled off.

Half an hour later the visitor was finished.

The visitor stood up, satisfied with the job, then pulled a fresh set of clothes out of the bag. Stripping, the visitor put on the new clothes and put the old ones in the bag. The clothes would be deposited in the incinerator.

Humming, the visitor left the apartment.

A job well done.

The plants, their leaves spattered with blood, remained in silent testimony to Bethany Carraval's loneliness, so cruelly and finally ended.

Dorothy let herself into the hotel room, and tried to tell by the light from the corridor whether or not anyone was sleeping in the bed. No, it was empty. She turned on the light and shut the door. She looked at the alarm clock. Funny, she hadn't realized it was that late. Somehow she had lost over an hour or else she'd misread her watch at some point during the evening. She checked to make sure that she hadn't forgotten to rewind it but it was okay. *Strange.*

Where was Jimmy at this hour? Not that she had a right to complain. She had been getting in pretty late herself these past few days.

It had been a wonderful night. The ladies at *L.A. Women Together* had arranged for her to attend a meeting for victims, for women who had been raped or brutally assaulted, or who were the loved ones of people who'd suffered violent deaths. She had sat back at first, strictly an observer, not wanting to do anything more than record what was said and freely absorb the emotions that were aired. But after a while she realized that she was not there just as a journalist; she had been a victim herself. She had, of course, attended other rape victim support groups in New York, but she should have joined a group like *this* long ago. Probably she'd thought that the circumstances of her parents' deaths had been so atypical that no one would quite understand how she felt.

But at this meeting, she finally opened her mouth and let it all out, so gratified to talk to people who appreciated and empathized with what she had gone through. The meeting was supposed to have ended at ten, but there had been so much to say, so much to do, that it had lasted until nearly midnight.

She didn't tell Jimmy much about *L.A. Women Together*, knowing that he thought the outfit was just a bunch of hypersensitive censors like *Women Against Violence in the Cinema*. There are some of that type in this organization, particularly those who were dedicated to eradicating porn and gory movies, but many others saw the group simply as a network for women —abused, battered, frightened women—to help one another, to find support they couldn't find anywhere else. The organization's merits outweighed its faults, she was convinced of that.

Dorothy sat down on the bed, rubbed the aching spots on her neck, and tried hard not to surrender to the urge to just lie back fully dressed and fall asleep.

As she washed up in the bathroom, she wondered again where Jimmy could be. She frowned. Probably out drinking, living it up in his vulgar, star-spangled Hollywood. Well, he could have Hollywood. She couldn't blame him for going out, though. Too bad he was always so late getting back from his appointments at the studio. Her method was just to go in, see whoever she had to see, take her notes, and leave. Jimmy had to stand around taking pictures, making friends, getting involved and absorbed in the whole filmmaking process. Well, she supposed that was what he'd come out here for. He had a job to do and she couldn't complain. But neither would she sit idly in her hotel room waiting for him to come back to her.

It would be nice, though, if they could have dinner together for a change. See the town. Maybe even go sightseeing again like she had the other night or something similarly corny. She looked at the clock again and hoped he was all right. Murderers were loose in this city and he was prowling the streets full of liquor. The ninny.

The phone rang. She grabbed it. "Jimmy, where are you?"

It wasn't Jimmy. The woman at the other end of the line introduced herself as Madeline Moses. "We met at the *L.A. Women Together*'s office the other evening," she said. "Perhaps you remember?"

Of course Dorothy remembered. Madeline was an elderly woman, early seventies probably, whom she had met at a meeting Tuesday night. She was a volunteer; answered the phone, did some typing and other light office work. A very pleasant woman, very alert and companionable. Dorothy and she had gone out for a cup of coffee afterwards, talked about so many, many things. Why did they want to put old people out to pasture when some of them were still so alive, so vital?

"What can I do for you Madeline?"

"I'm sorry to call so late. I've been thinking and thinking about it all evening. The other night when we talked . . . you told me what you were in town for. You said things that got me thinking, that made me wonder if at last I'd found someone I could trust, someone I could talk to. Dorothy, it's extremely important that I see you tomorrow afternoon. Would it be possible for you to come to my apartment?"

In spite of her concern, Dorothy frowned. There went another day she could have been with Jimmy. Maybe this business with Ms. Moses wouldn't take too long.

"Of course, I'll come." She grabbed a pen and paper and jotted down the time and the address. "Tell me, Madeline, is everything all right?"

"I'm very tired and I don't want to talk over the phone. But when I tell you what my real name is I'm sure you'll understand why what I have to say should be of interest to you."

She paused. "My real name is Janice Evans."

And then the old woman hung up.

Part Four: *"The Claw"*

14

Fall 1987.
Los Angeles and environs.

Jimmy woke up and opened his eyes slowly, afraid to discover that he was not in the bed he was supposed to be in. No, it was all right; he recognized the wallpaper of the hotel room, the bureau across from the bed, the cheap, rectangular mirror up above it.

For a moment he thought that after all his carousing last night he might have gone home with one of the women he had talked to, danced with, and yes—he had to admit it—even made out with. He hadn't the slightest idea of how the evening had wound up—it was all a blank. He had no recollection of taking a taxi or walking back to the hotel, no idea if Dorothy had been here when he got in. Well, she sure wasn't here now.

He saw a note tucked underneath the alarm clock. He would wait to read it until after he washed up; he wasn't ready for it now, some note about how she'd be gone all day, had a meeting to attend in the evening—or worse—a scolding missive about how drunk and disheveled he had been when he finally got back to the room. As he got up out of the bed he realized that he was still wearing the clothes he'd had on last night. Or was he? Had he worn the blue shirt and the black trousers? He couldn't remember, but he must have. The clothes were redolent of sweat and other odors, sweeter ones such as perfume or cosmetics.

What *had* he been up to last night?

He found more clues when he looked in the mirror. There was a tear in his shirt, one of the buttons had popped or been pulled off. There were stains of some kind on the collar. Was that lipstick? He also saw vague smudges of something on his neck and around the mouth which he rubbed off with his hand and some hot water. None of the stains were that distinct. With any luck, Dorothy might not have noticed.

His eyes were bloodshot and his stomach was churning. He was nauseated and his mouth tasted horrible. He must have literally drunk himself blind, stumbled back to the hotel and passed out.

He stripped out of his messy garments and stepped into the shower. The water rushing over his body felt terrific; it woke up his senses and made him more alert. *Boy, what an evening!*

When he was through in the bathroom, he went over to the night table and picked up Dorothy's note.

She had to be kidding.

She had written that she was having tea with Janice Evans. Wasn't that the woman who had lived with Désirée Fontana, the roommate who had survived Paul Wilson's attack in 1940?

Very funny, Dorothy. That's one for you.

He went over to the dresser and picked out a clean white shirt to wear.

As Dorothy pressed the downstairs buzzer of "Madeline Moses'" apartment, she still couldn't believe that she had had coffee the other evening with one of the principals of the infamous Désirée Fontana murder case and not even known it. For a moment she wondered if this was a joke; maybe even something Jimmy was behind. But she rejected the idea almost immediately. Ms. Moses had not appeared to be the kind of woman who'd be bothered with such foolishness, and she had sounded most sincere on the phone.

A buzzing noise rang out in the foyer, signaling that the door was now unlocked. Dorothy pushed her way into the lobby. She braced herself before walking up the short staircase to apartment "B"—this might well be the most fascinating interview she had ever been given.

The woman welcomed Dorothy into her home warmly, and led her over to the sofa. The apartment was small, but cozy; old-fashioned furnishings were crammed together in the tiny living room—couch overstuffed chairs, a table with plants on it—leaving little space to walk in. The walls were painted beige and a small air conditioning unit in the window was running.

"I'm sorry the place is so messy," the old woman said, smiling. "I cleaned up a bit before you got here, but I really am such a slob."

Dorothy waved off the suggestion. Aside from some scattered books and magazines, an out-of-place item here and there, and a few empty candy and cookie wrappers on the floor, the place wasn't really *that* bad. "You should see my apartment" she said.

Madeline Moses—or Janice Evans—was a fairly slender woman of medium height, with short gray hair and green eyes. She carried herself proudly, as if optimism and courage were racing through her system instead of blood. Probably she had never been beautiful, but she had the kind of face that got more attractive with the years, that settled and gained character. Her teeth were slightly crooked and her nose was too big and she had what looked like a smattering of acne scars on her face, around the cheeks and forehead. But these were not terribly noticeable and could easily have been covered with makeup had she chosen to wear any. She was a large-breasted woman, and may have been something of a sex pot in her heyday; some of that casual sensuality still remained.

Janice pressed her thin lips together for a second and studied her visitor. Dorothy couldn't help but notice the indecisiveness that was playing across her hostess' face. "Madeline Moses" was not anything like what Dorothy had imagined Janice Evans would be. This woman sitting beside her on the couch had been part of a notorious murder trial—her life had been publicly exposed, sensationalized, exaggerated. Janice Evans had seen her best friend brutally murdered, had witnessed the whole grisly tableau. The murderer himself had been a friend of hers, too. Wasn't that the sort of thing that changed people for life, that warped them, made them withdrawn and nervous, even hostile toward others? Dorothy hadn't actually seen her parents being murdered, but she still hadn't gotten over it. Of course, she was much younger than Janice who had had more time to recover.

Finally Janice said, "Thank you so much for coming." There was a pot of tea, two cups, and a plateful of cookies on the table in front of them. "Please help yourself. If you're hungry I could also make you a sandwich."

"This will be fine, thank you," Dorothy said, picking up the pot, after first offering to serve, and pouring some tea for both herself and her hostess. "What is it you wanted to talk to me about? I assume it has something to do with *Vicious Two* and my article?"

Dorothy had mentioned why she was in L.A. when the two women had talked in the coffee shop the other night. Dorothy recalled that Janice had not reacted in any particular manner, but then, someone who had hidden from society to the extent of moving to another coast and changing her name would probably have learned not to give herself away.

"Yes, I suppose it has to do with *Vicious Two*. You did recognize my name when I told you what it was last night, didn't you?" Dorothy nodded. "Believe me, there are very few people who know who I really am. After Désirée's murder, after the trial, I got so tired of writers and reporters—no offense intended—all these people wanting interviews, badgering me with questions I couldn't answer. I didn't have the answers. Over forty-five years later—God, has it been that long?—there are still things I don't understand about that night. Who ever thought a dumb Iowan farm girl could get mixed up in so much trouble!"

She paused to sip her tea and pick up a cookie. Dorothy put her cup down and focused all her attention on her hostess. Janice Evans sighed, wiped her forehead, and continued. "I was afraid that *Vicious*, Winteroth's movie, was going to start the whole thing up again. But by then two decades had passed, I had already changed my name, altered my appearance in what little ways I could, and moved to Hollywood"—she rolled her eyes—"to make a fresh start. I still thought I could make it in show business. I was one of those silly people who move to California to escape their troubles and discover that their troubles have moved with them."

"Under my new name I did get a few small roles, did work as an extra, toiled as a waitress, the usual things, but it never really happened for me. Just as well, I suppose. Had I become a 'star,' it would all have resurfaced—the murder, the scandal. I stopped working when I hit sixty-five, volunteered at various places such as the Senior Citizens' Center and *Women Together*, just to fill my time, to be less lonely."

She nibbled on a cookie and wiped crumbs off her thin dry lips with a knuckle. "When *Vicious* came out a lot of articles appeared about Désirée's murder, but no one ever found me or bothered me. Thank goodness. Maybe a shrewder person would have used their notoriety to get someplace—God knows everyone seems to do that today—but I guess I was never the smartest person in the world."

She could see the quizzical look on Dorothy's face. "Why am I unburdening myself to you, a writer, after all these years, you wonder? It was the things you said at those meetings, and during our talk over coffee. You've been a victim yourself—someone close to you has died and like all of us you don't even know why. Your life has been touched by violence. I share your dismay at how violence has become—commercialized—become entertainment in the form of books and movies. Oh, I realize a lot of it isn't meant to be taken seriously: horror stories, ghost tales, things that go bump in the night, monsters and raving lunatics. It's all so silly. But a lot of what they make today does bother me, though I haven't made it my 'cause.' What botheres me most of all is that the horrible thing that happened to Désirée . . . and Paul," she added softly, "has been turned into some kind of carnival sideshow. First *Vicious*, then *Vicious Two*—and all the others, the imitations." She closed her eyes for just a moment and sighed, "And Désirée herself, her tragedy, has been largely forgotten, as if she never really existed but was only a character in some movie. It just isn't fair."

She took another sip of the tea, then continued. "So you see, when you mentioned the article you were working on, the murder of your parents and its effect on you, I saw a way in which we could help one another. Any article on *Vicious Two*—no matter its context or perspective—should mention the *real* Désirée Fontana. She should not be forgotten. Her pain should not be reduced to some mindless thing for mindless people to get a few sick thrills from." She shifted in her seat and glanced quickly, almost guiltily at Dorothy from the corner of her eye.

"Oh, I know what you're thinking. Yes, I have a personal stake in this, too. You see, I've seen Winteroth's *Vicious*—took me five years to get up the strength to do it—and I've waited twenty years to tell people that I'm not some kind of psychotic murderess, that I'm not like that 'Yvette Cummings,' the woman in the movie who was supposed to be me." She rubbed a spot above her left eyebrow with a lingering finger, as if she were trying to erase a memory.

"I'm the only one alive who can tell the story. Désirée's dead. Paul is dead. Our landlady, my parents, all the others even remotely involved are dead. I want to set the record straight. Even those books written about the case made mistakes. I even cooperated with one author, but he just went ahead and wrote what he wanted to. Oh, I'm not expecting you to build your whole article around me, but as long as you're writing about the case, about *Vicious* and *Vicious Two*, about women who are victims of violence," she smiled, "surely somewhere there's room in there for me."

Dorothy reached over and patted the woman's hand; the skin was papery and lined with blue veins. "Of course there's room, Mad—I mean Janice. Remember, besides doing pieces for *Women Now* I also free lance. I'm sure any number of magazines would be interested in your story."

Janice grinned. "I must confess I even thought of a book. Unfortunately, I may be a good typist, but I'm a really lousy writer."

Inside Dorothy's mind, the wheels were turning. "We can talk about that, too," she said. She didn't know if there were room on the market for yet another book on the Fontana case—even one from Janice's unique perspective—but she *had* been thinking of doing a book on victims, the forgotten victims of violent crimes, the loved ones who were always left behind to deal with their anguish, as well as the stunning lack of concern, and concern for justice, shown by others. Certainly Janice's story would fit in there. And there was also the possibility of doing a book on the whole web of violence surrounding the *Vicious* movies—including the murders of the Longbanks. There was no limit to what she could come up with.

For a moment the rush of writer's excitement had superceded her distaste for sleazy exploitation, and she almost felt disgusted with herself for what she had been thinking. She gave her full attention back to her hostess.

"Can I ask you a few questions?" Dorothy said, taking a pad and pencil out of her bag. It was at times like this she wished she used a tape recorder, but her stenography was excellent and she knew that being taped made a lot of people edgy.

"Anything," Janice replied. "That's what I asked you here for."

"I know I've read written reports," Dorothy said. "But, if you could, if it isn't too difficult for you . . . could you tell me about that night, what *really* happened?"

It was a familiar story by now, but there were subtle differences in the published accounts and Janice Evans' narrative, and enormous differences between what she told Dorothy and what Winteroth had put on the screen. The biggest change came with the murder itself and how it had happened.

"I didn't actually rush into the room with Mrs. Prout until Paul had stopped . . . hitting her with the axe . . . but there was never any question in my mind, in anyone's mind, that he had done it. The way he had been acting just before . . . it was clear that something must have happened to him, to his mind.

"But I've always had these doubts . . . Was Paul out of his head, in the usual sense of the phrase, I mean, or—forgive me for saying this—did someone else take over his mind at the time, *make* him do that awful thing to Désirée. . . .?"

"Someone else?" Dorothy asked. She had read that Paul and the others had shared an interest in the occult—although Janice insisted the only time they ever held a seance or even talked about the spirit world was that night—but surely Janice didn't seriously think that there could be a supernatural explanation?

Janice saw the puzzled, disbelieving look on Dorothy's face. "Yes, this is where I usually lose everyone. How can I explain it so you don't think I'm crazy?" She looked heavenward and shook her fists, trying to come up with the right words. "Paul had been characterized by the media as a neurotic, psychotic crazy, an immoral black . . . *sensualist* . . . who took over the lives and bodies of two white girls, made them his slaves, and chopped one of them up when she rebelled. The movie *Vicious* changed his race, and made *me* the actual killer—but only served to perpetuate that same falsity by making Paul's filmic counterpart some kind of conscienceless stud."

"I know that Paul was gay," Dorothy said, trying to make things easier for the woman. "At least that's what some published reports have said."

"Yes, I'm sure he was," Janice nodded. "Looking back on it, he was gay in a very stereotypical way, not a 'screaming queen' necessarily, but delicate, dainty. God knows not all gay men are like that, I know. But at the time that's what we thought. The whole subject was so very shocking then. When I testified that he had never laid a hand on us I only made it worse. I think people would have preferred he was a hustling stud who preyed upon women than a blatant homosexual who kept his hands to himself. Suddenly he was a pervert in their eyes. Everyone knew that 'queers' weren't normal; they had sick tastes and passions. A colored homosexual? Paul didn't have a chance. The press painted him as a sick, sadistic woman-hater; just the kind of fantasy that appealed to the terrified white jurors. The *private* story that was passed around was hardly any better."

"But *didn't* Paul commit the murder, as you said earlier?"

"His were the hands that held the axe, that smashed it into Désirée's body, yes, but. . . ."

"But?"

Janice clenched her hands together, the years of strain, frustration and anguish evident on her face. "Dorothy, even when I was on the witness stand no one believed me when I told them about the things that happened in that room that night. I told you earlier that Paul seemed to go into a trance, that he then went berserk. What I didn't tell you—what I haven't told anyone since the trial"—she paused, reddened, then continued in a rush—"was that the *floor fumbled, the table shook, the air got cold*! All the cliched things that are supposed to happen during seances, I know. But they *did* happen. All these years later and I'm still as certain now as I was then—they *did happen!*" Bursting into tears, she dabbed at her eyes with a napkin but was soon under control again.

"Couldn't Paul Wilson have staged all that stuff? Somehow?"

"Aside from the fact that there was no reason for him to do that, that he wouldn't have had time, I don't see *how* he could have done it. I haven't told you how his voice changed, became impossibly deep, how his *features* changed: his mouth became wider and he vomited out gallons of this stuff, ectoplasm, I still don't know what it was. I spoke to him several times during the trial, though my parents and the lawyer didn't want me to. He had no memory of killing Désirée, I'm sure of it."

She added in a weak, tiny voice, "And I had such premonitions that night, before the seance. I passed it all off on my mood. But I knew something was going to happen. Somehow I knew. . . ."

Dorothy wanted to be sympathetic and understanding, but this all sounded like something out of a Hollywood movie, something like that *Demoniac*, in which a little boy is possessed by the devil and murders his family. "Are you trying to say that you thought Paul was *possessed*?"

Janice just looked at her for a moment, then she blurted out: "Yes, yes yes yes yes! Yes, he was possessed. That was the only possible explanation. Something took over his mind. He was a dear, sweet man, a gentle man, he was fond of us, loved Désirée—there was no reason for him to have done what he did. No reason at all." And the tears started falling again, this time so freely that it seemed like a liquid curtain had formed in front of her face. She pressed the napkin to her nose, and her shoulders shook with the agony of the memory.

"Dorothy, I know how crazy it sounds. My parents sent me to psychiatrists, the neighbors shunned us, my whole life changed for the worse. I've never forgotten that night. Never. I still have nightmares. Every time I'm alone with someone, I wonder—will the devil take them over too? Will they start gnashing their teeth and foaming at the mouth?" She calmed down a bit, crumbling her napkin in her fist. "Oh, it's not as bad now as it used to be. For a while there I was really on the edge of sanity." She let out a mirthless laugh, a bark of self-contempt. "Now you're *really* going to think I'm a reliable witness."

"Living through what you did would be enough to drive anyone—" Dorothy stopped short and looked down awkwardly at her hands. "It just sounds so . . . unbelievable. I don't mean to be unkind, Janice. I can imagine what you've been through."

"I don't think anyone can imagine what I've been through. To have your own family think that you're a liar. To be called a slut and a deranged, neurotic woman. To watch the most horrible, most significant event in your life turned into a vulgar, distorted piece of fiction. When I read about *Vicious Two* in the paper, I thought: Oh no, here it comes again. The barrage of fantasy and innuendoes. I must admit no one but Anthony Winteroth ever made me a *suspect* in the case. I'm not pleased to confess this, but when I read about what happened to his wife and son, I was almost *glad*. I thought 'Now you'll see how it feels; let them turn *your* life into a freakshow, let someone suggest that *you're* the one who killed them.' How I hated that man! Everyone connected to that picture."

It was scary. The way Janice Evans looked now, the rage and torment on her face, Dorothy could almost believe that she *could* have murdered her roommate, though she didn't really think that was the case. She touched the old woman's hand again. "Janice, stop upsetting yourself. I'm here and I'm listening to you, and I'm not going to make any judgments. I just want you to talk to me—calmly—and get it all out of your system." People wouldn't buy the demon-possession aspect of her story, but her thoughts on how the tragedy of Désirée Fontana's short life and horrible death had been turned into the stuff of popular entertainment could be important material. Certainly it was just the extra touch Dorothy's article could use. "Here. Take some more tea. Calm down. Then let it all out. I'm listening."

"There's not much more to say, I'm afraid. There's still so many unanswered questions." A faraway look came into her eyes and she talked in such a subdued tone that Dorothy had to strain to hear her. "Was I really so easily fooled? Was it all a game cooked up by Paul and Désirée, a game that went wrong?" Dorothy saw that under the strong, self-sufficient shell was a person who was barely keeping it together.

Janice pulled herself up straight again and looked Dorothy square in the eye. "Of course, there were all those years after the trial that I spent looking for answers. First, the psychiatrists—to help me 'adjust,' to help me regain my 'lost sanity.' They helped some. Got me back into the mainstream of life, I suppose, but they never got to the root of the problem. Then I turned to religion, but that was only a salve at best. Faith wasn't enough for me. I wanted to *know*, I wanted to *see*. Not having any answers wasn't good enough, as it never has been. To make matters worse, I was terrified of normal relationships, terrified of losing people who were close to me again, sick of unhappy love affairs, afraid that— as with Paul and Désirée—my closest relationships would turn out to be something *else*, something sinister. I couldn't trust anyone, not even myself.

"After my parents passed away—cancer and heart attack respectively, the same year—I went into hibernation again for a while, until some friends, who didn't know my true identity, got me back into the swing of things, going to auditions, what-have-you. I never married. Then," she paused to light a cigarette she had picked out of a gold case lying on the table near the cookies, "I turned to the occult."

Dorothy said nothing. Her tea was cold but she sipped it anyway. She didn't write anything down on her note pad, not sure if anything the woman was now saying would be worth remembering.

"I went to mediums, psychics, fortune tellers. I was convinced that something supernatural had happened the night Paul murdered Désirée, and I would not rest until I had been exonerated, in my own mind if no one else's. I met mostly fools and charlatans; had I been rich they would undoubtedly have sponged off me for years, told me anything I wanted to hear. Finally I met one man—not a psychic, but a 'professor of the occult,' you might say—who said something that reminded me of a detail about that dreadful night that I had almost forgotten.

"His name is Brian Asquith. He lives here in Los Angeles. I had been given his name by a friend, and was told he could tell me all about demonic possession. We sat and talked for hours—so nice to have someone who didn't think I was crazy, and who didn't seem crazy himself. It was when he told me the story of the four-fingered demon that I recalled something I had noticed during all the hysteria that night back in 1940."

She leaned closer to Dorothy and said: "Paul's hand. His left hand. Suddenly it was *missing* a finger. It was shrunken and shriveled, with long, thin nails and scaly flesh. The whole arm was affected. The hand was like a *claw*. But afterwards, it was normal; I noticed. He had all five fingers again. He didn't know anything about it."

This was getting more insane by the moment. Dorothy wondered if anything the woman said could be believed.

"And *then* I knew," Janice said. "That everything I'd thought I'd seen was *true*."

"What about this demon, this four-fingered demon? What is that?"

Janice stood up abruptly and held her hands together in front of her as if she were just about to pray. "I'm going to let Brian tell you about that. Brian Asquith."

"Janice, I—"

"Please, Dorothy. I know you're kind and understanding, an open-minded woman, but I also know that I've stretched both your patience and your belief. Oh, don't apologize. I would be surprised—and alarmed—if it were otherwise. But nothing I say from now on is going to sound real to you, not coming from me."

She went over to a desk in the corner and came back with a white slip of paper. "Please, for my sake, go talk to Brian

Asquith. Here's his address and number. If you're really interested in what happened that night—and I think you are—he may give you some answers. His story is incredible, but I think it's true. Remember, I was there. I saw with my own eyes, and I remember. There may be a story here that will make *Vicious* One and *Vicious* Two look like a collection of tired old recipes."

Janice took Dorothy's hand and held it for a moment, an old lady's way of telling this younger person to give her a *chance*. "Come back again, Dorothy. We'll talk some more. About the book. About women. About victims in general."

Well, what did she have to lose? Dorothy took the paper, thanked her hostess for the tea and cookies and the fascinating interview, and was escorted to the door.

Dorothy put the white slip in her bag and quickly made her way out of the building.

Strange, she thought.

Very Strange.

15

Harold Watson sat in his office and waited for his headache to subside.

Four aspirins, three shots of nasal spray, nothing would work on his sinuses. Damn it! He always got these debilitating attacks just when he had to be at his most alert. He had thought he had that location sewed up for next Friday's shooting on *Hell Warriors Part Three*, but now it looked as if the arrangements had still not been finalized. Where was Bethany? She should have taken care of this for him.

The main headquarters of Watson Productions, Inc. was on Montrose Avenue, a large cluttered establishment on the fifth floor with three big offices, a storage room, and a modest but attractive reception area. Every hour there was a bustle of activity in the office—several pictures were being worked on at once—and there were stories to read (submitted by agents), budgets to prepare, actors, directors, and writers to interview and hire, publicity campaigns to organize, costumes and set designs to go over and a hundred other things to do by the day before yesterday. If everyone didn't hold up their own end, there was havoc.

Watson dialed Bethany's number for the eleventh time that day. He knew that she had not intended coming in that morning;

she'd a full schedule of appointments around town. But she had promised to be back by one at the latest. Here it was two thirty, and she hadn't arrived, hadn't called the office, and hadn't gone home, if her unanswered telephone was any indication.

He wondered briefly if she could be sick or incapacitated. He thought about calling up the people she'd planned to see, but that would look as if he were checking up on her, as if one hand of his operation didn't know what the other one was doing. Besides, she had looked fine yesterday at quitting time. Flus and colds and whatnot didn't come on *that* suddenly. And that wouldn't explain why she hadn't used the telephone.

His secretary came in with a batch of the afternoon's mail. He flipped through it quickly, but saw nothing of outstanding importance. Damn—Bethany should be taking care of her end of things. If that location wasn't confirmed by the end of this week, the delay would be costly and annoying. And it all could have been avoided. Bethany was fast and efficient, normally punctual and courteous. But ever since her divorce she'd had this defensive manner about her that could really turn people off. It might have been *that* which was causing the problem. Maybe by not calling in she was trying to assert her independence or some such foolish notion.

He dialed her apartment one more time. If she didn't get in touch with him soon he would have to do her work for her.

A moment later he slammed down the phone. He swore that in the future he would doublecheck everything his associates did even if Wonder Woman herself flew in through the window on that robot plane of hers and asked him for a job.

Vivienne Cherneau wondered what on earth had compelled her to come here. These affairs were so dull and so difficult without dear Charlie at her side.

She sat on a long, decorated dais with several people, most of whom, like herself, were borderline stars from the forties. None of them were doing as much work currently as she was, but then, none of them had ever taken on such ill-advised projects as *Sweet Psychotic* or *Vicious Two*. She had hoped to stay out of the public limelight—and away from her peers—until that awful business in the *Hollywood Reporter* had faded away, but she'd forgotten the promise she'd made to attend this stupid convention.

The master of ceremonies was talking about her. They were going to give her an award, expect her to make a speech. She would have ducked under the table had there been room, an unlikely prospect considering her bulk. "Ladies and Gentlemen," a chubby Jewish man with a bald spot and a mustache pronounced, "I give you *Miss* Vivienne Cherneau."

The two-hundred or so nobodies sitting at their little round tables with plates of pale chicken and undercooked stringbeans applauded with gusto, that she had to admit. She wasn't sure if it were they or she who was the more pathetic.

"Thank you, thank you, you wonderful people," she said with all the theatrical insincerity she could muster. "I can't tell you how much this award from the"—she squinted at the inscription on the tiny plaque the man had given her—"*Movie Lovers Society of America* means to me. Out of all the awards I've received," she lied, "this one, perhaps, has touched me the most." *Oh, brother.*

There was more applause from the little people, in appreciation for which Vivienne did a rather grotesque curtsy. She curtsied to the right. "Thank you." She curtsied to the left. "Thank you." She curtsied to the center of the ballroom. "And thank you." She walked back to her seat with a comical flourish.

At least the people at *this* film convention looked normal. There had to be at least three dozen of these gatherings every year, film societies devoted to every kind of picture and every era of movie-making imaginable. Huge groupings of lonely people from the sticks came into the big city to goggle wide-eyed at long-forgotten stars—the only ones who'd attend their banquets—and trade stills and celebrity autographs with other people who shared their love of oldtime movies.

Gladys Cornbee, another old gal who had done a few pictures forty years ago, staggered out of her seat and did an arthritic stumble across the dais to receive her own plaque. Vivienne wondered where these societies dredged up these ancient losers. God, how low had she sunk in the past few years? Was she in the same category as Cornbee? At least Vivienne was still making movies. She was surprised to see that Cornbee was still breathing. And that vicious remark the old biddy had made earlier. "I'm so pleased you're being considered for an Academy Award, dear," Gladys had told her, referring to that ad in the *Hollywood Reporter*. "Of course, those kind of movies make me sick so I'm afraid I'll have to take the word of the critics as to the sterling caliber of your performance."

Get lost, Cornbee, you haven't made a picture since Washington crossed the Delaware, and if that's your own hair I'm Farrah Fawcett.

She'd almost sworn off these conventions—which her ego dragged her to each season whether she'd admit it or not—when the *Sinister Cinema Society* had held its Vivienne Cherneau Film Festival in 1984. She had gone with eager anticipation to the festival banquet on opening night, thrilled at the thought of being so honored, of not having to share the dais with a bunch of old has-beens. She figured they'd be showing some of the wonderful *film noir* thrillers she'd made in the forties, the detective melodramas in which she was usually cast as the lovely femme fatale who got the hero into trouble. She looked forward to meeting appreciative older film fans who had seen her in her heyday, to having them lavish her with love and affection.

Instead the "society" catered mostly to teenagers with punk hair cuts and leather jackets. These conventions always attracted some of the worst collections of freaks, fuck-ups, cretins and losers she had ever seen in her life, but the *Sinister Cinema Society* took the cake. There were people in the audience she wouldn't have wanted to meet in broad daylight, let alone a dark alley. They wore odd outfits and monster masks, made a terrible racket, and threw food and liquor into the air like demented children. The films of hers they liked included *Death Row Dolly* (1978); *Die, Die, My Lovely* (1974); *Attack of the Giant Fleshopods* (1957); *Pallbearer's Nightmare* (1983—Spanish with subtitles); *Slashed to Ribbons* (1979); and *Night of the Bloody Cleaver Part Five* (1983). Trash, trash, and more trash.

Worse yet, they admired Vivienne only as a camp figure, as some kind of macabre, bloated mischief-maker. She grabbed a copy of the society's newsletter and realized that these people *hooted* at her larger-than-life performances, *made fun* of her face and her figure. Halfway through the first screening—of *The New Orleans Hatchet Slaughter* (1979)—she had fled the premises, not caring that she was supposed to have talked about the movie and answered questions afterwards. If those were her fans these days, maybe it was better to be unknown like Gladys Cornbee.

There were still six people on the dais tonight who had not yet received their plaques. They had taken an endless time to get started, taken forever to get the food served, fussed around with mikes and chairs and the seating arrangements until she thought that she would scream. Vivienne couldn't take much more of this. Some of these people were nice enough, sincere admirers of both her and the movies' golden period. But as much as she would have liked to return to the past, she was frankly tired of living in it. Wasn't that why she had taken jobs like *Slashed to Ribbons*, anything to keep working and stay in vogue?

Surreptitiously, she put her plaque in her bag, and slowly eased out of her seat, pretending that she was answering a call of nature and would be right back in a moment.

Outside the ballroom she got her coat from the coat check and headed swiftly for the elevator.

I did it I did it I did it, she giggled as the car descended to the lobby.

She was snapped out of her mood of freedom and exhilaration when she got back to her apartment.

Hester was standing by the door holding a broom in her hand like a weapon, chattering a mile a minute and shaking like a jackhammer.

"Hester! Shut up! What is it?"

"Oh, Mrs. Cherneau. He was trying to force the lock, trying to get inside. It was horrible."

"*Who*, Hester? Hester, *what happened*?"

Hester lifted her tear-stained face and stared morosely at her employer. "Mrs. Cherneau. Someone tried to break in!"

Lord! In the middle of the day yet! "These hoodlums get more brazen every day," Vivienne said. Then she thought: *Suppose it wasn't a burglar? What if it was the maniac? The maniac who killed Doug and Edna Longbank?*

"I scared him off, Mrs. Cherneau. I screamed and banged on the door with my broom. He ran down the hall before I could call the police."

Good, Vivienne thought. If the police had come this would have wound up as an item in the *National Inquisitor*.

"You said 'he.' Did you see who it was, Hester?"

"No. I just figured it was a man. Burglars are usually men, aren't they?" She scrunched up her face and tried to hold back the tears. Vivienne had never realized the girl was quite so nervous and hysterical.

A burglar, she thought. *If that's only who it was.*

She gasped.

A few minutes sooner and she might have ran into him in the hall. And what if he came back tonight, when she was fast asleep in her bed and Hester was home safe in hers; when dear Hester wasn't there to 'scare him off?'

"Quick, Hester," she said. "Make me a martini. A double."

She rushed to the bedroom to change her clothes.

Brian Asquith was not the freak Dorothy had expected him to be. She expected a dapper, slender phony with a silken voice and an English accent, wearing a dressing gown, oozing insincerity by the cartload, and sizing up her bank account with his beady little eyes. His apartment would be in an old brownstone and have red curtains and eerie, awful paintings of quaint medieval atrocities covering the walls, and maybe an empty suit of armor in the corner. The only illumination would come from candles, of course.

Brian Asquith was actually a very contemporary kind of fellow. He was of medium height, possibly in his mid-forties, though his features were unlined and youthful. He had a round open face and dark blue eyes, lips just short of being full and a nose just short of being bulbous. His short brown hair was parted neatly to one side and his face was cleanshaven. The way he walked, his mannerisms, suggested a confident, easy masculinity.

He took her down the hall of his condo and led her into a large living room with blue walls and modern furnishings. The only things he had on the wall were a mirror over the sofa, and two small paintings—of Montmartte in Paris, and the Piazza Navona in Rome—on either side of a large brown bookcase. As Janice had, he shared the sofa with Dorothy and suggested she put her bag down on the wooden table in front of them. The top of the table, as well as the shelf underneath, were crammed with magazines and pamphlets.

"Can I get you a drink?" he said.

"If you're going to have one yourself. . . .?"

"Yes. I drink Scotch. Is that all right with you?"

"Yes. On the rocks. With a little soda if you have it."

"Of course."

As he prepared the drinks at the bar in the corner, she studied him more closely. He was wearing tan jeans and a tee shirt, not the fancy robe and peaked sorcerer's cap she'd expected. His accent was definitely mid-American, with just a hint of California.

"Were you born in Los Angeles, Mr. Asquith?"

"England, actually," he replied, stirring the drinks with a cocktail straw. "But I was brought to America when I was just a babe. I grew up mostly in Chicago; also lived on a lot of Air Force bases. My mother and I went where my father was posted. It was fun, most of the time. And you?"

She gave him an expurgated version of her life and times in Glendale, New York. When he handed her her drink and sat down beside her, she said, "Thank you for seeing me on such short notice. But as I told you on the phone, I'm really here only as a favor to Madeline—I mean, Janice. You know her real name of course."

"Yes, I know Janice very well. And I know why you're here, too. Janice called me about five minutes after you did. She'd been trying all afternoon, as you had, but as you know I only got back a little while ago."

"Yes."

"Janice was very pleased when I told her you had gotten in touch with me. Now, shall I just start at the beginning? Or do you have a particular question?"

Dorothy stopped sipping her drink and nodded with vigor. "Janice mentioned something about a four-fingered demon. Said it had something to do with Paul Wilson. That she thought he had been possessed when he murdered Désirée Fontana. She told me that you could explain what she was talking about."

"Before I do that, let me ask you: what is your interest in the Fontana case? Aside from a writer's curiosity."

"I'm not sure I *am* interested in any of this," she said. "My belief in the supernatural isn't terribly acute. I admit there are things we don't know about, but that's about as far as it goes."

She took another sip of the Scotch. "But Janice practically begged me to see you. So . . . here I am."

"Hmmm. A non-believer. This will be fun. Well, I might as well warn you that what I'm going to tell you now isn't going to make you any less of a skeptic. In fact, it will probably make it worse."

"Is the story *that* incredible?"

"Four-fingered demons? What do you think?"

"But you believe it? You believe Janice's story?"

"Let's just say I've seen things with my own eyes that would make your hair stand on end." He narrowed his eyes and looked at her intensely for a moment. "Can I tell you a little bit of my background before I begin?"

"Be my guest."

"At first I was just as skeptical as you are. I spent very little time even thinking about the occult. When I first moved out here fifteen years ago, I was just another aspiring young actor who had to wait on tables or starve."

Dorothy frowned. "There's an epidemic of that in L.A., isn't there?"

"And in New York everyone's a starving writer," Asquith countered.

"Touché."

"Anyway, I soon realized that my talents and chances were extremely limited, and realized I would need a second 'career' to fall back on. A friend of mine was very interested in spiritualism: tarot cards, ouija boards, seances, astral projection—you name it, he did it. Or at least he said he did."

"Your friend was a phony?"

"Like a dollar bill with Dolly Parton's picture on it."

"Nice guy."

"Well, I wasn't so nice, either. His intensity and pretentiousness used to annoy me. One night at one of his seances, I jumped up and discovered the tape recorder from where the 'mysterious voices' we were hearing were coming from. I exposed all of his tricks one after the other. You must understand—this was worse than merely breaking up someone's parlor trick. This guy was actually beginning to make a living at milking the rubes. His mistake was in numbering me among them."

"I take it you and he are no longer speaking?"

Asquith was silent for a moment, as if wondering if he should say what he was thinking. Finally he said, "Yes. You might put it that way." He rubbed his brow as if trying to repress an unpleasant memory and continued. "My friend lost his vocation, but I had found one. There are a lot of phony spiritualists and mediums in California, bilking an awful lot of people, literally stealing millions of dollars a year. What would those same foolish people pay to someone who could prove they were being cheated? My friend had inadvertently taught me the tricks of the trade, so it was a cinch for me to expose them. Why become another phony medium when there were already so many in town. Why not become a—"

"—ghostbreaker?"

"Yes, Dorothy, a ghostbreaker, instead. Which is what happened. But now comes the odd part of the story." He finished his Scotch in a few gulps and leaned back comfortably on the sofa. "At first I found quite a lot of resistance. Here were these pathetic people, people who wanted to make contact with their loved ones who'd 'passed on,' people who needed guidance, some assurance that there was life after death and that husbands and wives could be reunited. I had to tread very softly, approach them with the utmost of care. I had to convince them that just because the world of occultism was a tub of bullshit didn't necessarily mean there was no God, no life everlasting.

"But, eventually, I got through to them. I got my first clients by attending seances and approaching the participants afterwards. Later my reputation spread by word of mouth. I never told all of a particular medium's clients that he or she was a phony—only the ones who paid."

Dorothy gave him a playful smirk. "Now is that ethical?"

"Wait a moment." He held up his hand. "Do you realize how many enemies I would have made? How many people would have been out to get me? Some people think if someone is so gullible and desperate as to go to a medium, they deserve being taken in. I don't. But there *are* a lot of people who will only believe what they want to believe.

"Anyway, after a while clients began coming to me, wealthy men and women who were paying out thousands to these mediums, making business decisions according to their whims, building them temples and letting them rule their lives. They wanted to know if these people were legit. And ninety-nine times out of a hundred, they weren't."

This story was interesting, but Dorothy couldn't see what it had to do with Janice Evans. Was Asquith deliberately holding back, trying to build her anticipation? " 'But?' " she asked. "There is a 'but,' isn't there?"

"The 'but,' as you put it, is the hundredth time, the one time out of a hundred when I *could not prove* that the medium was faking."

"Maybe they were just more clever than you."

He nodded. "Yes, yes. I'm humble enough to admit that that was a possibility. In *some* cases. But not in all of them. By that time, I knew every scam and con in the book. All these mediums use the same bag of tricks, with an occasional, subtle variation. I could smell a phony the minute I saw one."

"So you're telling me there *is* something to the occult."

"Well, a lot of it is a matter of public record," he said. "There has been documented proof of ESP, telekinesis, other paranormal activities."

"But that's a branch of science," she argued. "We're talking about the supernatural."

"Ah yes, but that's just my point. Listen, if a person can muster enough will power to bend a metal spoon without touching it, to send a message mentally to someone else in another room, or another town, to pick up thoughts and feelings about a missing person just from that person's glove, isn't it possible that a person could also project himself into a dimension that we can't see, could keep his energy—or soul, if you will—alive after his body had died? To me everything supernatural is just a branch of science, a branch that human beings are only just beginning to perceive, let alone understand."

Dorothy chuckled. "Something tells me we're leading up to demons."

He laughed. "Yes, I'm afraid so. I believe there are alien intelligences, forces of will and energy, that exist all around us—but we can't see them. Whether these are the leftover energies of dead people, or the life forces of other-dimensional beings—or both—is something I can't tell you. But I've seen too many things over the years that have absolutely no other explanation."

"Like the four-fingered demon?"

"*No*, thank goodness. That's a force I could very well do without encountering."

"What *is* it?"

He paused. "Finish your Scotch and let me get you another. My dear, this is a story that will positively curl your hair."

Harold Watson parked his car down the street from Bethany's apartment and disembarked. She hadn't called in all day, hadn't answered her phone, and he was worried. It was not like Bethany to be so inconsiderate.

She kept a set of spare keys to her apartment in a desk in the office. Harold had taken them with him so he could open her door—just in case, just in case she had met with an accident, or, God forbid, foul play. After what had happened to the Longbanks. . . .

He had thought of calling the police, asking them to accompany him or investigate on their own. But he was afraid he might inadvertently get Beth into trouble. Everyone knew about her drug problem; she said she'd licked it, but you never knew. What if he walked in with the police and there was Bethany on her couch or in the bathroom, zonked out on some sort of illegal substance? The poor woman had had enough trouble these past few years without him making things worse.

He only hoped she hadn't O.D'd on whatever she might be taking.

He opened the lobby door, went quickly to the elevator, and went up to the third floor where her apartment was located. As he walked down the corridor he was struck by the building's total silence. He heard no noises at all: no TV sets or stereos, no children at play. He smelled no cooking odors, either. Bethany hadn't been kidding when she'd said the walls were so thick you could get murdered and no one would know it. Harold shuddered and sent the morbid thought back where it came from.

He rang the bell repeatedly, waiting five minutes in case she was on the toilet or in the shower. Then he fitted his key into the lock. The door opened a crack. "Bethany, are you there?" No answer. He repeated his query. *Silence.* He decided to investigate, just to make *sure*

The moment he stepped into the living room he knew that

something had happened. He saw plants all over the floor, dirt crushed into the carpet. There was a bloody footprint over near the wall. And, on the other side of the room near the sofa, *so much blood*. Everywhere.

He backed away, horrified. To see something like this, to have something like this happen in the movies was bad enough, but to have it happen *for real* to someone you knew . . . Harold felt the bile rising in his throat, his pulse racing. He had to get out, had to get out of this abattoir. He didn't want to see what the killer had done to Bethany, didn't want to have to live with the memory of it for the rest of his life.

He was at the door, trembling with fear and disgust, when he thought that perhaps Bethany might still be alive. *All that blood.* Yet she could have merely injured herself; she could be lying unconscious somewhere, helpless and dying. If by his inaction he was responsible for her death he would never forgive himself. Hadn't he ought to make sure? He could call the police straight away, but what if they got there too late? He was no paramedic, but he did know how to apply tourniquets—in case she had cut herself. He could lift a person's face up out of the water if it had flopped down into a bathtub. Yes. He made up his mind. He had to do it for Bethany's sake.

He went quickly through the living room and headed for the hallway that led to the bedroom and the bathroom. He was sure he'd find Bethany somewhere in that section of the apartment.

The smell was horrible. There was blood all over the walls. *It's bad*, he told himself, *awful bad*. There was no way she could still be alive. *Get out of here, for God's sake. Get out of here! You know you don't want to see this!*

Too late. His eyes widened in shock and horror and he could feel his mind and stomach convulsing.

Bethany. Pieces of her. Arranged helter skelter along the hallway from the bathroom to his feet.

Watson bent over, knelt down, and threw up all over the floor.

When he had sufficiently recovered, he pulled himself back up to his feet and ran screaming out of the apartment.

16

At the hotel room, Jimmy picked up on the first ring.
"Hello?"
"Jimmy, it's Dorothy."
"Where have you been? It's—"
"I was talking to Janice Evans, the real Janice Evans."
"You mean that wasn't a joke?" He heard a noise in the background. A man's voice, laughing.
"No, it wasn't a joke, Jimmy."
"Where are you now?"
"I'm talking to a man who's giving me more information about the case. I tried getting you earlier, after I spoke to Janice, but you must have been out at the studio."
"Yeah, I was. Just got back a minute ago. Are we going to eat together tonight or what?"
"Jimmy, I've already eaten! The man I'm talking to lives in the same neighborhood as Janice Evans, but he wasn't home until now. I didn't feel like going all the way back to the Bellmore so I had an early supper at a place around here to kill some time, hoping he'd eventually show up—and I got lucky." The man that Janice was with made another indecipherable noise in the background.

"What's going on, Dottie? Where the hell did you run into Janice Evans. And who's *this* guy?"

"I'll tell you all about it later. Have to go now." She made a kissing sound. "Bye."

"But—" She hung up. Jimmy replaced the receiver and went into the bathroom to take a shower.

Damn. Another day that the two of them were running around in different directions. Some vacation. He made up his mind: he was going to go back to that club tonight—or maybe another like it. Maybe more than one.

He was beginning to enjoy the feeling of being single. Beginning to enjoy the nightlife, the cruising, meeting strange, seductive women, touring the bars alone.

Alone.

He was really beginning to like it.

Dorothy put down the phone and thanked her host again. "I didn't want him to worry." Though he had sounded more angry than worried.

Brian gave out again with that funny laugh of his, a sort of half-giggle, half-snort that would have been offensive had he not done it with such conviviality. "You just wanted to make sure someone knew where you were. And that *I* knew someone was expecting you later." He handed her a fresh Scotch and soda. "Are you afraid I might poison your drink and have my way with you?"

"If I was afraid of that," she said, taking the drink as she leaned back on the couch's spongy cushions, "I would have given him your name and address."

He looked at her peculiarly. "Why didn't you?"

"Jimmy doesn't have to know where I am every minute." She wondered: was Asquith flirting with her, trying to get her drunk; was he getting ready to make a pitch? She couldn't figure him. He'd seemed so nice when she'd first arrived, so nice and normal. He was still nice—too nice—but an element seemed to have been added that hadn't been there before. Or was it just the liquor? But was it going to her head or to his? She had to admit she was beginning to find Brian Asquith quite attractive. "You were going to tell me about the four-fingered demon," she said.

"Ah yes." He revolved the cocktail glass in his hands, looked down at the golden liquid that was shining in the sunlight from the window. "The story is very famous in occult circles. With just enough tantalizing proof—of sorts—to make it all the eerier. Mind you, Dorothy, I'm not saying this is true. Only that it could be."

"Go ahead. I'm listening."

"The four-fingered demon has no name. At least none that I know of. But it's supposed to be a mischievous, diabolical—what would you call it?—creature, life force, that can take over the minds of susceptible human beings and force them to commit unspeakable atrocities against themselves and their loved ones. It's said that this four fingered demon—also known as 'the claw'—has existed for at least a century."

"Pretty young for a demon."

"I suppose so." He grinned. "But you know how cruel children can be. Anyway, there has been documented evidence over the past hundred years, recorded in books on the occult, of course, which suggests that the story of the demon might be more than just an old wives' tale."

"What evidence?"

"I'm getting to that. It's been said that when the demon possesses a person's body, a miraculous physical change comes over them. *Besides* acting strange and taking axes to their friends, that is. There's one particular detail that crops up in all the recorded cases. The left arm of the person being possessed, no matter what condition it may have been in before—the age, sex or race of the person makes no difference—shrivels up, becomes wrinkled and bony like that of an old woman. The hand becomes a claw, with the middle finger missing—and develops long, sharp nails that can literally tear off a person's flesh." He paused to let it sink in and sipped his Scotch.

"Brian!" She hadn't meant to use his first name, but it had just slipped out. "I'm sorry, but that's the most ridiculous story I've ever heard."

"Yes, it is. Far-fetched, ridiculous, crazy, imbecilic. But *I* think there's something to it."

"You can't be serious." She took another good, healthy swallow of her drink. It was strong. She reminded herself to go easy. But she was feeling so good, so comfortable.

"Yes, Dorothy, I'm serious." He got to his feet and paced around nervously, avoiding the intensity of her stare. "I was lying a minute ago when I said that this story *might* be true. With all my heart and soul, I believe it *is* true. The four-fingered demon exists. It's real. And it's been responsible for countless murders, for the damning of dozens of innocent people over the decades. I've devoted a lot of time in the past few years to finding out as much as I can about the demon. I've made a lot of money as a ghostbreaker, almost enough to retire. Now I spend most of my time doing something I thought I'd never do. Trying to *prove*—instead of disprove—that the four-fingered demon is real."

Dorothy was confused. "This is certainly a reversal, Mr. Asquith, isn't it? From what you were telling me before? About how it was all a lot of bunk?"

"Not *all* of it, remember? I told you I came up against things I couldn't explain. I spent years studying the occult, reading every book I could get my hands on, going into dusty bookstores to seek out ancient tomes and parchments, just to be able to know more than my opponents, the fake mediums, did. I had to be one up on all the fakes, because they knew their territory well. But as I read the more recent material, the story of the four-fingered demon kept appearing. I became as much of an expert on it as anyone."

Dorothy was getting impatient. "What has this got to do with Désirée Fontana? Are you saying that it was this four-fingered demon that possessed Paul Wilson? Really, Brian—haven't you ever heard of multiple personalities? *Sybil*, *Three Faces of Eve*, and others. *That* I could buy. Paul Wilson's 'second self' comes out for some reason and murders his closest friend for Lord knows why." She muttered, "The only one who'd know would be that second personality, and *it* died when Paul Wilson did." Then, in a stronger voice: "But *demons*, Brian? Be serious! This *is* the twentieth century, after all."

He sat back down and patted her hand like a principal

counseling a backward student. "Dorothy, let me go a little further, okay? All that I ask is that you keep an open mind. All right?"

Annoyed at his patronizing manner, she nevertheless agreed.

"Let's look at the facts. Janice Evans—an eyewitness—says that Paul Wilson's hand transformed itself into a claw while he was murdering Désirée Fontana. She saw it. She remembers it."

"That was over forty years ago and Janice Evans is a very mixed-up lady," Dorothy argued. "Not that I blame her. How do you know all of this claw stuff wasn't *planted* in her mind? The power of suggestion? Isn't it odd that she would repress that detail, as she told me she did, until you just *happened* to tell her about the demon? Brian, Janice Evans is an emotionally disturbed woman looking for answers. She'll cling to anything. Maybe you took advantage of her the way all these charlatans you exposed took advantage of their clients." Why was she sitting here listening to this when Jimmy was at the hotel waiting for her?

"Dorothy, will you listen to me! Don't you think I considered that possibility? But there's more. It so happens that Anthony Winteroth's brother-in-law, Stephen Chambers, is a friend of mine. He has access to information about the murder of his sister, the apparent suicide of his nephew, that no one else has. Details that were never released to the public. You're familiar with the case?"

She nodded, but Asquith insisted on repeating the details. "There's a *darker* connection between the murders of the Winteroths and Désirée Fontana." He got up again and stood over her dramatically. "Stephen told me that when young Gerald Winteroth was laid out in his coffin, they had to cover up his neck—because of the throat injury—*and* his left arm. You know why? Because what had once been the normal limb of a healthy seventeen-year-old boy, had become a shriveled, bony appendage with a four-fingered hand, a *claw*, on the end of it. No one could explain it. The man saw this with his own eyes, Dorothy. His own eyes.

"Gerald died while still in the demon's posession, that's why his arm didn't change back to normal. Paul Wilson, on the other hand, was still alive when the demon departed his body—leaving him to face the music of the murder *it* had actually committed—and that's why his arm reverted to normal, and why no one ever saw it but his victim and Janice Evans. Stephen Chambers told me what he saw late one night when he was drunk and rambling, long before I ever told him about the demon. The next day when he was sober I pressed his about it and he confirmed it. He's never understood what really happened. Just as his late brother-in-law, Winteroth, died without ever knowing what happened. Because what happened is beyond belief."

He put down his drink and went over to a file cabinet in one corner of the living room. "I've contacted police departments all across the country, even Europe. There have been hundreds of cases like this. Eyewitnesses who swear they noticed something odd about the murderer's hand. Killers who can't remember why they did things they did. Corpses in the morgue—of people who suddenly go berserk after years of contentment, who kill themselves after murdering their spouses or their offspring—that have *claws* instead of hands. Claws with four fingers. It's all documented here, Dorothy. Every bit of it."

In spite of her disbelief, Dorothy was getting frightened. "There are always explanations—rational explanations—for everything, Brian. Evidence can be faked, can't it? Witnesses can be led, can see things during their hysteria that weren't really there. There's *no such thing* as demons! For God's sake, my parents weren't murdered by a demon—"

"What? *Oh*, yes," Brian said. His forehead crinkled with sudden realization. "Janice told me about your tragedy. I *am* sorry, Dorothy. But I never said that the man who killed your parents was possessed by the four-fingered demon. Every year there are tens of thousands of homicides in this country. Most of them are committed by angry relatives or muggers or psychopaths. Not by demons, four-fingered or otherwise. Wouldn't it be nice if we could blame all of mankind's cruelty on demons? No, I may be talking about a lot of cases here, but they're merely a fraction of the number of violent crimes that have actually been committed."

Dorothy was still bugged. She had spent years hating crazy, demented Lawrence O'Connell—the thought that he might have been under the spell of some demon, that some fancy lawyer could have gotten him off on such an utterly absurd defense, was enough to enrage her. Then she wondered what it would have been like for O'Connell, in the institution, if he really hadn't done it, if he had no memory of doing it, and had been imprisoned unjustly. But no, O'Connell had never claimed innocence: he'd been proud of his crimes. And no one had seen any claws, on his left arm or elsewhere. O'Connell and her parents, at least, had not been victims of this crazy four-fingered demon.

"I'm sorry, Brian," she said. "But I just can't believe any of this."

Asquith tapped the file cabinet. "Want to see proof? I've even got pictures."

Dorothy had drunk the Scotch and soda too fast; she felt flushed, too warm, in spite of the air conditioning. "No, I— maybe there's something to what you say. It's just that . . . that it's tough enough to deal with *people* hurting one another without dragging demons into it, too." She started to get up. "I think I'd better be going."

"One last thing," he said, coming over and taking the glass from her hand. "I'm sorry I've upset you, and I'm only going to make it worse, but this I've got to say."

Dorothy didn't want to listen, but he was giving her no choice. "This demon apparently has a sick sense of humor." Asquith said. "It not only killed Désirée Fontana, but it murdered the family of the man who made a *film* about the crime. I can't explain its motives or its actions, how it chooses its victims—although I have theories—but I can tell you one thing: The deaths of Ms. Fontana and the Winteroths may not have been mere coincidence. They could be part of a pattern. . . ."

"A pattern. . . .?"

"What I'm trying to tell you, Dorothy, is that this film you're reporting on, this *Vicious Part Two*? Well, it could be a hot potato."

Dorothy grabbed her pocketbook. She was about to turn to

him and say goodbye, but what he was saying could not be ignored.

"Two people connected with the movie have already been murdered," Asquith continued. "Doug and Edna Longbank. Two people killed by a maniac. *How many more will there be?*"

Brian stood so close to Dorothy that they were practically touching noses. She could smell the liquor on his breath and it was much too sweet and provocative. "What if that maniac is someone *else* associated with the movie?" he suggested. "Someone you might see every day. Someone you've already talked to. Someone who's been possessed by the demon at least once—and doesn't even know it. Someone who may be possessed *again*—at which time they will undoubtedly murder someone else.

"Please, Dorothy." He grabbed her hand and pressed it inside his own, his face alive with surprising concern and frustration. "Be careful. Very careful.

"You could be in terrible danger."

George Piedmont had been having the most pleasant dream—an erotic one involving Marilyn Monroe *and* Marilyn Chambers—when he was awakened by someone knocking on his door. His head shot up off the pillow, visions of Marilyns dissolving behind his eyelids. "Coming," he yelled. Now who the hell could this be?

When he opened the door he was surprised to see who his visitor was. "Well, hello there," he said embarrassed. The place was such a mess, hardly fit for company. He hadn't the slightest idea what his visitor could possibly want with him anyway. George stood there awkwardly in the doorway. Funny, his guest didn't look too good.

"Come in, come in," he said, moving aside so the visitor could step in from the hallway. "Sorry this place is such a dump. What can I do for you? Can I get you some water?"

The visitor said yes to the offer. George went over to the large sink in the corner kitchen area to get the water. He had just the one large room, which was filthy, plus a tiny bathroom at the end of a short, narrow hallway. The furnishings consisted of a battered TV, old rolltop desk, two chairs, and a convertible sofa-bed against the wall in which he slept. He saw with dismay that his visitor was sitting down on the sloppy, unmade bed, and wished that he bothered changing the sheets more than once a month. They were full of crumbs and dirty underwear, and stained from booze and his bodily fluids.

He came over with the water and handed it to his visitor, who still looked rather pale. The visitor had a shopping bag, which had been placed on the floor near the bed. "Finished my scenes in *Vicious Two* today," George said. "Think I did pretty good. All I had to do was stand there and get murdered. Had a few drinks too many at Telly's down the street afterwards. Came home to have a nap before dinner. Say, what time is it?" George looked at his wristwatch. "That late. Good thing you came by. I might have slept till morning." Which is exactly what he had planned to do until this completely unexpected interruption. "Now what is it I can do for you, hmmm? Are you feeling better?"

"Better," said the visitor. "Thank you for the water." The visitor spoke like a zombie, like something out of *Bloody Day of the Diabolical Dead*. And that strange expression on the face. The visitor reached into the shopping bag and came up with a long, thin instrument with a sharp, pointed tip. "Say, is that the prop they used on me this morning? Sure looks like it." As George bent down to look at the ice pick his visitor was holding, he noticed something strange about the hand that was holding it.

"Hey, what's the matter with your hand?" His eyes lit up as he reached out and touched it. "Feels *real*. Say, your whole *arm* looks funny!"

That's when the visitor's hand dropped the ice pick and shot out to grab George's face with its four withered fingers.

"Hey—whatcha doin'! Let go!" There was surprising strength in those fingers, unnatural strength and uncanny ferocity. "Hey! You're hurting me!"

The pain he felt was so intense he couldn't make a move to free himself. His arms made feeble efforts to pull the hand away, but were unsuccessful. The-hand-that-was-a-claw held tight to George's face, digging its long, sharp nails into his skin.

"*Arghhh!*" George felt such incredible agony. "Whatcha

doin'!" His features were all squished together so that his lips looked blubbery and comical. His pinched cheeks were flattened up against his crooked teeth, and the visitor's grip was almost *crunching* his jaw. He'd never felt such pain.

"My face, my face," he screamed, but it came out sounding something like *memphis memphis*. The nails of the claw were puncturing his skin, scratching against the gums inside his mouth, slicing his tongue to ribbons. Blood was pouring out of his face and dripping down over the hand that wouldn't let go. "Arghhhh!"

This was real this was real this was real. Real blood. Real flesh being torn. Not like this morning when Eddie Petrano had sat him down and dabbed this stuff all over his face, and Eddie's assistants had brought out a dummy head that they would use for the closeups when the killer shoved an ice pick into his eyes.

The ice pick!

George's visitor had picked up the ice pick in the other hand, was now lifting it up and positioning it in front of George's face. "Heaven help me!" George screamed, but the sound that came out was just a muffled wheeze of hysteria.

The ice pick stabbed out. Once. Twice. Puncturing first one eyeball, then the other. George couldn't see. *I've been blinded.* How much pain could a human being endure? Why couldn't he fall into blessed unconsciousness? *Help me, help me, help me!* Blood was dripping onto his feet, he could feel it. *Why me?*

With a sudden, ferocious squeeze, the claw tightened on his face and his mind went as black as his eyesight. There came a crackling, *squishy* sound, and George dropped like a stone to the floor.

The visitor reached down into the shopping bag and pulled out a heavy, black claw hammer.

Holding the hammer in the four-fingered hand, the visitor got up off the bed and knelt down beside the unconscious Piedmont. The actor's breathing was weak, his face smashed beyond recognition. The visitor made repeated blows to the scalp with the round, blunt head of the hammer. Finally, the skull caved in, unleashing a gruesome stew of blood and brain matter.

Then the visitor used the prongs of the hammer to pull the

soggy brain out of its cavity. Alternately pounding and clawing, pounding and clawing, it turned the head into an indescribable splattering of grisly bits and pieces.

17

The next morning Dorothy woke up feeling refreshed and with only the vaguest sense of uneasiness. It was only when she remembered the events of the day before that she started to really feel unsettled.

Jimmy was still sleeping, but she wouldn't wake him. It was obvious from his condition that for the second night in a row he'd gone out drinking. A lot of drinking—and what else? she wondered. They weren't married, she was not his jailer, but they did have a commitment to each other and she did not treat that commitment lightly. She'd always told him that if he fooled around she just didn't want to know about it. Well, he should have cleaned himself up and changed his clothes before passing out. He may not have slept with another woman, but he'd certainly been in the vicinity. Was this his "seven year itch" starting to come in a little early?

As she washed her face and got into her clothes, the thoughts of yesterday's strange conversations came back to her. Janice Evans, Brian Asquith. That awful story about a four-fingered demon. The murders. Brian's warning. *You could be in terrible danger.* The thought of a world in which invisible demons walked about and from time to time, without warning, arbitrarily turned people into monsters, was so unreal and scary that she could scarcely deal with it. She refused to accept even the suggestion that it was true. A person could sleep easier that way.

She'd had no rape nightmares since she'd come to Los Angeles, no dreams about her parents or Lawrence O'Connell. Was it because she was coming to terms with those awful occurrences, that she had finally met other women who'd suffered as she did and had talked it all out to understanding listeners?

Two people dead. Killed by a maniac. How many more will there be?

She left the room and went down to the coffee shop to have a late breakfast. She bought a paper, which she intended to read in a booth while she consumed a mushroom omelet, but found her mind wandering in so many directions that she couldn't follow the words on the page. She closed the paper and let the thoughts wash over her.

What if that incredible story of Brian's was true? Poor Paul Wilson. To be—in one sense—entirely innocent of the crime, to have no memory of having committed it. Yet to be on trial before hateful, unsympathetic jurors, having your protests fall on deaf ears. She wondered if any demonologists like Brian had been called in to testify; psychiatrists, even. There was still the possibility that Wilson had had a split personality. But if he actually had been taken over by an otherworldly spirit, a malevolent life form, his last weeks on earth must have been agony for him. Everyone thinking he was crazy until he had probably thought so, too. And the poor man died without knowing the truth.

She let the busboy refill her coffee cup. It was just too grim and fantastic a subject to dwell upon for long. Better to plan the day's activities. That talk with Janice Evans, and Asquith, had thrown everything out of whack. Should she bother talking to Janice Evans again? How could Dorothy sell the woman's story to any serious publication when she insisted on sticking to that silly demonic fairy tale? It was just no good that way. Dorothy had no desire to write a book that would make her the laughing stock of the publishing industry, though she had no doubt many people would buy it—both the book *and* Janice's theory, that is. Well, she wasn't *that* desperate for money.

She was about to ask for a piece of apple pie, when Jimmy slid into the seat next to her and gave her a kiss on the cheek. He had showered and changed his clothes. She was not going to ask where he'd been last night. Better not to know.

"Not finished eating, are you?" he asked, smiling.

"No. I'm going to have some pie now."

"That sounds good." The waitress came over. "Pie and coffee, that's all I want."

The woman took their orders and walked away.

"So, what have you been up to?" he asked.

"If you're in the mood and wide awake enough, I have quite a story to tell you."

"I'm listening."

So she told him about Janice Evans and Asquith and the demon with the hand with four fingers. He took it all without saying a word, aside from asking for clarification or elaboration on some points. His expression registered neither amazement nor disbelief. On the contrary, it was as if he had *no idea* of how to take it all.

"So, don't just sit there!" Dorothy said. "Are those people crazy? Or *did* a demon murder Doug and Edna Longbank? Are there going to be more murders? There's nothing anyone can do for Paul Wilson or the Winteroths any more, but if there's a chance to keep someone else from being murdered. . . .?"

Jimmy put down his cup and assumed a thoughtful pose. "It's pretty incredible. And yet, if there's one thing I believe, it's that there are lots of things that are outside the range of human experience. Things that we can't understand."

"You think the story is true?"

"Not necessarily. I'm just open-minded about it. If we can believe in God and the Devil, if we live in an age where people can change their sex, create new life forms through genetic engineering, send space probes to distant planets—what's so terribly strange about a malevolent creature from an alternate dimension that likes to slay people on occasion?

"That's what always kills me about people," he said, folding his arms across his chest. "They'll put their faith in unseen supreme beings, devils even, but find it so hard to believe in ghosts and goblins. If you look at the supernatural with scientific objectivity, maybe it's not as crazy as it sounds."

"Yes, Brian suggested that. That the supernatural was simply a more esoteric branch of science."

"Brian is probably right," Jimmy said, deliberately pronouncing the name with a somewhat hostile emphasis.

Well, let him be jealous, Dorothy thought. *Brian is a damned attractive man, even if he is a little weird.* And she had to admit that part of her wanted *strongly* to see him again, to show Jimmy that he wasn't the only one who could fiddle with "outside entertainment."

"It gives me the shivers," Dorothy said out loud, "just to think about it. To think that at any time some demon could possess you and make you murder people you loved and no one would ever believe you didn't do it. The grief you'd feel, the confusion, the horror. Brian said there's only been a few cases like that out of thousands of 'regular' murders, but even a small percentage over a century adds up to a lot. And this is only *one* demon we're talking about." She wiped her lips and threw her napkin down on the table. "Listen to me! Talking as if I *believed* this! I have an article to finish, more interviews to do." She put her head on Jimmy's shoulder. "It's almost time to go home, drat."

Jimmy had picked up the paper and was idly flipping through the pages. "Yeah, I know. And we've hardly done anything together. Monday is the last full day of shooting so I'll be on the soundstage most of the time. How about Sunday for us?"

"No, not tomorrow," Dorothy said. "*Tonight* for us. I promise you. I've got nothing on the agenda. How about you?"

"This afternoon Eddie Petrano promised to show me the workshop they set up for him off the soundstage, but tonight I'm free." He patted the top of his own head. "But boy, I don't want to do any more drinking."

"*Good.* We'll go see a play or go out for a fancy dinner. Okay?"

"Okay." Suddenly Jimmy froze in his seat. His eyes were widening, staring at something he had seen in the paper.

"Oh God, Dorothy. It's happened again. Someone else! This *is* getting scary!"

"What? What is it? Let me see!"

She grabbed the paper from him.

And read about how Bethany Carraval had been murdered.

"It was just like a scene out of the movie," Watson was saying between gasps as he squeezed back the tears. "Body parts everywhere. I still can't believe it was Bethany. That poor, poor woman. No one deserves to have that happen—"

He was lying on the sofa in his living room, where he had been for much of the time since reporting Bethany Carraval's murder. His wife sat beside him holding a hand, applying a hot compress to his forehead. His headache had been pounding without letup, and heat was the only thing that worked. Around him in the living room stood Livingstone Stoner—who had temporarily halted production to come find out more about the murder and its possible effect on *Vicious Two*'s schedule, in person—Ellen Rue, and two stone-faced detectives from the L.A.P.D.

One detective was stocky and burly, the other tall and more pleasant—a literal Mutt and Jeff act. "We're afraid the body has been positively identified," said the short detective. "It's Bethany Carraval, all right."

"Oh God," Watson said. So did Ellen. She was clutching at Stoner and chewing gum furiously. Her eyes jumped from speaker to speaker as if an invisible ball only she could see was playing "connect the dots" with their faces.

"Terrible, terrible," Mrs. Watson muttered.

The tall policeman told Stoner that he was glad the director was there. "We'll have to ask you a few more questions, too," he said.

"Me?" Stoner exclaimed. "I don't know anything. I had very little to do with Bethany Carraval. She worked with Harold. I hardly ever saw her on the set. She, Mr. Watson, and their assistants usually work out of their office on Montrose Avenue. And I certainly never saw the woman socially."

"Mr. Stoner, please," the tall detective said with infinite patience.

Stoner seemed not to have heard him. "They said she was killed Thursday evening. I was with Ellen and a few crew members. You can ask them if you want."

"No one's accusing you of anything, Mr. Stoner," the burly cop interrupted. His voice was surprisingly melodious. "It's just that Ms. Carraval was the second person connected to this picture you're making who's been murdered. The third, if you count Longbank's wife."

The tall one said, "We don't want to make anyone uneasy, but it's hard not to see a pattern emerging. First the screenwriter gets himself killed. Now the associate producer. These murders may have no connection to each other whatsoever—the only thing they really have in common is the uncommon viciousness—" He realized what he'd said and put his fingers briefly to his lips, hiding what would have been an inappropriate grin. "Pardon me, the uncommon brutality involved in each case. These murders have been incredibly savage."

"You mean, we're *all* in danger," Ellen said. It was clear she would have much preferred that Bethany had met her end at the hands of some junkie or bar pickup who was already out of town and halfway across the country.

"Not necessarily. Whoever's committing these murders—assuming it's the same person—seems to be going after the big guns, though."

Upon hearing that, Mrs. Watson shuddered and fiddled with the beads of her necklace. She gave her husband an anxious look.

"Now I don't want to get anybody scared—"

The short one broke in. "Yes, yes we do, Harry. Scared people stay out of trouble." He folded his arms and shifted his weight from one leg to the other. "If any of you can think of any person who'd have a reason to kill either Carraval or the Longbanks, who'd have a reason to want to shut this picture down, you'd better let us know. And soon."

Ellen turned pale. "Is the picture being shut down?" she asked nervously. "So close to finishing?"

"No, no," Watson replied. "*I'll* be out of it, I'm afraid, but filming will continue as scheduled." Watson had been done in by the horror of what he'd seen in his associate's apartment. "Bethany can handle things while I'm—" He stopped short, filled with realization. "I can't believe I said that." He shook his head. "I mean, Walter and Jennifer will take over for me at the office. It'll mean more work for them but they can manage. Anyway, I'll be here if anyone needs me. I just . . . *can't* go into work for a few days." He saw Stoner give him a worried look. "I'm sorry, Livingstone. I won't let you down, I swear. The picture will go ahead without any hitches."

Ignoring her husband's dirty looks, Mrs. Watson asked the detectives "Do you think these murders are directed at the production company, at the people making *Vicious*? Do you think they're an attempt to prevent the film from being completed?" Before either of the cops could answer, she looked at her husband and added, "Because if that's the case, Harold, I wish you *would* shut down the production." She burst into tears. "I don't want anything happening to you like what happened to. . . ." She couldn't finish.

Stoner and Ellen glared at the woman while the detectives exchanged unreadable glances. Finally Stoner stepped closer to the couch and said, "Look, what happened to Bethany is ghastly—an outrage! Whoever did it should be drawn and quartered. But. . . ." His hands flew out in inarticulate gestures of frustration. "Look, I know I sound like a callous director who doesn't want anything interfering with his precious motion picture, but a lot of people are employed on this project, a lot of time and money has been expended." Stoner looked at the detectives as if trying to convince them of his sincerity.

"Beth's death is a tragedy, you won't get any argument from me on that. But how do we really know it had anything to do with this picture? Or the Longbanks' deaths, for that matter. The Longbanks surprised an intruder. Maybe Bethany picked up the wrong guy. I know how it sounds, but that's what I think. There's no *reason* anyone would want to shut down this picture. Who'd want to?—except for a few frantic activists who hate horror movies. And they're not likely to protest a splatter pic by going out and *killing* somebody."

There was silence for a moment. Then Watson shook his head wearily and said, "There's just one problem, Livingstone, the rest of you. One thing we—all—have been overlooking in our desperate hope that these dreadful murders have nothing to do with the movie."

He looked up at the tall policeman. "Detective Hansen. The papers—one of the supermarket tabloids at any rate—said that the Longbanks had probably been killed by someone wearing a sheet with eye holes cut out of it and using a scythe for a weapon." His eyes fell upon the director. "Livingstone. *Look at me*, Livingstone—what does that sound like to you?" Ellen was staring at her boyfriend with a funny, scared expression on her face.

"And Bethany—someone used a power drill on her before they cut her up. With a saw."

The tall cop shook his head and muttered. "We tried to keep the bit about the drill quiet to avoid false confessions—we always get 'em—but somebody leaked it to the paper."

"What does that sound like, Stoner, hmmm?" Watson prodded. "Like a scene right out of *Vicious Two*, no? Someone costumed as the grim reaper commits murder, kills a husband and his wife in a motel. And the murder with the drill and hacksaw . . . that little beauty is also one of the new scenes you added to Longbank's screenplay, isn't it?"

Stoner ignored Watson and turned back to the police. "I had nothing to do with those murders. That's just coincidence—"

Harold Watson's thunderous outburst was doubly startling because of his weakened position on the sofa. "*Coincidence*! Exact duplicates of the murders, Stoner? *Your* murders? Come on now—who are we kidding?" Mrs. Watson gasped and put her hand to her mouth.

"All right, all right," Stoner said. "I saw a resemblance, I admit it. But I didn't want to believe it. I still say I honestly thought it had to be a coincidence. People use drills to break into apartments. People get cut up with all kinds of crazy weapons. The stories I read in the papers weren't all that detailed." He paced back and forth frantically. "All right, all right, I admit it.

I'm freaked, really freaked. But what the hell do we do about it? I've got a picture to finish, just a day or so of shooting left, all these actors and crewmen sitting around. . . ."

Stoner suddenly faced the detectives and exploded: "Why don't you do something about this? Why don't you find the killer? Look, making a movie is a business. Somebody starts bumping off the executives of an insurance firm, you don't sit around and make them close up shop until the killer is finally caught. Business goes on as usual—and you cops work overtime to catch the creep so nobody *else* gets hurt. That's what you should be doing *now*. We shouldn't be shutting down production. I for one will not be bullied by this maniac." He sat down on the nearest chair, pulling Ellen onto his lap and grumbling.

"You're forgetting something else, Stoner," Watson said from his makeshift sickbed. "I never said—or thought for one minute—that *you* were reenacting the scenes of violence you put in your script with real victims. But someone *is*; we have to face it. Someone has seen that script and is using it as a blueprint for murder."

"How many people have copies of this screenplay?" asked Chalmers, the short policeman.

Stoner kneaded his forehead with stubby fingers and sighed. "The whole cast, I guess. Except bit players and extras. People with small parts just get copies of the scene they're in. Some of the crew have specially marked copies of the screenplay. Harold has one. So did Bethany. Two dozen or more altogether? That's not counting whatever copies may have been lost or stolen. You know, Doug Longbank and Bethany Carraval both had copies of the script in their homes. How do we know the killer, or killers, didn't come in, see their scripts and decide to imitate what they had read while he killed them?"

Watson snorted. "Pretty farfetched, Livingstone. A killer doesn't sit down and read a screenplay while he's in the process of robbing a house or murdering somebody."

"I only meant—these killings still may not have anything to do with the picture." Stoner looked as if he were about to collapse into tears. "I—I really wouldn't want to think that anyone would ever get murdered because of me, because of something I wrote. Those murder scenes—they just came out of my head. I deliberately made them exaggeratedly ghoulish, larger than life. That's what movies are about. . . ." Even Ellen seemed surprised that the man was so upset.

Watson sighed heavily. "If you had only seen it, Livingstone. If you had seen that poor woman—" His voice caught, and before he knew it he was crying in spite of his attempts not to do so. "We weren't close, Bethany, but—no one deserves something like that . . . Poor woman. She hadn't had an easy life. I know people always say this when it's too late, but I worked with her for years, yet was never her friend. I wish I had bothered finding out what was troubling her. I knew she was lonely after the divorce, after losing the kids—and I never even had her out here to dinner. I'm ashamed. She put up this cold front, this defensive austerity, only because she'd been so hurt. She did drugs because. . . ."

Watson put his hands over his face. "I'll never forget it. Oh God, I'll never . . ." He looked at his wife. "It's not like on the TV, like reading it in a book . . ." He turned to the two detectives. ". . . not even like what you see in the movies today, the ones like *this* one that are so damned explicit. When it's for real . . . God, I don't understand how you fellows can go through it every day, body after body, death after death. I can't understand how you do it. I wonder what you think of when you see movies like *Vicious Two*, when you see bloody fake corpses and people being murdered and people getting axes in the face—when you've seen all that *for real* day in and day out. I wonder what goes through your minds."

The tall detective grinned and cracked his knuckles. "My girlfriend wanted to see a picture called *Sweet Psychotic* the other night," he said. "I told her, go by yourself. I get enough of that on the job."

He pulled a hardbacked chair up closer to the sofa and indicated that his partner should find another chair and do the same. "Now, we had better put our heads together here and have a good, long talk about this screenplay and these murders.

We're going to have a little talk with everyone—and I do mean everyone—who's had *anything* to do with *Vicious Two!*"

18

Brian Asquith listened excitedly to the voice on the phone and nodded enthusiastically. "Again, thank you so much for this information. I can't possibly tell you how much it means—" He listened for a few beats, then added, "Of course. If I need you again I'll be sure to get in touch with you."

What a stroke of luck! He couldn't believe that the car was actually in California. It was like spending a lifetime looking for a hidden treasure and discovering it was buried in your backyard all along. *The railroad car was in California!*

He was about to make another phone call when the doorbell rang. He pressed the intercom switch and asked who it was. Probably UPS. He was always getting books and boxes from across the country and overseas.

"It's Dorothy Hunter. I called but your phone has been busy for over an hour."

Yes, he had been talking for quite a bit longer than he'd intended. The man he'd hired to track down the missing railroad car had insisted on giving him every minute detail of his search, the name of every city, every person . . . every dollar that had to be accounted for.

Well, he could afford it and it had been well worth the expense. And from what he'd read in the paper about the hideous murder of that poor young woman, time was of the essence. . . .

"Ms. Hunter. Come right up," he said, pressing the buzzer to admit her.

Asquith was surprised that she had come back to see him, but it was a welcome surprise. He had liked Dorothy Hunter, felt something for her, more than pity, certainly much less than love, but something. . . .

And then she was there before him, looking wary, hesitant, anxious, a little frightened maybe—but also strong and resilient, eager to get things done and to expand the boundaries of her consciousness. *Was there something else there, too? An undefinable attraction or interest of some kind?* Yes, he liked Dorothy Hunter.

He led her to the couch and offered her something to drink. "No, thanks," she said, "the two I had yesterday were enough."

"I was referring to coffee this time."

"Oh, in that case, yes."

He went into a small kitchen area that was divided from the living room by a broad wooden counter. As he poured coffee from a coffeemaker into two large mugs with trees on them, he asked "And what brings you here today, Ms. Hunter?"

"Several things," she said. "First, to apologize. I did walk out of here rather rudely yesterday."

"*Run* is more like it."

"Yes, well, your story began to scare me, even if I didn't want to admit it. You see, deep down I've always believed in demons, monsters, the boogie man. In that sense I guess I've never grown up."

"Join the club."

She paused while he handed her the coffee. "But the main reason I left was because—well, it wasn't your fault, I was the one who brought it up—but I'd started thinking about my parents again. . . ." She was about to go on but apparently the sympathetic look on his face assured her that she didn't need to.

"I understand," Asquith nodded. "All of us have things in our pasts that are very difficult to deal with." *Wasn't that true, Brian?* "Let me get you some cream and sugar." He came back in a jiffy with the condiments, and sat beside Dorothy as he had done the day before, stirring his own large mug of steaming coffee. "That was the first reason you came. What's the second?" *Was she blushing?*

Dorothy reached into her bag and took out the newspaper she'd been reading during brunch. *"This,"* she said, opening it to the account of Bethany Carraval's murder.

He waved it away. "Yes, I know. The afternoon news on TV didn't spare any details. They said the killer used a drill on her and a saw to cut her body up. It's monstrous." He made a fist out of his right hand and hit himself on the forehead. "God, I'm sorry! I didn't mean to be so graphic. How insensitive of me!"

Dorothy seemed to tremble for a moment, but finally said, "It's all right." She managed a weak smile. "I'm stronger than I look. But that's why I'm here. Because you said someone else might be murdered and someone else *has* been murdered.

Lord, did she think that *he* might have killed Carraval and the Longbanks? Then she was certainly braver than he could be, walking right back into the den of the lion. "I thought you didn't believe my explanation," he said. "So I'm not quite sure why you're coming to me about *this*." He indicated the paper.

"Because you sounded as if you knew how to stop this slaughter from continuing," she said. But in spite of her pleading, almost whining tone of voice, Asquith wasn't convinced. From her brief remarks about her boyfriend the other day, he suspected there was some kind of tension or resentment going on between the two of them, and the last thing he wanted was to get caught up in the middle of it. Then again, he might only be flattering himself. Dorothy Hunter was a writer, a journalist of sorts, after all. Maybe she just sensed a good story. Or maybe she honestly wanted to do something to help.

"You mean," he said, "now you believe me?"

"I don't know. Let's just say I'm willing to concede the possibility, whereas before I wasn't. You've piqued my curiosity, all right? This whole business is scaring the life out of me and part of me wants to run back to New York and forget I ever met you, but I'm afraid my writer's nature won't let me do that. So here I am. Wanting to know more. I want to find out who this maniac is and I want him stopped. And if it's a demon who's controlling him, I want to stop the demon. I won't let another woman be brutalized the way I was." She thought of drills and hacksaws and added, "Worse, much worse than I was. I won't let another child lose her parents. I couldn't fight back when it happened to me, but this time I have to. So stop sitting there with that silly grin on your face and tell me: do you know how to stop these murders?"

"I think so," he said, although it was one of the few times during his life that Asquith wasn't sure of himself. "But I'm not certain. There are—ways, means—of overpowering demons, exorcising them from people who are under their control. But it's . . . not easy. And not foolproof. It's not exactly a common, everyday occurrence, mind you."

"If we find out who it is we can exorcise this demon-killer? How?"

"There are spells and rituals, but I *think* it all comes down to catching them when they're unaware, when the demon inside is in a dormant stage. It's really very simple. You just have to complete the operation before the demon can completely take over. Once it emerges, you're in trouble. Possessed people have remarkable strength, far above ordinary levels. There's not a lot they can't do."

She thought for a moment, then said, "How do we know that this demon isn't flitting from person to person, that it uses different shells to commit each murder?"

"Unlikely," Asquith said. "The four-fingered demon, once it enters a person's body, likes to stay there safe and sound and comfortable until something forces it out, strips the host of freedom: such as exorcism, the host's suicide, the host being caught in the act or captured and imprisoned. Then it isn't fun any more and the demon—poof—runs away to fight another day. But if the person kills himself while the demon is still inside, the demon loses some energy, a little part of itself; the person's arm becomes withered for real and remains that way."

"You mean the claw is just an illusion?"

"Not necessarily, no. A temporary metamorphosis might be a better way to put it." He looked at her, wondering if she was really ready to hear all of this. Making converts could be as tedious as it was challenging. And few had the intestinal fortitude to stick it out for long. "Are you sure you believe what I'm saying?"

"I'd be lying to you if I said I believed it all. *Yet*," she admitted, "perhaps I'm waiting for you to convince me." She sat up straight in her chair and put her hands primly in her lap. "I want to see your files. I want to see the proof you have. And the pictures. I mean it, Brian. Let me see what you have."

He paused, studying her, looking for signs of insincerity, but saw none. For some reason this woman trusted him, believed in him, though he wasn't sure why. "All right," he said. He got up and walked over to the filing cabinet. A few moments later he came back with a thick, heavy batch of material.

For the next half hour she looked at newspaper clippings, handwritten eyewitness accounts and affadavits, newspaper reports—and most terrible of all—police and journal photographs of murder victims. Brian did his best to shield her from the worst, covering the more horrible parts of each picture with his hand, letting her see the important part—the claw—for herself. Many of the morgue shots were so old and yellowing they resembled etchings or daguerreotypes and their shock value was considerable diminished by the passage of time. Brian wondered: did Dorothy think there was a book in this? Was that why the woman was so curious?

When she was through reviewing the material, Dorothy sat back, ran her fingers through her hair, and sighed. "It's incredible. Just incredible. If it's *not* a demon, what is it? There could be perfectly rational explanations for all the nice quiet men who suddenly went berserk and shot up their families, but for all those corpses with unexplainable claws on their left arms. . . .? Why hasn't anyone bothered investigating before this?"

Asquith explained: "Because it happened in so many different places across the country and overseas. No one ever made the connection—until I started digging. And I'm afraid people would simply rather not deal with things they can't explain. I'm sure I'm not the first to be curious about all this. But how many other people, particularly policemen—who must have on the average a dozen different *contemporary* cases to work on every week—how many people would have time to sit down and go over all this material? It's my line of work, however. Or at least it's become my line of work.

"There's too many incidents for it to be mere coincidence, I'm certain of that. Just as I'm also certain that the murders of the Longbanks and Bethany Carraval are connected to the murders of Désirée Fontana and Anthony Winteroth's family. And not just because of the obvious connection between *Vicious One* and *Vicious Two*. For some reason over the years, in addition to its dozens of other victims, the demon has picked people connected to the Fontana case and the movies that were inspired by it. Had it never done that—had it stuck *exclusively* to victims who had no connection whatsoever to one another—I may never have caught on to what was happening."

"But *why* is it doing it? Taking over people? Killing people? It all seems so fantastic."

"Granted. Perhaps possessing people's bodies is just its natural function, as normal to it as sleeping and breathing are to us. Who knows? One thing I've learned about the occult world is that it operates by different rules from ours and there are never easy answers. One theory is that demons—whatever they might be and whatever form they might take—are attracted to people with some form of psychic power or special sensitivity."

"If there's someone like that working on *Vicious Two*," Dorothy said, "how can we find out who it is? Better yet, is there a way to send this demon back to wherever it came from and stop it from killing others in the future?"

Asquith tapped his lips thoughtfully. "I'm not sure if anyone other than the police are capable of finding out the former. As to the latter, sending it back to where it came from, that all depends on its origins. And I received some information just before you arrived that may shed some light on the subject."

He leaned back and put his arm casually across the sofa behind Dorothy. "Have you ever heard the story of the Sumarian ghost train? It's quite a famous supernatural event."

"Yes, I have. But I really don't remember any of the details."

"Well, in the late 1800s in Sumara, a train packed with hundreds of sick passengers was lost en route to a hospital outpost in Benpor. Rescue workers later came upon the train sitting there quietly on the tracks undisturbed. Except that every single passenger had vanished without a trace. Ever since then it's been one of the greatest unsolved mysteries of our time. No one ever found out where those hundreds of passengers disappeared to. They didn't wander off into the desert or mountains to die; no bodies were ever found. None of them ever showed up at their homes in other cities in Sumara. They were gone—every last one of them."

Brian took a good, long swallow of his coffee, found it cold, and grimaced. "Anyway, this incident occurred in 1887. The first recorded case of the four-fingered claw that I have in my files occurred a year later in late 1888. I may be clutching at straws here, but those dates are too close together to be without significance. I've tried in vain to discover incidents involving the claw before 1887, but so far I've drawn a blank. And nothing else as bizarre or mysterious as the disappearance of that train's passengers happened just before what I call the 'claw killings' began."

"So you think there's a connection?"

"Let's just say I can't ignore the possibility. Though I haven't *any* idea of what the connection could be. In any case, I've spent a great deal of money hiring people to track down the last remnant of that train, the only railroad car from it that has survived intact to the 1980's."

He paused to refill their coffee cups, then resumed. "The train was undamaged, and was soon chugging hundreds of people to and from Benpor again, though few of them were aware of what had happened. But a very eccentric British millionaire and student of the occult named Hamilton Davies, believed the train was a source of supernatural power, and in 1902 he bought it lock, stock and barrel from the railroad company. Apparently he wanted to have his underlings give it a thorough examination to see if they could find some clue to all the missing passengers.

"Davies fancied himself an 'amateur psychic' and was certain that one car in particular contained the most residual occult energy. He had the other cars torn up for scrap and saved this car as a sort of giant lucky penny or good luck charm. It soon became famous in occult circles as a sort of psychic storage battery or talisman. Psychics from around the world would travel to Davies' estate outside London to explore the car, to feel all its myriad sensations for themselves. Apparently, what they felt, touched, tasted, *saw* in the car was too much for them, and none ever stayed inside it for more than a few moments."

"And what happened to the railroad car?"

"After Davies died, it was inherited by his son, Judson, who sold it. Unfortunately, his grandson had no idea who might have bought it, as he was only an infant at the time and no record of the transaction has survived. A while ago I finally found out that it was sold to a man by the name of John Ruston, an occult aficionado whose own son came to America some years back. You've probably heard of *him*. Edward Ruston? He owns all those Ruston hotels and restaurants that you see on the highways. Ruston brought the car over to the states in the 1950s when *he* inherited it, but was never sure what to do with the damn thing. Like Judson Davies before him, he didn't share his late father's interest in supernatural matters. But unlike young Davies, he didn't want to part with such an unusual family 'heirloom.'

"What I'm leading up to is that he finally put the car on a storage barge, along with other discarded vehicles and equipment, just to get it out of the way. The barge is, right this very minute, only a short distance away in the San Pedro Harbor."

He could tell that his guest was almost as fascinated as he was. "Do you have any idea what this means to me?" he asked her. "A chance to actually *look* inside that car myself. The car that in some way my mind can't even conceive may have had something to do with the four-fingered demon."

"The thought of it alone is terrifying me," Dorothy said.

"I know," Asquith admitted. "Me, too. But it's an opportunity I simply can't pass up. Besides it's really just an old railway car, empty now, full of dust and cobwebs and probably nothing else." He wondered if he weren't trying to convince himself. "I'm not a psychic, so even if there is residual supernatural energy inside the car, it can't affect me. That's what I was about to do when you arrived: contact the car's current owner, Ed Ruston, and ask if I could go aboard that barge."

"I still don't see how it will stop the *Vicious Two* killings."

"It might not help in the least." He reached for the phone. "But I won't know that until I get inside that car and have a look at it for myself."

Dorothy reached out and touched his hand, a determined look on her face.

"I want to come with you," she said.

And Brian knew she meant it.

Eddie Petrano stretched out on the couch and sighed happily. Mrs. Blim had been nice enough—with the added incentive of a twenty dollar bill—to take his mother out for a late supper and shopping afterward, so that Eddie could have a little peace and quiet. The old lady's hearing was so bad that she always had to have the sound of the TV or radio, sometimes both, up so loud that it reached ear shattering decibels. If he was working in his shop it didn't matter, but when he just wanted to lie around the house and relax it was definitely a bummer.

He had to chuckle at the thought of Mrs. Blim strolling down the street escorting his mother—thumping along on her walker at a rate of two feet per minute—and trying her damnedest not to lose patience.

Eddie had been so busy on the set—he'd practically moved into the workshop at the studio—that he was really looking forward to this night of uninterrupted nothingness. Everything was so hectic on the set, all the work and then those terrible murders. Shooting had come to a temporary halt while Livingstone conferred with the producer. He'd been able to leave early for a change—after another interesting session with that Jimmy Radley from *Frames and Directions*—but this cold he'd gotten was still nagging at him and a good night's rest was just what he needed. Mrs. Blim had been told to keep the old lady out until ten even if she had to funnel twenty cups of coffee down her throat. Ma would be so tired when she got back from her "outing" that she'd go to sleep without doing any of her usual nagging or fussing no matter how much caffeine was in her system.

When the doorbell rang, it awakened Eddie from an unexpected nap.

Eddie figured it had to be his mother and Mrs. Blim coming back. He checked his wrist watch. *Damn.* She'd brought the old bitch back too early. He got up and wondered why they didn't let themselves in. They both had a key and he'd left all but one lock open.

His eyes squinted in puzzlement when he opened the door and saw who the visitor was, not to mention that terribly strange expression on the visitor's face. "Hi. How are ya?" *No answer.*

Eddie was too startled to mind his manners. "What do you want?" he said. This had to have something to do with the movie, he assumed. When the visitor again took too long to answer—*weird*—he said, "So what I can do for you, huh?"

The visitor asked to come in. Eddie said it was okay. He

stepped back to let the visitor pass through the portal. The visitor's face was drawn and tired, frighteningly white, very tense and rigid like someone who'd received an electric shock. The visitor's right hand held a shopping bag.

The left hand dipped down into the bag even as the visitor pushed backwards to slam the front door closed. It made Eddie feel as if he were being *cornered.*

Strange. It was odd enough that the visitor should have come here unannounced in the first place, without also acting in such a peculiar manner. Eccentricity was one thing, but. . . .

"Are you sick?" Eddie asked. "Pardon me for saying this, but you look like shit. C'mon, sit down. I'll get you a glass of water, okay?" He held out his hand. "Then you can tell me what this is all about."

Swoosh.

Eddie realized with shock that the tips of four fingers on the hand he'd been holding out were missing. Blood was busy dripping out of the ugly, trembling stumps. It had happened so fast he'd hardly seen the weapon, hardly had time to either run or react. He looked down and saw little fingertips lying on the rug like undercooked pieces of stringy link sausage.

"God! What have you done!" he screamed.

Then he saw the visitor's machete, saw the unearthly claw that was holding it, raising it up slowly for another slashing strike.

"Don't. *Don't!*"

The machete *swished* across his face, cutting deep into the bridge of the nose, slicing off a chunk of Eddie's cheek. Eddie, overcome with agony, dropped down to his knees and held his torn, flapping face in his hands. He pressed hard upwards, trying to keep his face from falling off.

The visitor took another step forward and raised the machete again, bringing it down swiftly on the exposed tender tissue at the nape of Eddie's neck. One stroke completely separated the head from the body. Gallons of blood gushed up out of the neck wound, spattering across the floor as the head rolled a few feet away and came to a halt, face upwards, near the sofa.

The visitor took fresh clothes out of the bag, changed, put the soiled clothes back in the bag. The visitor left the apartment.

Two women were getting out of the elevator just as the visitor disappeared down the stairwell around the corner.

Minutes later Mrs. Blim deposited her charge at the door to her apartment. Saying goodnight, she quickly ran down the hall to wash her hair—and have a nightcap or two.

Mrs. Petrano hoped Eddie had remembered to use only the one lock tonight; she didn't want to have to bother undoing the whole shebang, and her arms were getting too old to manage some of the tumblers. Eddie was probably fast asleep. Luckily the door opened with just a wrench of the one key. Using her walker, she entered the living room.

Mrs. Petrano's first impulse was to scream for Mrs. Blim.

But she didn't.

Eddie couldn't fool her again. No sir.

She closed the door behind her.

"Eddie," she called with a musical lilt. "Oh, Eddie. Thought you could play tricks on your ma, did you?"

She stepped over the fake blood—she'd have him clean this carpet till it was spotless or he'd buy a new one, the bastard—and ignored that silly headless dummy on the floor. He'd even gone to the bother of dressing it up in his own clothes. There were "bloodstains" on the wall, too, as if he'd stood there and simply hurled whole bottles of the stuff around the room.

And the smell! *Terrible!*

She stood there, trembling, on the verge of tears but refusing to give in to her terror. It was clear now how much he hated her, how much he wanted her to die. He was doing all this just to give her a heart attack. First that head on her chair the other day, now this. *If at first you don't succeed, try, try again.*

Well, she was a lot tougher than the little creep thought she was. She'd just say nothing, pretend it wasn't there, not let it raise her blood pressure. She'd sit there in her chair and watch TV, and sooner or later he'd come out of his workshop, admit defeat, and have to spend the whole night cleaning the place up. Even *he* wouldn't leave it looking this way.

"That's a nice touch, Eddie," she shouted, forgetting her edict to stay silent when she saw *another* head on the chair. She looked at it closely. Sure did look realistic, even better than the last one he'd tried to scare her with. This one had obviously been made from a mold of Eddie's features, 'cause the bloody ugly thing looked just like him.

Fake, fake, fake, she said to herself. *That boy is sick in the head but I will not be driven out of my apartment or out of what's left of my life by anyone!*

She pushed the head aside, leaving a gory smear on the cushion, and used the remote control box he'd bought her to turn the TV on. The head tottered over onto her lap. "There now," she said, patting it on the hair. The stupid thing was falling apart, flesh hanging free and bones all exposed. Looked like he'd been using it for a football. "There, there," she said, patting it and smiling while she watched her favorite programs. *She would sit there and pretend that all was right with her world, that she was not nearly overcome by loneliness and infirmity and old age, by her awful dependency on a son who did not love her.*

Mrs. Petrano wiped tears off her cheeks, and wondered where Eddie was. Was he hiding in his room, hoping to hear her cry out, praying she'd drop dead right then and there of a stroke? Well, she sure would surprise him, wouldn't she?

She sat there patting the head with perverse affection, trying not to think of what her son had done to their home. Mrs. Petrano did not read the papers or watch the news on TV. Neither Eddie nor Mrs. Blim had ever told her about the murders. She had not the slightest inkling of what she was actually touching as she watched a boring sitcom and played with Eddie's head. . . .

Until morning came.

And the light.

When she put on her glasses and started screaming.

19

It was two days later and the bodies of both George Piedmont and Eddie Petrano had been discovered.

Piedmont's work on *Vicious Two* had been over, and Petrano's two assistants could finish whatever work needed to be done for the last day of shooting. The *Vicious Two* murders were all over the papers in lipsmacking detail, and the story was the talk of the town.

"Watson and the studio won't shut down production," Jimmy said, as he put on his shirt in their room at the Bellmore Monday morning. Dorothy sat at the desk writing postcards for Aunt Maggie and her friends back in New York. "They're afraid they'd lose too much money. As morbid and inhumane as this sounds, the murders of these 'dispensable' people are providing a million bucks of free publicity."

He ran a comb through his hair and patted it approvingly. "I still can't get over it. I really was fond of Eddie Petrano. And that ol' George Piedmont seemed like an awfully nice fella. What a character."

Dorothy was finding the whole business so difficult to deal with she could hardly talk about it. "Isn't anybody scared?" she whispered. "Aren't they all afraid that the killer will get them next?" She felt like a character trapped in a neverending loop of

Body Count at Buzzard Bay, like the world had suddenly turned into a reflection of Jimmy's horror movies instead of the other way around.

"I'm sure they're scared," Jimmy said. "But they look at it this way: there's no guarantee the killer will stop picking them off even if they do shut down the production of *Vicious Two*. Also, there haven't been any incidents or killings at the studio itself, so a lot of people are clinging to the notion that these murders—which have all occurred in the victims' homes when they were alone—really might have nothing to do with the movie."

"But now it's come out that the murders were virtual re-enactments of the murders in the movie." And what Dorothy had read in the paper had been *unbelievable*. If anything like that happened to her. Or to Jimmy! God, those poor people. The pain, the mental anguish, they must have gone through.

Jimmy shrugged. "Who was it said people believe what they want to believe? It's a circus out there. Half the people want to quit and the other half refuse to face facts. A lot of them just think it's all a weird coincidence, a jinx, like the accidents on the set of *Demoniac* a few years ago, remember? What's left to do but continue filming and hope for the best? As long as none of the principal actors are killed, there's nothing to prevent them from finishing today. They have a security force out at the studio and some of the actors have even hired personal bodyguards."

Dorothy stopped writing and looked up thoughtfully. "I know the police aren't sure it's the same person who killed all four people, but I think it is. A killer who comes and goes, who in three out of four cases has been freely admitted into the victims' homes—indicating it was someone they knew." She scribbled an address on the front of a card showing the outside of Grauman's Chinese Theatre. "Why haven't the police come up with a suspect?"

Jimmy shook his head. "Each of the five victims may have had enemies, but not the same enemies. Aside from *Vicious Two* there's no real connection between them. Longbank never had anything to do with the others before this picture. Ditto for Bethany Carraval. Eddie may have done makeup effects for a picture or two that George Piedmont had bit parts in, but that's about it. They may not have even met before the day they shot George's murder. Everyone is stumped by the whole business."

Dorothy dug in her purse for a roll of stamps she'd bought and began affixing them to the postcards. Anything to keep busy. She wished it were she flying to the east coast and not these postcards, which would undoubtedly arrive long after she did. But Jimmy had insisted that he couldn't leave before the filming was over. "I'm beginning to wonder if everything Brian Asquith told me might be true," she said. How could she credit such a story? Just because she found Brian Asquith attractive, did that mean she had to find him so convincing, too?

Jimmy frowned. "If he's so confident in his theory, why doesn't he take it to the police?"

Dorothy gave him a you-should-know-better look. "Really. Do you think the police would for one minute believe a far fetched story like that?" *Why not?* she wondered privately. *I'm beginning to.* Hacksaws. Power drills. *Better a demon,* she thought, *than a human being.* She couldn't even bring herself to go to Bethany Carraval's funeral yesterday.

"You said Asquith has lots of evidence."

"Yes. Cases in other cities, other decades. Evidence that *could* have been faked, I must admit." Although she was somehow positive that the material was genuine, the police would probably question it. "Anyway, there's been no indication of any mysterious four-fingered claw in *these* killings. At least, not as far as we know. You can't expect a modern-day police department to seriously consider the super-natural as a possible explanation. They deal in facts, motives, *reality*. Besides, even if Asquith managed to convince them, what would they be able to do? Get all the potential suspects in a room together and see which one is the most sensitive to psychic suggestion? Give them a blood test for demonic possession?"

Was the horror of what was happening so intense, Dorothy wondered, so similar to what had happened to her parents that she had to seek shelter in Brian Asquith's comforting, terrifying *madness*?

Jimmy sat down on the bed and put on his shiny Italian loafers. "This is a real weird puzzle, all right. Possessed or not, demons or no, whoever's doing this has got to be discovered. If the police suspect anyone in particular they're keeping it under their hat."

"Did they tell you much of anything?"

He snorted. "A writer for *Frames and Directions?* I said I needed some information on the murders so that my piece on the film was as complete as possible, but they knew I was hardly an investigative crime reporter. But, damn—wouldn't it be something if I *could* get to the bottom of these murders?"

"Jimmy—"

"Relax, relax. I'm not that stupid. I know when I'm out of my league. I'm not in any hurry to come up against this maniac or demon or whatever it is, believe me. But I can't help wondering. . . ."

"Neither can I. Is it someone who has nothing to do with the picture? Or someone that we've met—spoken to—in the past couple of weeks? God, just the thought of it!"

"It's not unlikely," Jimmy admitted. "Whoever is killing these people has access to the script, probably knows most of the victims; didn't they let him into their homes? The only forced entry was at the Longbanks' house."

"Jimmy, do you suppose it could be Livingstone Stoner?"

"Come on, honey. Just because he likes to make gory movies? Why would he be crazy enough to kill those people in exactly the way he wrote some of his murder scenes?"

"*That's* why—he'd figure no one would ever think he'd dare to."

"I don't know. You would have thought that poor Eddie Petrano was a bit of a ghoul—you should have seen that workshop—but he was actually a pretty nice guy. And he didn't kill anybody. He wound up *getting* killed. I don't think our murderer will be someone quite so obvious. Stoner is a bit of a creep, but for all we know the killer could be a mild-mannered joe like Harold Watson."

Dorothy finished licking another stamp. Being a part of this whole business, even peripherally, was like walking around in a waking nightmare. "Do all these people have alibis?"

"Stoner says he was with Ellen Rue, but she could be covering for him. Watson was bar-hopping; people saw him in cocktail lounges, but I suppose he could have slipped away at some point and done the deeds. There's so *many* potential suspects. Dozens of people are working on that film, in all capacities. Burt Rawson, the cinematographer; his cameramen. Not to mention stunt men, makeup assistants, prop men, script girls, assistant directors, lighting and sound men; the set is a beehive of activity. The killer could be a lowly 'best boy' or grip, or someone in Avalon's publicity department who's seen parts of the script. There's just no telling."

"And if Brian is right—if the killer is simply a normal person who's been possessed by this four-fingered demon—even their everyday behavior might not give them away. The police are looking for people with motives. But a demon doesn't really *have* a motive."

"Aside from the victims being somewhat similar to the fictional victims in the film."

"What do you mean?"

"In the film a couple gets killed by the 'grim reaper.' Doug and Edna Longbank were killed by the grim reaper, according to the paper. A young, pretty woman gets it with a . . . power drill, same as Bethany Carraval. Do I have to go on?"

Dorothy shuddered. "No. Except . . . Wasn't George Piedmont killed in real life almost the same way he was killed in the movie? Say, now that you mention it, why hasn't the murderer killed off the *other* actors who were in those fictional scenes? Why Bethany and the Longbanks and Eddie Petrano?"

Jimmy shook his head. "Haven't the foggiest. But imagine how petrified those actors must be! We're either dealing with a deranged mind—or a demon's—and any kind of logic they'd adhere to would be too twisted for us to figure. The victims may have been chosen at random, their deaths dependent on where they lived, if they were alone, what they were doing. Where the killer was and what *he* was doing. All he needed was a married couple, a young woman, an old man, and a young man. And he found them. Choosing George Piedmont to re-enact his own death scene may have been sheer coincidence. The killings were out of sequence, by the way. In the film a young woman is murdered first. Not that it makes much difference I suppose."

"Jimmy, have you seen the script? How many more victims are there?"

"I managed to get a few peeks at the screenplay. Although all the murders have been filmed already, about a dozen or so people get killed. *Anyone* could be the next victim: young or old, black or white, male or female."

"*Wonderful.* By the way, have you found out who plays the

killer in the movie?"

"Nobody knows. To avoid leaks, Stoner's keeping it a secret. Only the actual participants in the final scene will ever find out, and some of the crew, of course. He wants his twist ending to have the same impact that Winteroth's did twenty-five years ago."

A twist ending? A mystery? Dorothy found all the parallels between the movie and the murders most unsettling. "Jimmy, what if the killer is someone very similar—just as the victims were vaguely similar—to the murderer in the movie? If only we knew who it was—we could put two and two together."

"I don't even think Stoner knows who it is. The rumor has it that he has about six possible endings in mind. He may wind up filming them all and then choosing the one he wants to use just before the film is released."

"I wish I could get my hands on that script."

"Don't bother. I can tell you that in the movie the only serious suspects are 'Yvette Cummings'—Vivienne Cherneau's character; the nurse—Jocasta Sullivan's character; another mental hospital escapee; and a weird-looking old man—I forget the actor's name. Also, the landlady of the building where Yvette goes to live. And this young jock who tries to hustle Yvette and then disappears. And Stoner may pull a fast one and bring the killer in from out of nowhere."

From out of nowhere. *Just like a demon.*

"Say, I thought Asquith was supposed to call you about that train of his. I still say it's a crazy idea, going with him to see it. I don't see what possible connection it could have to all this."

Dorothy was wondering about that herself, but only said, "I can't help it, Jimmy. I'm just so darned curious. Maybe I'm tired of being dull and rational and pragmatic all the time and need some excitement in my life." But what kind of excitement was she looking for?

"Excitement, huh? Aren't these murders more than enough?" He gave her a sly grin and a wink. "Is this Asquith fellow good-looking?"

"Don't be silly." Or was he all too accurate? "He's attractive, I suppose. In his own way. Anyhow, he said he'd get in touch with me as soon as he secured permission to go on board the barge."

"He'd better hurry. We're going home tomorrow."

On impulse, she asked. "Want to come with us if he calls?"

"No thanks. If they'll let me I'm going to watch them shoot the final scenes today."

Good.

"There'll be a wrap party at the studio tonight if they finish on time. When you get through with Asquith, why don't you come join me? I'll leave word at the gate. You can even bring Asquith if you want to."

"We'll see." *I just hope nobody else gets killed tonight.*

The wrap? she thought. *Maybe that means the wave of murders is over.*

That the demon will move on.

I can't believe I'm doing this.

But Dorothy was doing it. She was getting ready to take a trip into the Twilight Zone with a nice-looking comparative stranger.

They were on the side of a channel, one of many man-made canals in and around San Pedro Harbor. Rutson had leased several storage barges on the 22nd Street landing. This particular area was fairly deserted at this hour, late afternoon, and was filled with forboding warehouses and concrete walkways. The barge itself, one of a grouping of about twenty, sat low in the water a few feet from the dock, tied to the pier by several lengths of strong rope.

In the distance Dorothy could see small battered ships and tugboats, and across the channel, a row of silent, shuttered buildings and towering silos. For some reason she felt as if she were standing on the edge of the world. The *normal* world.

Asquith had called earlier in the afternoon with the news. "I finally tracked down the restaurant tycoon and got his permission. I said I was interested in the historical value, might be interested in buying it, all the usual bullshit, so he wouldn't think I was a nutcase and say no. He didn't sound very interested or concerned. I thought he might insist one of his people accompany us, but he made all the arrangements with a few phone calls."

A harbor employee had escorted them to the proper barge, and left them to their own devices. Apparently, they would have to climb over the side. Even in the afternoon the place looked spooky. The weather had suddenly turned cold, and both of them wore jackets. In spite of the overcast sky, which threatened rain and wind at the very least, the water was so tranquil it looked solid enough to walk on.

Most of the barges in the area were empty, though a few held rusting junk or garbage. Some had corrugated metal shacks on them that made them seem like floating warehouses. The small ripples made by the slightly shifting barge as Brian and Dorothy slipped aboard were like the vague stirrings of a slumbering liquid giant, as if something deep below the water level out of sight were slowly becoming conscious.

After Asquith had clambered aboard, he turned around to help Dorothy do the same. There was a huge grease smear across the front of his pants. "Watch it," he said. "This thing is filthy."

Try as she might, Dorothy was unable to keep from dirtying herself. Losing her grip and balance, she tumbled into the barge and collapsed, laughing, at Brian's feet. He helped her up off the greasy bottom. "What an entrance!" he said. For those few moments that their bodies touched, Dorothy felt a tingle of subdued but vivid excitement.

She shrugged it off. She had come here to see things for herself, to find out if all this talk of devils and demons could possibly be true; not to enter into an ill-timed, ill-fated romance. She was too mature to fling herself into the arms of the first man she met just because Jimmy might have "indulged" a little bit while out on the town in wild, wicked Hollywood. If only Brian hadn't those intense dark eyes, that penetrating way of looking into hers. She reminded herself that some men were that way whether they were "interested" or not. She might be completely misreading his signals.

She looked around. The railroad car took up most of the space on the barge. At least she hoped that's what it was. It was entirely covered by a heavy, bulky gray tarpaulin. Brian had told her that early railroad cars were wood-burning, steam-powered structures, first made of rickety wood, then iron, finally steel. This was an "iron horse," about twelve feet wide and forty feet long. She imagined it was covered with soot and debris and probably looked like a huge derelict boiler that had been left out in the trash too long. The grime on its surface must be at least an inch thick. She bent down to inspect the wheels, which were visible below the tarpaulin, while Brian proceeded toward the uncovered entrance at the other side. Two axles. They didn't make trains like this anymore, that was for sure.

Dorothy told herself that all they were going to do was peek inside an antique railroad car. There was nothing to be scared about. *But people are being hacked to pieces and this railroad car might have something to do with it.* Although she still couldn't imagine *what*. Asquith seemed so sure of himself, so vigorous and full of strength. *So mature and adult.* She told herself to stop comparing him to Jimmy. Was a man who believed in demons any more mature than one who liked to watch horror films?

Brian called to her and she went over to where he was standing. He was at the bottom of the entrance platform, beaming nervously. "Are you ready to go inside?"

She couldn't shake her feeling of apprehension. *Silly.* "I suppose so. Brian, the light won't go through this tarpaulin, will it? How will we be able to see anything?"

Brian pulled a flashlight out of his jacket pocket. "*Voila!* One torch." He flicked it on, then off. "Still working. Good. Ladies first? Or shall I?"

"You go first."

For some strange and irritating reason she found herself thinking about the four-fingered demon again, about *Vicious Two*. She'd sworn to herself that she'd think of this expedition strictly as a trip to an unusual "seaside museum" and nothing more, that it was her curiosity that needed sating and not her sense of danger. But even as she got ready to follow Brian up the steps into the car, she couldn't stop the rush of thoughts that streamed through her mind like an irresistible mental flowtide.

The killer—the demon—could be anyone. Someone who would kill and not even know it. The killer might not even know who he or she was. The killer would have no memory of what he or she'd done. *Even Dorothy herself could be the killer!* Hadn't she lost an hour or two of time one night? Couldn't she have wandered off between meetings and appointments and served at least once as the demon's savage messenger? To think that she could be forced—her body, her vessel—*forced* into committing such vile and atrocious acts against other human beings!

Another thought entered her mind. One that she hadn't taken seriously before! *Could Brian be the demon?*

What did she know about Brian Asquith, really? He'd said the demon had a sense of humor. Well, wouldn't it be funny if Brian were the demon, if he'd been playing with her all the time, if he'd taken her to this isolated place, to this isolated 'talisman,' just to have his way with her? And wouldn't the demon laugh if it knew that she'd had a dream about just such a thing? About Brian having his way with her. Only it had been mutual and pleasurable, full of warmth and affection—not depravity and violence. And if Brian were the demon, that would be all he'd offer, violence and pain in their infinite varieties, no tenderness, no affection, no love.

"Are you coming?" Brian was holding out his hand impatiently. The shadows caused by the overhanging tarpaulin hid his face and for a moment he looked like a satanically grinning imp.

She paused, took his hand, and jumped up onto the platform. Then she followed him into the darkness of the car.

20

When Jimmy arrived at the studio he expected to discover that the set was closed to all press and visitors due to the secretive nature of the filming. Today was the day Stoner filmed his "mystery ending," after all. Jimmy had follow-up interviews to finish and didn't want to run around looking for and cornering people at the wrap party. But to his delight the guard at the gate and at Soundstage "B" only nodded in recognition and allowed him through. They were used to seeing him, knew he was doing a major piece on the film and had been given *carte blanche* by the producer. He remembered to leave Dorothy's name at the gate.

Still, Jimmy knew that his being allowed admittance to the soundstage today was an oversight brought about by Harold Watson's incapacitation, Stoner's increasing hysteria as the minutes toward the deadline of shooting ticked away, and the relative inexperience of Stoner's and Watson's suddenly overworked assistants. Good. He was dying to see exactly how *Vicious Two* was going to wind up.

Yet Jimmy knew if Stoner saw him he'd probably politely request that he leave. Jimmy decided to stay out of the busy director's sight, if at all possible. He pulled out of his pocket the blue souvenir hat that the studio made up—with the words

Vicious Two emblazoned on it—and put it on his head. He quickly headed away from the set and into the maze of plywood corridors and dressing rooms spread out in the back of the enormous rectangular soundstage.

The set, as ever, was a bustle of hectic activity. Cameras were moving, lights were being rearranged, actors were running through their lines in preparation for the final shooting. The few people Jimmy passed either did not recognize him or were too used to his presence to question why he was there. He *had* been on the set virtually every day since he'd come to L.A. That was his method: to interview almost everyone who worked on a film regardless of capacity or importance, then plow through the material later and pull out whatever nuggets he could find. Sometimes a chance remark made by a bit player or electrician was more telling than anything in the director's or actors' prepared speeches.

The door to Vivienne Cherneau's dressing room was wide open. There was no one inside, no one in sight along the corridor created by her trailer and the one—usually unoccupied since her part had been rewritten—for Jocasta Sullivan. A script was sitting there unguarded on the dressing room counter. What if it now contained the final scene? Jimmy couldn't resist taking a peek.

He went quickly into the dressing room and touched the tattered copy of the screenplay. Underneath it there were a few loose pages. *The final scene!*

Oops. Jimmy reached out frantically. His grabbing of the screenplay had caused the loose sheets to slip off the edge of the table. Jimmy tried to catch them but wasn't fast enough. Kneeling, he gathered the sheets together quickly, put them in correct order—they were numbered on top—and got back to his feet.

As he raced through the pages his eyes widened. So that was it! Stoner's "final twist" was that there *was* none. The ending was just what logic dictated.

He put the pages back under the copy of the screenplay and started toward the door.

"What are you doing here?"

Vivienne Cherneau stood in the doorway, a can of cola clenched in her chubby hand. Though he had spoken to her briefly before, she didn't remember who he was. He didn't want her calling security. Although his press pass and familiar face got him past the security chiefs, the extra underlings they'd recently hired might give him some trouble.

"Just finished, Ma'm," he said, touching the brim of his cap and looking at the ceiling. "Had to change the lightbulb." In his dungarees and white shirt he did look somewhat like an Avalon Studios maintenance man.

He got out of there before Vivienne had time to wonder why a perfectly good lightbulb would need to be replaced.

They were hit by the raw, steaming atmosphere the moment they entered the railroad car; it seemed to surround them like a wet, living thing, to enter their mouths and lungs, to sheathe their bodies and drip by osmosis through their pores. For a moment it was as if they'd been transported back through time.

Asquith's light illuminated a large portion of the inside of the car. Although the original owner, Harrison Davies, had faithfully preserved the vehicle, since it had fallen into new hands it had been allowed to sink into a deplorable condition. The dust was inches thick, a spongy carpet of gray and black matter. The wooden seats were chipped and cracked, and the walls—alive with mildew or fungus of some sort—seemed in spots to actually secrete a dripping pus-like liquid. The odor in the car was fulsome: dank and acrid, but strangely not *entirely* unpleasant. There was a sweetness to the odor, an aroma of metal, wood and oil layered atop a stench of vegetative corruption. Like the fragrance of fresh flowers and rotting garbage blended together.

Dorothy broke the oppressive silence. "What exactly are we hoping to find in here?"

"I'm not sure." He looked at his watch playfully. "Well, thirty seconds have gone by and we haven't run screaming out of here. I guess neither of us is particularly sensitive to vibrations from the other world."

"Assuming there are any."

"Don't go all logical and level-headed on me now, dear."

"It's better than being scared to death."

He reached backward. "Hold my hand then if you want to."

"Really Brian. I'm not a five-year-old."

"Then don't act like one. This is simply a scientific expedition. Look at it that way and you'll be fine." He shone the light up to the ceiling, across the walls and the square, dirt-encrusted windows, over the seats and flooring.

"Just an ordinary old railroad car," he said, disappointed. "No clue whatsoever as to where or why all those people disappeared, or what connection they could have to. . . ." He muttered something unintelligible.

In her mind Dorothy filled in the blanks . . . *the four-fingered demon*. She forced the frightening thought away and instead chided him goodnaturedly. "Did you think after all this time, after all the people who've been in here, that *you* would discover the answer to one of the 'greatest mysteries of our time?' "

Brian *tch tched tched*. "Everybody thinks they could solve a great mystery if only they had the opportunity. Well, let's move down to the end of the car, knock on a few walls. You never know." He started forward, Dorothy close behind him. "Seriously, Dorothy. Doesn't it make you wonder—what *did* become of all those people?"

"Couldn't they have simply abandoned the train? It must have broken down—what else could they do?"

"In the middle of the desert, miles from civilization? Why didn't any of those hundreds of people ever show up at the depots on either side of the point where the train was later found?"

"They walked off, got lost, died in the mountains. . . ."

"400 people! *None* of whom chose to stick to the tracks and follow the railway bed to their destination? I can't believe that!"

"Well, what else makes sense? Even this demon of yours couldn't have murdered 400 people in one stroke, could it? And buried all the bodies?"

"I don't know. But I have a sinking feeling that whatever may have happened to those people, the answer won't be found today."

They had reached the opposite end of the railroad car. It was suddenly very cold, chilling. Dorothy pulled up the zipper of her jacket. Asquith was affected, too. "Brr, cold," he said.

Suddenly Dorothy screamed. "Brian! I saw something move! Something in one of those seats."

She was pointing to the right, toward a row of seats down near where they'd entered.

Brian gasped. There *was* a figure there. It was slowly sitting up in the seat as if it had formerly been leaning over in sleep and been awakened by their voices. Brian shone the light on it.

The light went right through the figure.

But the figure was still there.

All hopes that it might have been a bum or drifter who'd turned the barge into his private condominium were evaporated. "Brian. *What is it?*"

Before he could answer her, Dorothy told Brian she was inexplicably dizzy. Sleepy. "Brian. What's happening?" She seemed so sleepy he suspected she didn't have the *energy* to be scared. "I'm so tired, Brian. It's getting hard to see you."

Brian was beginning to feel the drowsiness, too. And the temperature was steadily dropping. His hand felt feeble—the flashlight was *so heavy.* He tried to hold onto it for *the darkness was their enemy!* In the glow of the torch—which was getting weaker by the moment—he saw that *all of the seats of the railroad car were now full of silent, staring figures.*

Ghosts!

And Brian knew: if he and Dorothy fell asleep in this car, they would be completely at the specters' mercy.

Dorothy was moaning. She was beginning to totter. Her hand was pressed against her forehead, she was swaying like a willow caught in a thunderstorm, like a dangling puppet whose separate strings were slowly being severed.

"Dorothy!" He grabbed her, held onto her, tried to keep her from falling to the floor and taking him with her.

While holding her in one arm, he pulled back the hand of his other arm and slapped her full in the face. "Wake up, Dorothy! Wake up! We've got to get out of here! Something's happening!" He slapped her gently a few more times until she started coming out of it.

She came fully awake then, enraged, clawing for his eyes.

"No, no, stop it!" Did she think he was trying to hurt her? "Dorothy, stop it!" Then he realized she was no longer looking at him. Her eyes were wide and full of terror, and her mouth made funny mewling noises.

The ghosts were moving, rising up out of their seats, coming for the both of them!

There must have been a hundred of them, at least; men, women and children squeezed into the car, all with tormented expressions, their filthy brown bodies and pale, ghastly faces a testament to their lifetime of despair, disease and poverty. *Once they had been alive, as alive as Brian and Dorothy, but they'd been stripped of their lives, stripped of a normal existence, stripped even of a normal ending. Some of them had cared little, at first, hadn't cared that their lives of misery and hunger were finally over. Until . . . until they knew that the peace and contentment, the nothingness, they had cried for, were still out of reach, that they had been doomed to an eternity of servility and entrapment under the power of the she-devil with the four-fingered claw.*

The demon had wanted to get him, to stop Brian from digging up things that were better left buried, to stop him from exposing the truth. And Brian, like a fool, had walked straight into the demon's trap, straight into the clutches of a hundred agonized, fear-maddened souls who were caught tight in the demon's power . . . who would do anything the demon said in the desperate hopes that it might free them!

Dorothy's screaming had an unexpected side effect: the jangling terror in her voice completely dissipated their drowsiness.

"Dorothy, they can't hurt us. We have to get out of here."

Brian sensed that the specters in front of him were intangible, incapable of rending them limb from limb although their outstretched arms and ghoulish faces—all sunken eyes and open mouths with rotted teeth and thick black tongues—indicated that that was what they would have liked to do. Yet on a *psychic* level they could do great injury, could drive them—especially Dorothy, who had never witnessed even minor types of occult manifestations such as this before—straight into insanity. Even Brian could feel the vivid fear and icy terror gripping his heart, the almost insurmountable urge to scream and cry, to close his eyes and thrash about in a panic that would only result in grievous self-injury.

Dorothy twisted and turned in his arms, screeching and sobbing, too horrorstruck to know what to do or where to turn. Brian tried the door behind them, which led out to the exit platform on the opposite end of the car from where they'd entered, but it wouldn't budge no matter how hard, how furiously, he yanked it. The only way out was through that gauntlet of transparent horrors behind them. And he was not sure even *his* heart would be able to stand the strain that the sheer terror of walking past them would entail.

The ghosts were becoming less and less translucent, and the more solid they became the more Dorothy screamed and wriggled her body. Her mind was incapable of coping with what she was seeing. There was no way this could have been a trick, a macabre tasteless joke, and she must have known it. Brian could imagine how she had to be feeling. He could hardly deal with his own fear as it was.

If they stayed here they would succumb to the terror. They might drop dead from sheer fright or fall into deep occult comas, lie in unblessed unconsciousness until the elements or time or starvation brought them to a natural death, or until a truly alive human host of the demon could arrive at the barge from wherever it was now and make short, swift work of them. It would ravage their bodies without mercy as they lay there unknowing and helpless, as they lay drifting in an unending nightmare of grasping claws and dark, haunted, hollow faces. As they were cut to pieces they'd be dreaming of eyes that beseeched and beckoned, eyes that made promises of unimaginable bliss and unendurable agony. It would do to them what it had done to all the others.

Brian ordered Dorothy to close her eyes and gripped her by the shoulders. "They aren't real," he shouted, "they're just images. They can't hurt us." She would have to believe his falsehood or they would both die here together.

Steeling himself for the ordeal, he pushed Dorothy forward and walked her slowly, slowly down the narrow passageway. He tried not to look at the long-dead people all around him. He could sense how envious they were of his condition, of the life he exuded, of the rich, red blood that was coursing through his veins; his ability to come and go in the daylight and to leave this dank, stinking enclosure whenever he so desired. They wanted him, they hated him, *they would never let him go.*

In his mind's ear, a chorus of 400 voices cried out to him. They pleaded for his help; they threatened and they cursed. They made sinful, wanton promises and offered him their bodies and their love. He felt psychic kisses on his cheeks, phantom lips on his mouth, saw their hands—now looking as fully formed and three-dimensional, albeit thin and unhealthy, as his own—

reaching out as fingers touched him in even the most indelicate places.

The ghosts had stepped out of their seats into the aisle as he moved forward; they were blocking his advance. He shoved past them, telling himself that their tangibility was only in his mind, that they were spirits and could not hurt him, mere afterimages of the people who'd sat in this train on that mysterious day a century in the past. He turned away from the pleading, desperate faces, the solemn, hurt eyes of the children, *the lusting countenances of the older men and women.*

But they were *not* after-images, they were plaintive human souls, and they were offering him anything, *anything* they could give him, if only he would help them and *set them free*, if only he would exchange his own fine body for their shriveled, wasted pods. If only he'd take their places in this hellhole and be the demon's servant in their stead.

Save us, help us, we implore you.

The further down the aisle he went, the worse the journey became. The sights and sounds of a hundred years ago were becoming real to him. Dorothy, his hands still gripping her shoulders, leaned back in terror against his body, whimpering and shaking, her eyes tightly closed. She was lucky. She couldn't see what he saw, couldn't see the terrible faces, the twisted, ravaged bodies, the eyes alive with anguish and *maggots*

There were more and more of them in the aisles that he had to push his way past. They could offer no resistance; their flesh was too weak, their bones too insubstantial. Brian could almost feel their skin rubbing against his own. Dorothy was spared that because she wasn't looking, her mind had no chance to imagine the spotted, papery tissue scraping repulsively against her flesh. The odor was getting fouler every second; the hot, enclosed sweat of the multitude—underarms, feet, clothes that hadn't been washed in ages. *The sour smell of the dying and diseased.*

They were getting closer to the end of the car, but the ghouls were determined. Brian noticed that the odor in the air was getting worse; added to the smells already existing was a putrid blast of feces and urine, of rotting meat that was filled with pus and larvae. *It was the passengers!* The faces and bodies of the people around him had undergone a change, from men and women who were merely unhealthy, to fetid and decomposing corpses. He saw heads on their way to becoming skulls, saw putrifying flesh falling in folds off of skeletal bodies, saw hollow eye sockets filled with tiny, squirming worm-things. The corpses still walked, still moved. They still held out their hands in desperation. *Help up, help us, help us.*

They had no intention of letting them leave the car.

The power of the demon had to be *enormous.* Brian, who was not and never had been a psychic, was experiencing things only possible for a true psychic. Unless "the claw" had somehow stimulated his natural ability, the repressed ability, that all average humans supposedly had inside them.

The corpses were blocking the door. *They would not let them leave!* In spite of the decomposing flesh, they looked more solid than ever. He could feel their foul, hot breath, almost *taste* the fiendish odor emanating from their gaping, toothless mouths. As one they opened their jaws as wide as they could and said, *Help us; Help us; Help us!* They had no faces now—only skulls with bits of hair and skin still clinging in red, disgusting tatters. Some of them still had eyes, white eyeballs that looked as if nothing held them in but a thin sheathe of gruesome jelly. Even as Brian watched, the eyes began *falling out,* plopping to the floor, onto his shoes. *Dorothy,* he prayed, *keep your eyes closed.*

Help us, Help us, Help us.

But to help them was to die. *And, once dead, he would simply become a part of them, doomed to spend the rest of eternity as a disembodied spirit in a railway car that had long since been forgotten by the rest of the world.* Couldn't they understand that? The only way he could help them was by freeing them, and the only way he could do that was to—

Kill the demon, Kill the demon, Kill the demon. . . .

Had he *heard* it—or was it merely a thought that he'd had?

The corpses were only skeletons now. No flesh remained on their bones.

He realized with startling, shocking clarity: they had never really meant him any harm.

Kill the demon, Kill the demon. . . .

Fading, fading, the words like an unholy echo in his mind, fading away even as the bones began to disintegrate, as the skeletons blocking his path fell to pieces and the pieces turned to dust.

It was over.

But he had heard enough. All in an instant of utter revelation.

He stepped over the carpet of dust—which was undisturbed by anything except for the footprints they'd left upon entering—and took Dorothy out into the daylight. He lifted her up bodily in his arms and walked down the steps until his feet touched the dirty surface of the barge.

He set Dorothy down on her feet. "You can open your eyes now. It's over."

Dorothy was still crying, trembling uncontrollably.

"Dorothy, stop it. It's over now. We're safe."

She opened her eyes, looked around. "Got to get off," she murmured. She ran to the side of the barge.

It wasn't until they were safely on the deck again that she was able to speak rationally. Her teeth wouldn't stop chattering. "Never so terrified—never seen anything—Is that—what the demon can do?"

He explained to her what had happened, how the spirits on the car had been pleading for his assistance. "They were never trying to kill us, to scare us—except perhaps at the very first. Then a change came over them."

"Not trying to scare us!" She must have been thinking of the terrible things she'd witnessed when her eyes had been open at the beginning. "'How can you say that?"

Brian explained: "They were communicating with us the only way they knew how." He felt tears forming in his eyes. He thought of all those people, those doomed souls, thought of the children—babies, some of them—and the pain they'd had to suffer. "I made a mistake, that's all. I thought they were prisoners, slaves of the four-fingered demon."

"Weren't they?"

"Not entirely. In part they *are* the four-fingered demon. It came to me—they *told* me—while we were inside. I have no psychic power, but they were able to reach me because they knew what I'd been doing, knew I'd been following the demon's 'career.' From the moment I stepped into the car, they knew I was on their side."

"But you said they *were* the demon." She rubbed her arms to get warm. "I can believe *that!*"

"I didn't get the whole story of how it happened, but the demon is made up of more than one consciousness. One of those consciousnesses is the dominant one. It gives all the orders while the others must suffer in silence, trapped in some hellish nonexistence. *It* ordered the others to attack us, but they finally rebelled—the demon must be preoccupied elsewhere or they might never have been able to disobey it. They gave me the information I need to destroy the miserable creature forever." He paused. "They also told me who the demon has possessed this time around."

He told her who it was. Dorothy was shocked at the identity of the host. "That's someone I never even suspected," she said numbly.

They didn't speak again until they were back in his car, on the way to Avalon Studios. Time was of the essence. This was the time to make a move against the demon, while it was still in its dormant stage.

"The demon," Dorothy said. "It did more than just make those spirits appear. *It made me see my mother and father.* It tormented me—with a vision of my parents. They were crying and they were bleeding and they seemed so lost and frightened." She added in a fainter voice, "I've always wondered if they'd known that something awful was going to happen to them that night. If they'd had a premonition . . . if all people who died that way have premonitions. I think they must. . . ."

Brian reached over and squeezed her hand; it was still trembling. "That was only an illusion and nothing more," he told her. "Your parents haven't anything to do with this. It was—as you surmised—just an attempt to terrify and destroy you. Your parents, wherever they've gone, passed on a long, long time ago and are at peace. Believe me."

She looked at him, a study in misery. "Are you sure?"

He patted her hand. "I'm sure." He could imagine how she must have felt. The demon had taken a memory very precious to her and made it vile and perverted. It hadn't shown Dorothy her parents—their love, their lives, their happiness—it had shown Dorothy her parents' *deaths*.

Something else had happened to Dorothy Hunter, he knew. Something both wonderful and terrible. A portal had been opened to her and she'd stepped through it before she'd even realized what had happened.

For better or worse, Dorothy Hunter had *seen*.

Dorothy Hunter was now a *believer*.

21

They'd had some equipment trouble and the filming had run overtime. The cast and crew should have been resting up, preparing for the wrap party, but instead they were still at work, setting up for the final scene.

There was tension in the air. Everyone was tired and it had been an awfully long day. Everyone had anticipated an end to the work on *Vicious Two* and freedom from the fear that the macabre events surrounding the filming had engendered. No one—not even those who could use the extra work and the money it entailed—wanted the picture to extend another *hour*, let alone a day. They were all doing their best to get it over with.

Jimmy had found a fairly unobstructed view of the proceedings back in an alcove where a pile of thick rubber cables had been plugged into the wall. He hunkered down and tried to remain as inconspicuous as possible. It wasn't hard to do. Everyone on the soundstage was preoccupied, running in every direction. In the catwalks overhead they were adjusting lamps and changing wires. On the floor they were operating boom mikes and dollies, darting in and out of partitions, wires and complex banks of machinery.

Jimmy couldn't shake the feeling that if something else were to happen it would happen tonight. Part of him wanted to run out of the soundstage—and the city—as fast as his feet could take him. Another part of him was unable to tear his eyes away, as if he were watching sinister history in the making.

He had to admit, he was hardly holding up any better than Dorothy was. These murders were really freaking him out, so much so that he had to make constant efforts to keep images of the grisly occurrences from intruding into his thoughts. He was cursed with too vivid an imagination. Seeing such things in a movie, faked with actors and clever makeup effects, was one thing. Jimmy did not get 'turned on' by the real thing *at all*. He was in a daze over it; his surface thoughts and body were doing one thing, but his subconscious was in another, more protective dimension for the duration.

He supposed he already had enough material and could have flown out of L.A.—and taken poor Dorothy with him—this morning, but how could he tell Dorothy to face up to, to confront, her fears, if he himself ran away from them? He *did* have a few minor interviews to complete later. If these people all around him could come here to do their jobs, why couldn't he? Besides, he doubted if the killer would strike on the soundstage in full view of dozens of witnesses.

Perhaps it was only part of the whole rationalization process, but he'd never really considered that he or Dorothy were in danger, were likely to become victims of the maniac. Was it that that sort of thing "only happened to other people," or because he and Dorothy were only peripherally connected to *Vicious Two*? Or was it simply something too horrible to contemplate? Bad enough *he* should be killed and dismembered, but if anything ever happened to Dorothy. . . .

Sure he'd danced, kissed a few women in the clubs while Dorothy was at her meetings. But he'd never slept with them. As intoxicating as his "freedom" had seemed, the thought of having Dorothy at his side to share, to comfort, to love and cherish, was even more attractive a proposition. God, how he loved that woman, neuroses, insecurities and all. Had there ever really been any doubt? He had to be fair to Dottie—she was not just a narrow, unconscionable prude. She was far too complex a person to be explained so simply.

He hoped she would be safe with this Brian Asquith character. Jimmy wasn't really jealous—Dorothy also had a right to a harmless fling now and then, didn't she?—but rather concerned for her welfare. Or so he told himself. He had expressed his reservations about her being alone with the "occult nut" but she would have none of it. She was pursuing a story—or so she said—and was convinced she could handle herself.

Just like Bethany, the Longbanks, Eddie and George had handled themselves? Damn! He should never have let her go. But she was a grown woman, not his prisoner. When her mind was made up, that was that.

Well, there was nothing he could do about it now. He just hoped she was safe. Life without Dorothy wouldn't really amount to much, that was for sure.

Dorothy had accused him of calling her a silly idealist. Yet in some juvenile Hardy Boys fashion hadn't he harbored the secret hope that during all his interviews and poking about he might uncover a clue to the killer's identity? Might he not solve the crime, stop the horrible murders—*stop the pain*—and become the hero of the hour?

He smiled. *So childish*. He concentrated on what was happening on the soundstage.

The cameras were focused on a small set of a greenhouse and adjacent patio. Exteriors had been shot on an estate in Beverly Hills many days before. This was the scene in which the film's heroine, played by Ellen Rue, was to unmask and have her final battle with the killer. In the original script, Ellen's part had been a small one; she'd been the murderer's first victim. In Stoner's revised screenplay, another woman, a hitchhiker, was murdered in Ellen's place, and she—playing a reporter—set about investigating the series of brutal slayings.

In the final full action scene (a brief epilogue showing Yvette back in the madhouse had already been filmed), the killer decides to pay a call on Ellen at her home and put an end to the young lady's snooping. Months from now when the film was released, the audience would be wondering—whose shadow is that filling up the foreground while Ellen is working in the greenhouse? Whose gloved hand is picking up those foot-long garden shears or hedge clippers? Stoner had made sure that his murderer would always wear gloves—that way the size and shape of the hand wouldn't give away the killer's identity. They'd gasp as the shadow of the killer moved closer and closer toward the entrance to the greenhouse. Was it Jocasta Sullivan's "nurse?" Was it the handsome young hustler? Certainly it couldn't be Yvette Cummings, the murderess in the original *Vicious*? That would be too obvious.

Well, apparently Livingstone Stoner didn't think so, because it was Vivienne Cherneau—playing the convicted murderess whose mind has once again become unhinged—who was wearing the gloves and holding the garden shears and moving in the heroine's direction. Jimmy craned his neck forward, fascinated. Maybe it wasn't such a bad idea. Everyone would assume someone else committed the murders, that Cummings' sanity had legitimately been restored. Then whammy—the truth would come out.

Jimmy tried to suppress the uncomfortable feeling he was getting from watching all of this. It was almost as if Stoner were directing a reenactment of some of the true horrible murders that had happned while the fantasy of *Vicious Two* was being filmed, instead of the other way around. Jimmy knew it was all fake—down to the phony backdrop behind the fake plastic windows of the greenhouse—but he couldn't dispel the uneasy feeling in his stomach.

Who was it really? he wondered. The *real* killer. *Was* it Stoner, the man with the unabashed passion for violent deaths and gruesome images? Was it Harold Watson or Jocasta Sullivan, or maybe Ellen Rue? Was actress Vivienne Cherneau identifying too closely with her role? Was it any of the assorted camera and prop people milling about in the enclosure?

Who?

The suspense was nearly killing him.

Vivienne Cherneau approached the girl in the caramel jumpsuit. She was in her Yvette Cummings persona now; Yvette Cummings, mass murderess, a deranged and tormented woman who had to murder people to still the "voices" in her mind, who had to hack and slash and mutilate until she once again felt peaceful and secure. Who had to slay all of her enemies as if they were menacing mythological dragons.

Vivienne's stomach was grumbling and she was annoyed at the long, costly delays they'd been having all day. She just wanted to get this atrocity over with. She had no doubt *Vicious*

Two would be a good-looking movie—solid production values, classy sets, handsome cinematography—but she wasn't so sure about anything else. If she had to look at one more dismembered body she thought she'd go out of her mind.

She thought she'd go out of her mind.

Stoner interrupted her reverie. "Okay, doll," he hollered. "We're ready for you. Just walk behind Ellen and slash out with the garden shears like you're going to stab her."

She nodded. She was ready. Ellen Rue—yechh! She hated that little bitch, wished she could have murdered her for real.

Jocasta Sullivan, who'd appeared with Vivienne in the scene they'd shot before this, sat on the sidelines glaring at her daughter. She'd been doing it ever since filming began, determined to make her daughter pay for her hand in reducing her role. Hand? Tits and ass was more like it, thought Vivienne. Careful, she had to concentrate now or she'd spoil the take.

As she walked closer and closer to the doorway, as she passed through the portal and entered the greenhouse, she could sense the camera tracking behind her. Vivienne felt hot all of a sudden, uncomfortable, so dizzy and tired and weak. *She heard an odd, distant voice in her mind as if something fat, toadish and terrible were squatting on her shoulder and whispering in her ear, whispering dark, debased thoughts that made her tremble.* She shook her head. She was just not herself today.

"CUT!"

"Vivienne," Stoner yelled. "What happened? Why are you shaking your head like that?"

"Sorry."

"Let's do it again, please. And no shaking. It screws up your shadow."

They set up the shot again and did a successful take. Now it was time to film the scene from Ellen's viewpoint. It would be the first time that the audience would realize that Vivienne was the killer as they saw her approach the heroine, raise her weapon, and snarl out her hatred and derangement.

They were ready.

"Yvette!" Ellen screamed, trying to give a reasonable approximation of mortal terror. *Fat chance.* "It can't be—it can't be *you*!"

"Yes, it *is* me, you little bitch—"

"CUT, *CUT*! Viv—that ain't in the dialogue, darlin'."

"Sorry."

They got ready to start again. Vivienne felt *so* hot now, so—no other word for it—*weird*. She'd been feeling this way a lot lately, but she didn't like to admit it. She hated even the thought of illness, just hated getting old. *Getting old. Oh, Charlie, I could bear it if you were with me.* She touched her left hand and scratched it. It was getting itchy under the heavy glove. The glove felt at least a size too small. Did the prop master give her the right one?

Then they were starting again and she was saying her memorized dialogue. The words came rushing out and she imagined that she must look quite menacing and horrible. *She must look like the monster she was.* She snarled: "Yes, it's me, Ramona. Me. It's been me all along."

Now Yvette was supposed to become weepy and melancholic, was supposed to sob and say, "Can't you see I had to kill them? It was either me or them. Can't you see?"

But instead, Vivienne could only repeat that one single line of dialogue. "Yes, it's me. Yes, it's me."

And then it hit her:

It is me.

It was me all along.

"Yes, it's me."

YES—IT'S ME!"

And then, something snapped open deep inside her. It all came rushing back to her in an instant, all the hurt and pain of the last few years, all the mortification she'd endured—the terrible realization that a once-beautiful and talented actress had been transformed into nothing more than a bloated ugly shadow of herself, a camp figure, something to laugh at, something to frighten little children. All the despair came rushing, rushing into her mind, overwhelming her, bringing out her secret side, the dark, sinister sharer who had been part of her all these days since the project began, the sharer that had at last emerged a few days ago when the Longbanks were murdered.

"Yes, it's me," she screamed, as the people on the set stared at each other in puzzlement.

In the space of a few seconds she saw it all in her mind: *her desire to slash out of existence everyone who made her feel fat and foolish and unwanted, anyone who contributed in any small way to her torment. She saw herself taking things out of the closet where she kept her late husband's tools, putting them in the perennial shopping bag in which she carried her belongings, the extra change of clothes she always kept so she'd be fresh in the early fall's humidity. She saw herself changing into these clothes after each murder, disposing of the old ones, always dripping with gore.*

She saw herself breaking into the Longbanks' home, murdering them, killing the man who'd written her another part as an ogre. Saw herself murdering the haughty Bethany Carraval, who'd been against her from the start, who'd wanted someone else for the picture and hadn't been above telling certain blabbermouths. She slaughtered that old drunken fool George Piedmont, who'd made the mistake of telling her how beautiful she'd once been, and chopped up that ghoulish, vulgar makeup man who splattered her with movie blood and forced her to touch and do depraved and disgusting things. She saw herself paying a call on George after leaving her apartment for the second time on the day of that dreadful convention—after Hester had gone home.

Yet it had really not been Vivienne who committed those murders—how odd!—but rather something inside her, something that compelled her even in those moments when she was in control of her actions to take note of the type of killings in the screenplay, to unobtrusively obtain the addresses of her victims.

But then that shadowy something in the dark corner of her brain took over again, crept in and possessed her, as the trauma of realizing all the terrible things she'd done forced Vivienne's consciousness to retreat, recede, into a hard, protective shell that nothing and no one could penetrate.

Yes, it's me, yes, it's me, it's me, it's meeeeee. . . .

Jimmy was confused. Why was Vivienne screeching at the top of her lungs like that? How had her features changed when the makeup artists had not yet come in to work their magic? He'd heard Stoner remark that it might be a nice touch if Viv looked a bit demonic toward the end of this sequence, but no one had had a chance to apply any makeup.

Stoner was yelling CUT and Ellen Rue was backing away and

it was clear that Viv was no longer sticking to the screenplay. From what he recalled of the script, Jimmy knew that at this point Vivienne was to make repeated stabs with the garden shears which Ellen would dodge until "Ramona" could get her hands on a gun and shoot Cherneau in the chest, disabling her. Yvette Cummings would not die, though; just in case they decided to make another sequel.

But though Stoner kept hollering CUT over and over again, Vivienne would not stop screaming.

Jimmy came out of his hiding place. Something was seriously wrong.

Instead of settling down and listening to Stoner, Vivienne kept shouting her line and shaking the hand holding the weapon.

It's me it's me it's me. . . .

Suddenly she stopped screaming and whipped the garden shears through the air and across Ellen Rue's startled face!

Ellen cried out in panic. Bowled over by the force of the blow, she dropped down to her knees and whipped her hands up to her injury.

"Oh my God, no!" Livingstone Stoner raced out onto the set.

Vivienne had pulled the shears open and was positioning the blades on either side of Ellen's neck.

The shears were not props. They were real ones.

Stoner tried to pull the shears out of Vivienne's hands. She let the left handle dangle and shoved him away with her strong, fleshy arm. She made a fist and rammed it into Livingstone's stomach.

Ellen managed to get up to her feet before Vivienne could snap the shears shut on her neck. Screaming and cursing at Vivienne, she tried to get away from the "greenhouse." Crewmen rushed to Vivienne's side and tried to subdue her, but no one really wanted to get too close to those nasty shears.

Out of breath, hunched over from the blow to his solar plexus, Stoner moved toward Vivienne with an intent to disarm her. On his way he had the misfortune to trip on a cable. He reached out for something to grab but there was only empty air.

Stoner fell headlong into the open, outstretched pair of garden shears, his face catching tight between the blades!

Vivienne put her hands back on either handle and pushed inwards with a sickening thrust. There came the crunch of crackling bone, the alarming hysteria of Stoner's high-pitched squealing. Ellen Rue started screaming and there was a startling cacophony of frenzied, frantic commotion. Chairs overturned, people screeched, crewmen ran in all directions. Security guards came running up, guns drawn, but none wanted to shoot and possibly kill one of the principal actors and later be held responsible for the action. It was impossible for them to tell that it was the director whose face was being cleft.

Jimmy stood stock still and took it all in. *Took in the man's head caught between the blades,* which were now buried deep in Livingstone's flesh. *The river of dripping blood gushing out of the wounds. The cracking, snapping noises the head emitted as the blades cut even deeper into the bones.* Jimmy held his stomach and tried to keep himself together, wondering what on earth he could do. He needed to vomit very badly.

Vivienne wrenched the shears open again and Stoner fell to the floor, dead, little bits of him still sticking to the blades. Vivienne looked around for more victims. She was growling and glowering, her face transformed into something out of a nightmare. The shears were opening, closing, opening, closing, a dark, metallic symphony of bloody anticipation.

From a safe distance, Jimmy looked at the woman's hand. Something was shredding the glove she was wearing—*did he see dark spots of mottled flesh in the places that were torn? Were those long, piercing, unnatural nails creeping, ripping out of the leather fingertips?*

Ellen Rue rushed over to Stoner's body and dropped down beside it, sobbing. "Murderer! Murderer!" she screamed.

Vivienne was at the girl's side so fast Ellen had no time to save herself. She thrust the closed metal blades downward through Ellen's hair and *into her head.* Blood gushed out of the girl's eyes, mouth and ears as she dropped over messily onto her face. Vivienne tore the bloodied twin blades out of the woman's head with a terrible *yank.*

Jocasta Sullivan cried out in horror and rushed toward Vivienne with her fists upraised. Before the actress could lay a hand on her daughter's killer, Vivienne slashed the shears in front of her like a sword and severed the woman's jugular. Jocasta's eyes went blank and she dropped to the floor spewing purplish blood and spittle.

Vivienne turned away from Jocasta's corpse and brandished her weapon at all those around her—the cameramen, the startled technicians, the impudent young security pups. *I'll Kill You All*, she screamed through gritted teeth. Her voice was completely inhuman.

A few shots rang out: the security men trying to disarm her. It had all happened so fast they'd hardly had time to aim, being afraid of shooting the wrong person. Vivienne turned her attention to them. Even a bullet in the arm, the shoulder—flesh popping open like blooming rose petals from the bullets' impacts—wouldn't stop her. She started stabbing and hacking mercilessly at the armed men all around her.

Once past the scattered, bleeding security men, Vivienne decided to trash the set. She ripped through the cables on the floor with her shears and smashed every camera lens she could reach. There was blood all over the soundstage, blood and mutilated bodies. Something fell over and a fire erupted, turning within seconds into a dangerous conflagration. Seeing the smoke, the helpless crewmen and wounded security guards forgot about the corpses and the killer and headed for the exits.

Jimmy was so scared he nearly wet his pants.

This was not a movie.

This was real.

Real blood. Real bodies.

This wasn't fun.

The smoke from the fire was beginning to be too much for him. He tripped on something in his rush for the exit and fell onto the floor.

He got up moments later in a daze. He must have hit his head on something because he'd blacked out for a while. From his perch on the floor he looked around groggily for some sign of Vivienne. Thank goodness he didn't see her anywhere, but there was so much smoke it was hard to be sure. He rolled over and prepared to get to his feet.

Vivienne Cherneau, still as mad as a hatter, was standing directly above him.

The claw, the four-fingered claw, which had by now completely ripped out of Vivienne's glove, was hanging in the air above his face.

Vivienne lifted the shears. In another instant they'd be swinging downward with the force of a guillotine.

Something hit Vivienne on the side of her head, distracting her. A wrench! It bounced on the floor near Jimmy's feet and he grabbed it. A feeble weapon but better than nothing. Then he saw with surprise who had thrown it.

Dorothy! She looked pale and frightened, disbelieving but determined—as did the man with her whom Jimmy assumed was Brian Asquith.

Jimmy stumbled to his feet. Vomit was dribbling down his chin onto his trousers.

"Dorothy! Get out of her. She'll kill you—" Then the smoke crept back into his lungs and he was too busy coughing and choking to be able to speak.

Dorothy and Brian ran to his side just as Vivienne continued her assault. *Too late*—the blades stabbed into Jimmy's shoulder. He pulled back and cried out in pain.

"Jimmy!"

Brian rushed the heavyset actress from the side when her face was turned, as she was gloating over the agony of her victim. She was deftly knocked to the ground by Asquith's agile tackle.

Brian screamed, "Get out of here!"

Dorothy tried to pull Jimmy away, but neither really wanted the occultist to face the killer alone. "Get out!" Asquith hollered at them. "I tell you I know what to do!"

The smoke was becoming too thick for breathing or thinking. The heat of the flames made the sweat pour out of them. "Get out, I said!"

Earlier, a dolly, abandoned by its panicked operator, had crashed into a piece of equipment, starting a chain reaction of disaster that finally overtook a series of heavy, overhanging lamps. The lamps, which had been dangling precariously for precious seconds, chose that exact moment to fall.

They fell right on top of Vivienne Cherneau.

One moment, Brian was looking at Vivienne's hand.

The next moment, Vivienne was no longer there.

She was underneath the shattered lamps, her body trembling and sizzling from the escaping electricity, sliced by huge shards of broken razor-sharp glass. Her bloodied legs were sticking out from beneath the hissing equipment. The shears had been knocked out of her hand and were lying several feet away from her body. There was no question about it. She was dead.

Jimmy couldn't help but feel relief.

The whole soundstage was burning, the equipment, the backdrops, the flimsy plywood partitions. Dorothy grabbed Brian by his collar, knocking him out of the trance he'd been in.

"Come on!" She helped the shivering, dazed Jimmy out of the building.

Brian Asquith followed, shaking his head and swearing.

The fire blazed and the smoke billowed. The bodies in the room began to burn.

The sound of fire engines filled the air.

22

"It isn't over."

They sat in Brian Asquith's apartment, drinking cool wine and trying to make sense out of all that had happened. Jimmy's shoulder injury was bandaged, but it had been comparatively minor.

Dorothy looked over at their host. "What do you mean, Brian? Poor Vivienne is dead. The demon is gone. How can you say it's not over? Because we don't know how the passengers became a demon in the first place?"

"Because the demon isn't dead." He lifted his glass. "All of us saw the claw, did we not?"

Dorothy and Jimmy nodded. Even now they couldn't believe that any of it had happened.

"Before the lamps fell on top of Vivienne," he said, "the claw had disappeared."

He waited a few moments for what he'd said to sink in.

"Vivienne was *herself* when she died, poor woman. She felt all the pain and confusion in those final moments. The demon had fled her body just a second before."

He leaned forward. "It still exists. It still lives. It's still out there, capable of doing this all over again."

"How do you know that?" Dorothy wanted him to explain.

"Doing what again?" Jimmy asked. "We found out that there'll never be a *Vicious Two*. The final scenes were never completed. The studio has no intention of resuming production, not after all those deaths—not to mention the devastation of the fire. So how can it start again?"

Brian shook his head wearily. "That makes no difference, Mr. Radley. This demon has murdered and caused misery for hundreds of people who have had nothing to do with *Vicious* or its ill-fated sequel. The battle isn't over, not by a long shot." He turned to Dorothy. "And you ask how I *know*? I know because I was told that by the spirits on the railroad car." He saw the look of disbelief on Jimmy's face. "If you don't believe me, Mr. Radley, ask Dorothy. She was a skeptic once, too."

Dorothy nodded. "It really happened, Jimmy," she said. "I saw it with my own eyes."

Jimmy kissed her on the forehead and squeezed her body. "Okay, guys. I believe you. It's just that it's such an *incredible* story."

Brian took a sip of his Chablis. "You saw the claw as well as we did. You saw what happened on the set before we even arrived." Brian was grateful that all the pandemonium on the soundstage had facilitated his and Dorothy's entrance after the studio gateman, who'd recognized Dorothy as Jimmy's associate and had her name in any case, waved them through. "Tell me," he said, "do you still have doubts?"

Jimmy scratched his palm. "I don't know *what* to think any more."

"The spirits and I became *one* for a short while. They told me what I would have to do to completely destroy the demon.

"*But I never had the chance to*. It fled, leaving Vivienne to face the music, leaving her to die only moments after we arrived. It's still out there. Waiting. Looking for more victims. *And* another human host."

Jimmy took Dorothy's hand in his own. "So what do we do?"

Brian leaned forward. "We wait. We wait and we

watch. . . .

"And when it makes its move, we'll be ready."

Part Five: *The Sisters of Mourning*

23

Winter, 1988.
Lennington, Illinois.

Sally Anne Hollister tossed her head back and ran her fingers through her long auburn tresses. "I mean, really, I'm just about to go out of my mind."

Chubby Lucinda reached across the space between their two beds and grabbed the joint out of Sally Anne's hand. She stuck it between her full red lips, and inhaled dramatically. Screwing up her eyes, she held her breath, exhaled a cloud of smoke a moment later, and started couching. "Ugh!" She pounded her chest above her sizeable bosom. "That's good stuff." Handing the joint back to her roommate she said, "Yeah, I know what you mean. I had no idea how it would be at this place. I know Dolby is supposed to be one of the best women's colleges in the country, but it's so out of the way, and there are hardly any boys around at all. The guys in town are so . . .?"

Sally Anne rolled her eyes. "I know. Yucchy, Carpenters and grocery clerks. Grease monkeys. Why did they plunk Dolby down in the absolute *toadiest* small town they could find." She looked at the young woman sitting on the hard-backed chair in the corner and grudgingly handed her the reefer. "Oh, sorry, Jane Paige. I forgot you were here."

Jane took the joint from Sally Anne's fingers and put it to her lips. She wasn't sure what irritated her more: Sally Anne's loathsome snobbishness, or her habit of constantly referring to her by using her full name. It was never "Jane" or "Paige" or "Miss Paige" or "Janie" it was always "Jane Paige" and nothing but. She knew Sally Anne didn't like her, but she had to put up with her because Jane and Lucinda were friends. Of course, Sally Anne *loved* Lucinda. Her roommate was short and fat and no competition as far as boys were concerned. Unless one counted personality. That was one area in which Lucinda had it all over her bitchy roommate.

As Jane let the marijuana rush through her system and add to the mild high she was feeling, she felt a sudden stab of depression. She hoped Lucinda wouldn't fall so completely under the influence of her roommate that she'd start to talk and act just like her. Lucinda was *nice*; she was likeable. It would be a shame for her to be spoiled by that silly young woman she was living with.

But Jane well knew how "nice girls"—not in a sexual or behavioral sense, but simply in how they treated other people—could be corrupted by their desperate desire to fit in with the popular girls, to be part of the gang. Peer pressure could have you doing and saying things you'd never say or do of your own volition.

Jane handed the joint over to Lucinda and looked up at the window. Over the tops of the school's other buildings—the dormatories, the classrooms, the glass and steel student center—could be seen the towers and spires of the Mourning Sisters' nunnery. "Sometimes I feel like I'm over *there*," she said, "instead of here."

Lucinda saw where she was looking and laughed. "Yeah. For all the action we get we might as well be nuns."

Of course, at seventeen, none of the three girls had had very much "action," their first time away from home and all. Jane had petted, made out, let a boy touch her, but that was about it. Despite the way Sally Anne presented herself as being world-weary and sophisticated, Jane suspected she, too, was a virgin. And Lucinda had admitted that she was one one night when she and Jane were alone. Going to an all-girl school did not do much to turn a young woman's fantasies into reality.

"What do you think they *do* over there?" Lucinda said. "That convent gives me the creeps."

"I bet they're dykes," Sally Anne said with a mean-spirited sneer.

"You mean *lesbians*," Jane said. Sally Anne's mind was so narrow it could have fit between two slices of bread and still have made an awfully thin sandwich.

"Lesbos, dykes, who cares?" Sally Anne said. "Yucch. Bet they sit over there all night and stick cucumbers up each other's pussies."

"Oh, *gross*," said Lucinda.

"I hate dykes. Half the teachers here are dykes. Did you see that Miss Esterbrook in Social Studies? Bet she's a dyke."

"Oh shut up, Sally Anne."

"*Grow* up, Jane Paige. If you don't like what Lucinda and I are talking about you can just go back to your room."

"She stays," Lucinda protested. "This is my room, too."

"Fuck you, Lucinda." She looked venomously at Jane. "Bet you'd like it over there at the convent, Jane Paige. Bet you'd enjoy hanging out with all those dykey nuns."

"Cut it out," Lucinda said. "Jane's my friend."

"Just don't be alone with her," Sally Anne warned her roommate.

"Sally Anne," Jane said. "Sometimes you are *such* an idiot." She knew why the girl from Poughkeepsie didn't like her. Because she had the guts to stand up to her, because they both knew Jane was prettier and smarter than Sally Anne was.

Sally Anne took the joint back from Lucinda, took a toke, and then handed it back. "You can't have any more, Jane Paige, for being insubordinate. Lucinda and I will finish it ourselves."

"Sally Anne!" whined Lucinda.

"Shut up, Lucinda, or you won't get any, either."

"Don't worry about it, Lucy," Jane said. "I don't want any more anyway."

Jane hoped this evening wasn't an omen of what the whole freshman year would be like. At least the weekends. The school term had only started a couple of weeks ago, but Jane hadn't made many friends. Late Friday afternoons half the girls in the dorm would jump in their cars and drive home to their parents' for the weekend. The other girls, girls like her and Sally Anne and Lucinda who came from halfway across the country, had to be content with seeing their folks only during school breaks. There were boys available—mostly young men who lived in the town and a few fellows who came from the nearest college fifty miles away—but most of them were already taken by the older girls at the college. The good ones, anyway.

And there was so little to do on the weekends. The college sponsored a few poetry readings and amateur theatrical productions on Friday or Saturday nights, but that was hardly the kind of excitement they were after. Just about the only man on campus was the security guard, a fortyish married fellow with Brylcreem in his hair and a limp in his right leg. At night the comparatively deserted campus was dark and foreboding, with long, long stretches of tree-and bush-lined pathways between the buildings. There had been talks of muggings, rapes, hushed up by the administration. There was a rumor that once a Dolby girl had been kidnapped by a bunch of townies and gang-raped for two hours behind the Rexall Drugs on Main Street. The thought of it made Jane shudder.

The dorms themselves were darkened and lonely at night, especially on weekends. Loud noises and music were forbidden, and half the rooms were empty. There were narrow corridors and stairwells where only shadows seemed to dominate, and the old floorboards and staircases creaked at the slightest footfall. Downstairs in her widow's domicile, the house mother, Mrs. Jessup, sat watching television, sniffling into her handkerchief and telling herself it was the plight of the characters on *Dynasty* and *Dallas* that made her cry. Late at night the muted tones of the Late Show were all that could be heard in Hubbard Hall.

"What time is it?" Jane asked, getting to her feet.

"Going somewhere?" Sally Anne sneered. "Good."

Lucinda looked at her wristwatch. "It's not nine yet. Why?"

"I think I'll go to the library. It's open until ten tonight. *Thank God.*"

"The library? Why do you want to go *there*, Jane Paige?"

"I want to go there, Sally Anne Hollister, to *read*. Have you ever tried it? Reading a book, that is? Or are you too sophisticated for that?"

Sally Anne rolled over on her back and flipped the joint's ashes onto the floor. "Fuck you, you *toad*."

"I'll go with you," Lucinda said quickly.

"*What*? You, too?"

"It's better than sitting around here doing nothing, Sally Anne. They get copies of *Glamour* and *Cosmo* every week. Why don't you come with us?"

And *Ms* and *Woman Now*, Jane thought. And books by Dickens and Oates and even Erica Jong.

"Go, then. I'll stay here. Maybe I'll go down to the TV room later and watch *Falcon Crest*."

Lucinda reached for her jacket. "Okay. See you later."

As they left the room Jane felt as if she'd achieved some sort of significant victory. Lucinda was her friend and she would not let Sally Anne spoil her. They went down to the Victorian-style lobby—polished brown floors, solid banister, heavy red drapes and carpeting—and out into the darkness. "I hate walking alone at night, don't you?" Lucinda said, stopping to pull up the zipper on her jacket.

"Yeah. Say, thanks for coming with me, Lucy."

"Don't mention it. Sally Anne gets on my nerves, too, sometimes."

Jane laughed. She put her arm around her friend's shoulder. Silently, they started off in the direction of the library. They'd walked a few minutes when Lucy said, "I wish they had some of the fan mags in the library. Every time I go to the drugstore they're sold out of *Tiger Beat* and *Teen*. And Tony Peters was supposed to be on the cover this month."

"Oh, I love him," Jane said. "What a hunk! But can you imagine Mrs. Groat putting *Tiger Beat* in the library. We're lucky we get anything halfway interesting."

"Mrs. Groat might have a crush on Tony, too, for all we

know."

The girls giggled at the thought of elderly, bulldog-faced Mrs. Groat with her spotted forehead and lantern jaw actually having *sexual feelings*.

Before they knew it they were approaching the bushes at the furthest edge of the long, white, rectangular library. The forest, thick with spindly trees and large, leafy bushes, was just a few feet away, scraping the back wall of the building and sweeping in an impenetrable arc all the way up to the convent.

Lucy stopped. "Shit. The lace on my sneaker is loose. Wait a minute."

Jane stood at the edge of the bushes while Lucy bent down with her back to her and set about trying to retie her shoelace. Struggling to see clearly what she was doing—she was farsighted and virtually blind when up too close to something—Lucy balanced precariously on her girth while Jane tried to keep from laughing.

Jane looked around the valley in which the campus was situated, and remembered that in the daytime the woods and gardens between the pathways with their bright shrubs and flowers were beautiful to look at, that the cold dark night would not last forever.

Perhaps it wouldn't be so bad here after all. She had come to Dolby to satisfy her parents' wishes, to escape her mother's hysteria, her father's indifference, the stifling pain of their loveless marriage; she'd come because she'd been told that the staff at Dolby could bring out the creativity and sensitivity that her writing talent indicated was within her. Suddenly the fresh air seemed cool and delightful, and she was filled with the thought of the unlimited promises that her life had to offer.

The next second she heard a *swooshing* sound and a thin, insulated wire was thrown around her throat.

"L—lllluuucccccc" was all she could get out before she was pulled back, back into the bushes.

Lucinda heard the sound her friend had made and turned to see what was wrong. Doing so made her lose her balance and she fell over onto her side. "Owwww." She was inspecting the scrape on her elbow when the frantic rustling of the bushes made her look once again in Jane's direction.

There was a figure in the distance, back at the far wall of the library where the forest began, and it was dragging Jane Paige into the woods. Jane was on her back, and struggling, her body being pulled helplessly over the underbrush and into the enveloping shadows.

Lucy was too thunderstruck to even cry out. For just a second one of the outdoor lights on the back of the library played over the struggling figures and Lucy had a quick distant look at the assailant. At *part* of the assailant. She saw the hands holding the garrote that was cutting into Jane Paige's neck, saw the peculiarly-shaped appendage on the right. *Funny. . . .?*

Lucinda screamed and ran into the library, her loose left sneaker falling off her foot and dropping forgotten onto the moist dirt at the side of the pathway.

24

Winter, 1988.
New York City.

Dorothy somehow managed to balance the grocery bag against her hips as she turned the key in the lock and thrust open the door to their apartment. "Jimmy?" she called out, wondering if he may have returned from work a little early. No, the apartment was empty. Drat. She brought the bag of groceries over to the kitchen counter. She was really feeling hungry and would have loved to skip all the fuss and preparation and go out to dinner. But if Jimmy was going to come home late and tired, he probably wouldn't want to go out again. She figured she'd have to start cooking for no other reason than to eventually satisfy her own appetite.

She took the groceries out of the bag and put some in the counter, some in the fridge, and some in the cabinets above and beside the oven. Of course, she could always go out to eat by herself and let Jimmy do the same—or fix a little something for himself—when he got home. Jimmy didn't mind cooking now and then; on occasion he'd even prepare elaborate dinners for the two of them. But she wasn't in the mood for sitting in a nice restaurant by herself, and there was nothing the local diner offered that particularly appealed to her.

So she turned on the radio to the easy listening station and got all the ingredients for a nice tuna casserole in order. She was putting the whole concoction in the oven when the door opened and Jimmy walked in waving a newspaper. "Hi," she said. He came over and kissed her on the neck. "How was *your* day?" he asked.

"Dull," she admitted. "Spent most of it in the library. I really felt like going out to dinner tonight, but I was afraid you wouldn't want to."

"That's not a bad idea. Where shall we go?"

"Oh, great. Right after I finish putting the tuna casserole in the oven."

"Thought I smelled something good. Well, as long as you've fixed something we might as well stay home."

"I was afraid you'd say that."

"Tell you what," he said, giving her another kiss. "Later on I'll take you over to Barnaby's for a drink. Would you like that?"

"That'll be nice, yes." She kissed him back and went to look for the lettuce while he went to the bedroom to change.

As she tore the head of the lettuce into chunks and held each piece under the running faucet to wash it, she thought for the hundredth time of how shallow their homey domesticity seemed, that underneath it was far deeper truth, one that they both tried to repress and always avoided talking about; they had touched the cosmic void and could never be quite the same again.

She didn't *feel* any different. She still had nightmares, worse nightmares than before, nightmares that hinted of dark, crawling things walking just out of her range of vision, dark creeping horrors that came forth to touch her the moment her back was turned. Visions of a silent, slashing *claw*.

Dorothy had to stop washing the lettuce for a moment. A harmless, mundane task—*yet the pieces of lettuce she had shredded in her hands had become strips of flesh peeling off of someone's screaming face; the head of lettuce had become a bleeding skull.* These visions came with increasing frequency—it seemed as if the terror of *Vicious Two* would always be alive inside her.

It was even worse for Jimmy, she knew. He had not spoken much about the things he'd seen on the last day of shooting, but she'd put the pieces together. The firemen had found several burned bodies amidst the smoke and carnage, and the details of their deaths had made the papers. Other people who had been on the set had seen how Vivienne Cherneau used the garden shears to smash Stoner's face, to kill Ellen Rue, to cut the throat of Jocasta Sullivan. All that blood, all that anguish. And Jimmy had *seen* it all. She and Brian had arrived only in time to save Jimmy's life, to watch Vivienne come to a comparatively bloodless end. All the bodies had been hidden in the smoke, all the blood and misery.

But Jimmy had seen it all.

The look on his face, the startled, stark whiteness, had not been caused by his mild shoulder wound. It had come from seeing the actual enactment of senseless bloodshed, the shock of sudden death. *Real death.*

She learned over the weeks afterwards that Jimmy's interest in fictional and cinematic terror, his apparently morbid preoccupations, had never truly been the sign of a callous or insensitive nature. The carnage on the set of *Vicious Two* that he had personally witnessed had affected him deeply; the blood, the tragedy, four people's lives snuffed out in less than the space of as many minutes. She realized fully for the first time that those terror films *had* been for him a means of escape, that his ghoulish appreciation and his constant chuckling over what seemed like the worst forms of inhumanity and torture were only his way of dealing with the world's real horrors. He looked forward to those films, relaxed with them, got away from his and the world's troubles for awhile.

Now he never looked at them. The *TV Guides* and cable station booklets—which at one time had been marked up with black magic marker circles indicating when and where a particular horror movie would be broadcast—were now completely untouched. He never stayed up late to look at them any more, never went on his journeys to Times Square to see two grisly pictures for the price of one. The films were no longer entertaining. Dorothy surmised that each crunching death, each hideous celluloid screech, would only serve as a reminder of the terrible things he had seen on the soundstage; he'd hear Livingstone

Stoner's squeals of agony in his mind, see the blood dripping from Ellen Rue's ears and nostrils. Now and then he woke up trembling, pulling himself out of the nightmare, and Dorothy would hold him and cry for him, remembering how she'd wanted him to understand how she felt, but realizing she'd never wanted it at such a cost.

He had faced his fear one night and watched videocassettes of *Vicious*, a few others, on the VCR. "Why do you have to get over your squeamishness?" she'd asked him. "It's not as if you're a nurse or a paramedic. It's not as if your job performance depends on it." But he'd insisted, trying to banish his nightmares and recover the lost joy that the films had once brought him. Ironically, Dorothy came to understand that her objection to the films had been entirely due to her personal experiences, just as Jimmy had always suggested. Now that Jimmy had had his own bad experiences—even if it had not been as personal as hers had been—he was unable to look at things he had once relished watching. The difference was that he had no moral or political objections to most of the movies—disregarding total sleaze with maniacs wrenching eyeballs out of women's sockets and popping them into their mouths—but he simply couldn't stomach them any more.

Eventually that would change, she knew; as time passed, wounds would be healed, emotional stability restored, along with his sense of balance and perspective. She viewed the inevitable with mixed emotions. Why? Jimmy had not really come over to her side, had he? In fact, in spite of everything, she had apparently come over to his. He had watched and enjoyed those movies and had never been a ghoul, had not been turned into one, or become inured to violence—true, real-life violence—because of them. Yet she and he would always argue, she feared, *hoped*, as to those pictures' essential wrongness, the basic sickness of their existence. She did know one thing: if his coming to enjoy terror films again meant that he was once more whole and healthy—as strange as that might sound—then she welcomed such a prospect with open arms.

That still left the One True Thing to deal with. The thing they found it so *difficult* to handle. The thing they thought Brian Asquith had brought into their lives, but which had really been there in the shadows all along.

The unknown.

The occult.

The four-fingered demon.

The *claw*.

As few others had been, Dorothy and Jimmy's lives had been touched by the supernatual. Dorothy had seen the ghostly visions on the barge, the shambling horrors in the seats of the ancient Sumarian train. Jimmy had seen the claw bursting from Vivienne's glove, and seen the hideous, demoniacal expression on her face. Jimmy had said a dozen times that he had no proof, he wasn't certain, wasn't even sure of what he'd seen. It had happened so fast, so furiously, the violence had been over in a matter of minutes. Yes, he had seen what appeared to be a claw hanging over him—four fingers, long nails—but it had only been for a second during an extremely hectic moment. He just couldn't swear to anything supernatural.

Dorothy, on the other hand, had no such escape mechanism. She'd *seen* her parents on the barge, seen the shuffling figures and felt their evil power, seen enough to last a lifetime before she did as Brian ordered and shut her eyes. Still, in the daytime, surrounded by the hustle and bustle, the somewhat appalling normalcy—or what passed for it—of New York City, she found it easier to believe that it had all been an illusion, a hallucination brought on by an overwrought and an over-vivid imagination.

But it was always there, deep in the back of their conscious minds, the possibility, the *certainty*, that there was more to this universe than the waking world—than the clattering garbage trucks, the honks of the automobiles, the thousands of rushing pedestrians, the rumble of the subway, the rustle of pigeons outside their window. What they saw with the naked eye was just one world. But there was another world that they knew they could never understand.

Dorothy finished fixing the salad, and started setting the table. The tuna casserole would not take long to bake. She could hear Jimmy moving about in the bedroom, whistling. She was filled with a sudden love for him, and a sadness that they'd seen two different sides of the same occult coin, instead of the same one, that they'd not been together to share their experiences. Instead of bringing them closer, these experiences had only driven a wedge of silence between them. Instead of something to share, it was a subject to avoid.

The first few weeks back from Hollywood, before a mutual unspoken agreement not to discuss what had happened, they had spoken practically of nothing else, awestruck by their experiences, by the feeling that their safe little world now seemed so vulnerable, and they so helpless. To keep away literal demons, to retain their sanity, they had thrown themselves into their work.

Vicious Two had been canceled, was kaput (*Frames and Directions* could no longer use the story of the film that would never be) so Jimmy worked up a free-lance piece on its ill-fated production—the murders, the strained temperaments, the eyewitness account of the last day on the soundstage—and sold it to *Playboy*. He never mentioned the claw, and only alluded to Asquith's theories very briefly—"some people feel there is an occult explanation for the murders"—for he had known that without solid proof there was no way he could introduce the four-fingered demon into any serious account of the production.

Dorothy had written a very long piece for *Woman Now*—a piece more in line with her original suggestion—stopping short of tastelessly (and wrongly) implying that the *Vicious Two* murders were an inevitable result of just the category of movies that *Vicous Two* belonged to. She was sure there were others who would do that. She focused instead on victims, on herself and Désirée Fontana, even the "madwoman" Vivienne Cherneau. Dorothy, too, made very brief references to the occult in her article. But without proof. . . .?

She did turn out other articles, however: a piece on Janice Evans for *Cosmopolitan*, downplaying the woman's demonic obsessions for which Dorothy felt like a traitor. And Brian Asquith had planted in her mind the idea of doing a full-length book on her whole Hollywood experience, or collaborating with him on a book about the claw and its many victims. She no longer believed that Asquith was crazy, that his theory was fit just for gullibles and crackpots. Still, she knew how everyone *else* would react. Her credibility would plummet to the basement, and her free-lance career might be irreparably damaged. She was known for her rational, practical insight, not for ghoulish flights of fancy.

She was caught in a dilemma common to many writers.

Should she write a book about victims, an expansion of her piece for *Woman Now*, a book that would probably garner good reviews and sell, if she was lucky, two dozen copies? Or should she write something more lurid and exploitative: *The "Vicious Two" Murders, The "Vicious Two" Demon*, something that might well become a blockbuster with proper handling? Months had gone by and so far nothing along those lines had been published or been announced by any firm. Neither Asquith nor Janice Evans had taken their stories to other writers. There was still a chance if she didn't delay.

Well, what was wrong with making money? And a book didn't *have* to be cheap and exploitative, not if it were written with taste and compassion. And she did believe the demon existed. It was not as if she'd be pulling the wool over her readers' eyes. So why not?

Yet the thought of doing talk shows, of having to defend her belief about the occult world . . .? Someone like Brian Asquith would be in his element: *she'd* squirm through every interview. *What to do, what to do, what to do . . .?*

"How's dinner coming?"

Jimmy, rolling up his sleeves, walked into the kitchen wearing bluejeans and a pale yellow shirt. "It smells good."

"It won't be long," she said. Now they would talk about the office, the new secretary who wore red plastic hot pants, the day to day strain of the whole operation, the new films he'd be writing about in the future. And she would tell him about the grumpy lady at the reference desk in the library, and the new flavor of ice cream she'd tried at Rumplemeyers, and mention the check she'd got from *Good Housekeeping* for her article on breast cancer recovery. And underneath it she'd be thinking: *A demon, a demon, there are demons in the world and what if it tries to possess me next? Has enough time gone by? Has it forgotten me? Will it leave me and Jimmy alone?*

"Honey. Are you all right?"

"Sure. I just have a headache, that's all." She got up, went over to the oven, and poked a fork into the casserole. The breadcrumbs on top were getting all brown and crunchy the way she liked them. "Almost ready."

She had managed—as she always did—to repress the bad thoughts and feelings, the paranoia, which she called her "demon fever," when the phone rang.

"Hello?"

"Hello, Dorothy. This is Brian Asquith."

Her hand went up to her chin.

"I think I've found it."

And the fear came rushing back again.

25

Winter, 1988.
Lennington, Illinois.

The hotel room was small but functional, with a large twin bed, grayish-brown bureau, and a pale turquoise rug on the floor.

Dorothy sat on the bed sipping coffee. Asquith was sitting on the chair by the writing desk. And Jimmy was pacing back and forth along the side of the bed, rubbing his fingers together as if to punctuate his dread and uncertainty.

"How can we be sure, Brian?" he asked for the seventh time.

"By asking questions," Asquith replied. Dorothy noted that the man didn't look good; he was frazzled and pale and seemed thoroughly worn by his exhaustive search for the four-fingered demon.

Dorothy and Jimmy had hesitated only a short while before deciding to fly out to the town of Lennington in Illinois to help Brian in his insane mission to stamp out the demon and free those hundreds of souls from its influence. Jimmy had gone along—or so he said—not out of any great belief or conviction, but rather to protect Dorothy. He swore he was not jealous of

Asquith, not jealous of their possibly spending days or weeks together in a strange city, but only feared for his lover's safety. "If all this stuff is really true," he'd said, "I figure you two will need all the help you can get."

Dorothy was not even certain why she was going. She had long since gotten over the silly "crush" on Brian Asquith, that was for certain. Jimmy was the only man she wanted or needed. As she packed her suitcase, she asked herself why then was she willingly running into possible danger, agreeing to help fight an alien force that was almost beyond her comprehension. Was it to get even? she wondered, was it to pay the monster back for tormenting her with visions of her parents' dying moments? Yes, that was it. She wanted the demon to pay for what it had done to so many people, but most of all she wanted it to pay for what it had done to her.

Of course, the reason she gave Jimmy was quite another matter. "I haven't yet abandoned the idea of writing a book about all this," she told him. "You and I could even collaborate, use all the material that Brian has collected. I'm sure he'd go along with it. Jimmy, this could be the biggest story of our lives and I'm going to see it through to the end. I have to."

It was a convenient time for them to get out of the city, too. Neither had any pressing reasons to stay behind. Jimmy was in the mood for a sudden, early vacation. To think six months had gone by since that trouble out in Hollywood. And they had almost succeeded in forgetting it.

Which brought them to the crux of the matter. What made Brian so certain he had tracked down the demon and located the site of its latest killing orgy? He'd given them some details, convincing details, over the phone, but not the whole story. After he'd picked them up at the airport, given them breakfast, gotten them a room at the motel where he was staying, he took them back to his hotel room and began to tell them why they were there.

"It all fits," he was saying. "A number of girls have disappeared. There have been two savage murders—of a young man and young woman. I think the killer is after women, but will kill a boyfriend if he gets in the way."

"Why does he kill some girls and kidnap others?"

Asquith shrugged. "Who knows? Anyway, the killer comes

and goes freely, which suggests it's someone the students know, someone they trust or can't possibly be afraid of."

"The most harmless and unlikely. . . ." Jimmy whispered. "Like Vivienne Cherneau."

"And Paul Wilson and young Gerry Winteroth, yes. Nice people, innocent people. People who would be freely admitted into any door, people no one would ever suspect of harboring murderous designs. There was one witness to a kidnapping, the first one"—he checked his notes—"a Lucinda Larabee. She saw her best friend get snatched practically out from under her nose. Only caught a glimpse of the killer, though—assuming the killer and the kidnapper are one and the same, a fairly good bet. According to the paper, she could only describe him or her as a 'dark figure.' But it's possible she saw more, one particular telling detail, if you know what I mean. At some point we must get to that girl and talk to her. It's essential. But she's visiting her family now. At least that's what the Dean said."

Dorothy knew what "the detail" he'd been referring to was: *the claw*. "But until we do talk to the girl," she argued, "I still don't see how you can assume the demon is responsible for the murders and disappearances on the campus. As you yourself said, most psychotics and murders are not possessed by demons, our demon or any other."

"That's true." Brian looked down at his hands. He was uncomfortable with what he had to say. "I—when we were in that railroad car, Dorothy, I was mentally *touched* by the people—the spirits—trapped within, as I've mentioned. I told you that I really don't have—and have never had—psychic power. I think if I *did* have, the same thing would have happened to me that happened to so many others. Genuine psychics couldn't pick up a 'message' the way I did, in part because they didn't stay inside the car long enough. They were overwhelmed by psychic feedback, or couldn't perceive the true message amidst all the psychic clutter."

He got up and walked over to the window, rubbing his face with his hands. "You have no idea how it's been. There's no way either of you can understand. The spirits won't let me go, won't give me any peace until I fulfill my promise and free them. And only by destroying the demon can I do that."

"Brian. What have—the spirits—been doing to you?"

"Nothing tangible," he answered, turning away from the window and meeting her gaze. "Dreams mostly. Every night, dreams. I see them—pleading, imploring, reaching out to me. There's no end to it." That certainly explained his frazzled appearance. "I've given up all hope of ever having a normal night's sleep again. And sometimes, during the daytime, I seem to hear voices. I see things. Nothing too vivid. Distant voices, distant scenes from other people's pasts. But not enough for me to ascertain *how* those Sumarian train passengers died and became what they are.

He rubbed his brow. "I have to set them free, have to finish this mission or I'll go crazy. I can't tell you what it means to me that you've come here to help. I don't care what ulterior motives you may have had. I really had no one else to turn to. Most mediums and psychics I know are charlatans, and as for the legitimate ones, their psychic power would actually make them more vulnerable to the demon, more susceptible to its evil. The few I got in touch with wanted nothing to do with it. They're scared. They've heard of the four-fingered demon and know what it can do. So you see, there was no one else I could turn to."

"How exactly can we help?" Jimmy asked.

"I'm not sure," Brian admitted. "By just being here, for one thing. It's important that someone be here to record what's going on—in case, in the event, something should happen to me. In case . . . well, it's unlikely the demon will possess me, I have all those other souls on my side. But I could conceivably be attacked by its—pawn, its messenger. We *all* could conceivably—" It seemed he'd realized for perhaps the first time just what it was they were up against. "Forgive me. I'm putting you both in such terrible danger."

"We've been in danger before, Brian," Dorothy said. "We've talked about this. I won't kid you. Jimmy and I are confused and frightened, but we'll stick by you. You can count on that."

"You *could* help me find out exactly who the demon has possessed this time," he said. "You see—this is what I began telling you—the dreams I've been having—I *saw* this place in my dreams. This town, this school. I had subscribed to a clipping service, told them what kind of newspaper accounts I was looking for. I went through the clippings I had and got a match. The girls' school, the convent squatting above it. This small dreary town in Illinois. And the murders and disappearances. Those souls planted it in my mind. *That's* how I know the demon is here. That's how I know that we're on target by being here."

He lowered himself to the windowsill. "But the identity of the killer, what it wants with those girls, *that* I haven't been able to figure. I was hoping it would come to me in my dreams. I see girls, lots of nuns, which in this town is to be expected. But which one—*which one* . . .? Perhaps even the spirits themselves don't know. Perhaps the dominant consciousness of the demon is keeping it from the rest of them."

"Could the demon be a nun?" Jimmy suggested. "Who would suspect a nun of committing these crimes?"

"Yes, I thought of that, too. However, the murders and disappearances have occurred on campus. A nun might stick out like a sore thumb amongst those well-bred but spirited girls. I was thinking it might be one of their teachers, a well-liked teacher who makes her way around the campus without arousing suspicion."

"That makes more sense."

"However, a nun *would* be able to go different places without being questioned. Especially since more people assume the party committing these atrocities is male."

"Which already makes it likelier that the demon has again possessed a woman."

"Yes."

"How is the college dealing with the murders?" Jimmy asked.

Brian went over to the bed and sat down beside Dorothy. "They've hired additional security," he said. "Girls are only allowed to go out in pairs. A very early curfew—no one allowed out after dark. And this time of year that means no later than five or five thirty. They're forbidden to go into town except in chaperoned groups. So far, it's worked."

Brian, blinking furiously as if to clear his mind of its fatigue, ran his hand back through his hair. "The first disappearance occurred in late January. The school figured it was an isolated incident. The parents raised unholy hell in spite of the administrations' efforts to keep it quiet. The trouble was that the witness, Lucinda Larrabee, had in the past told stories that were later proven to be untrue, I guess in an effort to be the center of attention. She has a whole history of doing things like that. Her story of the girl, Jane Paige, being snatched right off the path outside the library and pulled into the woods was considered the product of a fanciful imagination. But where *had* the girl disappeared to? She never went home. No trace of her was ever found.

"They had barely managed to quiet things down after that, when it happened again. Sort of. A 'problem girl,' Rosemary Woodside, was threatening to leave school—to anyone who would listen—and when she vanished one night everyone assumed she'd simply taken off, leaving behind some inconsequential belongings. The same with the third girl—according to rumor, she was pregnant and despondent. The most 'popular' theory has it that she threw herself into a 'bottomless' lake on the outskirts of town where her body will remain until summer.

"By that time it was mid-February and the murders began. A pretty senior who snuck out to town to have a soda was found with her throat slashed, practically beheaded, in a weed-filled lot on the edge of the campus. The following night, when everything was still in a state of panic, another girl—and her townie boyfriend—were stabbed and garroted in a field picnic area located somewhere between the campus and the convent. The very next night another girl disappeared. Everyone thought she had run back to her parents in fear, which was what she had apparently intended to do, but when her family was called they said she'd never shown up. That brings us up to date. Two girls and one young man murdered. Four girls missing."

Dorothy put her coffee cup down on the nightstand. "My God, it's horrible. Why hasn't the college closed down, at least temporarily? You'd think the parents would be grabbing their girls out of the school so fast—"

"Ah, you'd think that, wouldn't you? But so far it's 'only' been six girls out of 1500. Six girls who were loners or who were alleged to have 'bad reputations.' Six girls who—or so everyone tells themselves—were killed or kidnapped because they broke the rules and snuck off by themselves, although that certainly wasn't the case with poor Jane Paige. The human mind has an inexhaustible ability to rationalize. And remember, Dolby is a school for wealthy girls whose parents travel and run businesses; they're dumped into the hands of the faculty. No one ever thinks it will happen to them, not *their* child. They figure if the girls follow the rules, stay indoors out of trouble, the boogie man won't get them. A tragic mistake, I'm afraid."

Asquith folded his arms across his chest, and for a moment it looked as if he could handle anything, dare anyone, an unstoppable force of nature and energy.

"Now," he said, "here's what we're going to do. . . ."

But in the face of all of it he looked so terribly small.

Sister Margarita climbed down the narrow, dimly-lit stairs and opened the door to the chamber. *Hurry, hurry!* she told herself, *you must get back before Sister Absolum discovers you're missing.* She swept through the doorway, her long robe scraping the hard surface of the floor, and went over to the poor, frightened girl in the corner.

That makes four altogether, the sister thought, shuddering. Four young girls, innocent girls, to be used, she suspected, for the most hideous of purposes. The other three had already been 'cleaned' and taken from the chamber, might even have been killed. She had to do what she could to save this one, had to lesson her agony and see if she could aid in the girl's escape.

Sister Margarita gasped when she saw the condition of the young woman. She was completely naked, her body a mass of bruises and scars. Tiny little cuts covered almost the entire surface of her back. Her heart went out to her.

Sister Margarita had been born at the Convent of the Mourning Sisters; she was in the church but not *of* it. Had she any doubts about *that* they would have been erased by the events of the past few weeks.

Her mother had been one of the sisters. She had been raped, and died in childbirth. Sister Margarita was the result of that union. She was taken in by the sisters, raised by them; there'd been no question that she would eventually become one of them. She'd become a novice, then taken her vows. It was only then, only afterwards, that she realized that the Church—the Holy Messianic Church with which she'd entered into a covenant—was not quite what it appeared to be.

Beneath the simple lifestyle, the grace and holiness, the kind and loving demeanor on the surface, there was *something else*. Something corrupt and frightening, something only a few of the sisters dared speak about and then only in whispers.

Something to do with worship.

Something to do with *what* they worshipped.

Sister Margarita had always known that the Holy Messianic Church was different from other churches. It was not the Holy Roman Church, not Protestant nor Episcopalian. Having known nothing else, Sister Margarita had not thought their habits and rituals unusual. But unlike many of the other sisters, Sister Margarita was inquisitive. On the days when she was permitted to travel outside the convent, she would go to the library and bookstores of the town and eagerly devour as much knowledge of this bold new world that was around her as she could.

The sisters had taught her the basics of the world, and their part in it, the goals of the Holy Messianic Church. But her reading showed her that the Church—the *real* Holy Messianic Church—was like other churches only on the surface. They kept up a bold facade. Weren't the nuns at the Convent of the Mourning Sisters supposed to care for the sick and indigent, just as the nuns of the Catholic Church did? Didn't they wear similar clothing? (Although the Holy Messianic Church had never modernized their garments in so drastic a manner as the Catholic Church.) Didn't they dispense concern and kindness to everyone they met?

Everything had *seemed* normal—if that was the word—until several weeks ago, when the *awful things* started happening; the killings and disappearances on the campus down below. Sister Margarita had stumbled onto the truth only by accident, during one of her frequent explorations of the passageways and catacombs within and beneath the convent. She had been shocked to realize who was participating, to discover what was happening. Suddenly the church seemed abominable, a haven for obscenity. And she felt duty bound, if no one else would, to do what she could to fight the evil from *within*.

She pulled a moist warm cloth out of her garments and placed it on the young woman's head, then pressed it against the other wounds on the girl's face and shoulders. The girl was slowly reviving. She opened her eyes and looked at Sister Margarita.

And screamed.

"Stop! Stop it! I'm not one of them. I won't harm you, I—"

But the girl kept screaming. Even when the sister held out some fruit to eat, showed her the bandages she'd brought to bind her wounds with, the girl still would not stop screaming. She had been beaten, been injured, so badly. And Sister Margarita was sure she knew who had done it to her. Sister Margarita was filled with hatred for anyone who would so abuse such a helpless child.

Sister Margarita reached out her hand and tried to cover the girl's mouth with it. If Sister Absolum should hear. . . .? The girl's teeth bit down savagely into the hand, cutting into the knuckles. Margarita pulled her hand back and held the bleeding section up to her lips. "Stop," she whispered. *"Please be quiet!"*

Someone must have heard her by now. They might assume the girl was simply screaming for help and let her yell her heart out without bothering to investigate. But she couldn't take that chance. Margarita slapped the girl continuously until the child was stunned into silence.

"Forgive me, please, forgive me." She lifted the girl to her feet, and started stumbling with her over to the door. At the end of the corridor outside was a hidden door that led to a secret underground passageway.

"Just where do you think you're going?"

Tall, sturdy and demanding, the Mother Superior, Sister Absolum, stood before her. Sister Absolum stepped forward, raising the whip that she held forcefully in her hand.

"Sister Absolum, I—"

The whip lashed out, striking Sister Margarita in her hand. A welt began to form directly along the teethmarks that the whimpering girl had left in the sister's flesh. Crying out in pain, Sister Margarita let go of the girl, let her carelessly slip to the floor.

"Someone will have to teach you a lesson, Sister Margarita," the Mother Superior said. "You will have to be punished for what you've tried to do."

Sister Margarita could think of nothing to say. She stood there cradling her injured hand, trying to hold back the tears of fear and anguish.

The Mother Superior ordered the younger nun to undress.

Finished, the naked sister turned her back to the Mother Superior.

"Turn around!" Sister Absolum ordered.

And the terrified woman did as she was told, bravely offering her undraped breasts to the cold, stinging caress of the lash.

26

Asquith had had no luck talking to the police the day he arrived. They'd dismissed him as a crackpot and a nuisance. "The killer is some out-of-town psycho who's hiding out up in the woods," they'd told him. "We'll flush him out. Don't give us any malarky about nuns or faculty." He'd been lucky that they hadn't arrested him for the crimes. He was in the "suspicious stranger" category, after all. Apparently, they'd checked to make sure that he really had been in L.A. during the time the crimes were committed.

Asquith had suggested Jimmy have a try at talking to the police while he and Dorothy paid a call on the Convent of the Mourning Sisters. They were in Asquith's rented Chevrolet now, driving over a narrow country lane that wound halfway around the town proper before heading into the hills where the convent was located.

"Odd name for a convent," Dorothy said, enjoying the peace and quiet of the surroundings—forests gave way to fields, which in turn gave way to more forests, an unending cycle of green and tranquillity. "What's it mean, do you know?"

"Yes, it is an odd name. And I don't know what it means. Even the townspeople don't know much about the convent. Or the church it belongs too, for that matter, except that it's been here for decades. I suppose it means the sisters are mourning the failure of their Savior to return. That's what the whole church is supposedly based on: the second coming of Christ. That the world will not be whole and beautiful until Jesus comes again and saves us all."

"Doesn't sound any different from most churches," she noted.

"True. But the Messianic Church is unusual. It's not like the Catholic Church, aside from the similarity of its nuns. It holds no masses and has no lay members, no public churches, and only a few priests. They're like a very strict order of Catholic nuns, totally cloistered, isolated from society. Some of their nuns do volunteer work, like regular nuns do, work with sick people and similar duties. But it's a very private religion, very seclusive and secretive."

"How old is the church?"

"From what I've been able to ascertain, it's early incarnations under different names *predate* the Catholic Church. This convent we're going to—the building itself supposedly is a copy of one in Europe. It's like a medieval castle. There are only a few hundred members in the church, all of them priests and nuns who live in these isolated outposts across the world. There is only one Holy Messianic enclave in the United States currently, as far as I could find out. Apparently it was moved, members and all, lock, stock and barrel from Europe. There are about a half dozen enclaves scattered through Europe now, maybe an additional one in Canada."

"From where do they get their members?"

"Who knows? There are a lot of unfounded rumors." He chuckled. "Some say the church attracts loners, that it's a kind of peaceful foreign legion for the lost and friendless. They're not choosey who they take in. Aside from the occasional emergency, the convent ignores the townspeople, and the town ignores them. A few sisters have become known to, even friendly with, the residents. But most of the nuns never even travel into town. They have a nice, self-sufficient little world of their own up there." He craned his neck. "There. Do you see it? The convent? That's it at the top of the hill."

Dorothy saw it in the distance, and a chill went through her. The ancient building, with its Gothic ambiance and sheltered, fortified appearance, was as ugly as it was beautiful. She had a sensation as they drove up the winding mountain road that they were approaching the fortress of an enemy, entering another part of the abnormal, unseen world she wanted no part of. She turned to Brian. "Why do you think this particular order of the church chose here to relocate?"

"Beats me. It's quiet. The property must have been available at a reasonable price. They wanted to expand their horizons to the States from Europe, and the Midwest seemed ideal for their purposes. Who knows? Maybe we can ask them."

"Do you think we'll find our murderer here?"

"The question is: now that I know what to do when I find her —or him—will I be able to do it in time? And will it work?"

Then the convent was looming up in front of them, a massive structure that seemed to tower above their heads and oppress them simply with its size. It was enormous. The walls were high and turreted and curiously decorated with gargoyles that were the symbols of ancient pagan religions. There were arched doorways and windows covered with grills and many spires sticking up all around the roof. It consisted of two basic connecting structures: the high church itself, and the longer, lower, rectangular dormitory to the right of it.

They drove through tall stone pillars and approached a metal gate in the road. Brian stopped the car. Behind the fence that surrounded the property a slender young gardener pushed a power mower across the huge expanse of lawn in front of the building. Brian shouted, trying to make himself heard above the sound of the mower. Finally the handyman turned and noticed the car. He shut off the mower and strode over to the edge of the property. "What can I do for you?" he asked.

"You can open the gate for us," Brian said, giving Dorothy a quick look of exasperation.

The gardener appeared to be a mite slow-witted. "The sisters don't want no visitors." He took off his baseball cap and rubbed the sweat off his brow with his fist.

"It's important," Brian whispered. "Please let us inside and let us talk to whoever's in charge. If the sisters want us to leave—if *they* tell us to leave—then we will. We're not here to spy on them or invade their privacy, we just want to talk."

The gardener scratched his head. "Well, I don't know. They didn't say they were expecting no one. We don't get no deliveries today, either."

"Please."

He shrugged and went over to the gate. Then he thought better of it and said, "Hold on a minute. I'll be right back." He lumbered off in the direction of the convent.

"I think he's going to ask the sisters if we can come in," Dorothy said.

"Yes. But I wish he had asked who we were first."

Dorothy agreed but added, "Not that that would necessarily do any good. We should have thought of some cover story. What exactly are we going to say to them? Surely we can't tell them about . . . demons."

"I don't know. I had intended to play it by ear. I was hoping if the demon had possessed someone in the convent it would somehow become apparent to me, that there'd be a *sign* of some kind. . . ."

"From your spirit friends?"

"Yes. But nothing's happening. I'm not getting any feelings at all. Either because I'm way off track—or because I'm right on top of it and can't see the forest for the trees."

A moment later the gardener came back, embarrassed. He had an angry expression on his face, as if he'd just been scolded. He went right up to the gate and practically thrust his face between the bars.

"Sister Absolum says *no visitors*." Then he turned his back on them and went back to his mower, turning on the engine to drown out further conversation.

"Well, that's that," Dorothy said.

"I'm afraid so." Brian sat still for a few moments, considering his options. "We'll just have to go back to the motel and try to reach them by phone again. That Sister Absolum is always busy —or so they tell me. Well, I'll get her to listen to me if it's the last thing I do."

He started the car again. "I think this road winds around the convent and goes back to town on the other side of the mountain." He backed out of the driveway and turned onto the road they had come in on, continuing along it instead of turning around. "Let's see where this takes us."

The road turned a little to the right and they found themselves riding along the property line of the convent, the metal fence

326

partially obstructing their view of the magnificent structure.

"I wonder who that is," Dorothy said.

A nun had come out of a side of the building and was running across the lawn in their direction, waving, trying to keep pace with the vehicle as they rode in a semicircular path around the convent.

"Brian. I think she's yelling at us. I think she wants us to stop."

Brian brought the car to a halt and backed up so that the woman wouldn't have so far to run. In the distance across the lawn, the gardener had his back turned and was walking his mower in the other direction. The nun raced breathlessly up to the fence and thrust something between the bars.

Dorothy got out of the car and walked over to the nun. The papers the woman held dropped out of her hands and fell onto the ground. As Dorothy approached she got a quick glance at the woman: nervous, frightened eyes, pale skin, a bruise on her dainty cheek. Were those scratches on her chin? The sister looked terrfied.

Dorothy bent down to pick up the papers that the nun had dropped.

When she stood up again the sister was gone, running across the lawn back in the direction she had come from.

Dorothy got back into the car. "Did you ever . . .?"

"What did she give you?" Brian asked.

The first small sheet was just a note consisting of two words: *Please help*.

Dorothy went quickly through the other pages. "Brian, this one is a diagram. I think it shows a secret entrance to the convent!"

The other sheet fluttered out of her hands and fell to the floor of the authomobile. Brian lifted it up off his shoe.

"Dorothy! Look at this!"

On the sheet of paper someone had drawn a crude approximation of a *claw*.

Brian had received his sign.

Jimmy walked swiftly across the campus toward the administration building, hoping he could arrive there before being accosted by campus security or frightening to death some of the young ladies who peered anxiously at him as they did any strong-looking male stranger.

He had spent a fruitless hour at the police station waiting for the sheriff to give him an interview, but the man—an old, grizzled fart with glaring eyes and a deeply suspicious nature (understandably)—wasn't interested in cooperating with "big city" reporters, especially one who didn't have the proper press credentials.

There was no way Jimmy would have told the man about the four-fingered demon; and if the witness to the first on-campus snatching had noticed a claw on the assailant, and told the police about it, the sheriff was not the obliging type who'd pass the information along to just anyone. Jimmy had to be content with learning nothing. Had he mentioned the claw, they probably would have wondered how he knew or why he *thought* he knew something about the case and have put him behind bars. Jimmy was just glad to get out of the sheriff's office in one piece. Now he was on his way to find out if Lucinda Larrabee had finally returned to school and if he might be allowed a word with her.

For the fiftieth time since he and Dorothy had received Asquith's phone call, Jimmy wondered what he was doing in the town of Lennington. It was most unspectacular, a typical clone of millions of small hamlets across the country, with nothing to distinguish it from a similar town in, say, New England or California. It had a fairly busy main street, tasteful brick houses on assorted side streets, and then opened up to form farms and highways with scattered motels and restaurants.

Jimmy had decided that the easiest way to deal with this madness was to put that certain part of his brain on hold as he had done in California, particularly when on the soundstage before Vivienne Cherneau's attack. Fictional, fake violence had lost its appeal for him; he could no longer achieve catharsis or garner appreciative amusement out of slashing maniacs and busty, screaming co-eds. *So what was he doing in Lennington about to co-star in his own fucking horror movie?*

Perhaps because he'd been so *helpless* on that soundstage. He'd just stood there getting ill, would probably have died had Dot and Brian not come along to save him. *Perhaps he needed a chance to prove that, given the opportunity, he could summon up as much courage and heroism as anyone.*

Jimmy would need permission to have a chat with Lucinda

Larrabee. No way would he search her out on the campus and talk to her without prior consent and a written introduction. The poor girl would probably scream at the sight of him, wondering if he were the man who had snatched her friend away. *Then again, he wondered if it had ever occurred to Asquith that a frightened little schoolgirl might be the perfect host for the demon's scabrous consciousness. Perhaps little Miss Larrabee was the one they were after.*

Fifteen minutes after he walked into the building's administrative offices, he was ushered into the office of Miss Susan Giddons, the assistant to the Dean. She was a pale, pretty woman of about thirty-five, with short, brown hair and green eyes. Underneath her well-tailored business suit and sensible shoes, that quietly dignified exterior, Jimmy imagined a much more exciting, sensual creature just waiting for the right person to set it free. Miss Giddons was cordial and friendly on the surface, but there was also an element of wariness and discomfort with his presence and objective. She sat him down in a couch across from her desk and stood at his side clutching a pencil in her fingers.

"You say you want to interview her? Really, Mr. Radley, I would probably need her parents' permission for that. We've had reporters—"

"I'm not a reporter. I'm a magazine writer. And I'm therefore a little more sensitive to the people I interview than someone from a daily paper or supermarket tabloid. I really just have one particular question that I want to ask Miss Larrabee."

"Why don't you speak to the police?"

"I tried. They weren't too sympathetic, I'm afraid. I told you I'm a crime writer," he lied. "These murders and disappearances have similarities to other cases that I've done pieces on. You know how small town police are, Miss Giddons. They resent help from 'city slickers.' All I need do is ask the girl one question, here, in your office, with you present and anybody else you might like. Call in some of the security guards. I have nothing to hide. Believe me, I'm well aware of how traumatic this has all been for the young lady, but if I can help get to the bottom of things, wouldn't it be worth it? What's there to lose? Ask her if she's willing to see me. If she refuses, then I'll leave and that will be the end of it."

Maybe he had a kind face, warm and trustworthy like a Boy

Scout's, he didn't know, but in ten minutes Lucinda Larrabee was sitting beside him on the couch, tugging at the ends of her sweater, and looking at him with a mixture of determination and leeriness. She was chubby but not unattractive, dressed in a nice, frilly outfit and radiating a mild but obvious arrogance that was probably a cover-up for the insecurity and confusion she must have felt. It was clear she wanted very badly to find out what had happened to her friend *and* to exonerate herself from the charge that her story was a lie. Jimmy felt sorry for the girl. What kind of parents could have sent her *back* here while all this was going on? It was true—no amount of money was a substitute for love.

Jimmy looked at her with compassion and said, "Lucinda, thank you for seeing me. What I'd like is for you to tell me everything—every little detail, even things you may not have told the police—that you remember about the person you saw the night your friend was assaulted." He wondered as she studied him if she thought he might be the assailant, if she thought he might be trying to discover how much she'd seen of *him*, and if it would prevent her from giving an honest answer. Instead she scrunched up her face and said, "It was dark. It happened fast and it was in the shadows. I hardly saw anything. That's what I told the police."

"Do you remember anything else? Clothes? Mannerisms? Was it a man or woman who assaulted your friend?"

"I couldn't tell. It was too dark to see. They stepped into the light only for a second." She was beginning to whine, twisting her fingers and looking at Miss Giddons for support. She was probably tired of trying to get people to believe her.

"Anything, Lucinda. Any detail—no matter how weird, how bizarre. I'm not going to laugh at you or tell you you were seeing things. Did you notice *any*thing unusual—"

He was getting to her. Yes, there was something there. All he had to do now was bring it out.

"Like what?" She looked at Miss Giddons again.

He caught and locked into Lucy's eyes as she turned back to face him, and said, "You tell *me*, Lucinda."

There was an interminable pause. Then she said slowly, cautiously, "there was . . . a hand."

"A hand?"

"I thought I saw—just for a second—one of the hands holding Jane. . . . it looked funny."

"What did it look like?"

"It—It looked like a *claw*."

"A claw, Lucy? A claw!"

"*Yes.*"

"How many fingers did this claw have?"

"Four!" she screamed. "It only had *four*!" And then she ran to Miss Giddon's outstretched arms and collapsed into tears.

Miss Giddons looked at Jimmy reproachfully. "I think you'd better go now," she said.

But it was all right. Jimmy had found out all he needed to know.

Dorothy sat on the bed in her motel room sipping a cup of machine-made hot chocolate from the lobby while Asquith stood at the window watching for Jimmy's car. "Are you sure we shouldn't take this to the police?" she said, referring to the papers they'd gotten from the nun.

"No," he said emphatically. "That's the last thing we should do. How could we prove we got these papers from someone at the convent? What do they consist of, really? Crude diagrams. A childish 'please help' note that anyone could have written. And a drawing of a four-fingered claw. It means a lot to us; to anyone else it means nothing. I told you the sheriff is a pig-headed idiot and wouldn't listen to a word I had to say."

"But this should convince him to at least go out to the convent and look around, to ask a few questions. Why did that nun *give* us the diagram? Who was she? Did she ever think it could be because the girls, the missing girls, are being held out there?"

"Look at it this way, Dorothy. This *is* a convent we're talking about. A convent full of nuns. You really think the police are going to believe that *nuns* have anything to do with this?"

"But the underground passageway on this diagram," she argued, "seems to be way *below* the level of the convent. Someone could be using it, hiding the girls down there, without the nuns even knowing. The 'please help' notes makes it official, doesn't it? We don't have to show the sheriff the drawing of the claw. But *someone* should go out there and look around."

"I agree. And that 'someone' is going to be me. I'll leave as soon as it's dark. I don't want the police or campus security to see me wandering through the woods, detaining me while they ask a lot of stupid questions I can't answer."

"Why do you have to do this alone? I just don't understand—"

"Dorothy, I—and I alone—know what has to be done to destroy the demon."

"And you won't tell us *what* no matter how many times we ask you."

"For the simple reason that you wouldn't want to know. *Trust* me on that. And if the police saw me doing what I'm going to have to do, they wouldn't just stand there and let me. Finding the person who the demon has possessed in Lennington is only half the battle. This note indicates that the host is inside the convent, and is probably one of the other nuns. When I go in there and confront the host, I'll have very little time to do what I have to before the demon escapes from the host's body and gets away from me again.

"Let's just say that we do tell the cops about this and they decide to take a run up to the convent. Okay, they find the missing girls, maybe even have a tangle with the murderer. Bingo—the demon takes leave of its host and we're right back where we started. The girls are saved, there'll be no more murders in Lennington. But the demon will still be *at large*. My whole purpose in coming here is to prevent that, to prevent that monstrosity from ever doing this again."

Brian slammed his fist into his palm. "Can't you see my way is the *only* way? The only way those girls will be rescued —if they're still alive—the only way the town will be saved, and most important of all, the only way the demon will be destroyed, *freeing* those four hunderd souls so they can finally rest and I can breathe easy again. I have to do this *on my own*." Calming himself, he sat down on the bed beside her.

"Okay, Brian, okay. I understand most of what you're saying. But I don't understand why you have to do all this alone. Jimmy and I flew out here all the way from New York. Let us go with you. Like you said, God forbid something should go wrong. . . ." She touched his shoulder. "You might need us."

He nodded his head and reached out on impulse to hug her. She squeezed him back, patting his shoulder. It was a simple show of affection only, an innocent, honest sharing of strength and energy.

"Thank you, Dorothy, you and Jimmy both. Thank you for being here. For helping me. You're right, I couldn't do this on my own. To be the only one in this town who knew the incredible truth. . . . It would have been too difficult. I'm really glad you came."

"That's what friends are for," she said.

He sighed then, letting it all out, all the tension and fatigue, letting it all wash out of his body in an abrupt cathartic flow. "Why is it me, why does it have to be *me*?" he said. "I've asked myself that a hundred times. Why me? To have this burden. Why did I ever go into that railway car? Why do I care?"

"Because you're a compassionate human being," Dorothy told him. "A decent one. Because you care about innocent victims and realize this is an evil that the police, the everyday authorities, can't handle."

Of course there was truth in what she said. But he only replied: "Decent, am I?" He rubbed his eyes. "I suppose so. I have to tell you, though—part of me is doing this for selfish reasons. To atone, to repent. To make up for something lousy I once did. Part of me thinks if I get rid of this demon I'll have paid the debt I owe, have a clean slate, be able to sleep at night. I've had nightmares for a long time, Dorothy, long before I went into that damnable railroad car."

He thought a moment, then decided he might as well unburden himself to a sympathetic listener. "Remember I told you about that friend of mine, the medium? The one I exposed, and how it led into a whole new career for me?" Dorothy nodded.

"That friend of mine . . . was actually my lover. Jack Cotter." There was surprise, a mild embarrassment in Dorothy's eyes, but no sign of disapproval. "Jack and I had been together about . . . five years . . . two struggling actors. We met a few months after my first and only marriage went to pot. First we shared an apartment just to save rent. Then something more developed between us. It was good. I make no apologies for it. What we had was good."

"But Jack—couldn't handle—the constant disappointment, the hurts, the way he'd get so close to a good job, *this close* to the break he needed, only to fail—in his eyes, at least—only to lose it. He couldn't handle it happening over and over again, couldn't stand always watching people with less talent and better connections getting ahead while he had to take dehumanizing jobs and die inside a little more as he got older. Every year his chances of finding success got slimmer and slimmer.

"He didn't want stardom, Dorothy. He just wanted to *survive*, make a respectable living doing what he loved and did best. And, oh God, was he good at it! I never really had it, you know, the talent, the persistence, but *he* had it all. He was a real artist. But they just wouldn't give him a chance.

"When that happens to such a person it drives them crazy. Slowly, painfully. He lived in a city of glamour and illusion, with his nose always pressed up against the window, surrounded by symbols of the good life, the life of ease and comfort that everyone else seemed to have. It wasn't yachts he needed, not condos or fancy restaurants, but just enough money in the bank to know he could grow old without worrying about what might happen to him. A little security, that's all." He sighed and muttered, "They wouldn't even give him that."

Brian leaned forward, put his elbows on his knees. "He was up for a big role in a movie—it would have *transformed* his life, given him everything he wanted. Instead it went to a studio head's nephew, the son of a big TV celebrity. Guy gives interviews and tells everyone how unhappy he is making 250,000 dollars a year." He chuckled sardonically. "My heart bleeds for him, I tell you."

"So, just to take his mind off things, Jack got into all this occult stuff, started doing readings, palm readings, holding séances. But it started scaring me, the whole business; he wasn't treating it like a joke any more. He wasn't conning people, you understand; he actually thought he could make contact with the spirit world. Slowly Jack was losing touch with reality, faking these voices and manifestations on one hand, and denying it with his dying breath, denying it even to himself, on the other. I was scared he was losing his mind. He wouldn't be honest with himself; he wouldn't be honest with me.

"The night I did it—the night I exposed him, showed everyone there just how he pulled off his tricks—something snapped inside me. It was as if I had stripped him of all dignity, delivered the final blow to his ego. But I was so worried and angry. We had a big fight afterwards. I went out for a while, hoping he'd cool off. When I got back home he was dead. Cut his wrists." He added softly, "I don't think I've ever gotten over it."

Dorothy put her hand over his, her face full of concern. "Oh, Brian. I'm so sorry. But you can't blame yourself. You were trying to help him. You didn't do anything wrong—how were you to know? You were trying to snap him back into reality."

"Yeah, yeah, that I was. And it worked too well, didn't it? Why didn't I realize those little games of his kept his mind off what his life was really like? You see, his despair over his career colored everything. He wasn't hung up with his life-style, wasn't unhappy with me—he was just being beaten down by the city and his lack of success until he couldn't take it any more. Funny, if I'd sat there and done nothing that night, he might have gone on fooling himself and everyone else—but he'd have been living with it, *living*—he woud have been a cheat and a fake and a charlaten, but he would have been *alive*. He might have been so preoccupied with his new career that he might not have brooded so much on how he hadn't found fulfillment as an actor.

"I think I went around as a ghostbreaker afterwards not just to pay the rent, but to keep reliving that night over and over again as my punishment. I did something rotten—I handled it all wrong. If something goes wrong tonight at least I *tried* to make things better. If it doesn't work. . . ."

"You're telling me that you gave up on life when your lover died?"

He shrugged. "Part of me did. But no, not really. Surprise! I'm still reasonably young, got money in the bank, friends. I have no doubt I'll find love again, when I want it, when I'm ready for it. I'm in no rush to die. Tonight or any other. It's just a chance I'll have to take."

"You won't die, Brian. Jimmy and I won't let you. You're *not* going in there alone."

He leaned back on the bed and relaxed. "Y'know it's funny. When Janice Evans told me about Paul Wilson and that seance, I was struck by the similarity. Do people turn to the occult because the real world is just too depressing? Probably. Isn't it funny how the occult world—what we've seen of it—is just as bad, maybe even worse than day-to-day living? Makes you wonder what the hell it's all about. I got interested in Paul Wilson because of Jack. Now, Jack was a big, burly fellow—not the least bit effeminate like Paul Wilson. And there were a hundred other differences. But they both chose the occult as a way out of their pain, the pain of failure, and it meant the end for both of them. Funny, huh?"

Dorothy reached out and hugged Brian again, comforting him.

Jimmy chose that moment to come rushing in the door.

He took it all in as they moved apart and said, "You two look cozy." His voice betrayed a touch of hostility.

Dorothy grunted. "Oh, for Pete's sake, Jimmy. Not now."

Brian stood up and said, "It's okay. Look, Jimmy, Dorothy was only consoling me 'cause I'd just told her how my lover— my *male* lover—committed suicide a few years ago. Now if that's difficult for you to deal with, I'm sorry, 'cause I have too much on my mind now to worry about your attitudes toward the subject. In any case, I'm not some cowering nelly queen who is desperate for your approval, *nor* am I some swaggering stud who has designs on your beautiful girlfriend. Nor you, for that matter, as long as we're on the subject. Frankly, I've been too keyed up for months now to even think about sex."

Jimmy just looked at him. "Oh."

There was a space of a few heartbeats, then Dorothy and Brian looked at each other and burst out laughing.

Jimmy watched them for a few seconds, perplexed, then finally joined in with them. "Well, *I've* sure been told off," he said. "Though I'm not sure why. Really, Brian, I'm not all *that* unsophisticated."

Brian relaxed. "Well, now that that's out of the way, how

are you at navigating underground? We're going to need flashlights, a compass, maybe rope, too."

Jimmy noticed the papers spread out on the bed. "What's this stuff?"

Brian handed him the material the nun had given them and filled him in on what had happened. Jimmy listened with increasing interest, then hit them with his own news. "I spoke to Lucinda Larrabee," he said. "She saw the claw."

"Then there's no doubt," Brian said. "This is the right place, all right."

Jimmy then went over his futile conversation with the sheriff and agreed that this was something they'd have to do on their own. "But how *are* we going to stop this demon?" he asked.

Dorothy moaned. "Brian won't tell us."

"It's something I have to do by myself. I don't want you two mixed up in it, do you hear me? Bad enough I got you involved this far. Even in the event that whatever we plan goes awry, I am the only one who is even going to attempt to destroy the demon."

Dorothy and Jimmy exchanged anxious, puzzled glances, but they agreed.

"Okay. Now let's make up a list of what we need."

And outside, as the sun was setting, the day grew darker and colder.

27

Sally Anne Hollister was more upset than she'd been in a long time.

"So a few toady nobodies decide to wander off in the woods, and a couple of 'em get hacked up by their boyfriends," she argued. "Why do the rest of us have to get punished?"

Sally Anne stood in the TV room trying to garner support from the crowd of twelve or so girls gathered before her. Few of them seemed to entirely agree with her and it was making her so *mad.* . . .

"Listen! There is no proof that these killings and disappearances are connected, y'know." She counted on her fingers, her gum snapping loudly in the cramped acoustics of the room. "Let's see: There was Jane Paige. She never fit in at Dolby, did she, girls? She probably ran back home to Mommy and Daddy and when they told her to get lost she joined a convent. Maybe she's up there with the sisters right this minute making nice-nice."

One of the girls groaned and another said, "Sally Anne, her parents were here looking for her. They were very upset, remember?"

Sally Anne sucked up something deep inside of herself and regurgitated it verbally. "Some parents will *say* anything, *act* any way, if they think that's what's expected of them. Believe me, *they're glad she's gone.*" That done, she pulled her hair out of her eyes. "Now, let's see, Rosemary Woodside told all of us that she hated it here. She ran away, that's all. Of course she didn't go home to her parents; they would only have sent her back. Or worse. Believe me, if I know Rose she's probably in California right now soaking up the sun and getting laid every night by the lifeguards."

Some of the girls giggled. It was not an unpleasant prospect.

"And as for Carolyn Kastner, everyone *knows* she got herself pregnant. She told Ella Evans she was madly in love with the boy and he didn't want to marry her. It's sad about Carolyn, but should we have to suffer because *she* decides to kill herself?"

A tall, slender young lady in the back raised her hand as if she were still in the classroom, and Sally Anne acknowledged her. The girl's voice was hard and stony, though a tremble betrayed her apprehension. "Carolyn Kastner was not pregnant, Sally Anne, and you know it. She was still a virgin. She only told that story to get attention. We all know what she was like. I don't think she killed herself. She didn't even like that boy back home. *I* think something happened to her."

Sally Anne couldn't stand it when anyone dared to contradict her. "Shut up, lesbo," she said. "Nobody asked for your opinion. I'm the one who called this meeting."

The tall girl muttered something in disgust and walked out of the room. Two other girls followed.

"Who needs them anyway?" Sally Anne snarled.

A short, squat girl in pigtails and pajamas raised her hand—Sally Anne was pleased to see that the habit was catching on—and said, "But what about the murders, Sally Anne? What about *them*?" The other girls in the room nodded their heads in agreement and started murmuring amongst themselves.

Sally Anne was in a dither. She pulled herself up to her full height and put her hands on her hips. "*Shut up*, everyone! You want to know about the murders? I'll tell you about the murders! Deirdre Hampton was a slut who said she was sneaking out for sodas, but was really sneaking out to see guys. Yeah, I know she was fat and ugly, but when a guy is horny and a girl is willing. . . . She got killed by some toad in town, that's all. Probably a handyman or even some creepy married guy. That's her problem, not ours.

"And as for Faye Edwards and her boyfriend: my theory is that Faye's boyfriend *back home* found out about them—do you hear me, Evelyn Barrington?—and came to the campus one night to kill them both. None of the so-called crimes are related, and I for one am sick of being quarantined in this dump night after night. You girls are in the same boat as me—your parents live too far away for you to go home on weekends, and they aren't pulling you out of school. I say we band together and *order* them to lift the curfew and let us get on with our lives!"

Half the girls cheered enthusiastically—though mutedly, as they didn't want to disturb the house mother—but the other half was unconvinced.

"This is the day of emancipation, girls," Sally Anne said to her cronies. "I don't know about you, but I'm going to get dressed in my Saturday night best and go down to the Lennington Tavern for a drink. Then I'm going to pick up a six pack and go swimming in the pool, naked. Anyone want to join me? Well, are you women or are you *slaves*?"

She pushed her way out of the crowd and went up to her room to change, followed by four or five other girls who said they were with her all the way. The rest dispersed or stayed in the TV room to continue talking. Sally Anne was such a scandal!

Ten minutes later, wearing heavy makeup and her fabulous "fuck me" pumps, her hair dangling over one side of her face like a latterday Veronica Lake, Sally Anne emerged from her room and proclaimed. "Ladies, I am going to get fucked tonight!"

Jean Timmons and Osa Peters joined her at the top of the stairs and whooped with laughter. "You look like a slut," Osa said admiringly.

Jeannie agreed. "You look fabulous!"

Sally Anne looked around querulously. "Where are all the others?"

Osa shrugged. "Guess they chickened out, huh?"

"Silly cunts. And dumb Lucinda is still moping in her room."

By the time they reached the bottom of the stairs, Sally Anne had lost another one of the troops. "Hey, guys," Jeannie said, looking nervously at the lighted doorway behind which the house mother sat, "this is fun and all, but I don't really think it's such a good idea, y'know?" She gave them a weak, apologetic smile and darted up the stairs into her room.

Sally Anne sighed in exasperation. "Are *you* still with me, Osa?"

Osa, a cute brunette with quaintly teased hair and light blue lipstick, wiggled her behind and said, "I'm ready for anything."

Actually, as they sneaked out the front door and ran for the cover of the bushes, Sally Anne herself wasn't sure if this was such a good idea. She really didn't want to get fucked for one thing, though she may have tried to create that impression. She had tried sex once and hated it, had only done it so that she would no longer be a virgin. Truth to all, making love didn't appeal to her all that much. She liked making out with guys, but as for the rest, it was positively gruesome. Besides, it was sex that had brought all those other girls to ruin, she was sure of it. No way would they catch *her* fooling around with some disgusting townie.

They made their way from shrub to shrub, heading for the dent in the fence where they could sneak out into Main Street. The campus security force was out, but most of them were too old and too dumb to find their socks in the morning let alone a killer. Sally Anne was convinced there was nothing to worry about. As long as they didn't get caught.

Afraid of what might happen in that grungy working-class bar around the corner, Sally Anne suggested they buy a couple of six packs in the package store and head straight back for the swimming pool. To her great relief, Osa seconded the motion. "We might run into some teachers in the bar," she said. Sally Anne hadn't even thought of that.

In makeup Sally Anne looked old enough to buy liquor without having to show an I.D. She flirted casually with the middle-aged proprietor as she bought the beer. Using virtually the same route as before, the girls made their way back to the dorm, then went past it toward the Student Activities building and on to the gym.

"We forgot the gym is locked at this hour," Osa groaned. "Sally Anne, how are we supposed to get in?"

Sally Anne opened up her purse and lifted up a key ring that glittered in the moonlight. "Never fear," she said. "Sally Anne thinks of everything."

"The *keys*. Where did you get them?"

"The first week I was here I stole or made copies of practically every key to every building I could get my hands on in case I ever needed them. I'm not some kind of *servant*. I don't need *permission* to go to the bathroom or use the gym. These teachers and handymen boss us around, and *they're* just middle class. Well, I wasn't going to allow that." She dangled the keys in her hand. "This big yellow one opens the door to the gym. Let's go."

"I wonder why they didn't change the locks?"

"Are you kidding? The slow way things move around here? Besides, extra keys are disappearing all the time. They can't change a lock every time it happens."

In a moment they were inside the building. It was spooky. Luckily enough moonlight came in through the huge grated windows so that they could see their way across the gym and into the room with the swimming pool. The walls were aglow with shimmering blue and green patterns, the moonlight reflecting off the surface of the water. The pool was surrounded by a tiled, turquoise floor and the smell of chlorine was pervasive.

Osa groaned. "We forgot our suits."

"Silly." Sally Anne stripped down to her underwear. "We're going to swim in the nude, remember?"

Osa hesitated. "Uh, let's have a beer first, okay?"

"Okay." Sally Anne dipped her toe into the water. "Not bad," she said.

Osa opened two beers and handed one to her friend. "Don't worry. We'll get used to it fast."

"Well, c'mon, take your clothes off."

Osa tensed. "*Shhhh*. Did you hear that?"

"What?"

"I thought I heard a noise."

"Shit! Are you sure?"

"Stay here. I'm still dressed. Let me go check."

"Okay." Standing there in her underwear, Sally Anne wondered again if this was such a good idea. She took a few gulps of the beer and felt warmer. What was keeping Osa? If a security guard *had* come into the building he would have found her by now. In any case, they'd have heard his footsteps, his whistling —he'd have turned on the lights and looked around. Damn that Osa—Sally Anne was sure the girl was trying to scare her.

Well, Sally Anne wasn't falling for it. If she stood there half naked any longer she'd get too chilly and be unable to force herself into the water, where it was probably warmer. She removed the rest of her undergarments and slowly eased herself into the pool. There was a shock to her system at first, then it just felt awfully good and not cold at all. There—she had done it! Gone swimming at night without permission, thumbed her nose at the curfew. If this didn't make her the *baddest* girl on campus nothing would.

She floated around for awhile, treading water, staying away from the deep end where the diving board was because she was really not that good of a swimmer. Where the hell was Osa? Surely she must have realized Sally Anne wasn't going to go look for her. She was not about to fall into her trap by stepping inside the next room, and having Osa jump out of the shadows shouting "boo." What if something had happened for real, though? Osa had been gone for such a long time.

Sally Anne swam over to the edge of the pool and grabbed her beer from where she'd left it lying. She drained half the can, burped, and put it down again. She wasn't really crazy about beer, but at least it was cheap. Her parents didn't send her nearly as much money as they could have. She was getting chilly again. Now where the hell was Osa?

With mounting horror she realized that someone was walking into the room from the gymnasium.

Osa! Had the girl put on some kind of robe or cloak? No—it couldn't be Osa. Osa wasn't that tall; Osa's build was entirely different. She couldn't tell if it were a man or a woman, really. Or was it the beer, the reflection from the water, playing tricks?

"*Osa*," Sally Anne whispered. "Stop it! You're scaring me!"

The figure didn't answer. It looked around at the sound of her voice, *spotted* her, and moved over to the edge of the pool. It was heading toward the large, broad, concrete steps that led into the water at the end of the pool. Was it going to get into the water with her? Sally Anne swam over to the metal steps at the side and climbed hastily out of the water. *She had to get out. Get out of there fast.* Now that the figure was down at the other end of the pool, there was nothing between Sally Anne and the exit.

As Sally Anne, dripping and terrified, climbed out of the water and pulled herself naked onto the tiles surrounding the pool, she realized that the figure had anticipated her move and even now was approaching from behind her. Screaming, the frightened girl forgot her clothes and dashed away from the water's edge toward the door.

Just as the intruder reached out to grab her, she slammed the door in the pursuer's face. Sally Anne stopped to get her bearings, her breathing so loud and frenzied, the beating of her heart so rapid and pounding, that she could swear it echoed across the length of the room. She heard a muffled sound, a groaning. Turning toward the right, she looked with surprise at its source:

Osa was writhing on the floor a few feet away from Sally Anne. Her hands and feet were bound and there was a gag in her mouth.

Sally Anne was just about to try and untie her friend when the door to the gym burst open and the intruder's hands were reaching out only inches from her face. Forgetting Osa, Sally Anne screeched and headed toward the gymnasium door. Opening the door with one panicky wrench, she ran out screaming into the night.

Help, she had to get help. One of the security guards had to be in the vicinity. Someone had to save her and Osa from the killer.

Sally Anne tried to scream again but her chest was pounding and she was finding it difficult just to breathe. She raced down the path from the gym and ran in the direction of the cafeteria. The guards might be inside having coffee. *Please, please, someone be there.* Although the February snow had been plowed off the pathway and would have melted since the last blizzard anyway, the tarred ground was cold and rough on her feet. She was too frightened to feel the frigid air as it rushed past her naked body.

The security force was a joke. Since no one had been actually murdered on the campus itself or in any of the dorms, the guards spent all their time circling the streets directly around the college looking for trespassers. *Where were they when she needed them?*

The outside lights of the cafeteria were on—as well as the low night lights inside—but the building seemed deserted. Sally Anne ran up to the double doors in front and tried to wrench them open. Locked! She pounded on the doors with her fists. *Oh, please, please, help me!* She turned and saw the intruder running toward the steps. Sally Anne slipped over the black railing and jumped down into the bushes lining the building. She got up quickly and dashed around to the back, desperate to get away from her determined pursuer.

Sally Anne's nude, shivering body was smeared with dirt and leaves. She could hardly stop trembling, though it was more from terror than from the temperature. Reaching the back of the cafeteria, she looked around for a place to hide. There was a small loading dock and an inclined driveway leading down to the storage garage below the building. To her left were brick steps leading up to the back door and the kitchen. If only she had her keys!

Hide, hide, she told herself. *Where* could she hide? There weren't even any cars or trucks she could duck behind. *What was she going to do?*

In desperation she ran up the steps and pulled at the door to the kitchen. It moved. It was open. *Thank God.* She darted into the corridor beyond, slamming the door behind her. Damn! The only way you could lock it from the inside was with a key. That meant her pursuer would be following her inside at any moment. She ran down the hall past the "Food Manager's" office and the restrooms, and entered the large, cluttered kitchen to the right.

There she discovered why the door had been unlocked. Arnold Matson, the head cook and a borderline alcoholic, was curled up on a cot in a corner near the freezer, a half-empty bottle of Scotch in his hand. He still hadn't left for the evening, the drunk! She could have kissed him. She went over to Matson and tried to wake him, but it was no use. *Idiot!* She heard the sound of footsteps running down the corridor. *Oh God.*

She darted through swinging doors into a storage room beyond the kitchen. Perhaps she could hide behind the boxes, maybe shove some of them on top of her pursuer. She realized too late that she should have headed for a phone, gone into the manager's office where she could have *locked the door* and called for help. Why had she been so stupid? At the very least she could have grabbed a weapon from the kitchen. All those knives and forks. . . .

She hid behind a large carton and heard the sound of rattling cutlery. Her pursuer had had the same idea she'd had, and was implementing it, grabbing a sharp knife or something like it to use on her. The young woman shook with terror, afraid she might even lose control of her kidneys. There must be a way out of this mess. *Wait a minute.* There!

Her eyes had fallen upon the trap door that led down to the basement garage where some of the delivery vans pulled in to unload. The boxes of food and supplies were handed up or carried from the garage to the storage room through the trap door. *That was her way out!*

The trap door consisted of two sheets of metal which rose up off the floor electronically to a vertical, parrallel position several feet apart. Sally Anne saw the controls, but wouldn't have to touch them as the trapdoor was open now, the metal doors sticking up like giant twin bookends. Clearly Matson had been about to go downstairs for something when the boozing had become too much for him. Sally Anne stepped out of her place of concealment and ran over to the hole.

Someone stepped through the swinging doors and pressed a button on the wall.

Sally Anne started to carefully lower herself onto the first rung of the narrow metal stairs to the basement.

The heavy metal doors started closing.

Sally Anne screamed.

The doors came down, catching her body tight, trapping half of her above floor level, half below, pressing against her shoulders. Try as she might to struggle out of the trap, Sally Anne was held as fast and hard as if she'd been caught in a vice. The doors had stopped moving, crushing her, but she still couldn't wiggle free.

The dark figure moved out of the doorway where it had been standing, waiting. A throaty chuckle escaped its sneering lips. For the first time Sally Anne saw who it was. . . .

She didn't understand. It simply made no sense.'

"God! Oh no! It can't be! It can't—"

And what was wrong with the hand, that outstretched hand that looked like a claw?

As the victim writhed and struggled between the pinching metal slabs, the figure stepped closer to the trap door.

Sally Anne saw what her pursuer was holding, the object that had been removed from the kitchen. "Please—*don't!*"

It was a cleaver. A meat cleaver. Her assailant was going to chop her into pieces. Sally Anne began to screech.

The hand holding the cleaver went up higher and higher into the air. Sally could only watch helplessly as her assailant sadistically stretched the deathblow out for as long as possible. Perhaps the worst thing of all was the constant chuckling that issued from the maniac's lips.

And then the cleaver was crashing downward, slashing through the air with a whistling *whoosh* that almost drowned out the sound of the front door opening, the footsteps rushing to the rescue. . . .

Thank God, I'm saved, thought Sally Anne.

And then the cleaver sliced through her neck.

The security guards who had finally heard her screams raced into the storage room where the sounds had come from. They did not see the figure in black run down the hall and out the back door into the night. All they saw was a headless body caught in a trap door, spewing blood from the neck, arms outstretched in a macabre manner, shaking like a jackhammer.

And a large bloody pebble, a ball—*a pretty painted easter egg with red lips and green eyes and long auburn hair*—rolling across the floor to come to rest at their feet.

28

Dorothy, Jimmy, and Brian Asquith left Brian's rented car parked in a clearing at the side of the road that he and Dorothy had taken up to the convent that afternoon. Brian held the map, Dorothy, the flashlight, and Jimmy carried a hammer he had bought in a hardware store "for protection."

They were not far from the Dolby campus, whose lights they could see shining through the trees of the woods they were about to enter. Only this motley group would be heading away from the school and up in the direction of the convent. Brian pointed over to a narrow, gurgling brook that crossed under the road through a culvert and disappeared into the forest. "According to this diagram we'll have an easier time getting through these woods if we stick to the stream."

Dorothy groaned. "Why didn't I bring boots?"

Jimmy gave her an affectionate shove. "You don't expect us to carry you, do you?" She punched him gently on the shoulder.

She and the others had decided that the only way to survive this ordeal was to keep the tone light, to keep up a friendly banter until the last possible moment, to keep themselves from thinking about what they might be getting into. If jokes, phony punches, and goofy smirks were the things they needed to keep their sanity, then that's what they would do.

Brian rechecked the nun's diagram and made an estimate. "The abandoned shack that we're looking for is about half a mile into the woods."

Jimmy was confused. "But if we follow this stream it's going to take us in the opposite direction."

"Not really. True, it does veer away from the cabin once we're deep in the woods, but then we can use the compass. I'm only saying that if we just head into the woods at any old point, we may not only find it rough going, but also take the risk of getting ourselves lost. The stream will be safe and easy. And faster. It will take a long time to push our way past those thick branches."

He pointed to a spot on the map and indicated to Dorothy that she should bring the flashlight closer so Jimmy could see. "There's an abrupt curve in the stream at this spot here. See? The cabin is almost exactly at that point, only over to the left. When we reach the curve we'll leave the stream and head into the woods. It should be a fairly short walk to the cabin from there." He didn't mention what would come afterwards. They all knew. And no one wanted to think about it.

Dorothy tried to hide what she was feeling. She said cheerfully, "Okay guys, this is it. Let's go."

There could be no more delays. They started off into the woods by sticking to the bank of the stream. There was so much moonlight that Dorothy only had to put the flash on low power, if at all. "Conserve it for when we're in the tunnel," Brian suggested.

Dorothy was glad now that they'd had this ready made "path" waiting for them—the woods on either side of the brook seemed almost impenetrable, with sharp, clinging branches that looked good for scratching flesh and tearing clothing. Dorothy saw hardly any vegetation, due to the season, she supposed. She just hoped she wouldn't blunder right into a path of unseasonal poison ivy.

There were spots along the stream where the woods grew so close to the water that they had to step into the water and get their feet wet. Dorothy's sneakers were soaked and squishy before they'd even walked five minutes, and soon after that the jacket she wore didn't seem warm enough to keep out the chill.

"Should be coming to that curve in the brook any minute now," Brian said.

Dorothy nodded. *Demons, demons, we're chasing after demons. We should be home safe and sound in Manhattan, safe and warm in our beds. We must be crazy, all three of us—looking for a demon in a nunnery!*

A few minutes later and they were at the curve shown on the map. The three of them came to a halt. "Now we go into the woods," Brian said.

"Terrific," Dorothy muttered. The woods looked just as spindly and impassable here as they did everywhere else. "Just how are we supposed to cut our way through these brambles?"

"Wait a minute." Jimmy took hold of the end of the flashlight. As he lifted it, Dorothy's arm went with it. "Shine the light over there. Isn't that a path?"

Dorothy's eyes followed the beam from the flashlight.

There *was* a path.

"And it's going in the direction we want to go, too," Brian said. "Why, I bet it leads right to the cabin."

It made sense, thought Dorothy. Anyone coming from the cabin would probably have followed the stream out of the woods just as they had followed it in. A path from the cabin to the brook, well-worn by years of travel, would certainly come in handy. *For us as well as them.*

As they walked along the pathway Dorothy noticed how dark the area was. Although the moonlight shone down on the passageway, it seemed to be absorbed, swallowed up, by the thick barrier of narrow trees and shrubbery on either side of them. It was as if they were walking within an unending expanse of blackness. Thank goodness she wasn't doing this alone. Thank goodness she and Jimmy had refused to let *Brian* do it alone.

Five minutes later and the cabin—signified by the crude drawing of a tiny house on the map—came into view. It sat silently in the middle of a clearing, and looked as if it had been undisturbed for half a century.

"We'll need the flashlight now," Brian said. "We have to find the 'X' on the map, the trapdoor in the cabin's floor."

The cabin was very old and in a state of disrepair. It was one story high, with a tiny attic room, broken windows, and shutters that hung down crookedly on rusted hinges. Broken steps led up to a small roofed porch. The front door was missing, giving the house a disturbing sentient quality; the entranceway was like a black jagged maw beckoning them to enter.

"It's a sure bet no one lives here," Dorothy said, trying to sound like one of those comediennes on television, something out of *Kate and Allie* or *Mary Tyler Moore*. It didn't work. The boys were tense now, too tense, and didn't laugh. Once they were inside, below the ground, on their way to the convent on this insane mission of rescue and assassination, there would be no turning back. *No more jokes, Dottie*, she told herself. *This is serious business. One misstep, one mistake—and it's over.*

She wondered not for the first time if they were doing the right thing. Perhaps they were fooling not only with the forces of nature, but the very cosmic balance itself. Perhaps this demon—for all its apparent evil—was actually part of the natural order of things, and by destroying it they would let loose an even worse holocaust. But what choice did they have? If someone—man, woman, or demon—went around killing people, kidnapping children, you couldn't just stand there and let it happen.

As for her own part of it—well, she had done a lot of yapping about horror films and evil—but this was *real* horror, *real* evil, with actual victims. If she was half the woman she thought she was she would have to do her part to stop it. What went on in a few sleazy movies didn't seem terribly important up against something like this, something *real*. There was nothing controversial or ambiguous about it: "the claw" was *murdering* people. For once in her life she needed to take positive action. To get her hands good and dirty.

She was still confused over the demon's actions. What was the common thread among its victims, particularly those who had nothing to do with Désirée Fontana, *Vicious*, and *Vicious Two*? Why did it kill only one person at times, and then evolve into a full-fledged serial killer at others? Why did it possess some people during séances and then others who had no occult leanings?

Brian had theorized that the demon was attracted by misery, by heartache, frustration and anger. As to why each host body was killing more and more people than the one before, Brian said, "Simple. The demon is getting stronger. The evil is growing. As for how it chooses its hosts and victims from such a rich, human field? Well, think of the demon as being in a totally dark room—our conception of the astral plane. Then imagine that the walls of that room are being punctured by holes, holes that let in narrow streams of white light. The demon goes after that white light, squeezes through the tiny apertures, and comes into this world. Some streams are brighter than others so he goes to those first. Where he'll wind up nobody knows. More than that I can't even guess at."

Dorothy concentrated on the task at hand, but one phrase kept running through her mind:

The evil is growing.

They walked up the steps and entered the doorway, stepping gingerly in case there were rotting floorboards. Moonlight streamed in through the windows, showing a large front room with a bare table, two wooden chairs, and a dilapidated couch from which poured white stuffing. There appeared to be at least two other smaller rooms, devoid of furnishings, in the rear.

They entered a short narrow hallway leading off from the main room. Brian pointed to the small room on the right. "The trap door should be in here."

There was a small rectangular rug on the floor. Brian reached down and lifted it. The wooden floor beneath was dissected by four lines forming a square. "This is it, folks," He dug his fingers into one of the cracks and pulled upwards. There was a creaking metallic whine and the section of floor rose up and clattered noisily onto the rug beside it. A black pit yawned before them; metal rungs sunk into the wall led downward. "Now we'll have to climb down. I'll go first. Dorothy, keep shining the light down. I want to see exactly what I'm getting into."

Dorothy held the light steady as Brian descended into the darkness. She looked at Jimmy but said nothing. They were both more apprehensive about this than they cared to admit, but there was no need to say it out loud.

Brian had reached the bottom. "There's a tunnel down here," he said. "Just like it shows on the map. Seems safe enough." He was only a few feet below the level of the floor. He reached up his hand. "Give me the flashlight, Dorothy. I'll hold it while you and Jimmy come down."

Dorothy went first. The rungs were metal and seemed both encrusted with dirt *and* greasy. She reached out to feel the wall to which the rungs were attached and found it surprisingly wet and bumpy. A couple of times she nearly slipped. Another few seconds and she was standing in what felt like a patch of drying mud. There was a comforting, rich-earth aroma in the air and for the moment Dorothy felt at ease.

When the three of them were standing together at the bottom, Brian looked at them and said, "If you want to go back now, I'll understand. You can still change your mind, and I won't hold it against you."

Again Jimmy and Dorothy exchanged anxious glances. "No," Dorothy said. "For my prospective book, if for nothing else, I want to see this to the finish."

Jimmy grinned. He put his arm around Dorothy and squeezed her. "I wouldn't miss it for the world."

Brian smiled back and clapped them both on the shoulders. "Well, let's get going." He turned to Dorothy. "If you don't mind, let me hold onto the flashlight. The passageway is narrow and we'll have to walk single file. I think it's better if I go first."

Dorothy didn't argue. She was in no hurry to meet up with whatever they might find at the end of the tunnel.

The conduit was dark, dank, and, for Dorothy, brought on a touch of claustrophobia. The ceiling seemed only an inch or two above Brian's head—and he was the tallest. There were spots when the passageway, which seemed to have been cut out of rock as well as dirt at certain points, became so narrow that they had to squeeze past protruding stone surfaces. The corridor was relatively straight—whenever it did curve to the right or left it swerved back to its former position only a few feet later. There was a little trickle of water running along the hard dirt floor.

Fifteen stifling, oppressive minutes went by as they traversed the underground corridor, fifteen minutes during which no one spoke and Dorothy's fantasies threatened to overwhelm her. Several times she almost cried out, told them to stop, told them she wanted to go back. It wasn't fear of the demon so much as her terror of being buried alive, a phobic reaction to the thought of being trapped beneath tons of rock. Though Brian was in front of her and Jimmy right behind, she had the sensation that something just out of reach was watching her, that at any moment she'd feel fingertips on the back of her neck and they would not belong to anything human.

But then they had reached the end of the passageway, and

Dorothy felt temporary relief. Whatever was going to happen, they were out of the dark, above the ground, ready to face it once and for all. Brian pushed open an old wooden door at the end of the tunnel; they felt a blast of warmer air as they went through and found themselves in a broad stone corridor that reminded Dorothy of something out of a Universal horror film from the forties.

The walls were formed of huge blocks of yellowing quarry stone and were dotted with burning torches set in holders. The odor in here was less "comforting" than it had been in the passageway—stuffier, more oppressive, harsher. They walked along the corridor until they reached a wooden door that was set into the wall to their right. A few yards beyond it was a dark, winding staircase, built into the wall itself, that led, presumably, up to a higher level of the convent. "This must be a subbasement," Brian said. Dorothy nodded but was thinking: *Now that we're here, what do we do—what do we look for?*

They went into the doorway on the right first. Brian said, "If those missing girls are being held captive anywhere, it must be down on this level." The arched wooden door had a large metal latch and for a moment Dorothy thought they'd find it locked, but when Brian pushed on the door—slowly, carefully—it eventually moved inward.

The chamber inside the door was fairly large, lit by torches and a huge stone fireplace at one end. There were shadowy recesses in the walls that looked like cells without bars. Dorothy could see chains and iron bracelets, attached to rungs on the walls, that were draped across the filthy stone floor as if waiting for victims. Against the walls there was a grisly collection of medieval torture devices: a rack, an Iron Maiden, spikes and rods and pokers of all shapes and sizes. There was a great deal of dust in the air. The particles caught the light and created the illusion that everything could be seen only through a curtain of gauze or mist.

Dorothy was appalled. *This place is a dungeon.*

And then she gasped.

For there was someone in the room with them, someone who had been bending over another figure lying on a cot against the right wall. Even now the vertical figure was turning around to see who the intruders were.

Brian's eyebrows lifted when he saw the familiar costume the woman was wearing. Then they saw the young girl on the cot behind the nun. Her hands and feel were bound with rope. *One of the missing girls!* Was this nun the demon? Dorothy wondered.

Brian seemed to be in a trance. Dorothy was about to grab the flashlight from him, shine it directly in the woman's eyes and effectively blind her, when the nun cried out in recognition.

"Thank God you've come! My prayers have been answered!"

The woman stepped away from the cot and rushed over toward Dorothy and the others. As she came within a few feet of them Dorothy realized who she was. Yes, she had seen that face before. She turned to Asquith and said, "Brian! This is the nun who gave us the map!" The fear in Brian's eyes seemed to diminish—but not his excitement.

Jimmy was about to close the door to the dungeon when the nun cried out, "No! Leave it open. Or else we won't be able to tell if anyone is coming."

A moment later Dorothy and the nun, who had introduced herself as Sister Margarita, were embracing like blood relations. The nun started to cry. "I was so scared—I didn't think this nightmare would ever. . . ." She looked back at the girl on the cot, who appeared to be unconscious. "Another one. I looked in here tonight and found *another* one."

"Where are the other missing girls?" Jimmy asked. "Are they here?"

"Dead. All of them. *Sacrificed.*"

The others looked at one another in defeat. All this trouble and they'd come too late.

Dorothy broke the silence. "I don't understand," she said. "If you knew about this, if you knew someone in the convent was responsible, why didn't you go to the police yourself?"

The sister wrung her hands and pleaded with her eyes for understanding. "They're watching me, always watching me, don't you see? I have no access to a phone. I was *beaten* after running out to your car this afternoon. I'm *always* beaten. If they had known what I'd given you they might have *killed* me."

"What about the secret passageway?" Jimmy asked. "Why didn't you escape the way we came in?"

She shook with frustration and gathered the folds of her

garment in her hands, twisting, turning the material, as if by tearing it she'd free herself from her miserable situation. "I didn't want to leave without taking one of the girls with me," she said. "But whenever I managed to sneak down here to the dungeon the girl would always be asleep or groggy. Unconscious. They're drugged once they get here. I know I should have run directly for the passageway the moment I managed to sneak away from the others, but I thought of the girls. I always had to *try* and see if I could take one with me."

Poor woman, Dorothy thought. She seemed barely out of her teens herself. And so scared of the other sisters it was a wonder she'd accomplished as much as she had.

There were footsteps on the stairs outside the chamber.

"*Ssshhh*," said Sister Margarita. "Someone's coming!" She pulled herself up to her full height. "Follow me. I know another way out of here. Thank God they're still at the top of the stairs so we have time."

The sister motioned to Jimmy and Brian. "Please carry the girl. We can take her with us now."

"Why should we leave?" Jimmy asked her. "Can't we overpower a few nuns?"

"This is *not* a 'few nuns,' " the sister snapped. "This is a whole cult of strong, dangerous men and women. I suggest you keep that in mind. Let's get away while we can and talk about this later."

Sister Margarita was nervous and anxious, yet so confident in her commands that the others didn't hesitate to follow orders. While Jimmy and Brian lifted up the girl between them—she was slowly beginning to revive—Sister Margarita told Dorothy to assist her in pulling a large round grill off the floor. It was about twice the size of a manhole cover but not nearly as heavy. The hole beneath the grill stank of sewage, and the grill itself was dripping a gooey brown liquid. "This is the way I've been coming in late," the nun explained. "I can push the grill up by myself, but it makes so much noise."

She and Dorothy put the grill to one side, and began to slither one by one into the opening. The hole was also greased with that brown gunk and Dorothy virtually slid through a narrow tube until she hit a soft bottom. She found herself in a small, smelly conduit that stretched in either direction with no end in sight.

Dorothy didn't even want to think about what this chamber was used for.

Brian and Jimmy lowered the girl down into the opening so that the two women could grab her, then darted in after her. Jimmy had just pulled the grating back into position when they heard the chamber door opening and footsteps entering the room. *Talk about close calls!*

Dorothy held the flashlight as they proceeded to the left. "I know my way around in the dark," the sister bragged. "Just a little ways further and we'll enter another part of the convent."

Dorothy heard a highpitched squealing and looked down to see a rat skittering across her sneaker. There seemed to be several more of the rodents hiding in cracks and spaces along the walls, silent witnesses to this parade of unlikely partners. Just as Dorothy thought she'd be overcome by the fetid odor in the conduit, the nun opened a tiny door for them and they proceeded into a narrow stairwell in a rounded enclosure. It appeared that they were in one of the servant's several towers.

Sister Margarita waited until the whole group was assembled, then closed the door firmly behind her. She gently touched the face of the semiconscious schoolgirl, her compassion apparent in her wide, glowing eyes. "Poor child," she said.

Shining the flashlight to one side of the girl, so as not to blind her, Dorothy got her first good look at the teenager. She was pretty, rather short, wearing heavy make-up. At first Dorothy was alarmed at the girl's blue lips—*why she must be freezing*—until she realized it was only a more esoteric shade of cosmetic. Kids these days. . . . Dorothy could imagine how terrified the young woman had been, and felt a thrill at the thought that they had saved her and were finally getting to the bottom of the mystery. Perhaps solving it—*ending it*—forever.

Sister Margarita stopped stroking the girl's face and turned to look at the others. "We're still underneath the ground," she explained. "We have to go up three levels, and into another narrow passageway." She apologized to Dorothy. "This one is full of spiders, I'm afraid." Dorothy shuddered but said nothing. "At the end of the passageway, there'll be another staircase to a very special secret chamber. It's the library, the hidden archives of the Church. Hardly anyone goes there. We'll rest there, compare notes, and decide what we're going to do."

She saw Brian opening his mouth and raised her finger. "Save your questions for later. There's no way to get back to that tunnel you came in through from here, or else I'd let you take the girl and run. Bear with me—I'll answer all your questions shortly."

And then they were following the nun up the winding stone steps, into another creaking door and through a passageway that was, as she had promised, full of sticky cobwebs. They clung to faces and clothing and were alive with dozens of tiny, eight-legged creatures that jumped about, darted off and onto the intruder's bodies, and scurried out of the path of their footsteps.

The group finally entered another small, square enclosure; this one had a series of broad, flat steps that led up to an oaken doorway recessed into the wall.

"Welcome to the library," the sister said dramatically. "The Archives of the Order of the Mourning Sister of the Holy Messianic Church."

She pulled open the heavy wood door.

"Step inside," she said. "It's time the world knew the truth about this church."

29

"It was here that I first learned the truth about the church I had been born into."

Sister Margarita had ushered them inside, then gone about putting a match to several candles until there was enough light in the dark chamber to see by. The octangular room was small, with a very low ceiling and no windows. The musty air was fragrant with lavender or violets. Along the walls of the room were beautiful antique furnishings, handsome wood bookshelves, and several round tables. There was a large solid desk and a long brown table in the center, both of which were piled high with massive tomes and manuscripts.

Sister Margarita and Brian removed some books from the long table, and the moaning youngster was gently deposited on top. Sister Margarita stood protectively by the girl's side, stroking her forehead, looking down at her to comfort her when she whined or stirred fitfully. "There, there. It will be all right."

To the others, she said, "The girl will be all right. She's had a bad fright, that's all."

"You don't think she requires medical attention?"

"No," she told Brian. "I've had nurse's training. I would know. She'll be all right. The drug they gave her just has to wear off, that's all." She quickly looked at each of them in turn and said, "In the meantime let me thank you from the bottom of my heart for coming, and let me tell you why you're here and what has happened." The others each chose one of the room's several chairs and sat down to listen to her story.

Sister Margarita waved her hand in the air to indicate all the books surrounding them. "Much of what I'm about to tell you I read for myself in these diaries, these historical accounts of the Church. I found this room the same way I originally blundered into the dungeon downstairs. My inquisitive nature. While I was growing up here I amused myself by traveling through all the secret passages—and there are many—in this convent, and came upon at least half a dozen secret rooms. This by far was the most interesting. I found the blueprints of the building, even that diagram I gave you, in a drawer in that desk over there. Apparently it was accurate or you wouldn't be here.

"The Holy Messianic Church is usually thought of—when it is thought of at all—as a sort of strange bowdlerization of the Holy Roman Church. Nothing could be further from the truth. Originally, under a different, forgotten name, our church was devoted to *paganism*—the Messiah it worshipped was not Jesus Christ, but a demonic god of whom the sisters are earthbound followers. They prayed to this demonic god and hoped that one day he would reappear to bring order and discipline to the people, a new age of kind and just *subjugation*.

"But as the Judeo-Christian ethic slowly obliterated the pagan religions, the Messianic Church went underground. On the surface it seemed no different from other religions; it even molded its new incarnation after the Roman Catholic Church, half in mockery, I suppose, half in self-defense. Its nuns seemed no different from Catholic nuns. They too were sent on missions of love and charity across the world. Many of the sisters were not even aware of who the other sisters were actually worshipping. Only certain nuns were taken into the fold, while the rest were used as cover. Their love of the "God" we know today was legitimate."

Brian kneaded his chin. "Fascinating."

"But as the years, the centuries, went by, the Church began to change. There remained a small core of faithful fanatics, those who still worshipped the demonic god and were its 'brides,' but most of them were worshippers of the God of today. The

Church began to lose its uniqueness, its place in the world. Gradually it transformed into a conventional religion as the old fanatics passed away without first winning any converts. The old knowledge died," she patted a book on the table, "even as it was collected into dusty, rotting tomes where it would soon be ignored and forgotten. For all intents and purposes, the Church was exactly what it seemed to be."

She paused to check on the girl again. Satisfied that her breathing was regular and all seemed in order, she continued. "But . . . there were still some who remembered what its original mission had been, who and what the Church had originally believed in and worshipped. Those few remaining 'faithful' formed an inner circle, a secret society, you might say, and carried on their own activities, pagan worship, witchcraft on the sly, in secret ceremonies that only the members of this inner circle were privy to. And slowly, surely, the pagan aspects of the Church began to flourish once again, until the inner circle grew so large that it needed its own order. The Order of the Mourning Sisters, those who mourned the world's, their Church's, loss of what they called the One True Faith."

Jimmy stirred restlessly. "But why didn't this inner circle start its own church then?"

Again Sister Margarita had to snap at him. "What? And be persecuted, subject to inquisition, burned at the stake? No, they needed to remain part of the Holy Messianic Church for *cover*, for safety's sake. It was rather ingenious of them when you think of it. They had their own order, could do as they pleased, in privacy, could always play a game of pretense if any of the Church superiors should happen to visit. And they still sent out their own nuns to do mission work, often," she smiled with bitterness, "stupid, gullible nuns who had no idea of what the church really stood for. Or those who were privy to the inner workings but so isolated and naive that they didn't realize until they went out into the world and saw for themselves that their beloved Church was not at all like the others. That they were pariahs, outcasts and heathens as far as the world was concerned."

Brian lifted his hand to get her attention. "Are you saying these nuns are Satanists? Devil-worshippers?"

"No. Their religion predates the very concepts of God and

Satan; hence they worship neither—not God but *a* god, a powerful god who commands the forces of nature and can create and send out demons to do his bidding. According to our beliefs, he has lost much of his power because so few will worship him any more. The Mourning Sisters hope that someday that will change, but must wait until they feel the time is right to spread their message openly. Their God is known only as *Abbiscyste*, the Blood God. As to its origins, even I can not say. But it is very, very ancient."

The young girl moaned and Sister Margarita stopped for a moment to comfort her. "Sshhh. Sshhh. It will be all right."

She resumed. "The Sisters do not think of themselves, see themselves, as being evil. They want basically the same thing other religionists do: peace on earth, all people worshipping the same god, strict obediance to that god's laws, complete and unquestioning allegiance to their Lord. When that occurs, they feel a golden age will come upon the world, an age similar to other religions' concepts of heaven. They are fantasies.

"At first when I learned the truth, I was shocked. I felt like such a fool. The reading I did, my increasing sophistication as I watched films, as I talked to and worked with the college students and attended lectures at Dolby and elsewhere, revealed to me that the Mourning Sisters were out of step with the times, completely cut off from reality. And they didn't seem to realize or even consider it. They walked around smugly believing that theirs was the only true faith."

"They don't sound so different from everyone else," Jimmy noted.

Sister Margarita seemed not to have heard him. "Many sisters here are not part of—aren't even aware of—the activities of the cult, the Church's inner circle. The cult members refer to them as stupid cows. They are here only to help present a normal facade to the world." She shook her head sadly. "I tried to accept, and I almost did. The sisters had been kind to me. So what if my life suddenly seemed like a joke? I don't know if I believe in anything any more."

Her face grew dark. "But then, a few weeks ago, the disappearances began, the *murders*, and—God help me—I realized that someone, maybe everyone, at the convent was behind it. I heard cries coming from the dungon. I hid in the shadows, watched the Mother Superior and some others take the girl away and bring her to a room with an altar. I saw them beat her, butcher her, offer her up in sacrifice to their god.

"There was no one I could turn to. I got that diagram out, the one showing the secret way into the convent—I think that's how they bring the girls in—and planned to slip it to someone when the groceries were delivered. I was constantly stymied. Always I had duties that kept me indoors on delivery days. Then I started watching for cars, any passing cars, whenever I was working in the kitchen." She looked at Dorothy. "When *you* came this afternoon, I took a chance and ran out to give you the material."

Brian jumped to his feet. "But the claw—what about the claw? The *drawing*. We have to know who the demon has possessed *this* time."

The nun looked at him blankly. "The claw? The drawing?" Sister Margarita blinked in puzzlement. "I don't remember any drawing. And *which* demon are you referring to?"

Brian and Dorothy, taking turns, filled the nun in on what they knew of the four-fingered demon. "We thought surely you knew," Brian said, "that *you* had drawn that picture. It's obvious that the demon has possessed someone in this convent, possibly the Mother Superior herself. That's why these killings and kidnappings have been occurring. Don't you see how it fits!"

"I don't remember any drawing or any claw," the sister said, "but if a demon has taken over the sisters—perhaps that *would* explain everything. Perhaps the sisters have been right all along. Perhaps the Blood God *has* created a demon for them as a sign of his love and devotion." She didn't seem anxious to elaborate.

The girl on the table was whimpering, about to wake up. "If that's a sign of love he can keep it," Jimmy muttered.

Sister Margarita leaned against some of the books on the table and wiped tears out of her eyes. Then she gave up trying to hold it in and began sobbing in such a way that the whole room echoed with her anguish. Dorothy tried to comfort the woman, but Sister Margarita held up her hand to keep her away, to tell her she'd be all right in a moment. She sniffled, wiped her eyes and nose with a tissue she'd pulled out of her pocket, and got herself together.

"I'm all right now. It's just been . . . so difficult these past few weeks." She finished drying her eyes and attended to the girl. "Wake up, darling," she cooed. "Wake up. Everything will be all right now."

Perhaps because she saw that she was not alone in the room, that what appeared to be sane and normal people were standing there watching her with obvious concern, the young lady did not cry out in panic.

Dorothy went over to her and took her hand. "You're safe now, dear." *For the time being, at least.* "Can you tell us what happened?"

"Where am I?" the girl asked, the fear returning in spite of the two women's efforts to reassure her.

"What's your name, child?" asked Sister Margarita.

"Osa. Osa Peters." Shivering and sniffling all the while, she gave them an abbreviated version of what had happened at the college. "I didn't see who it was, though," she said. "Someone snuck up behind me in the gym and threw their hands over my mouth. I smelled a funny odor." *Chloroform*, Dorothy figured. "And the next thing I knew I was all tied up. I woke up for a second and thought I saw Sally Anne—that's my friend—but everything gets foggy after that. I'm still groggy. I can't believe it's all happening."

Sister Margarita helped the girl to her feet. "I'm going to get this child out of here. I failed with the others, but I won't fail with this one."

Brian looked at Jimmy and Dorothy. "*We* can't leave yet. Our work isn't done. My job isn't finished."

He stepped over to the sister and said, "Where is the Mother Superior now?"

"Sister Absolum is probably organizing a search for the girl. Later on, there'll be a service—with or without a sacrifice—in the underground temple." She went over to a desk and got out pen and paper. "There's a vault deep in the mountain, a natural cavern that was converted to a temple for pagan worship when the sisters arrived." She started writing instructions on the paper. "I'm going to try and get the girl out of here. It will be easier if the two of us attempt it on our own. I'll go get the police. They'll listen to me when they hear the girl's story.

"In the meantime," she finished scribbling on the paper, "this is a route you can take to reach the temple, though God only knows why you'd want to go there. You'll have to enter the nuns' chambers at one point, but most of them will be elsewhere when you do. Be careful, though."

A few moments later, she and the girl were gone.

Brian looked around the library at his two friends. "Well, are you ready to step into the lair of the dragon?"

"Or the Blood God," Jimmy smirked. "This whole business is the *weirdest*. . . ."

"Weird or not, we've run into a cult of child murders, people with a penchant for human sacrifice. I can't believe our demon has nothing to do with it."

Dorothy tried to swallow her fear. "Do you think this 'Abbiscyste' *is* the demon?" She was struck by how small and hollow her voice sounded.

Brian shook his head negatively. "Not if the four-fingered demon is only a century old, and Abbiscyste has existed for *eons*. If there is a connection, we won't find out until we reach this temple."

Dorothy summoned up her courage. "Let's get it over with. Brian, you've got the directions. Take the flashlight and show us where to go."

They left the library and reentered the passageway with all the spiders. Dorothy paid no attention to them; what were spiders when you were up against murderers and Blood Gods and assorted demonic horrors? This time they headed in the opposite direction, away from the tower they had ascended earlier and into the heart of the building.

They traversed the narrow passage and other connecting passages for at least half an hour; they must have been walking *within* the walls of the convent. The passages were filled with dust as well as cobwebs and Dorothy nearly had a coughing fit. *Don't!* she warned herself. *Hold it in! You don't want them to know we're here.*

They came out through a wooden doorway indicated in the sister's directions and found themselves in the living quarters of the convent. Dorothy was at her most nervous at this stage, as were the others. They had to go from one bedroom, down a corridor, and into another room where there was a staircase behind a closet. Crooked wooden steps led downward from the level of the hidden library.

Dorothy was surprised at how well-appointed the living quarters were. The sisters were certainly not accustomed to a particularly modest lifestyle. Drapes, chairs, beds, lamps and other furnishings, far from being humble accountrements, were fit for royalty. Only the very best fabrics and antiques were in evidence. The Holy Messianic Church certainly did not lack for money, which had probably been accumulated over the centuries until it had reached impressive proportions.

At the bottom of the staircase they had to enter several more connecting staircases and passageways. *It's like a maze*, Dorothy thought, contemplating the sorry possibility that they might wander about inside these enclosures for the rest of eternity. Neither Brian nor Jimmy seemed in a conversational mood, which meant that she was alone with her thoughts—and apprehensions—more than she cared to be. *She did not want to think about what was coming.*

Finally they came upon a winding stone staircase that seemed to descend several levels below the ground floor, even below the dungeon where Osa had been imprisoned. Dorothy sensed that this was the last leg of the journey. *They were going down into the pit.* Dorothy could feel herself trembling to the very core of her being, but refused to give in countenance. *Chin up, lady!*

At the bottom of the stairs was a long, narrow hallway that led up to what appeared to be a solid stone wall. A sickeningly sweet odor permeated the air, and the enclosure was quite cold and damp. Brian played his flashlight over the wall.

"Did we take a wrong turn?" Jimmy asked. "Brian, take another look at the directions."

Brian read the sheet of paper again under the light and shook his head. "No. We followed her directions exactly. No wrong turns, no detours. The temple is supposed to be right beyond this wall."

Dorothy pushed her way past the two men. "Guys, this is supposed to be a *secret* entrance, right? We can't expect them to have an open door waiting for us, can we?" She stepped over to the wall and ran her fingers over it, searching for chinks or crevices that might contain hidden springs or handholds. "Let's see if we can find a way to make this *open*."

Jimmy hesitated. "What happens if we stumble out right in the middle of the altar?"

"That's a chance we have to take," Dorothy replied. "Besides, Sister Margarita would have warned us if that were the case, right? C'mon. Help me." She didn't voice her fear that in her rush the nun might have left out *other* essential instructions.

The two men followed Dorothy's suggestion. Brian ran his fingers along the surface of the wall, carefully looking for hidden notches, while Jimmy used his hammer to search for hollow spots behind the stones. Brian was bent over a section in the middle of the wall when he said, "Found something." He began pulling on a loose stone, yanking on it with increased urgency until finally the whole small section came away from the wall. It left an opening big enough for them to crawl through.

"Hand me the flashlight," Brian said. He stuck the beam in through the hole and discovered a small storage room with a wooden door on the opposite side. "That door over there across the way leads into the temple, I'll bet. Let's go."

After crawling through the opening, they replaced the loose section of wall and clambered over several boxes in their path until they reached the doorway opposite. Brian carefully opened it a crack and peered through. Dorothy noted the look of amazement that crossed his face, and was filled with curiosity in spite of herself. He turned back to the others. "It's the back of the temple. And it looks empty." Dorothy allowed herself to exhale.

They went through the door into the subterranean vault and were astonished at its elegance and vastness. Its dimensions were enormous, with a ceiling about thirty feet above their heads, and a smooth marble floor that stretched out twenty yards up to an impressively frightening altar at the opposite end of the chamber. The roof of the vault was supported by several massive columns and flying buttresses.

They descended three stone steps to the floor, which was sunk below the level of the room they'd just come from. To their right was the main entrance to the temple, two huge wooden doors adorned with curlicues and gargolyes. The only illumination in the chamber came from torches set into the walls and Brian's flashlight. There were no pews or seats of any kind, and the floor was covered with strange indecipherable markings and lurid drawings.

Brian shone his light over the altar. It was adorned with pagan drawings etched right into the stone, figures entwining, copulating, in a river of gushing blood. "Look at that craftsmanship, the detail. It's incredible." For a moment Dorothy forgot where she was and what she was doing; it was like they had wandered into another time, another century. But then she got a good look at the sculptured face atop the altar and her fear returned tenfold.

The head of the altar, which stuck out several feet over the floor of the temple, was about ten feet high, six feet wide, and another ten feet deep from the neck to the tip of the nostrils. It had cold, penetrating eyes, red as rubies, that followed the spectator no matter where in the room he or she traveled. It had more of a snout than a nose, fangs than teeth—a wolfish cast— and seemed to emanate a force of pure, unharnessed energy and violence. It was made of a polished bronze that seemed to have dark crimson undertones glittering beneath the surface. Directly under the nasty grinning head were two broad stone slabs about the size of small tractors.

"So that's the Blood God," Jimmy remarked, staring up at the head. "Pretty scary fellow." He was trying to sound brave and unimpressed, but Dorothy knew he was just as spooked by all this as she was. "So what do we do now?" he asked.

Brian turned to face him. "We hide, Jimmy. And wait. I have to make absolutely certain that the Mother Superior—or someone else—is actually possessed by the demon. A horrible tragedy would occur if I were to pick the wrong person. There can't be any doubt in my mind."

Jimmy gestured helplessly. "Look, Brian. An old nun is one thing. But what if the demon takes over her body while you're trying to destroy it? Remember, I've seen firsthand what this monster likes to do to people. Do you honestly think any one person will be able to stop it by themselves? Hell, Vivienne Cherneau was shrugging off bullets, man! Like they were pebbles!"

Brian kneaded his brow worriedly. "I don't know, Jimmy. But I have to try. I have to. I know this won't work if the demon's in a dormant stage. Besides, I won't be sure *which* nun is possessed until I see proof of the demon's presence within her with my very own eyes. Now, don't argue with me. I know what I have to do, believe me, and I know it won't be easy. But I'm prepared for that. And I'll get the job done if it kills me."

"That should be very interesting to see."

A nun was walking out from behind the altar. She was leading a procession of about twenty people, most of them nuns, and a few men dressed in priestly garb. Dorothy realized there had to be another entrance to the temple behind the altar, and had a sickening feeling. There was nothing inordinately strange about these people, nothing blatantly menacing, yet she had never been more terrified in her life. Only the ghosts on the railroad car had had a worse effect. *Now what were they going to do*?

"I am Sister Absolum of the Order of the Mourning Sisters," the woman said. *The Mother Superior!* She was tall and graceful, older than Sister Margarita, but younger than Dorothy had expected. She was dressed entirely in flowing black robes. Her wimple hid most of her head, but what could be seen of her face was determined, hard and attractive. Thin lips, small chin and nose, big eyes that seemed to be bright wet pools shimmering with quiet fury. Walking up to the trio she pulled something from the folds of her garment. Dorothy smelled a sweet, fragrant odor, and immediately began to feel tired. She could tell that Brian and Jimmy were similarly affected. The hammer and flashlight dropped out of their hands to clatter onto the floor.

Even in the midst of a direct confrontation with the members of the cult Sister Margarita had warned them about, Dorothy could still not believe this was happening. Her mind refused to accept that these people were out to do her any harm.

Smiling, Sister Absolum continued waving something in front of their eyes. It was from there the smell came, as well as a bluish-gray fog or mist. The mist was clouding, *clouding* Dorothy's eyes.

As she lost consciousness and fell to the marble floor, the last thing Dorothy heard was Sister Absolum saying, "Welcome to our temple, my friends.

"You will not leave here alive."

30

The Wicked Witch was sitting before them and she was smiling, a tight smile and a cold one, and her eyes were shining in the firelight. Brian was eleven years old. The Witch was their mean homeroom teacher and she was telling them scary stories by the campfire. "Let me tell you a story," she was saying. And Brian wanted to get up and walk away because he already suffered from nightmares; he wanted to plug his ears up and make her voice go away, but he couldn't, so he had to just sit there and listen.

"Let me tell you a story," Sister Absolum said. Brian was lying drugged and helpless beneath one of the stone slabs under the head of the snarling Blood God. Dorothy was draped over the top of the slab, eyes open, but clearly not in possession of her faculties. Jimmy, with his back up against the other slab, was resting against the floor like a blurry-eyed drunkard.

"The drug you inhaled will not harm you," the sister was saying. "It makes you feel dizzy, weak, unable to control your limbs or take any kind of action. It does away with the necessity of ropes. But you can hear me and understand me. Before you take the places of the sacrificial victim that you undoubtedly helped escape from the convent, I want you to know all about us, about our methods and our purpose. It will help you attain grace. It helps you accept us, if you willingly offer yourselves up to our Lord, Abbiscyste, it will mean the salvation of your souls."

She has to be the demon's host, Brian thought. *This is the one. The one I must take care of.* He looked at her hands, tightly clasped together in front of her as she spoke. But if it were the demon within her who was speaking to them now, why was the claw not in evidence? *Where was the claw*, the ultimate proof of who Brian's victim had to be?

"This story takes place over a hundred years in the past. It concerns a young nun named Sister Venicus. She was quite different from the woman she was named for, Venicus, the earthwoman that our God took as his bride when he first walked our planet many centuries ago. A strong-willed, opportunistic young lady, *Sister* Venicus made a lot of enemies among her peers and superiors. To punish her, she was sent on an assignment normally reserved for those children of the Church who were unaware of its original purpose. She was sent to minister to the needs of the sick in Sumara. And she was angry and hurt, utterly miserable, because of it.

"Sister Venicus had had a childhood accident; it stripped her of one finger, the middle one of her left hand, and her arm became withered and useless. Her gnarled hand looked just like a claw. People were cruel. Even the other sisters. Sister Venicus had a lot to be bitter about.

"So she prayed and prayed to her Lord, the Blood God, for help and comfort and guidance. And the Blood God answered!

"*She was on a train in Sumara when the Blood God sent a meteor or comet sailing down from the very heavens. The train Sister Venicus was on rode into the heavenly body's gaseous remains after it landed some distance from the tracks. The radiation the gas emitted was extremely potent, capable of disintegrating human flesh and bone, leaving no trace whatsoever. Like a neutron bomb, the radiation left the train itself and the surrounding territory untouched, but vaporized the passengers.*"

At last, Brian thought. The mystery of the ghost train had been solved!

"*Can you imagine the horror, the shock, the outrage and sorrow all those souls must have felt? They were sick and miserable, but none of them wanted to die. Even Sister Venicus didn't want to die. So they didn't die. Instead they merged, their immortal souls came together as a type of living energy, became a life force that could virtually live forever. Among the passengers on that train, Sister Venicus was perhaps the healthiest, with the strongest, most indomitable will. She became the dominant consciousness of all those that made up the life force. Sister Venicus had prayed that her God send her a demon to strike down her enemies, but it did better than that. It transformed Sister Venicus herself into a demon. The Demon Venicus, whose sign is the four-fingered claw, the hand of the late sister who died and was transformed like no human being ever before her."*

Brian wasn't sure if there were any truth to the "Blood God" part of the story. He doubted that a supreme being of any kind had been responsible. But all the rest—it made sense. As horrible and fantastic as it was, it made sense. Sister Venicus and her fellow traveling companions had not come up against the wrath—or blessing—of a Blood God, but an accident of nature, a scientific nightmare. Of course, the insane woman who stood there calmly telling them all this would never believe that.

"The Demon Venicus found itself on a new plane of existence. Time—our time—passes very quickly for a demon, as it does for our Lord, so it took Venicus many of our years to assert her total superiority over the other spirits, to turn them into her slaves. She traveled about in the ether, occasionally making contact with living mortals . . . always to those mortals' regret. Her world, the laws that govern it, are not the same as our own. It took her all this time to 'come home,' as it were, to reach her cherished goal, this convent in America. She knew that it was within this order that the worshippers of the Blood God still existed."

Brian figured that Sister Venicus—the claw—had started her killing spree right off the bat in the late 1800s, but had not been able to control the physical laws of the other-world or the wills of the other passengers enough to reach her ultimate destination. Until now. Her rage at having her wishes denied had led her to torment and possess, to slaughter, helpless humans.

"Not long after her arrival here, the Demon Venicus appeared to us in one of our ceremonies, where she told us everything. She possessed one of us, entered one of us, and told us what we must

do if we were to make our faith the dominant faith on earth once again. At first we were appalled, repelled, but then . . . we knew we had to listen to the demon for it was the voice of our Lord, and no matter how horrible its commands might be, we had to fulfill them without question. We had to have faith in our Lord."

Brian was disgusted. Didn't the fools realize that Sister Venicus was a crazy old psychopath who took orders from no one but herself, that her ordeal a century ago had completely twisted her mind? Venicus' deviant energy was attracted to people who exuded misery and rage, people susceptible to its vile insinuations. It was more a force of pure evil than any kind of benevolent intelligence. Couldn't they see that? Couldn't they see that no supreme deity was ordering—or would order them—to go out and butcher young girls?

"We had to make sacrifices, human sacrifices," Sister Absolum continued. *"Which we had not done for a great many years. Using the body of its host, Sister Venicus went out and captured young women"*—the pretty young women she had probably always been jealous of and hated, Brian surmised—*"and brought them back to the convent. Some struggled too hard, could not be captured, and had to be killed instead. She gets strength from killing, you see. Our Lord says it must be done, though, and we cannot question."*

Sister Absolum lifted her eyes toward the bronze head of Abbiscyste. *"No one has suspected what is happening here. Not even Venicus' host—until recently, that is. When the demon inside her is dormant, she is completely unaware of its presence. Some of the college girls know her, this sister. They have seen her around town and they like her. The one the demon Venicus chose to possess is perhaps the most innocent, the most trusting of us all."*

Brian was getting a sinking feeling. The demon had *not* possessed the Mother Superior! It was someone else. But who? The tools he needed to destroy the demon were concealed on his person, but he needed to know *who* to attack. He also needed to have freedom of movement, to have his strength back, and he was barely able to move his fingers or to keep his eyes from closing.

"In her natural state, the sister would try to fight against her possession, without realizing what she was doing. She tried to

escape from us here several times, but always the demon took over before she could get too far. Deep in her subconscious she knew what was happening; out of self-protection, she would not go herself to the authorities. So she would go kill or kidnap instead, and come back here with her booty. To keep up the charade, as the demon wishes, I would beat her for her transgressions."

Brian felt ill. *Oh no. Don't tell me. It can't be . . .*

"The demon let her contact you, Mr. Asquith, told her when you and your friend were in the vicinity. For it knows of you, knows of your presence here. It wanted you here. So that we could dispose of you. We will not let you and your friends remain a threat to our Church, to Venicus, to our Lord, any longer.

"Yes," she said, smiling, sneering, *leering* at him. *"Yes, Mr. Asquith, it's true. The nun whom the Demon Venicus has possessed is Sister Margarita!"*

And Brian thought of Osa, poor Osa, who thought she was getting out of danger. And the sister—the sweet, helpful sister— who was carrying inside her a weapon more dangerous than an H-bomb.

And who didn't even know it.

Osa was feeling much better by the time they'd traveled halfway through the tunnel that led to the abandoned cabin in the forest. She was still scared, downright terrified, by all that happened, but the sister was so kind and concerned, so full of quiet strength and dignity, that she felt ashamed of herself for being such a sissy.

Osa felt bad about making fun of the sisters all the time, she and Sally Anne. Sister Margarita was really nice, helping her out like this. She remembered that the sister spent a lot of time at the college. She'd seen her in the library, having coffee in the cafeteria, at the drama club presentation. She'd even heard that the nun took the time to talk to some of the girls about their problems. Osa herself had seen the sister having a quiet chat with that creepy cook, Arnold Matson, when she and Sally Anne had stormed into the kitchen to complain about the food. Now *that* took compassion!

At first Osa couldn't understand why they had to go through

this spooky tunnel. Why didn't they just go to the Mother Superior's office and have her call the police? But the sister had explained, she'd said that a gang of thugs had taken over the convent, were dragging girls off campus and bringing them up to the nunnery and that the place wasn't safe. Osa was sure that the sister was holding something back, but who was she to question a nun?

She felt awful—those poor nuns at the mercy of rapists and hooligans. Thank God they had escaped from there. Sister Margarita also said that the woman and two men who'd been with her were special police called in to break up the mob.

Gee, she hoped Sally Anne was okay. She hoped they didn't get her, too. Well, when she got to town she'd check to make sure her friend was all right, then tell the police to send lots and lots of men—the National Guard, maybe—up to the convent to save those poor sisters and free the other missing girls.

Sister Margarita had been whispering comforting things to her all the time, but she fell silent not long after they'd entered the tunnel. Osa hoped they'd reach the end of it soon. Sister Margarita was carrying a torch, but it was still damp and scary down here. The sister strode ahead of the girl, lighting up the way, her left hand stretched behind her to pull Osa along in a hurry. Osa wished the nun wouldn't hold her hand so tightly, though; it was beginning to hurt. And she wished the sister would get a manicure, too. Ouch, her nails were long.

Finally they reached the steps that led up to the trapdoor in the cabin. Sister Margarita let go of Osa's hand and instructed her to climb up and wait for her. Osa did as she was told. The nun handed the torch up to Osa, then the girl stood back to make room for Sister Margarita as the woman climbed up out of the hole.

Suddenly Osa saw the sister's face in the torchlight; it was hideous, distorted, bulging with red and purple blotches. The teeth had grown and were sticking out obscenely from between her thickening lips. And the eyes—God the eyes.

But then the sister turned her head to look downward, as if checking to make sure no one had followed them. Osa's rapid heartbeat began to slow—surely it had only been a trick of the light, the shadows playing over the sister's face?

But then Osa saw the hand, the claw, its nails clattering on the hard wood surface of the floor as the sister pulled herself up into the room.

Osa screamed.

31

Venicus knew that she could not let the woman-child go. She had to be destroyed. She would walk, tell everyone what she had seen. It had taken Venicus a while to assert control over this pitiful human wretch it was possessing, the other souls that made up its sustenance fighting its influence all the way. Damn them. Venicus reached out her host's hand—the withered, long-nailed claw which had so much strength, so much surprising resilience—and grabbed the woman-child's throat with her fingers.

Osa struggled, tried to scream, but she couldn't get any air. The demon wouldn't let her. Venicus thrust the nails of its four-fingered claw deeper and deeper into the girl's neck, drawing blood, a lot of blood, cutting into the jugular vein.

With a casual wrench, she tore the girl's head off. It smacked against a corner of the room and plopped into a puddle on the floor.

Too late—Venicus had made a mistake. It had killed the girl before it had complete control over Sister Margarita. Hence it was Sister Margarita who watched in horror as her hand— seemingly of its own accord—reached out and brutally, mercilessly, killed an innocent young woman. A moment later, against all Venicus' efforts, Sister Margarita was again in con-

trol.
And she remembered.

"Oh My God!"

Recoiling, vomiting, Sister Margarita turned away from the carnage on the floor of the cabin and wept and shook with outrage.

She remembered.

She knew.

What she had done. What was happening.

She had drawn the picture of the claw.

She *was* the claw.

And she had killed so many people.

Assisted in the murders of many more.

Sobbing, stumbling, Sister Margarita climbed down through the trapdoor. *She could see herself throwing the wire over Jane Paige's head, dragging her into the woods and over to the cabin. And all the others. Coming upon Rosemary on her way back home from town, attacking her even as she opened her mouth to say hello. Seeing Faye Edwards and her boyfriend sprawled across the lawn of the picnic area, using her knife and her wire to send them out of this world because they had seen her face, seen what she looked like when the demon possessed her. She saw herself slapping a chloroformed handkerchief over Osa Peters' mouth—the other girls had put up too much of a struggle—binding her with rope in case the chloroform didn't work.*

At some point she had drawn the picture of the claw, hoping that it might end this madness if she herself could not.

She saw herself hacking off the head of Sally Anne Hollister, stepping back just in time to avoid getting the girl's blood spattered all over her clothing.

She saw herself committing all these atrocities and it made her ill in body and spirit.

And the worst thing was. . . .

She wasn't through.

The Mother Superior had removed her clothing.

Her body was much more beautiful and sensual than Jimmy had expected. The breasts were large and firm, the abdomen smooth and flat. She knew she had the power to excite him. Her hair, which had been pinned up beneath the wimple, was now flowing down to her shoulders in seductive auburn locks. She looked at him, beckoned him.

She lacked the true beauty, the true sexual confidence, of a wanton. For one thing, her eyes were dead and the face was cold. She ignored Brian and Dorothy; she came over to Jimmy's side and ran one finger down his cheek. It felt as if she had drawn blood.

"Do you know how the Church, this particular order, at least, has kept alive while others have not? Do you wonder how we 'recruit' new sisters? They are born into our order. Yes, we are allowed to have lovers. To have children. We can do this in many ways. Some of us leave the convent for a brief time, have intercourse with a stranger in another town, come back here to have the baby and are never seen by our 'lovers' again."

She indicated the priests, pale, blank-eyed men who stood about silently in obvious deference to the Mother Superior. "Our priests also service us. Some of them have fathered more than two dozen children over the years. In the days when we had frequent sacrifices, the men would first serve us before being slaughtered for the glory of Abbiscyste."

Jimmy was too weak to resist. She put her hand under his chin and gently, gently, lifted him up to his feet. He could not believe what she was about to do. He tried to turn around, to see Dorothy, but she was outside his sightline. This bitch was going to do this to him and make Dorothy watch. Which was worse? he asked himself. Seeing your lover having sex with someone else? *Or watching them die right in front of your eyes?*

He looked around. The other nuns were removing their garments. Not all of them were in as good condition as Sister Absolum. They seemed drugged, hazy, bleary-eyed. Perhaps the demon was in part controlling, influencing all of them. They got down on the cold marble floor, and began to touch themselves—only themselves, not one another—in their private places. Fingers dipped into vaginas, hands stroked bellies. Breasts were cupped and lips pursed in a grotesque impersonation of arousal.

The priests had undressed and stood masturbating, their eyes locked into the eyes in Abbiscyste's bronze cranium. Apparently the only one who would be allowed to enjoy actual fornication was the Mother Superior herself.

Jimmy was helpless, unable to stop them from removing his clothes. *Were those bloodstains, dried bloodstains, discoloring the stone?* He shuddered; the only actions his body seemed capable of making were involuntary ones. He was pulled up and onto the other slab, face upward, beneath the Blood God.

Sister Absolum reached out and touched his penis. It was hardening, growing, against his will. Her fingers pulled the pliable flesh and she grinned. Jimmy felt sensation in his groin but nowhere else. His mind was completely dead except for the fear.

He felt so helpless, so abandoned by everything natural and normal, his complacency shattered. What might have been under other circumstances the fulfillment of a wonderful, if bizarre, erotic fantasy, was instead only a time of turmoil and terror.

The Mother Superior climbed onto the altar stone and mounted him. Her buttocks began thrusting up and down against his torso.

"Fuck me," she screamed. *"Fuck me!"*

Jimmy did nothing; the woman did it all. The shadow of the Blood God's frozen face fell over them, obliterating all joy and all hope. This was insanity personified—*not* the sexual act, the molestation—people giving up their minds, their lives, *other people's lives*, in the service of some mythical monster, an evil, unworthy god.

Jimmy tried to get his arms and legs to move—not to make love to this creature sitting on top of him, but to be able to fight back against the inevitable, when she would attack his body with knives instead of fingernails, draw blood instead of semen. He had to fight back, save himself, save Dorothy and Brian. *Had to fight back!*

From the corner of his eyes, Jimmy saw that several of the nuns and priests had lifted up a circular grating in the floor in front of the altar. This was much, much larger than the one in the room where they'd found Osa. From his vantage point, the black pit beneath the grating seemed to be without bottom, and the odor it emitted was so thick and foul as to be indescribable. Jimmy tried not to gag, to regurgitate. With his muscles and nervous system affected as they were, he might literally drown in his own vomit.

He reached orgasm.

Is this how Dorothy felt when she was raped? Used, helpless, a mere receptacle for somebody else's passion, a device, a machine, a sex toy? *You wonder how many pieces he'll leave you in*, she'd once told him. Jimmy was scared, so scared. The sexual act itself had not harmed him, not physically or emotionally. But the fear—the fear of what would come later. *That* was slowly destroying him.

The nuns and priests, now clothed again, crowded around the altar as Sister Absolum dismounted. Someone handed her her robe. It was nearly time.

There was a small murmuring, a commotion, as someone pushed past the gathering and approached the Mother Superior. Was it help? Someone who could save them?

No.

It was Sister Margarita.

While Sister Absolum and Jimmy had been occupied with that travesty of intercourse, Brian Asquith had been working to get free. It was those souls, those tormented souls, in the railway car who were helping him, who had helped to clear his mind. They were part of the Demon Venicus, too, and the demon was near, he knew it.

He lay there gathering his wits, building his strength. There was still time, still time while the nun had her pleasure. He knew what he had to do. His hands dug into his pockets while the attention of the gathering was focused elsewhere, and slowly began pulling out the hammer and rivet. The hammer was smaller than the one Jimmy had been carrying; the rivet was a polished rod with a sharp tapered end at the bottom and a rounded knob on top. It would do the job.

He remembered what he had to do to destroy the demon, recalled the thoughts that had entered his consciousness that day he and Dorothy had been on the barge.

You must drive a spike into the host's brain as the demon emerges. You must rip out the beating heart of the host. The host may return to life, intact, once the demon is dead—but there is no guarantee. You may kill the host, but you have no other choice. The demon will live again and again throughout time everlasting if it is not stopped now.

He and Dorothy had raced to the studio those long months ago with those "words" still ringing in his ears. He'd had no idea where he'd find a spike, how he'd rip out a heart—how he'd be *able to*—but tonight he was prepared. If only he would be able to do it, to actually kill the host, even if she were human. He told himself that Sister Margarita, to all intents and purposes, was already dead. That his act would be a merciful one.

He heard the murmuring, saw the jostling, in the gathering around the altar stone, and saw who was the cause. Sister Margarita. She was still in control of her body; her left hand was normal. She was crying, shouting, screeching at the Mother Superior. She knew. *She knew.*

Brian had to do it now. Any second, before the precious Mother Superior could be hurt by the demon's host, Venicus might take control of Sister Margarita's mind again. It was then, while it was active but before it was *fully* in control, that Brian would have to strike. He got up, holding out the hammer and rivet, and began to move slowly toward the crowd of cultists.

Too late—the demon was already emerging. Sister Margarita's hand was growing, changing. How would he be able to stop her once the transformation was *complete*!

The Mother Superior no longer wore a frightened look. She was smiling now, the victor, sure that if she served the Blood God faithfully, its demon would not harm her.

Fight it! Brian screamed the words inside his mind. He felt the power of the four hundred joining with his own. *Fight It! Fight It! Fight It!*

Sister Margarita's hand remained a claw, but it was the nun who was in control. Yet the ferocity, the violent, vicious nature of the beast was *still inside her.*

"Sister Margarita," Sister Absolum said. "You may have the honor of slaying this young man." She scornfully indicated Jimmy Radley, still prostrate on the slab.

Sister Margarita stood there trembling, a thousand and one feelings flickering across her tormented features. The claw lifted, dropped, lifted again. The nun took a step toward Jimmy.

The Mother Superior smiled.

The claw lashed out and in one stroke ripped away half of Sister Absolum's face.

White bone and teeth glared through the bleeding flaps of flesh on the Mother Superior's countenance. Sister Absolum screamed, tottered backwards. . . .

She was only a step or two away from falling into the pit. The congregation gasped. A priest reached out, tried to grab her—but was too afraid to get close to the feral Sister Margarita.

Sister Absolum swayed, grabbed the air, dripped blood. Her one remaining eye grew wider as she realized it was too late.

She fell into the pit.

They could hear her screeching all the way down, so far down into the vast deep underground well full of the putrifying corpses of animals and humans.

They never heard the woman hit bottom.

Venicus and Sister Margarita wrestled mentally for control of the latter's body. Brian ran up, past the frightened, scattering crowd of cultists, and lifted up the rivet in his hand. He prepared to use the hammer to drive the rivet into the woman's buckling forehead.

"Give . . . to . . . me. . . ."

Sister Margarita reached out, grabbed the rivet—and using her ferocious strength—rammed the metal spike into her own brain. The left hand, the four-fingered claw, dug into the cloth of the sister's habit—still wet with Osa's blood—dug deep through flesh and bone and sinew, and pulled out a throbbing, blood-drenched heart from the yawning cavity of her chest.

On the altar stone, Jimmy fainted.

Brian's eyes looked into those of Sister Margarita. Yes, she was only—and all—Sister Margarita now as she lay dying, sustained momentarily by the demon's residual energy. Brian knew that the sister had believed no longer in God *or* Abbiscyste—but in the will and beauty and courage of the undying human spirit. She did not really know if there were a hereafter, and if there were, what kind of hereafter would it be. Yet she had killed herself in order to kill the demon. *The woman had made a magnificent sacrifice.*

The demon Venicus was breaking up into its respective souls. The soul of Sister Venicus was no longer any stronger than any of the others. Brian felt the force of four hundred consciousnesses going off to wherever souls went, wherever they belonged. *Perhaps merely a state of peaceful nonexistence.*

But Venicus would not go easy.

It wasn't over.

There was an ominous rumble in the temple, a chilling, vibratory clatter that *hummed* through the air like a devilish adagio, and a hot wind sprang up from nowhere. Tiny hairline cracks began to form in the marble columns and buttresses. The vault was beginning to quake, to die an unnatural death.

Then the walls themselves were shaking and the stone floor began to crack open. Venicus' energy, collected and multiplied over the years, strengthened by each new death, was playing havoc with the temple. Several nuns, too close to the edge of the pit where the Mother Superior had fallen, also tumbled in to their deaths. A huge chunk of stone separated from the wall and came crashing down on a group of screaming cultists. Everywhere there was dust and bedlam. Huge gaping fissures opened in the floors, walls and ceilings, fissures that swallowed human bodies whole and closed again to crunch those bodies to powder between gnashing stone jaws.

The Blood God looked as if it were crying. The huge metal head wrenched partly off the wall with a clanging groan, dipping its chin toward the melee below. The head slid farther and farther down the altar until it cracked completely off the wall and began rolling across the floor. Cultists who were too slow to get out of its way were squashed underfoot.

Sister Margarita's body was once more whole and intact—but still she was dead. *Thank God I was not the one who had killed her,* Brian thought. He bent down at her side and looked for signs of life, a pulse, breathing—but her soul had fled with the others. Brian went over to Jimmy and Dorothy, who were fully awake now, beckoning him and hollering. They were heading toward the back of the altar, hoping to find the entrance that the Mother Superior and her minions had used before.

"Brian!" Jimmy waved. "Hurry! We've got to get out of here!" Sheltered from the falling debris by the god's head jutting out above them, they had been spared the early effects of the devastation. As soon as they'd seen the head start to crack and totter, they had gotten out of the way. Jimmy had grabbed up the tatters of his clothes and covered himself as best he could.

They found the exit behind the altar. There was a rectangular opening cut into the rock and steps leading upwards, a narrow passageway to the surface.

"Let's go!" Jimmy screamed.

Dorothy and Jimmy were about to dart through the opening when they realized that Brian wasn't following. They turned back to see what was keeping him.

The man stood transfixed a few feet away, watching what was happening in the temple. In spite of their terror, Dorothy and Jimmy had to peer out to see for themselves. They were drawn to the miasma of blood and horror like moths to a flame.

The torches on the walls had started to shimmer, to explode, sending forth huge geysers of fire and a multitude of burning, stinging sparks. The clothes of the cultists caught on fire as they screeched and bellowed in agony. Smoke filled up the chamber, smoke and heat and burning embers of both flesh and clothing.

The flames began to fill the room, darting across the floor as if following traces of oil. The tongues of fire whipped out, as if mentally directed, to *snatch* at the people who ran every which way to escape.

And there above their heads, a vision in the smoke, was a face, a woman's face, the pale, shriveled, demented face of the long-dead Sister Venicus.

She had cared nothing for the church, for their ridiculous god—she was beyond such mortal concerns. She had used the church the same way she had used the others, used it to create misery and horror, to stalk and kill for pleasure, her pleasure, to get even for the fate she had not chosen for herself, to make the world pay for her suffering.

The face was getting fainter and fainter as a demonic screech filled the air. The Blood God's huge head had turned to molten slag; it was pouring across the cracked, buckling floor, combining with melted stone and flesh to form an unearthly wave of malevolent liquid. Some of it seeped into the fissures, but most was heading straight for the spot where Dorothy and her companions were standing. The demon Venicus would not cease to exist without first attempting to destroy those who had interfered—*they were the ones she hated most.*

Brian, Dorothy, and Jimmy ran into the stairwell just as the sizzling, burning liquid washed over the area before the altar. When they thought it would actually begin climbing the steps after them, the wave of molten death receded.

It was draining away into the "bottomless" pit and could follow them no further.

Racing at a breakneck pace they soon reached a corridor upstairs, part of the convent proper. The entire building quivered again, and an ungodly screech of frustration and vengeance denied rent the air. Venicus had been an unnatural being, one created by the purest of chance, a freak accident of the most grotesque in nature. Nature had finally reclaimed its mistake and neutralized it forever.

The many souls of the demon had dissipated.

Venicus was no more.

EPILOGUE

The phone rang.
Dorothy got up from the couch where she had been resting and went to answer it. "Brian?" she said. "Hello! When did you get into town?"

They had stayed in touch through all the months since the night the Demon Venicus was destroyed, deciding that to pretend none of it had happened, which they really wanted to do, would be neither healthy nor realistic. The only question was: now that they alone knew the truth about the murders in Lennington, the truth about the "earthquake" that tore through the mountain and nearly obliterated the Convent of the Mourning Sisters, should they tell the story to everyone else?

Dazed and numb with disbelief, that night they had fled down the road from the convent, still afraid the entire building might collapse on top of them. When they finally reached their car at the side of the road, they drove to the police and told them an earthquake had rattled the ground near the convent as they drove past and the sisters might need assistance. No one asked what they had been doing driving up that road at that hour of the night.

What the police found beneath the building was a loathsome chamber full of melted stone, torn human bodies, skeletons from which the flesh had been singed. Half of the sisters were missing. The town, which had scarcely paid them much attention when they were alive, made a big show of public mourning. The sisters who survived—those not members of the Blood God cult—sought refuge in prayer, completely unable even to comprehend what had happened to the others.

No one understood how the earthquake could have occurred just in that spot—"structural faults of the building itself," someone said (which did not explain why the building was still standing and the subterranean vault was not)—nor how molten lava could have appeared when there was no volcanic activity in the area.

In any case, the Blood God cult was gone and no one was bothering the schoolgirls any more. The Sisters of the Mourning Convent carried on as they had before, little lost lambs in a country that ignored them. There were no more murders and no more disappearances, and if anyone made a connection, they certainly didn't say so. The only people who could have told them the true story had fled the town in the middle of the night, never to return.

For weeks the three of them had shivered in their beds at night, reliving the terror they had seen and experienced in that temple. Brian had assured them that the demon had truly been destroyed—he felt nothing from those four hundred souls any more. Wherever they had gone, they no longer existed on this earthly plane or even the astral one. There was nothing to fear any longer.

Eventually they simply accepted what had happened—what else could they do?—and went about the normal, everyday business of their normal, everyday lives. Brian would call or write now and then from California. They'd chew the fat: he had found a new lover and the relationship was going beautifully; he'd 'ghostbusted' for a prominent senator. And so on. The three of them shared something together that was a tighter bond than mere friendship. That closeness would always be there, no matter how hard they might try to forget the cause of it.

And then: the book. It would perhaps raise more questions than it would answer—but they had, after all, committed no wrongdoing. Brian had not used his rivet and hammer on the sister. (Imagine the police standing by, had they accompanied them into the convent, letting him do *that*?) If anything, they had been victims. They were going to sit down together and write the book, Dorothy's byline—she'd do the actual writing; Brian's exhaustive research—he was good at it and had loads of material. Jimmy's input would be his more practical impressions of what they had seen and done. (Ever one to rationalize, but it made life easier.) The whole story. Not just parts of it. Not just Janice Evans *Vicious* or *Vicious Two*, the movies that the demon had, in part, brought into being as if it needed to see its exploits turned to myth and glamorized. *Insane*. But *all* of it. Even the Mourning Sisters. That, too.

Dorothy chatted with Brian for a while, asked which hotel he was staying at, then invited him for dinner. She was anxious to show him the parts of the manuscript she had completed; curious to see what more of the history of the Mourning Sisters, the Holy Messianic Church, the dubious Blood God—ah yes, he figured in it, too, poor soul—he had uncovered. To think: all that material just gathering dust in the library of that convent; all that rich historical information out of bounds. Never would she, would any of them, go back inside there. . . .

Jimmy and Brian shook hands, traded stories, as Dorothy prepared the dinner. Jimmy was so busy these days; Bart Hamilton had died—heart attack—and Jimmy was Acting Executive Editor of *Frames and Directions*. There was a strong possibility that the promotion would be permanent. He had no time for free lance work any more, couldn't even work on the book if he had wanted to. Part of Jimmy wanted to forget the whole thing had happened. Dorothy was annoyed by this—(threatened?)—but she said she understood.

They sat sipping cocktails. "I've been thinking a lot," Brian said. "About life and death, the afterlife. I've come to the sobering conclusion that *our* experiences . . . don't really prove the existence of an afterlife, or even a deity."

"Brian," Dorothy said. "Those people on the train—Sister Venicus—were *dead*. Their bodies had been vaporized a century ago. And yet their minds and thoughts were still alive, still active in 1988. Isn't that afterlife?"

"Another *kind* of life, perhaps," he countered. "They—the

demon—was a product of a once-in-a-lifetime cosmic accident. It had—as farfetched as it may have been—a *scientific* explanation; 'Abbiscyste' had nothing to do with it! It doesn't necessarily indicate that under *normal* circumstances the mind lives on after the body dies. And even if it does, our friends were in some kind of purgatory, neither dead nor alive, not here on earth, not in heaven nor hell, whatever those concepts truly signify. I sensed the four hundred souls, Sister Venicus, 'moving on' when it was over. But moving on to *where*? It *could* have been oblivion."

"Well," Jimmy said, "I for one don't doubt after all we've been through that there is something, the *possibility* of something, happening to us after death, a continuation—an alternative, you might call it—or how did you put it, Brian, 'another kind of life.' Call it the soul, call it electromagnetic energy, something in us *can continue*. Even under normal circumstances, I think. Isn't that what people mean by an afterlife? Only it's as you say, scientific in nature, not necessarily theological. But I'm not sure if I'm *comforted* by the thought—or frightened. I'd hate to wind up some sort of *thing* like the demon. Or worse, one of the souls it enslaved."

They had a good dinner, talked a lot about the book, other projects, the world situation. Always it hung over them: the enormity of what they'd witnessed, their aloneness—even most people who professed an interest in the occult or parapsychology had never seen what they had seen, did not know what they knew. This book might be a revelation, or it might turn them into a national joke. That was the chance they had to take. Dorothy *had* to write it. While Jimmy did some work in his bedroom/office, Dorothy and Brian went over each other's material. The book was coming along well; it was going to be a sensation. Even people who didn't believe would be hard put to resist its chilling, hypnotic spell.

Dorothy said good night to Brian and went in to check on Jimmy. He had fallen asleep on his desk. Poor boy—working himself so hard, trying so hard to pretend that the world was the same as it had always been. *Had never been.*

She was not tired. She sat on the couch and read the paper, trying not to think about the supper dishes soaking in the sink.

Jimmy came out, yawning, stretching, just as she began going through the entertainment section. He said hello, but something in the paper had caught her eye. *Something terrible.* She gasped.

"Did Brian leave already? Honey, what's wrong?"

Dorothy tried to control herself. "Jimmy. It says here in the *Film Slants* column . . . they're going to make—*God!*—a movie about the New York Slicer." Tears began to fill her eyes. " 'A serious study of the most horrible series of slayings to hit this city in fifty years.' " She threw the paper down. " '*Serious!*' Sure, I'll bet!" Thoughts of her parents filled her mind and all of a sudden she was in such despair. . . .

She looked up at Jimmy helplessly. "No one *cares*, Jimmy. Not about my parents. Not about Lawrence O'Connell's other victims. No one cares about them any more." *If they ever did . . . or about Paul Wilson and Desiree Fontana. Gerry and Suzette Winteroth. Vivienne Cherneau and Bethany Carravel and George Piedmont . . . Sister Margarita . . . so many others. So many victims. . . .*

"Oh God, Jimmy. Does it ever end?"

"No, it doesn't," he answered sadly, grabbing her hand, resting it on her shoulder as he stood behind her, holding it, warming it, letting his love flow from his fingers into hers. "But you keep on going in spite of it, and try to get as much happiness as you can."

Dorothy smiled. He was right. Love and happiness were all that mattered.

With Jimmy, she thought, *she'd probably get more than her share.*

From a New York Newspaper:

DEMON MADE HER DO IT

Marjorie Berrans, who is alleged to have slaughtered her husband and children at their home in Larchmont last Friday night, today told police it was a demon that forced her to murder her family.

"It took over my mind and made me kill my children," she told investigating detectives, according to one source. The three children, aged six months to seven years, were attacked with a baseball bat as they slept, after Mrs. Berrans had alledgedly slashed her husband to death with a straight razor.

Mrs. Berrans is thirty-seven. Her husband, Philip, forty-three, worked as a copy writer at the advertising firm of Otis and McGuade on Lexington Avenue. Police officials stated that Mrs. Berrans will receive a full psychiatric evaluation.

"Marge hadn't been right for months," a friend of the family told reporters. But neighbors of the Berrans' are shocked. "She was the sweetest, kindest person you would ever want to know," said Lillian Crabtree, who lived next door to the family for six years. "I just can't believe it happened."

MORE BLOOD-CHILLERS FROM LEISURE BOOKS

2329-6	**EVIL STALKS THE NIGHT**	$3.50 US, $3.95 Can
2319-9	**LATE AT NIGHT**	$3.95 US, $4.50 Can
2309-1	**EVIL DREAMS**	$3.95 US, $4.50 Can
2300-8	**THE SECRET OF AMITYVILLE**	$3.50 US, $3.95 Can
2275-3	**FANGS**	$3.95 US, $4.50 Can
2269-9	**NIGHT OF THE WOLF**	$3.25
2265-6	**KISS NOT THE CHILD**	$3.75 US, $4.50 Can
2256-7	**CREATURE**	$3.75 US, $4.50 Can
2246-x	**DEATHBRINGER**	$3.75 US, $4.50 Can
2235-4	**SHIVERS**	$3.75 US, $4.50 Can
2225-7	**UNTO THE ALTAR**	$3.75 US, $4.50 Can
2220-6	**THE RIVARD HOUSE**	$3.25
2195-1	**BRAIN WATCH**	$3.50 US, $4.25 Can
2185-4	**BLOOD OFFERINGS**	$3.75 US, $4.50 Can
2152-8	**SISTER SATAN**	$3.75 US, $4.50 Can
2121-8	**UNDERTOW**	$3.75 US, $4.50 Can
2112-9	**SPAWN OF HELL**	$3.75 US, $4.50 Can

DARE TO ENTER THE DEMONIC WORLD OF JOHN TIGGES

2350-4	**THE IMMORTAL**	$3.95 US, $4.50 CAN
2309-1	**EVIL DREAMS**	$3.95 US, $4.50 CAN
2265-9	**KISS NOT THE CHILD**	$3.95 US, $4.50 CAN
2225-7	**UNTO THE ALTAR**	$3.75 US, $4.50 CAN

ELECTRIFYING HORROR AND OCCULT

2343-1	**THE WERELING**	$3.50 US, $3.95 Can
2341-5	**THE ONI**	$3.95 US, $4.50 Can
2334-2	**PREMONITION**	$3.50 US, $3.95 Can
2331-8	**RESURREXIT**	$3.95 US, $4.50 Can
2302-4	**WORSHIP THE NIGHT**	$3.95 US, $3.95 Can
2289-3	**THE WITCHING**	$3.50 US, $3.95 Can
2281-8	**THE FREAK**	$2.50 US, $2.95 Can
2251-6	**THE HOUSE**	$2.50
2206-0	**CHILD OF DEMONS**	$3.75 US, $4.50 Can
2142-0	**THE FELLOWSHIP**	$3.75 US, $4.50 Can

Make the Most of Your Leisure Time with
LEISURE BOOKS

Please send me the following titles:

Quantity	Book Number	Price
_____	_____	_____
_____	_____	_____
_____	_____	_____
_____	_____	_____
_____	_____	_____

If out of stock on any of the above titles, please send me the alternate title(s) listed below:

_____	_____	_____
_____	_____	_____
_____	_____	_____
_____	_____	_____

Postage & Handling _____

Total Enclosed $_____

☐ Please send me a free catalog.

NAME _____
(please print)

ADDRESS _____

CITY _____ STATE _____ ZIP_____

Please include $1.00 shipping and handling for the first book ordered and 25¢ for each book thereafter in the same order. All orders are shipped within approximately 4 weeks via postal service book rate. PAYMENT MUST ACCOMPANY ALL ORDERS.*

*Canadian orders must be paid in US dollars payable through a New York banking facility.

Mail coupon to: **Dorchester Publishing Co., Inc.
6 East 39 Street, Suite 900
New York, NY 10016
Att: ORDER DEPT.**